THE RED BADGE OF COURAGE

AN AUTHORITATIVE TEXT
BACKGROUNDS AND SOURCES
CRITICISM

SECOND EDITION

W.W. NORTON & COMPANY, INC.
also publishes

THE NORTON ANTHOLOGY OF AMERICAN LITERATURE
edited by Nina Baym et al.

THE NORTON ANTHOLOGY OF CONTEMPORARY FICTION
edited by R. V. Cassill

THE NORTON ANTHOLOGY OF ENGLISH LITERATURE
edited by M. H. Abrams et al.

THE NORTON ANTHOLOGY OF LITERATURE BY WOMEN
edited by Sandra M. Gilbert and Susan Gubar

THE NORTON ANTHOLOGY OF MODERN POETRY
edited by Richard Ellmann and Robert O'Clair

THE NORTON ANTHOLOGY OF POETRY
edited by Alexander W. Allison et al.

THE NORTON ANTHOLOGY OF SHORT FICTION
edited by R. V. Cassill

THE NORTON ANTHOLOGY OF WORLD MASTERPIECES
edited by Maynard Mack et al.

THE NORTON FACSIMILE OF
THE FIRST FOLIO OF SHAKESPEARE
prepared by Charlton Hinman

THE NORTON INTRODUCTION TO LITERATURE
edited by Carl E. Bain, Jerome Beaty, and J. Paul Hunter

THE NORTON INTRODUCTION TO THE SHORT NOVEL
edited by Jerome Beaty

THE NORTON READER
edited by Arthur M. Eastman et al.

THE NORTON SAMPLER
edited by Thomas Cooley

STEPHEN CRANE

THE
RED BADGE OF COURAGE

AN AUTHORITATIVE TEXT
BACKGROUNDS AND SOURCES
CRITICISM

➤➤➤ ⫷⫷⫷

SECOND EDITION

➤➤➤ ⫷⫷⫷

Edited by

SCULLEY BRADLEY
PROFESSOR EMERITUS OF ENGLISH
UNIVERSITY OF PENNSYLVANIA

RICHMOND CROOM BEATTY
LATE OF VANDERBILT UNIVERSITY

E. HUDSON LONG
PROFESSOR EMERITUS OF AMERICAN LITERATURE
BAYLOR UNIVERSITY

Revised by

DONALD PIZER
PIERCE BUTLER PROFESSOR OF ENGLISH
TULANE UNIVERSITY

W · W · NORTON & COMPANY
New York · London

Second Edition

Library of Congress Cataloging in Publication Data
Crane, Stephen, 1871–1900.
    The red badge of courage.
    (A Norton critical edition)
    Bibliography: p.
    1. United States—History—Civil War, 1861–1865—
Fiction. I. Bradley, Edward Sculley, 1897–   . II. Title.
PZ3.C852R48 [PS1449.C85] 813'.4 76–18237
ISBN 0-393-04435-1
ISBN 0-393-09182-1 pbk.

W. W. Norton & Company, Inc., 500 Fifth Avenue, New York, N.Y. 10110
W. W. Norton & Company Ltd., 10 Coptic Street, London, WC1A 1PU

4 5 6 7 8 9 0

Contents

Preface

Stephen Crane's *The Red Badge of Courage* is an acknowledged masterpiece of American literature, and Crane himself is one of our most closely examined late-nineteenth-century authors. Whether read as an exciting war story, a psychological study of fear, or an allegory of man's condition in an inhospitable world, the novel has always had a large and involved audience. One proof of its permanence lies in its responsiveness to the distinctive interests and needs of each new generation of readers and critics. And Crane himself has had a similar protean resourcefulness for those seeking to identify characteristics of the modern consciousness. He has been discussed as naturalist, impressionist, symbolist, existentialist, and ironist, and each new emphasis has contributed to an understanding both of Crane's work and of our own preoccupations.

This second edition of *The Red Badge of Courage* is a revision by Donald Pizer of the edition published in 1962 by Sculley Bradley, Richmond Croom Beatty, and E. Hudson Long. As earlier, the editor seeks to place before the reader an authoritative reading text of the novel and a body of material bearing on its interpretation. In the decade and a half since the Bradley, Beatty, Long edition, much work has been done on the complicated problem of the text of *The Red Badge*, and there have been several important shifts in scholarly and critical approaches to the novel. The present edition attempts to reflect these changes and is thus a substantial rather than a minor revision of the 1962 edition.

As in 1962, the text of the novel is that of the first edition, published by D. Appleton in 1895, conservatively emended. This emendation has been greatly aided by the publication in 1972 of a facsimile of the manuscript of the novel. As before, Crane's uncanceled but unpublished manuscript passages are presented in an appendix to the text of the novel; in addition, and for the first time in the Norton Critical Edition of *The Red Badge*, Crane's discarded Chapter XII is included in the appendix. (See "A Note on the Text," preceding the text of the novel, and "The Manuscript of *The Red Badge of Courage*," following the text.) The annotation of the text has been revised, though, as before, information necessary to understand obscure terms and allusions is provided. Rather than annotate the text repetitiously for Crane's use of a specific Civil War battle, the editor has thought it best to direct the reader at the opening of the novel to Harold Hungerford's " 'That Was at

Chancellorsville' : The Factual Framework of *The Red Badge of Courage*."

The Backgrounds and Sources and the Criticism sections have been extensively revised. The first portion of the Backgrounds and Sources section, "Stephen Crane: An Introduction," provides an introduction to the biographical, historical, and critical context of *The Red Badge*—in particular, to Crane's life and times, to the nature and origin of his literary beliefs, and to the major tendencies in the criticism of the novel since its publication. The last essay in this section, on Crane criticism and scholarship, can also serve as an introduction to the varying approaches to Crane's work found in the Criticism section and as a guide to further reading in Crane studies. The second part, "Sources," reflects the movement in recent Crane scholarship away from an emphasis on specific literary sources and toward an interest in determining Crane's reliance on the battle of Chancellorsville and on a generic tradition of war fiction. And although the controversy over the origin and meaning of Crane's wafer image continues occasionally to liven the critical scene, it has been thought that one example of a wafer study and numerous references within the essays in the Criticism section would be a sufficient introduction to this subject.

The Criticism section attempts to present the best that has been written about *The Red Badge of Courage* and to do so as much as possible in complete essays and chapters. There has been no effort to have the selections reflect the history of Crane criticism either by a full representation of earlier criticism or by the presence of criticism from all "schools" of interpretation, though in fact the most significant schools are represented. Thus, the "Early Estimates" portion of the section is comparatively slight, with the stress on those critics who isolated permanent strains of interest in *The Red Badge*. (Crane's story "The Veteran" is offered as Crane's own estimate not of the novel but of Henry's character.)

Modern critical interest in Crane begins in the early 1950s with John Berryman's biography and with the editions and long critical essays of R. W. Stallman. The problem of Henry's growth or maturity has always been central to this criticism, as has been the related difficulty of identifying Crane's literary allegiances in the novel. "Does Henry mature?" and "Is Crane a naturalist, symbolist, or ironist?" are the questions most critics appear to be answering. Recently, Crane's narrative voice and the structure of the novel have increasingly served as a means of discovering meaning. And there has been a return by some critics to the deeply absorbing problems of the war theme in the novel and of the relation of Crane's underlying vision of life to the configuration of nineteenth- and twentieth-century American life and thought.

DONALD PIZER

The Text of
The Red Badge
of Courage

A NOTE ON THE TEXT

There are three significant texts for *The Red Badge of Courage*: portions of a discarded draft; an almost complete manuscript; and the 1895 Appleton edition. (Portions of the draft survive because Crane used the clean sides of its pages for his final manuscript version.) Until the early 1950s, when the manuscript versions of *The Red Badge* became available, the Appleton text had sole authority. Soon afterward, however, editors began to use the manuscript versions in several ways. Since the completed manuscript contains uncanceled passages which do not appear in the Appleton version, some editors incorporated these passages in the text of their editions (usually in brackets) on the assumption that they were omitted without Crane's approval. Other editors adopted the technique of publishing these passages as notes to the text, and in some instances also publishing as notes or appendices canceled passages from the completed manuscript and sections from the discarded draft.

There is no doubt that the manuscripts of *The Red Badge* are a great boon to Crane scholarship. They permit us to see Crane's imagination at work in a way not usually permitted us, since no other Crane novel is extant in manuscript form. And they permit us to correct errors in the Appleton text. But there is some doubt whether they should lead to any major revision or annotation of the Appleton text when that text is offered as a "reading" text, as was the fashion in the 1950s and early 1960s. It is generally accepted that one or more lost typescripts intervened between the completed manuscript and the Appleton text, that one such typescript probably served as printer's copy for the Appleton text, and that Crane revised the Appleton text in proof. In short, except for obvious errors which occurred in the transmission of the text from the manuscript to the typescript to print, we should permit Crane the last word—that of the Appleton text—and not attempt to return the novel to a state which he had rejected or revised in the course of composition.

For this edition of *The Red Badge of Courage*, therefore, uncanceled passages in the manuscript do not appear in the text or as footnotes but rather are reproduced in a list at the close of the text. And the text of the edition is that of the 1895 edition, conservatively emended. Emendations either correct obvious typographical errors in the first edition or supply a manuscript reading when the typist or compositor clearly failed to follow Crane's copy correctly. I have not emended or noted grammatical and spelling lapses in the first edition which are confirmed by the manuscript except in instances when such lapses might cause confusion. A list of all emendations of the 1895 Appleton text can be found at the close of the novel.

I wish to thank Joseph Katz for a valuable contribution which aided me in the preparation of the text of *The Red Badge of Courage* for this edition.

The Red
Badge of Courage

Chapter I

The cold passed reluctantly from the earth, and the retiring fogs revealed an army stretched out on the hills, resting.[1] As the landscape changed from brown to green, the army awakened, and began to tremble with eagerness at the noise of rumors. It cast its eyes upon the roads, which were growing from long troughs of liquid mud to proper thoroughfares. A river, amber-tinted in the shadow of its banks, purled at the army's feet; and at night, when the stream had become of a sorrowful blackness, one could see across it the red, eyelike gleam of hostile camp-fires set in the low brows of distant hills.

Once a certain tall soldier developed virtues and went resolutely to wash a shirt. He came flying back from a brook waving his garment bannerlike. He was swelled with a tale he had heard from a reliable friend, who had heard it from a truthful cavalryman, who had heard it from his trustworthy brother, one of the orderlies at division headquarters. He adopted the important air of a herald in red and gold.

"We're goin' t' move t' morrah—sure," he said pompously to a group in the company street. "We're goin' 'way up the river, cut across, an' come around in behint 'em."

To his attentive audience he drew a loud and elaborate plan of a very brilliant campaign. When he had finished, the blue-clothed men scattered into small arguing groups between the rows of squat brown huts. A negro teamster who had been dancing upon a cracker box with the hilarious encouragement of twoscore soldiers was deserted. He sat mournfully down. Smoke drifted lazily from a multitude of quaint chimneys.

---

1. For Crane's reliance upon the events and geography of the Battle of Chancellorsville, see Harold Hungerford, " 'That Was at Chancellorsville': The Factual Framework of *The Red Badge of Courage*," in Backgrounds and Sources, below.

"It's a lie! that's all it is—a thunderin' lie!" said another private loudly. His smooth face was flushed, and his hands were thrust sulkily into his trousers' pockets. He took the matter as an affront to him. "I don't believe the derned old army's ever going to move. We're set. I've got ready to move eight times in the last two weeks, and we ain't moved yet."

The tall soldier felt called upon to defend the truth of a rumor he himself had introduced. He and the loud one came near to fighting over it.

A corporal began to swear before the assemblage. He had just put a costly board floor in his house, he said. During the early spring he had refrained from adding extensively to the comfort of his environment because he had felt that the army might start on the march at any moment. Of late, however, he had been impressed that they were in a sort of eternal camp.

Many of the men engaged in a spirited debate. One outlined in a peculiarly lucid manner all the plans of the commanding general. He was opposed by men who advocated that there were other plans of campaign. They clamored at each other, numbers making futile bids for the popular attention. Meanwhile, the soldier who had fetched the rumor bustled about with much importance. He was continually assailed by questions.

"What's up, Jim?"

"Th' army's goin' t' move."

"Ah, what yeh talkin' about? How yeh know it is?"

"Well, yeh kin b'lieve me er not, jest as yeh like. I don't care a hang."

There was much food for thought in the manner in which he replied. He came near to convincing them by disdaining to produce proofs. They grew much excited over it.

There was a youthful private who listened with eager ears to the words of the tall soldier and to the varied comments of his comrades. After receiving a fill of discussions concerning marches and attacks, he went to his hut and crawled through an intricate hole that served it as a door. He wished to be alone with some new thoughts that had lately come to him.

He lay down on a wide bunk that stretched across the end of the room. In the other end, cracker boxes were made to serve as furniture. They were grouped about the fireplace. A picture from an illustrated weekly was upon the log walls, and three rifles were paralleled on pegs. Equipments[2] hung on handy projections, and some tin dishes lay upon a small pile of firewood. A folded tent

2. An acceptable plural in late-nineteenth-century usage.

was serving as a room. The sunlight, without, beating upon it, made it glow a light yellow shade. A small window shot an oblique square of whiter light upon the cluttered floor. The smoke from the fire at times neglected the clay chimney and wreathed into the room, and this flimsy chimney of clay and sticks made endless threats to set ablaze the whole establishment.

The youth was in a little trance of astonishment. So they were at last going to fight. On the morrow, perhaps, there would be a battle, and he would be in it. For a time he was obliged to labor to make himself believe. He could not accept with assurance an omen that he was about to mingle in one of those great affairs of the earth.

He had, of course, dreamed of battles all his life—of vague and bloody conflicts that had thrilled him with their sweep and fire. In visions he had seen himself in many struggles. He had imagined peoples secure in the shadow of his eagle-eyed prowess. But awake he had regarded battles as crimson blotches on the pages of the past. He had put them as things of the bygone with his thought-images of heavy crowns and high castles. There was a portion of the world's history which he had regarded as the time of wars, but it, he thought, had been long gone over the horizon and had disappeared forever.

From his home his youthful eyes had looked upon the war in his own country with distrust. It must be some sort of a play affair. He had long despaired of witnessing a Greeklike struggle. Such would be no more, he had said. Men were better, or more timid. Secular and religious education had effaced the throat-grappling instinct, or else firm finance held in check the passions.

He had burned several times to enlist. Tales of great movements shook the land. They might not be distinctly Homeric, but there seemed to be much glory in them. He had read of marches, sieges, conflicts, and he had longed to see it all. His busy mind had drawn for him large pictures extravagant in color, lurid with breathless deeds.

But his mother had discouraged him. She had affected to look with some contempt upon the quality of his war ardor and patriotism. She could calmly seat herself and with no apparent difficulty give him many hundreds of reasons why he was of vastly more importance on the farm than on the field of battle. She had had certain ways of expression that told him that her statements on the subject came from a deep conviction. Moreover, on her side, was his belief that her ethical motive in the argument was impregnable.

At last, however, he had made firm rebellion against this yellow light thrown upon the color of his ambitions. The newspapers, the gossip of the village, his own picturings, had aroused him to an uncheckable degree. They were in truth fighting finely down there. Almost every day the newspapers printed accounts of a decisive victory.

One night, as he lay in bed, the winds had carried to him the clangoring of the church bell as some enthusiast jerked the rope frantically to tell the twisted news of a great battle. This voice of the people rejoicing in the night had made him shiver in a prolonged ecstasy of excitement. Later, he had gone down to his mother's room and had spoken thus: "Ma, I'm going to enlist."

"Henry, don't you be a fool," his mother had replied. She had then covered her face with the quilt. There was an end to the matter for that night.

Nevertheless, the next morning he had gone to a town that was near his mother's farm and had enlisted in a company that was forming there. When he had returned home his mother was milking the brindle cow. Four others stood waiting. "Ma, I've enlisted," he had said to her diffidently. There was a short silence. "The Lord's will be done, Henry," she had finally replied, and had then continued to milk the brindle cow.

When he had stood in the doorway with his soldier's clothes on his back, and with the light of excitement and expectancy in his eyes almost defeating the glow of regret for the home bonds, he had seen two tears leaving their trails on his mother's scarred cheeks.

Still, she had disappointed him by saying nothing whatever about returning with his shield or on it.[3] He had privately primed himself for a beautiful scene. He had prepared certain sentences which he thought could be used with touching effect. But her words destroyed his plans. She had doggedly peeled potatoes and addressed him as follows: "You watch out, Henry, an' take good care of yerself in this here fighting business—you watch out, an' take good care of yerself. Don't go a-thinkin' you can lick the hull rebel army at the start, because yeh can't. Yer jest one little feller amongst a hull lot of others, and yeh've got to keep quiet an' do what they tell yeh. I know how you are, Henry.

"I've knet yeh eight pair of socks, Henry, and I've put in all yer best shirts, because I want my boy to be jest as warm and comf'able as anybody in the army. Whenever they get holes in 'em, I want yeh to send 'em right-away back to me, so's I kin dern 'em.

"An' allus be careful an' choose yer comp'ny. There's lots of bad men in the army, Henry. The army makes 'em wild, and they

3. A traditional injunction to the young warrior in Greek heroic literature.

like nothing better than the job of leading off a young feller like you, as ain't never been away from home much and has allus had a mother, an' a-learning 'em to drink and swear. Keep clear of them folks, Henry. I don't want yeh to ever do anything, Henry, that yeh would be 'shamed to let me know about. Jest think as if I was a-watchin' yeh. If yeh keep that in yer mind allus, I guess yeh'll come out about right.

"Yeh must allus remember yer father, too, child, an' remember he never drunk a drop of licker in his life, and seldom swore a cross oath.

"I don't know what else to tell yeh, Henry, excepting that yeh must never do no shirking, child, on my account. If so be a time comes when yeh have to be kilt or do a mean thing, why, Henry, don't think of anything 'cept what's right, because there's many a woman has to bear up 'ginst sech things these times, and the Lord 'll take keer of us all.

"Don't forgit about the socks and the shirts, child; and I've put a cup of blackberry jam with yer bundle, because I know yeh like it above all things. Good-by, Henry. Watch out, and be a good boy."

He had, of course, been impatient under the ordeal of this speech. It had not been quite what he expected, and he had borne it with an air of irritation. He departed feeling vague relief.

Still, when he had looked back from the gate, he had seen his mother kneeling among the potato parings. Her brown face, up-raised, was stained with tears, and her spare form was quivering. He bowed his head and went on, feeling suddenly ashamed of his purposes.

From his home he had gone to the seminary[4] to bid adieu to many schoolmates. They had thronged about him with wonder and admiration. He had felt the gulf now between them and had swelled with calm pride. He and some of his fellows who had donned blue were quite overwhelmed with privileges for all of one afternoon, and it had been a very delicious thing. They had strutted.

A certain light-haired girl had made vivacious fun at his martial spirit, but there was another and darker girl whom he had gazed at steadfastly, and he thought she grew demure and sad at sight of his blue and brass. As he had walked down the path between the rows of oaks, he had turned his head and detected her at a window watching his departure. As he perceived her, she had immediately begun to stare up through the high tree branches at the sky. He had seen a good deal of flurry and haste in her movement

4. A local school, not then necessarily a school of theology.

as she changed her attitude. He often thought of it.

On the way to Washington his spirit had soared. The regiment was fed and caressed at station after station until the youth had believed that he must be a hero. There was a lavish expenditure of bread and cold meats, coffee, and pickles and cheese. As he basked in the smiles of the girls and was patted and complimented by the old men, he had felt growing within him the strength to do mighty deeds of arms.

After complicated journeyings with many pauses, there had come months of monotonous life in a camp. He had had the belief that real war was a series of death struggles with small time in between for sleep and meals; but since his regiment had come to the field the army had done little but sit still and try to keep warm.

He was brought then gradually back to his old ideas. Greeklike struggles would be no more. Men were better, or more timid. Secular and religious education had effaced the throat-grappling instinct, or else firm finance held in check the passions.

He had grown to regard himself merely as a part of a vast blue demonstration. His province was to look out, as far as he could, for his personal comfort. For recreation he could twiddle his thumbs and speculate on the thoughts which must agitate the minds of the generals. Also, he was drilled and drilled and reviewed, and drilled and drilled and reviewed.

The only foes he had seen were some pickets[5] along the river bank. They were a sun-tanned, philosophical lot, who sometimes shot reflectively at the blue pickets. When reproached for this afterward, they usually expressed sorrow, and swore by their gods that the guns had exploded without their permission. The youth, on guard duty one night, conversed across the stream with one of them. He was a slightly ragged man, who spat skillfully between his shoes and possessed a great fund of bland and infantile assurance. The youth liked him personally.

"Yank," the other had informed him, "yer a right dum[6] good feller." This sentiment, floating to him upon the still air, had made him temporarily regret war.

Various veterans had told him tales. Some talked of gray, be-whiskered hordes who were advancing with relentless curses and chewing tobacco with unspeakable valor; tremendous bodies of fierce soldiery who were sweeping along like the Huns.[7] Others spoke of tattered and eternally hungry men who fired despondent powders. "They'll charge through hell's fire an' brimstone t' git

5. Sentries.
6. A euphemism for "damn."
7. A fierce Asiatic people whose raids

terrorized Europe in the fourth and fifth centuries.

a holt on a haversack, an' sech stomachs ain't a-lastin' long," he was told. From the stories, the youth imagined the red, live bones sticking out through slits in the faded uniforms.

Still, he could not put a whole faith in veterans' tales, for recruits were their prey. They talked much of smoke, fire, and blood, but he could not tell how much might be lies. They persistently yelled "Fresh fish!" at him, and were in no wise to be trusted.

However, he perceived now that it did not greatly matter what kind of soldiers he was going to fight, so long as they fought, which fact no one disputed. There was a more serious problem. He lay in his bunk pondering upon it. He tried to mathematically prove to himself that he would not run from a battle.

Previously he had never felt obliged to wrestle too seriously with this question. In his life he had taken certain things for granted, never challenging his belief in ultimate success, and bothering little about means and roads. But here he was confronted with a thing of moment. It had suddenly appeared to him that perhaps in a battle he might run. He was forced to admit that as far as war was concerned he knew nothing of himself.

A sufficient time before he would have allowed the problem to kick its heels at the outer portals of his mind, but now he felt compelled to give serious attention to it.

A little panic-fear grew in his mind. As his imagination went forward to a fight, he saw hideous possibilities. He contemplated the lurking menaces of the future, and failed in an effort to see himself standing stoutly in the midst of them. He recalled his visions of broken-bladed glory, but in the shadow of the impending tumult he suspected them to be impossible pictures.

He sprang from the bunk and began to pace nervously to and fro. "Good Lord, what's th' matter with me?" he said aloud.

He felt that in this crisis his laws of life were useless. Whatever he had learned of himself was here of no avail. He was an unknown quantity. He saw that he would again be obliged to experiment as he had in early youth. He must accumulate information of himself, and meanwhile he resolved to remain close upon his guard lest those qualities of which he knew nothing should everlastingly disgrace him. "Good Lord!" he repeated in dismay.

After a time the tall soldier slid dexterously through the hole. The loud private followed. They were wrangling.

"That's all right," said the tall soldier as he entered. He waved his hand expressively. "You can believe me or not, jest as you like. All you got to do is to sit down and wait as quiet as you can. Then pretty soon you'll find out I was right."

His comrade grunted stubbornly. For a moment he seemed to be searching for a formidable reply. Finally he said: "Well, you don't know everything in the world, do you?"

"Didn't say I knew everything in the world," retorted the other sharply. He began to stow various articles snugly into his knapsack.

The youth, pausing in his nervous walk, looked down at the busy figure. "Going to be a battle, sure, is there, Jim?" he asked.

"Of course there is," replied the tall soldier. "Of course there is. You jest wait 'til to-morrow, and you'll see one of the biggest battles ever was. You jest wait."

"Thunder!" said the youth.

"Oh, you'll see fighting this time, my boy, what'll be regular out-and-out fighting," added the tall soldier, with the air of a man who is about to exhibit a battle for the benefit of his friends.

"Huh!" said the loud one from a corner.

"Well," remarked the youth, "like as not this story'll turn out jest like them others did."

"Not much it won't," replied the tall soldier, exasperated. "Not much it won't. Didn't the cavalry all start this morning?" He glared about him. No one denied his statement. "The cavalry started this morning," he continued. "They say there ain't hardly any cavalry left in camp. They're going to Richmond, or some place, while we fight all the Johnnies.[8] It's some dodge like that. The regiment's got orders, too. A feller what seen 'em go to headquarters told me a little while ago. And they're raising blazes all over camp—anybody can see that."

"Shucks!" said the loud one.

The youth remained silent for a time. At last he spoke to the tall soldier. "Jim!"

"What?"

"How do you think the reg'ment 'll do?"

"Oh, they'll fight all right, I guess, after they once get into it," said the other with cold judgment. He made a fine use of the third person. "There's been heaps of fun poked at 'em because they're new, of course, and all that; but they'll fight all right, I guess."

"Think any of the boys 'll run?" persisted the youth.

"Oh, there may be a few of 'em run, but there's them kind in every regiment, 'specially when they first goes under fire," said the other in a tolerant way. "Of course it might happen that the hull kit-and-boodle might start and run, if some big fighting came first-off, and then again they might stay and fight like fun. But you can't bet on nothing. Of course they ain't never been under fire

8. "Johnny Rebs," or Confederate soldiers.

yet, and it ain't likely they'll lick the hull rebel army all-to-oncet the first time; but I think they'll fight better than some, if worse than others. That's the way I figger. They call the reg'ment 'Fresh fish' and everything; but the boys come of good stock, and most of 'em 'll fight like sin after they oncet git shootin'," he added, with a mighty emphasis on the last four words.

"Oh, you think you know——" began the loud soldier with scorn.

The other turned savagely upon him. They had a rapid altercation, in which they fastened upon each other various strange epithets.

The youth at last interrupted them. "Did you ever think you might run yourself, Jim?" he asked. On concluding the sentence he laughed as if he had meant to aim a joke. The loud soldier also giggled.

The tall private waved his hand. "Well," said he profoundly, "I've thought it might get too hot for Jim Conklin in some of them scrimmages, and if a whole lot of boys started and run, why, I s'pose I'd start and run. And if I once started to run, I'd run like the devil, and no mistake. But if everybody was a-standing and a-fighting, why, I'd stand and fight. Be jiminey, I would. I'll bet on it."

"Huh!" said the loud one.

The youth of this tale felt gratitude for these words of his comrade. He had feared that all of the untried men possessed a great and correct confidence. He now was in a measure reassured.

Chapter II

The next morning the youth discovered that his tall comrade had been the fast-flying messenger of a mistake. There was much scoffing at the latter by those who had yesterday been firm adherents of his views, and there was even a little sneering by men who had never believed the rumor. The tall one fought with a man from Chatfield Corners and beat him severely.

The youth felt, however, that his problem was in no wise lifted from him. There was, on the contrary, an irritating prolongation. The tale had created in him a great concern for himself. Now, with the newborn question in his mind, he was compelled to sink back into his old place as part of a blue demonstration.

For days he made ceaseless calculations, but they were all wondrously unsatisfactory. He found that he could establish nothing.

He finally concluded that the only way to prove himself was to go into the blaze, and then figuratively to watch his legs to discover their merits and faults. He reluctantly admitted that he could not sit still and with a mental slate and pencil derive an answer. To gain it, he must have blaze, blood, and danger, even as a chemist requires this, that, and the other. So he fretted for an opportunity.

Meanwhile he continually tried to measure himself by his comrades. The tall soldier, for one, gave him some assurance. This man's serene unconcern dealt him a measure of confidence, for he had known him since childhood, and from his intimate knowledge he did not see how he could be capable of anything that was beyond him, the youth. Still, he thought that his comrade might be mistaken about himself. Or, on the other hand, he might be a man heretofore doomed to peace and obscurity, but, in reality, made to shine in war.

The youth would have liked to have discovered another who suspected himself. A sympathetic comparison of mental notes would have been a joy to him.

He occasionally tried to fathom a comrade with seductive sentences. He looked about to find men in the proper mood. All attempts failed to bring forth any statement which looked in any way like a confession to those doubts which he privately acknowledged in himself. He was afraid to make an open declaration of his concern, because he dreaded to place some unscrupulous confidant upon the high plane of the unconfessed from which elevation he could be derided.

In regard to his companions his mind wavered between two opinions, according to his mood. Sometimes he inclined to believing them all heroes. In fact, he usually admitted in secret the superior development of the higher qualities in others. He could conceive of men going very insignificantly about the world bearing a load of courage unseen, and although he had known many of his comrades through boyhood, he began to fear that his judgment of them had been blind. Then, in other moments, he flouted these theories, and assured himself that his fellows were all privately wondering and quaking.

His emotions made him feel strange in the presence of men who talked excitedly of a prospective battle as of a drama they were about to witness, with nothing but eagerness and curiosity apparent in their faces. It was often that he suspected them to be liars.

He did not pass such thoughts without severe condemnation

of himself. He dinned reproaches at times. He was convicted by himself of many shameful crimes against the gods of traditions.

In his great anxiety his heart was continually clamoring at what he considered the intolerable slowness of the generals. They seemed content to perch tranquilly on the river bank, and leave him bowed down by the weight of a great problem. He wanted it settled forthwith. He could not long bear such a load, he said. Sometimes his anger at the commanders reached an acute stage, and he grumbled about the camp like a veteran.

One morning, however, he found himself in the ranks of his prepared regiment. The men were whispering speculations and recounting the old rumors. In the gloom before the break of the day their uniforms glowed a deep purple hue. From across the river the red eyes were still peering. In the eastern sky there was a yellow patch like a rug laid for the feet of the coming sun; and against it, black and patternlike, loomed the gigantic figure of the colonel on a gigantic horse.

From off in the darkness came the trampling of feet. The youth could occasionally see dark shadows that moved like monsters. The regiment stood at rest for what seemed a long time. The youth grew impatient. It was unendurable the way these affairs were managed. He wondered how long they were to be kept waiting.

As he looked all about him and pondered upon the mystic gloom, he began to believe that at any moment the ominous distance might be aflare, and the rolling crashes of an engagement come to his ears. Staring once at the red eyes across the river, he conceived them to be growing larger, as the orbs of a row of dragons advancing. He turned toward the colonel and saw him lift his gigantic arm and calmly stroke his mustache.

At last he heard from along the road at the foot of the hill the clatter of a horse's galloping hoofs. It must be the coming of orders. He bent forward, scarce breathing. The exciting clickety-click, as it grew louder and louder, seemed to be beating upon his soul. Presently a horseman with jangling equipment drew rein before the colonel of the regiment. The two held a short, sharp-worded conversation. The men in the foremost ranks craned their necks.

As the horseman wheeled his animal and galloped away he turned to shout over his shoulder, "Don't forget that box of cigars!" The colonel mumbled in reply. The youth wondered what a box of cigars had to do with war.

A moment later the regiment went swinging off into the darkness. It was now like one of those moving monsters wending with many feet. The air was heavy, and cold with dew. A mass of wet grass, marched upon, rustled like silk.

There was an occasional flash and glimmer of steel from the backs of all these huge crawling reptiles. From the road came creakings and grumblings as some surly guns were dragged away.

The men stumbled along still muttering speculations. There was a subdued debate. Once a man fell down, and as he reached for his rifle a comrade, unseeing, trod upon his hand. He of the injured fingers swore bitterly and aloud. A low, tittering laugh went among his fellows.

Presently they passed into a roadway and marched forward with easy strides. A dark regiment moved before them, and from behind also came the tinkle of equipments on the bodies of marching men.

The rushing yellow of the developing day went on behind their backs. When the sunrays at last struck full and mellowingly upon the earth, the youth saw that the landscape was streaked with two long, thin, black columns which disappeared on the brow of a hill in front and rearward vanished in a wood. They were like two serpents crawling from the cavern of the night.

The river was not in view. The tall soldier burst into praises of what he thought to be his powers of perception.

Some of the tall one's companions cried with emphasis that they, too, had evolved the same thing, and they congratulated themselves upon it. But there were others who said that the tall one's plan was not the true one at all. They persisted with other theories. There was a vigorous discussion.

The youth took no part in them. As he walked along in careless line he was engaged with his own eternal debate. He could not hinder himself from dwelling upon it. He was despondent and sullen, and threw shifting glances about him. He looked ahead, often expecting to hear from the advance the rattle of firing.

But the long serpents crawled slowly from hill to hill without bluster of smoke. A dun-colored cloud of dust floated away to the right. The sky overhead was of a fairy blue.

The youth studied the faces of his companions, ever on the watch to detect kindred emotions. He suffered disappointment. Some ardor of the air which was causing the veteran commands to move with glee—almost with song—had infected the new regiment. The men began to speak of victory as of a thing they knew. Also, the tall soldier received his vindication. They were certainly going to come around in behind the enemy. They expressed commiseration for that part of the enemy which had been left upon the river bank, felicitating themselves upon being a part of a blasting host.

The youth, considering himself as separated from the others, was saddened by the blithe and merry speeches that went from rank to rank. The company wags all made their best endeavors. The regiment tramped to the tune of laughter.

The loud soldier often convulsed whole files by his biting sarcasms aimed at the tall one.

And it was not long before all the men seemed to forget their mission. Whole brigades grinned in unison, and regiments laughed.

A rather fat soldier attempted to pilfer a horse from a dooryard. He planned to load his knapsack upon it. He was escaping with his prize when a young girl rushed from the house and grabbed the animal's mane. There followed a wrangle. The young girl, with pink cheeks and shining eyes, stood like a dauntless statue.

The observant regiment, standing at rest in the roadway, whooped at once, and entered whole-souled upon the side of the maiden. The men became so engrossed in this affair that they entirely ceased to remember their own large war. They jeered the piratical private, and called attention to various defects in his personal appearance; and they were wildly enthusiastic in support of the young girl.

To her, from some distance, came bold advice. "Hit him with a stick."

There were crows and catcalls showered upon him when he retreated without the horse. The regiment rejoiced at his downfall. Loud and vociferous congratulations were showered upon the maiden, who stood panting and regarding the troops with defiance.

At nightfall the column broke into regimental pieces, and the fragments went into the fields to camp. Tents sprang up like strange plants. Camp fires, like red, peculiar blossoms, dotted the night.

The youth kept from intercourse with his companions as much as circumstances would allow him. In the evening he wandered a few paces into the gloom. From this little distance the many fires, with the black forms of men passing to and fro before the crimson rays, made weird and satanic effects.

He lay down in the grass. The blades pressed tenderly against his cheek. The moon had been lighted and was hung in a treetop. The liquid stillness of the night enveloping him made him feel vast pity for himself. There was a caress in the soft winds; and the whole mood of the darkness, he thought, was one of sympathy for himself in his distress.

He wished, without reserve, that he was at home again making the endless rounds from the house to the barn, from the barn to the fields, from the fields to the barn, from the barn to the house.

He remembered he had often cursed the brindle cow and her mates, and had sometimes flung milking stools. But, from his present point of view, there was a halo of happiness about each of their heads, and he would have sacrificed all the brass buttons on the continent to have been enabled to return to them. He told himself that he was not formed for a soldier. And he mused seriously upon the radical differences between himself and those men who were dodging implike around the fires.

As he mused thus he heard the rustle of grass, and, upon turning his head, discovered the loud soldier. He called out, "Oh, Wilson!"

The latter approached and looked down. "Why, hello, Henry; is it you? What you doing here?"

"Oh, thinking," said the youth.

The other sat down and carefully lighted his pipe. "You're getting blue, my boy. You're looking thundering peeked. What the dickens is wrong with you?"

"Oh, nothing," said the youth.

The loud soldier launched then into the subject of the anticipated fight. "Oh, we've got 'em now!" As he spoke his boyish face was wreathed in a gleeful smile, and his voice had an exultant ring. "We've got 'em now. At last, by the eternal thunders, we'll lick 'em good!

"If the truth was known," he added, more soberly, "*they've* licked *us* about every clip up to now; but this time—this time— we'll lick 'em good!"

"I thought you was objecting to this march a little while ago," said the youth coldly.

"Oh, it wasn't that," explained the other. "I don't mind marching, if there's going to be fighting at the end of it. What I hate is this getting moved here and moved there, with no good coming of it, as far as I can see, excepting sore feet and damned short rations."

"Well, Jim Conklin says we'll get a plenty of fighting this time."

"He's right for once, I guess, though I can't see how it come. This time we're in for a big battle, and we've got the best end of it, certain sure. Gee rod! how we will thump 'em!"

He arose and began to pace to and fro excitedly. The thrill of his enthusiasm made him walk with an elastic step. He was sprightly, vigorous, fiery in his belief in success. He looked into the future with clear, proud eye, and he swore with the air of an old soldier.

The youth watched him for a moment in silence. When he finally spoke his voice was as bitter as dregs. "Oh, you're going to do great things, I s'pose!"

The loud soldier blew a thoughtful cloud of smoke from his pipe. "Oh, I don't know," he remarked with dignity; "I don't know. I s'pose I'll do as well as the rest. I'm going to try like thunder." He evidently complimented himself upon the modesty of this statement.

"How do you know you won't run when the time comes?" asked the youth.

"Run?" said the loud one; "run?—of course not!" He laughed.

"Well," continued the youth, "lots of good-a-'nough men have thought they was going to do great things before the fight, but when the time come they skedaddled."

"Oh, that's all true, I s'pose," replied the other; "but I'm not going to skedaddle. The man that bets on my running will lose his money, that's all." He nodded confidently.

"Oh, shucks!" said the youth. "You ain't the bravest man in the world, are you?"

"No, I ain't," exclaimed the loud soldier indignantly; "and I didn't say I was the bravest man in the world, neither. I said I was going to do my share of fighting—that's what I said. And I am, too. Who are you, anyhow? You talk as if you thought you was Napoleon Bonaparte." He glared at the youth for a moment, and then strode away.

The youth called in a savage voice after his comrade: "Well, you needn't git mad about it!" But the other continued on his way and made no reply.

He felt alone in space when his injured comrade had disappeared. His failure to discover any mite of resemblance in their view points made him more miserable than before. No one seemed to be wrestling with such a terrific personal problem. He was a mental outcast.

He went slowly to his tent and stretched himself on a blanket by the side of the snoring tall soldier. In the darkness he saw visions of a thousand-tongued fear that would babble at his back and cause him to flee, while others were going coolly about their country's business. He admitted that he would not be able to cope with this monster. He felt that every nerve in his body would be an ear to hear the voices, while other men would remain stolid and deaf.

And as he sweated with the pain of these thoughts, he could hear low, serene sentences. "I'll bid five." "Make it six." "Seven." "Seven goes."

He stared at the red, shivering reflection of a fire on the white wall of his tent until, exhausted and ill from the monotony of his suffering, he fell asleep.

Chapter III

When another night came the columns, changed to purple streaks, filed across two pontoon bridges. A glaring fire wine-tinted the waters of the river. Its rays, shining upon the moving masses of troops, brought forth here and there sudden gleams of silver or gold. Upon the other shore a dark and mysterious range of hills was curved against the sky. The insect voices of the night sang solemnly.

After this crossing the youth assured himself that at any moment they might be suddenly and fearfully assaulted from the caves of the lowering woods. He kept his eyes watchfully upon the darkness.

But his regiment went unmolested to a camping place, and its soldiers slept the brave sleep of wearied men. In the morning they were routed out with early energy, and hustled along a narrow road that led deep into the forest.

It was during this rapid march that the regiment lost many of the marks of a new command.

The men had begun to count the miles upon their fingers, and they grew tired. "Sore feet an' damned short rations, that's all," said the loud soldier. There was perspiration and grumblings. After a time they began to shed their knapsacks. Some tossed them unconcernedly down; others hid them carefully, asserting their plans to return for them at some convenient time. Men extricated themselves from thick shirts. Presently few carried anything but their necessary clothing, blankets, haversacks, canteens, and arms and ammunition. "You can now eat and shoot," said the tall soldier to the youth. "That's all you want to do."

There was sudden change from the ponderous infantry of theory to the light and speedy infantry of practice. The regiment, relieved of a burden, received a new impetus. But there was much loss of valuable knapsacks, and, on the whole, very good shirts.

But the regiment was not yet veteranlike in appearance. Veteran regiments in the army were likely to be very small aggregations of men. Once, when the command had first come to the field, some perambulating veterans, noting the length of their column, had accosted them thus: "Hey, fellers, what brigade is that?" And when the men had replied that they formed a regiment and not a brigade,[9] the older soldiers had laughed, and said, "O Gawd!"

Also, there was too great a similarity in the hats. The hats of a regiment should properly represent the history of headgear for a period of years. And, moreover, there were no letters of faded gold

9. A brigade normally comprises two or more regiments.

speaking from the colors. They were new and beautiful, and the color bearer habitually oiled the pole.

Presently the army again sat down to think. The odor of the peaceful pines was in the men's nostrils. The sound of monotonous axe blows rang through the forest, and the insects, nodding upon their perches, crooned like old women. The youth returned to his theory of a blue demonstration.

One gray dawn, however, he was kicked in the leg by the tall soldier, and then, before he was entirely awake, he found himself running down a wood road in the midst of men who were panting from the first effects of speed. His canteen banged rhythmically upon his thigh, and his haversack bobbed softly. His musket bounced a trifle from his shoulder at each stride and made his cap feel uncertain upon his head.

He could hear the men whisper jerky sentences: "Say—what's all this—about?" "What th' thunder—we—skedaddlin' this way fer?" "Billie—keep off m' feet. Yeh run—like a cow." And the loud soldier's shrill voice could be heard: "What th' devil they in sich a hurry for?"

The youth thought the damp fog of early morning moved from the rush of a great body of troops. From the distance came a sudden spatter of firing.

He was bewildered. As he ran with his comrades he strenuously tried to think, but all he knew was that if he fell down those coming behind would tread upon him. All his faculties seemed to be needed to guide him over and past obstructions. He felt carried along by a mob.

The sun spread disclosing rays, and, one by one, regiments burst into view like armed men just born of the earth. The youth perceived that the time had come. He was about to be measured. For a moment he felt in the face of his great trial like a babe, and the flesh over his heart seemed very thin. He seized time to look about him calculatingly.

But he instantly saw that it would be impossible for him to escape from the regiment. It inclosed him. And there were iron laws of tradition and law on four sides. He was in a moving box.

As he perceived this fact it occurred to him that he had never wished to come to the war. He had not enlisted of his free will. He had been dragged by the merciless government. And now they were taking him out to be slaughtered.

The regiment slid down a bank and wallowed across a little stream. The mournful current moved slowly on, and from the water, shaded black, some white bubble eyes looked at the men.

As they climbed the hill on the farther side artillery began to boom. Here the youth forgot many things as he felt a sudden impulse of curiosity. He scrambled up the bank with a speed that could not be exceeded by a bloodthirsty man.

He expected a battle scene.

There were some little fields girted and squeezed by a forest. Spread over the grass and in among the tree trunks, he could see knots and waving lines of skirmishers who were running hither and thither and firing at the landscape. A dark battle line lay upon a sunstruck clearing that gleamed orange color. A flag fluttered.

Other regiments floundered up the bank. The brigade was formed in line of battle, and after a pause started slowly through the woods in the rear of the receding skirmishers, who were continually melting into the scene to appear again farther on. They were always busy as bees, deeply absorbed in their little combats.

The youth tried to observe everything. He did not use care to avoid trees and branches, and his forgotten feet were constantly knocking against stones or getting entangled in briers. He was aware that these battalions with their commotions were woven red and startling into the gentle fabric of softened greens and browns. It looked to be a wrong place for a battle field.

The skirmishers in advance fascinated him. Their shots into thickets and at distant and prominent trees spoke to him of tragedies —hidden, mysterious, solemn.

Once the line encountered the body of a dead soldier. He lay upon his back staring at the sky. He was dressed in an awkward suit of yellowish brown. The youth could see that the soles of his shoes had been worn to the thinness of writing paper, and from a great rent in one the dead foot projected piteously. And it was as if fate had betrayed the soldier. In death it exposed to his enemies that poverty which in life he had perhaps concealed from his friends.

The ranks opened covertly to avoid the corpse. The invulnerable dead man forced a way for himself. The youth looked keenly at the ashen face. The wind raised the tawny beard. It moved as if a hand were stroking it. He vaguely desired to walk around and around the body and stare; the impulse of the living to try to read in dead eyes the answer to the Question.

During the march the ardor which the youth had acquired when out of view of the field rapidly faded to nothing. His curiosity was quite easily satisfied. If an intense scene had caught him with its wild swing as he came to the top of the bank, he might have gone roaring on. This advance upon Nature was too calm. He had opportunity to reflect. He had time in which to wonder about himself and to attempt to probe his sensations.

Absurd ideas took hold upon him. He thought that he did not relish the landscape. It threatened him. A coldness swept over his back, and it is true that his trousers felt to him that they were no fit for his legs at all.

A house standing placidly in distant fields had to him an ominous look. The shadows of the woods were formidable. He was certain that in this vista there lurked fierce-eyed hosts. The swift thought came to him that the generals did not know what they were about. It was all a trap. Suddenly those close forests would bristle with rifle barrels. Ironlike brigades would appear in the rear. They were all going to be sacrificed. The generals were stupids. The enemy would presently swallow the whole command. He glared about him, expecting to see the stealthy approach of his death.

He thought that he must break from the ranks and harangue his comrades. They must not all be killed like pigs; and he was sure it would come to pass unless they were informed of these dangers. The generals were idiots to send them marching into a regular pen. There was but one pair of eyes in the corps. He would step forth and make a speech. Shrill and passionate words came to his lips.

The line, broken into moving fragments by the ground, went calmly on through fields and woods. The youth looked at the men nearest him, and saw, for the most part, expressions of deep interest, as if they were investigating something that had fascinated them. One or two stepped with overvaliant airs as if they were already plunged into war. Others walked as upon thin ice. The greater part of the untested men appeared quiet and absorbed. They were going to look at war, the red animal—war, the blood-swollen god. And they were deeply engrossed in this march.

As he looked the youth gripped his outcry at his throat. He saw that even if the men were tottering with fear they would laugh at his warning. They would jeer him, and, if practicable, pelt him with missiles. Admitting that he might be wrong, a frenzied declamation of the kind would turn him into a worm.

He assumed, then, the demeanor of one who knows that he is doomed alone to unwritten responsibilities. He lagged, with tragic glances at the sky.

He was surprised presently by the young lieutenant of his company, who began heartily to beat him with a sword, calling out in a loud and insolent voice: "Come, young man, get up into ranks there. No skulking 'll do here." He mended his pace with suitable haste. And he hated the lieutenant, who had no appreciation of fine minds. He was a mere brute.

After a time the brigade was halted in the cathedral light of a forest. The busy skirmishers were still popping. Through the aisles of the wood could be seen the floating smoke from their rifles. Sometimes it went up in little balls, white and compact.

During this halt many men in the regiment began erecting tiny hills in front of them. They used stones, sticks, earth, and anything they thought might turn a bullet. Some built comparatively large ones, while others seemed content with little ones.

This procedure caused a discussion among the men. Some wished to fight like duelists, believing it to be correct to stand erect and be, from their feet to their foreheads, a mark. They said they scorned the devices of the cautious. But the others scoffed in reply, and pointed to the veterans on the flanks who were digging at the ground like terriers. In a short time there was quite a barricade along the regimental fronts. Directly, however, they were ordered to withdraw from that place.

This astounded the youth. He forgot his stewing over the advance movement. "Well, then, what did they march us out here for?" he demanded of the tall soldier. The latter with calm faith began a heavy explanation, although he had been compelled to leave a little protection of stones and dirt to which he had devoted much care and skill.

When the regiment was aligned in another position each man's regard for his safety caused another line of small intrenchments. They ate their noon meal behind a third one. They were moved from this one also. They were marched from place to place with apparent aimlessness.

The youth had been taught that a man became another thing in a battle. He saw his salvation in such a change. Hence this waiting was an ordeal to him. He was in a fever of impatience. He considered that there was denoted a lack of purpose on the part of the generals. He began to complain to the tall soldier. "I can't stand this much longer," he cried. "I don't see what good it does to make us wear out our legs for nothin'." He wished to return to camp, knowing that this affair was a blue demonstration; or else to go into a battle and discover that he had been a fool in his doubts, and was, in truth, a man of traditional courage. The strain of present circumstances he felt to be intolerable.

The philosophical tall soldier measured a sandwich of cracker[1] and pork and swallowed it in a nonchalant manner. "Oh, I suppose we must go reconnoitering around the country jest to keep 'em from getting too close, or to develop[2] 'em, or something."

1. Hardtack, a large, hard biscuit.
2. A military term meaning "to learn the   enemy's strength and position."

"Huh!" said the loud soldier.

"Well," cried the youth, still fidgeting, "I'd rather do anything 'most than go tramping 'round the country all day doing no good to nobody and jest tiring ourselves out."

"So would I," said the loud soldier. "It ain't right. I tell you if anybody with any sense was a-runnin' this army it——"

"Oh, shut up!" roared the tall private. "You little fool. You little damn' cuss. You ain't had that there coat and them pants on for six months, and yet you talk as if——"

"Well, I wanta do some fighting anyway," interrupted the other. "I didn't come here to walk. I could 'ave walked to home—'round an' 'round the barn, if I jest wanted to walk."

The tall one, red-faced, swallowed another sandwich as if taking poison in despair.

But gradually, as he chewed, his face became again quiet and contented. He could not rage in fierce argument in the presence of such sandwiches. During his meals he always wore an air of blissful contemplation of the food he had swallowed. His spirit seemed then to be communing with the viands.

He accepted new environment and circumstance with great coolness, eating from his haversack at every opportunity. On the march he went along with the stride of a hunter, objecting to neither gait nor distance. And he had not raised his voice when he had been ordered away from three little protective piles of earth and stone, each of which had been an engineering feat worthy of being made sacred to the name of his grandmother.

In the afternoon the regiment went out over the same ground it had taken in the morning. The landscape then ceased to threaten the youth. He had been close to it and become familiar with it.

When, however, they began to pass into a new region, his old fears of stupidity and incompetence reassailed him, but this time he doggedly let them babble. He was occupied with his problem, and in his desperation he concluded that the stupidity did not greatly matter.

Once he thought he had concluded that it would be better to get killed directly and end his troubles. Regarding death thus out of the corner of his eye, he conceived it to be nothing but rest, and he was filled with a momentary astonishment that he should have made an extraordinary commotion over the mere matter of getting killed. He would die; he would go to some place where he would be understood. It was useless to expect appreciation of his profound and fine senses from such men as the lieutenant. He must look to the grave for comprehension.

The skirmish fire increased to a long clattering sound. With it was mingled far-away cheering. A battery spoke.

Directly the youth could see the skirmishers running. They were pursued by the sound of musketry fire. After a time the hot, dangerous flashes of the rifles were visible. Smoke clouds went slowly and insolently across the fields like observant phantoms. The din became crescendo, like the roar of an oncoming train.

A brigade ahead of them and on the right went into action with a rending roar. It was as if it had exploded. And thereafter it lay stretched in the distance behind a long gray wall, that one was obliged to look twice at to make sure that it was smoke.

The youth, forgetting his neat plan of getting killed, gazed spell bound. His eyes grew wide and busy with the action of the scene. His mouth was a little ways open.

Of a sudden he felt a heavy and sad hand laid upon his shoulder. Awakening from his trance of observation he turned and beheld the loud soldier.

"It's my first and last battle, old boy," said the latter, with intense gloom. He was quite pale and his girlish lip was trembling.

"Eh?" murmured the youth in great astonishment.

"It's my first and last battle, old boy," continued the loud soldier. "Something tells me——"

"What?"

"I'm a gone coon this first time and—and I w-want you to take these here things—to—my—folks." He ended in a quavering sob of pity for himself. He handed the youth a little packet done up in a yellow envelope.

"Why, what the devil——" began the youth again.

But the other gave him a glance as from the depths of a tomb, and raised his limp hand in a prophetic manner and turned away.

Chapter IV

The brigade was halted in the fringe of a grove. The men crouched among the trees and pointed their restless guns out at the fields. They tried to look beyond the smoke.

Out of this haze they could see running men. Some shouted information and gestured as they hurried.

The men of the new regiment watched and listened eagerly, while their tongues ran on in gossip of the battle. They mouthed rumors that had flown like birds out of the unknown.

"They say Perry has been driven in with big loss."

"Yes, Carrott went t' th' hospital. He said he was sick. That smart lieutenant is commanding 'G' Company. Th' boys say they won't be under Carrott no more if they all have t' desert. They allus knew he was a——"

"Hannises' batt'ry is took."

"It ain't either. I saw Hannises' batt'ry off on th' left not more'n fifteen minutes ago."

"Well——"

"Th' general, he ses he is goin' t' take th' hull command of th' 304th when we go inteh action, an' then he ses we'll do sech fightin' as never another one reg'ment done."

"They say we're catchin' it over on th' left. They say th' enemy driv' our line inteh a devil of a swamp an' took Hannises' batt'ry."

"No sech thing. Hannises' batt'ry was 'long here 'bout a minute ago."

"That young Hasbrouck, he makes a good off'cer. He ain't afraid 'a nothin'."

"I met one of th' 148th Maine boys an' he ses his brigade fit th' hull rebel army fer four hours over on th' turnpike road an' killed about five thousand of 'em. He ses one more sech fight as that an' th' war 'll be over."

"Bill wasn't scared either. No, sir! It wasn't that. Bill ain't a-gittin' scared easy. He was jest mad, that's what he was. When that feller trod on his hand, he up an' sed that he was willin' t' give his hand t' his country, but he be dumbed if he was goin' t' have every dumb bushwhacker[3] in th' kentry walkin' 'round on it. So he went t' th' hospital disregardless of th' fight. Three fingers was crunched. Th' dern doctor wanted t' amputate 'm, an' Bill, he raised a heluva row, I hear. He's a funny feller."

The din in front swelled to a tremendous chorus. The youth and his fellows were frozen to silence. They could see a flag that tossed in the smoke angrily. Near it were the blurred and agitated forms of troops. There came a turbulent stream of men across the fields. A battery changing position at a frantic gallop scattered the stragglers right and left.

A shell screaming like a storm banshee[4] went over the huddled heads of the reserves. It landed in the grove, and exploding redly flung the brown earth. There was a little shower of pine needles.

Bullets began to whistle among the branches and nip at the trees. Twigs and leaves came sailing down. It was as if a thousand axes, wee and invisible, were being wielded. Many of the men were constantly dodging and ducking their heads.

The lieutenant of the youth's company was shot in the hand. He began to swear so wondrously that a nervous laugh went along

3. A guerrilla.   warning of approaching death.
4. In Gaelic folklore, a female spirit

the regimental line. The officer's profanity sounded conventional. It relieved the tightened senses of the new men. It was as if he had hit his fingers with a tack hammer at home.

He held the wounded member carefully away from his side so that the blood would not drip upon his trousers.

The captain of the company, tucking his sword under his arm, produced a handkerchief and began to bind with it the lieutenant's wound. And they disputed as to how the binding should be done.

The battle flag in the distance jerked about madly. It seemed to be struggling to free itself from an agony. The billowing smoke was filled with horizontal flashes.

Men running swiftly emerged from it. They grew in numbers until it was seen that the whole command was fleeing. The flag suddenly sank down as if dying. Its motion as it fell was a gesture of despair.

Wild yells came from behind the walls of smoke. A sketch in gray and red dissolved into a moblike body of men who galloped like wild horses.

The veteran regiments on the right and left of the 304th immediately began to jeer. With the passionate song of the bullets and the banshee shrieks of shells were mingled loud catcalls and bits of facetious advice concerning places of safety.

But the new regiment was breathless with horror. "Gawd! Saunders's got crushed!" whispered the man at the youth's elbow. They shrank back and crouched as if compelled to await a flood.

The youth shot a swift glance along the blue ranks of the regiment. The profiles were motionless, carven; and afterward he remembered that the color sergeant was standing with his legs apart, as if he expected to be pushed to the ground.

The following throng went whirling around the flank. Here and there were officers carried along on the stream like exasperated chips. They were striking about them with their swords and with their left fists, punching every head they could reach. They cursed like highwaymen.

A mounted officer displayed the furious anger of a spoiled child. He raged with his head, his arms, and his legs.

Another, the commander of the brigade, was galloping about bawling. His hat was gone and his clothes were awry. He resembled a man who has come from bed to go to a fire. The hoofs of his horse often threatened the heads of the running men, but they scampered with singular fortune. In this rush they were apparently all deaf and blind. They heeded not the largest and longest of the oaths that were thrown at them from all directions.

Frequently over this tumult could be heard the grim jokes of the critical veterans; but the retreating men apparently were not even conscious of the presence of an audience.

The battle reflection that shone for an instant in the faces on the mad current made the youth feel that forceful hands from heaven would not have been able to have held him in place if he could have got intelligent control of his legs.

There was an appalling imprint upon these faces. The struggle in the smoke had pictured an exaggeration of itself on the bleached cheeks and in the eyes wild with one desire.

The sight of this stampede exerted a floodlike force that seemed able to drag sticks and stones and men from the ground. They of the reserves had to hold on. They grew pale and firm, and red and quaking.

The youth achieved one little thought in the midst of this chaos. The composite monster which had caused the other troops to flee had not then appeared. He resolved to get a view of it, and then, he thought he might very likely run better than the best of them.

Chapter V

There were moments of waiting. The youth thought of the village street at home before the arrival of the circus parade on a day in the spring. He remembered how he had stood, a small, thrillful boy, prepared to follow the dingy lady upon the white horse, or the band in its faded chariot. He saw the yellow road, the lines of expectant people, and the sober houses. He particularly remembered an old fellow who used to sit upon a cracker box in front of the store and feign to despise such exhibitions. A thousand details of color and form surged in his mind. The old fellow upon the cracker box appeared in middle prominence.

Some one cried, "Here they come!"

There was rustling and muttering among the men. They displayed a feverish desire to have every possible cartridge ready to their hands. The boxes were pulled around into various positions, and adjusted with great care. It was as if seven hundred new bonnets were being tried on.

The tall soldier, having prepared his rifle, produced a red handkerchief of some kind. He was engaged in knotting it about his throat with exquisite attention to its position, when the cry was repeated up and down the line in a muffled roar of sound.

"Here they come! Here they come!" Gun locks clicked.

Across the smoke-infested fields came a brown swarm of running men who were giving shrill yells. They came on, stooping and swinging their rifles at all angles. A flag, tilted forward, sped near the front.

As he caught sight of them the youth was momentarily startled by a thought that perhaps his gun was not loaded. He stood trying to rally his faltering intellect so that he might recollect the moment when he had loaded, but he could not.

A hatless general pulled his dripping horse to a stand near the colonel of the 304th. He shook his fist in the other's face. "You've got to hold 'em back!" he shouted, savagely; "you've got to hold 'em back!"

In his agitation the colonel began to stammer. "A-all r-right, General, all right, by Gawd! We-we'll do our—we-we'll d-d-do—do our best, General." The general made a passionate gesture and galloped away. The colonel, perchance to relieve his feelings, began to scold like a wet parrot. The youth, turning swiftly to make sure that the rear was unmolested, saw the commander regarding his men in a highly resentful manner, as if he regretted above everything his association with them.

The man at the youth's elbow was mumbling, as if to himself: "Oh, we're in for it now! oh, we're in for it now!"

The captain of the company had been pacing excitedly to and fro in the rear. He coaxed in schoolmistress fashion, as to a congregation of boys with primers. His talk was an endless repetition. "Reserve your fire, boys—don't shoot till I tell you—save your fire—wait till they get close up—don't be damned fools——"

Perspiration streamed down the youth's face, which was soiled like that of a weeping urchin. He frequently, with a nervous movement, wiped his eyes with his coat sleeve. His mouth was still a little ways open.

He got the one glance at the foe-swarming field in front of him, and instantly ceased to debate the question of his piece being loaded. Before he was ready to begin—before he had announced to himself that he was about to fight—he threw the obedient, well-balanced rifle into position and fired a first wild shot. Directly he was working at his weapon like an automatic affair.

He suddenly lost concern for himself, and forgot to look at a menacing fate. He became not a man but a member. He felt that something of which he was a part—a regiment, an army, a cause, or a country—was in a crisis. He was welded into a common personality which was dominated by a single desire. For some moments he could not flee no more than a little finger can commit a revolution from a hand.

If he had thought the regiment was about to be annihilated

perhaps he could have amputated himself from it. But its noise gave him assurance. The regiment was like a firework that, once ignited, proceeds superior to circumstances until its blazing vitality fades. It wheezed and banged with a mighty power. He pictured the ground before it as strewn with the discomfited.

There was a consciousness always of the presence of his comrades about him. He felt the subtle battle brotherhood more potent even than the cause for which they were fighting. It was a mysterious fraternity born of the smoke and danger of death.

He was at a task. He was like a carpenter who has made many boxes, making still another box, only there was furious haste in his movements. He, in his thoughts, was careering off in other places, even as the carpenter who as he works whistles and thinks of his friend or his enemy, his home or a saloon. And these jolted dreams were never perfect to him afterward, but remained a mass of blurred shapes.

Presently he began to feel the effects of the war atmosphere—a blistering sweat, a sensation that his eyeballs were about to crack like hot stones. A burning roar filled his ears.

Following this came a red rage. He developed the acute exasperation of a pestered animal, a well-meaning cow worried by dogs. He had a mad feeling against his rifle, which could only be used against one life at a time. He wished to rush forward and strangle with his fingers. He craved a power that would enable him to make a world-sweeping gesture and brush all back. His impotency appeared to him, and made his rage into that of a driven beast.

Buried in the smoke of many rifles his anger was directed not so much against the men whom he knew were rushing toward him as against the swirling battle phantoms which were choking him, stuffing their smoke robes down his parched throat. He fought frantically for respite for his senses, for air, as a babe being smothered attacks the deadly blankets.

There was a blare of heated rage mingled with a certain expression of intentness on all faces. Many of the men were making low-toned noises with their mouths, and these subdued cheers, snarls, imprecations, prayers, made a wild, barbaric song that went as an undercurrent of sound, strange and chantlike with the resounding chords of the war march. The man at the youth's elbow was babbling. In it there was something soft and tender like the monologue of a babe. The tall soldier was swearing in a loud voice. From his lips came a black procession of curious oaths. Of a sudden another broke out in a querulous way like a man who has mislaid his hat. "Well, why don't they support us? Why don't they send supports? Do they think——"

The youth in his battle sleep heard this as one who dozes hears.
There was a singular absence of heroic poses. The men bending and surging in their haste and rage were in every impossible attitude. The steel ramrods clanked and clanged with incessant din as the men pounded them furiously into the hot rifle barrels. The flaps of the cartridge boxes were all unfastened, and bobbed idiotically with each movement. The rifles, once loaded, were jerked to the shoulder and fired without apparent aim into the smoke or at one of the blurred and shifting forms which upon the field before the regiment had been growing larger and larger like puppets under a magician's hand.

The officers, at their intervals, rearward, neglected to stand in picturesque attitudes. They were bobbing to and fro roaring directions and encouragements. The dimensions of their howls were extraordinary. They expended their lungs with prodigal wills. And often they nearly stood upon their heads in their anxiety to observe the enemy on the other side of the tumbling smoke.

The lieutenant of the youth's company had encountered a soldier who had fled screaming at the first volley of his comrades. Behind the lines these two were acting a little isolated scene. The man was blubbering and staring with sheeplike eyes at the lieutenant, who had seized him by the collar and was pommeling him. He drove him back into the ranks with many blows. The soldier went mechanically, dully, with his animal-like eyes upon the officer. Perhaps there was to him a divinity expressed in the voice of the other—stern, hard, with no reflection of fear in it. He tried to reload his gun, but his shaking hands prevented. The lieutenant was obliged to assist him.

The men dropped here and there like bundles. The captain of the youth's company had been killed in an early part of the action. His body lay stretched out in the position of a tired man resting, but upon his face there was an astonished and sorrowful look, as if he thought some friend had done him an ill turn. The babbling man was grazed by a shot that made the blood stream widely down his face. He clapped both hands to his head. "Oh!" he said, and ran. Another grunted suddenly as if he had been struck by a club in the stomach. He sat down and gazed ruefully. In his eyes there was mute, indefinite reproach. Farther up the line a man, standing behind a tree, had had his knee joint splintered by a ball. Immediately he had dropped his rifle and gripped the tree with both arms. And there he remained, clinging desperately and crying for assistance that he might withdraw his hold upon the tree.

At last an exultant yell went along the quivering line. The firing dwindled from an uproar to a last vindictive popping. As the smoke slowly eddied away, the youth saw that the charge had been re-pulsed. The enemy were scattered into reluctant groups. He saw a man climb to the top of the fence, straddle the rail, and fire a parting shot. The waves had receded, leaving bits of dark *débris* upon the ground.

Some in the regiment began to whoop frenziedly. Many were silent. Apparently they were trying to contemplate themselves.

After the fever had left his veins, the youth thought that at last he was going to suffocate. He became aware of the foul atmosphere in which he had been struggling. He was grimy and dripping like a laborer in a foundry. He grasped his canteen and took a long swallow of the warmed water.

A sentence with variations went up and down the line. "Well, we've helt 'em back. We've helt 'em back; derned if we haven't." The men said it blissfully, leering at each other with dirty smiles.

The youth turned to look behind him and off to the right and off to the left. He experienced the joy of a man who at last finds leisure in which to look about him.

Under foot there were a few ghastly forms motionless. They lay twisted in fantastic contortions. Arms were bent and heads were turned in incredible ways. It seemed that the dead men must have fallen from some great height to get into such positions. They looked to be dumped out upon the ground from the sky.

From a position in the rear of the grove a battery was throwing shells over it. The flash of the guns startled the youth at first. He thought they were aimed directly at him. Through the trees he watched the black figures of the gunners as they worked swiftly and intently. Their labor seemed a complicated thing. He won-dered how they could remember its formula in the midst of con-fusion.

The guns squatted in a row like savage chiefs. They argued with abrupt violence. It was a grim pow-wow. Their busy servants ran hither and thither.

A small procession of wounded men were going drearily toward the rear. It was a flow of blood from the torn body of the brigade.

To the right and to the left were the dark lines of other troops. Far in front he thought he could see lighter masses protruding in points from the forest. They were suggestive of unnumbered thou-sands.

Once he saw a tiny battery go dashing along the line of the horizon. The tiny riders were beating the tiny horses.

From a sloping hill came the sound of cheerings and clashes. Smoke welled slowly through the leaves.

Batteries were speaking with thunderous oratorical effort. Here and there were flags, the red in the stripes dominating. They splashed bits of warm color upon the dark lines of troops.

The youth felt the old thrill at the sight of the emblems. They were like beautiful birds strangely undaunted in a storm.

As he listened to the din from the hillside, to a deep pulsating thunder that came from afar to the left, and to the lesser clamors which came from many directions, it occurred to him that they were fighting, too, over there, and over there, and over there. Heretofore he had supposed that all the battle was directly under his nose.

As he gazed around him the youth felt a flash of astonishment at the blue, pure sky and the sun gleamings on the trees and fields. It was surprising that Nature had gone tranquilly on with her golden process in the midst of so much devilment.

Chapter VI

The youth awakened slowly. He came gradually back to a position from which he could regard himself. For moments he had been scrutinizing his person in a dazed way as if he had never before seen himself. Then he picked up his cap from the ground. He wriggled in his jacket to make a more comfortable fit, and kneeling relaced his shoe. He thoughtfully mopped his reeking features.

So it was all over at last! The supreme trial had been passed. The red, formidable difficulties of war had been vanquished.

He went into an ecstasy of self-satisfaction. He had the most delightful sensations of his life. Standing as if apart from himself, he viewed that last scene. He perceived that the man who had fought thus was magnificent.

He felt that he was a fine fellow. He saw himself even with those ideals which he had considered as far beyond him. He smiled in deep gratification.

Upon his fellows he beamed tenderness and good will. "Gee! ain't it hot, hey?" he said affably to a man who was polishing his streaming face with his coat sleeves.

"You bet!" said the other, grinning sociably. "I never seen sech dumb hotness." He sprawled out luxuriously on the ground. "Gee, yes! An' I hope we don't have no more fightin' till a week from Monday."

There were some handshakings and deep speeches with men whose features were familiar, but with whom the youth now felt the bonds of tied hearts.[5] He helped a cursing comrade to bind up

5. Crane apparently means "whose features were *not only* familiar, but with whom. . . ." In the manuscript, the passage reads, "whose features were only familiar but with whom. . . ."

a wound of the shin.

But, of a sudden, cries of amazement broke out along the ranks of the new regiment. "Here they come ag'in! Here they come ag'in!" The man who had sprawled upon the ground started up and said, "Gosh!"

The youth turned quick eyes upon the field. He discerned forms begin to swell in masses out of a distant wood. He again saw the tilted flag speeding forward.

The shells, which had ceased to trouble the regiment for a time, came swirling again, and exploded in the grass or among the leaves of the trees. They looked to be strange war flowers bursting into fierce bloom.

The men groaned. The luster faded from their eyes. Their smudged countenances now expressed a profound dejection. They moved their stiffened bodies slowly, and watched in sullen mood the frantic approach of the enemy. The slaves toiling in the temple of this god began to feel rebellion at his harsh tasks.

They fretted and complained each to each. "Oh, say, this is too much of a good thing! Why can't somebody send us supports?"

"We ain't never goin' to stand this second banging. I didn't come here to fight the hull damn' rebel army."

There was one who raised a doleful cry. "I wish Bill Smithers had trod on my hand, insteader me treddin' on his'n." The sore joints of the regiment creaked as it painfully floundered into position to repulse.

The youth stared. Surely, he thought, this impossible thing was not about to happen. He waited as if he expected the enemy to suddenly stop, apologize, and retire bowing. It was all a mistake.

But the firing began somewhere on the regimental line and ripped along in both directions. The level sheets of flame developed great clouds of smoke that tumbled and tossed in the mild wind near the ground for a moment, and then rolled through the ranks as through a grate. The clouds were tinged an earthlike yellow in the sunrays and in the shadow were a sorry blue. The flag was sometimes eaten and lost in this mass of vapor, but more often it projected, sun-touched, resplendent.

Into the youth's eyes there came a look that one can see in the orbs of a jaded horse. His neck was quivering with nervous weakness and the muscles of his arms felt numb and bloodless. His hands, too, seemed large and awkward as if he was wearing invisible mittens. And there was a great uncertainty about his knee joints.

The words that comrades had uttered previous to the firing began to recur to him. "Oh, say, this is too much of a good thing!

What do they take us for—why don't they send supports? I didn't come here to fight the hull damned rebel army."

He began to exaggerate the endurance, the skill, and the valor of those who were coming. Himself reeling from exhaustion, he was astonished beyond measure at such persistency. They must be machines of steel. It was very gloomy struggling against such affairs, wound up perhaps to fight until sundown.

He slowly lifted his rifle and catching a glimpse of the thick-spread field he blazed at a cantering cluster. He stopped then and began to peer as best he could through the smoke. He caught changing views of the ground covered with men who were all running like pursued imps, and yelling.

To the youth it was an onslaught of redoubtable dragons. He became like the man who lost his legs at the approach of the red and green monster. He waited in a sort of a horrified, listening attitude. He seemed to shut his eyes and wait to be gobbled.

A man near him who up to this time had been working feverishly at his rifle suddenly stopped and ran with howls. A lad whose face had borne an expression of exalted courage, the majesty of he who dares give his life, was, at an instant, smitten abject. He blanched like one who has come to the edge of a cliff at midnight and is suddenly made aware. There was a revelation. He, too, threw down his gun and fled. There was no shame in his face. He ran like a rabbit.

Others began to scamper away through the smoke. The youth turned his head, shaken from his trance by this movement as if the regiment was leaving him behind. He saw the few fleeting forms.

He yelled then with fright and swung about. For a moment, in the great clamor, he was like a proverbial chicken. He lost the direction of safety. Destruction threatened him from all points.

Directly he began to speed toward the rear in great leaps. His rifle and cap were gone. His unbuttoned coat bulged in the wind. The flap of his cartridge box bobbed wildly, and his canteen, by its slender cord, swung out behind. On his face was all the horror of those things which he imagined.

The lieutenant sprang forward bawling. The youth saw his features wrathfully red, and saw him make a dab with his sword. His one thought of the incident was that the lieutenant was a peculiar creature to feel interested in such matters upon this occasion.

He ran like a blind man. Two or three times he fell down. Once he knocked his shoulder so heavily against a tree that he went headlong.

Since he had turned his back upon the fight his fears had been wondrously magnified. Death about to thrust him between the shoulder blades was far more dreadful than death about to smite him between the eyes. When he thought of it later, he conceived the impression that it is better to view the appalling than to be merely within hearing. The noises of the battle were like stones; he believed himself liable to be crushed.

As he ran on he mingled with others. He dimly saw men on his right and on his left, and he heard footsteps behind him. He thought that all the regiment was fleeing, pursued by these ominous crashes.

In his flight the sound of these following footsteps gave him his one meager relief. He felt vaguely that death must make a first choice of the men who were nearest; the initial morsels for the dragons would be then those who were following him. So he displayed the zeal of an insane sprinter in his purpose to keep them in the rear. There was a race.

As he, leading, went across a little field, he found himself in a region of shells. They hurtled over his head with long wild screams. As he listened he imagined them to have rows of cruel teeth that grinned at him. Once one lit before him and the livid lightning of the explosion effectually barred the way in his chosen direction. He groveled on the ground and then springing up went careering off through some bushes.

He experienced a thrill of amazement when he came within view of a battery in action. The men there seemed to be in conventional moods, altogether unaware of the impending annihilation. The battery was disputing with a distant antagonist and the gunners were wrapped in admiration of their shooting. They were continually bending in coaxing postures over the guns. They seemed to be patting them on the back and encouraging them with words. The guns, stolid and undaunted, spoke with dogged valor.

The precise gunners were coolly enthusiastic. They lifted their eyes every chance to the smoke-wreathed hillock from whence the hostile battery addressed them. The youth pitied them as he ran. Methodical idiots! Machine-like fools! The refined joy of planting shells in the midst of the other battery's formation would appear a little thing when the infantry came swooping out of the woods.

The face of a youthful rider, who was jerking his frantic horse with an abandon of temper he might display in a placid barnyard, was impressed deeply upon his mind. He knew that he looked upon a man who would presently be dead.

Too, he felt a pity for the guns, standing, six good comrades, in a bold row.

He saw a brigade going to the relief of its pestered fellows. He scrambled upon a wee hill and watched it sweeping finely, keeping formation in difficult places. The blue of the line was crusted with steel color, and the brilliant flags projected. Officers were shouting.

This sight also filled him with wonder. The brigade was hurrying briskly to be gulped into the infernal mouths of the war god. What manner of men were they, anyhow? Ah, it was some wondrous breed! Or else they didn't comprehend—the fools.

A furious order caused commotion in the artillery. An officer on a bounding horse made maniacal motions with his arms. The teams went swinging up from the rear, the guns were whirled about, and the battery scampered away. The cannon with their noses poked slantingly at the ground grunted and grumbled like stout men, brave but with objections to hurry.

The youth went on, moderating his pace since he had left the place of noises.

Later he came upon a general of division seated upon a horse that pricked its ears in an interested way at the battle. There was a great gleaming of yellow and patent leather about the saddle and bridle. The quiet man astride looked mouse-colored upon such a splendid charger.

A jingling staff was galloping hither and thither. Sometimes the general was surrounded by horsemen and at other times he was quite alone. He looked to be much harassed. He had the appearance of a business man whose market is swinging up and down.

The youth went slinking around this spot. He went as near as he dared trying to overhear words. Perhaps the general, unable to comprehend chaos, might call upon him for information. And he could tell him. He knew all concerning it. Of a surety the force was in a fix, and any fool could see that if they did not retreat while they had opportunity—why——

He felt that he would like to thrash the general, or at least approach and tell him in plain words exactly what he thought him to be. It was criminal to stay calmly in one spot and make no effort to stay destruction. He loitered in a fever of eagerness for the division commander to apply to him.

As he warily moved about, he heard the general call out irritably: "Tompkins, go over an' see Taylor, an' tell him not t' be in such an all-fired hurry; tell him t' halt his brigade in th' edge of th' woods; tell him t' detach a reg'ment—say I think th' center 'll break if we don't help it out some; tell him t' hurry up."

A slim youth on a fine chestnut horse caught these swift words from the mouth of his superior. He made his horse bound into a gallop almost from a walk in his haste to go upon his mission. There was a cloud of dust.

A moment later the youth saw the general bounce excitedly in his saddle.

"Yes, by heavens, they have!" The officer leaned forward. His face was aflame with excitement. "Yes, by heavens, they 've held 'im! They 've held 'im!"

He began to blithely roar at his staff: "We 'll wallop 'im now. We 'll wallop 'im now. We 've got 'em sure." He turned suddenly upon an aide: "Here—you—Jones—quick—ride after Tompkins— see Taylor- -tell him t' go in—everlastingly—like blazes—anything."

As another officer sped his horse after the first messenger, the general beamed upon the earth like a sun. In his eyes was a desire to chant a pæon. He kept repeating, "They 've held 'em, by heav‧ ens!"

His excitement made his horse plunge, and he merrily kicked and swore at it. He held a little carnival of joy on horseback.

Chapter VII

The youth cringed as if discovered in a crime. By heavens, they had won after all! The imbecile line had remained and become victors. He could hear cheering.

He lifted himself upon his toes and looked in the direction of the fight. A yellow fog lay wallowing on the treetops. From beneath it came the clatter of musketry. Hoarse cries told of an advance.

He turned away amazed and angry. He felt that he had been wronged.

He had fled, he told himself, because annihilation approached. He had done a good part in saving himself, who was a little piece of the army. He had considered the time, he said, to be one in which it was the duty of every little piece to rescue itself if possible. Later the officers could fit the little pieces together again, and make a battle front. If none of the little pieces were wise enough to save themselves from the flurry of death at such a time, why, then, where would be the army? It was all plain that he had proceeded according to very correct and commendable rules. His actions had been sagacious things. They had been full of strategy. They were the work of a master's legs.

Thoughts of his comrades came to him. The brittle blue line had withstood the blows and won. He grew bitter over it. It seemed that the blind ignorance and stupidity of those little pieces had betrayed him. He had been overturned and crushed by their lack of sense in holding the position, when intelligent deliberation would have convinced them that it was impossible. He, the enlightened man who looks afar in the dark, had fled because of his superior perceptions and knowledge. He felt a great anger against his comrades. He knew it could be proved that they had been fools.

He wondered what they would remark when later he appeared in camp. His mind heard howls of derision. Their density would not enable them to understand his sharper point of view.

He began to pity himself acutely. He was ill used. He was trodden beneath the feet of an iron injustice. He had proceeded with wisdom and from the most righteous motives under heaven's blue only to be frustrated by hateful circumstances.

A dull, animal-like rebellion against his fellows, war in the abstract, and fate grew within him. He shambled along with bowed head, his brain in a tumult of agony and despair. When he looked loweringly up, quivering at each sound, his eyes had the expression of those of a criminal who thinks his guilt little and his punishment great, and knows that he can find no words.

He went from the fields into a thick woods, as if resolved to bury himself. He wished to get out of hearing of the crackling shots which were to him like voices.

The ground was cluttered with vines and bushes, and the trees grew close and spread out like bouquets. He was obliged to force his way with much noise. The creepers, catching against his legs, cried out harshly as their sprays were torn from the barks of trees. The swishing saplings tried to make known his presence to the world. He could not conciliate the forest. As he made his way, it was always calling out protestations. When he separated embraces of trees and vines the disturbed foliages waved their arms and turned their face leaves toward him. He dreaded lest these noisy motions and cries should bring men to look at him. So he went far, seeking dark and intricate places.

After a time the sound of musketry grew faint and the cannon boomed in the distance. The sun, suddenly apparent, blazed among the trees. The insects were making rhythmical noises. They seemed to be grinding their teeth in unison. A woodpecker stuck his impudent head around the side of a tree. A bird flew on lighthearted wing.

Off was the rumble of death. It seemed now that Nature had no ears.

This landscape gave him assurance. A fair field holding life. It was the religion of peace. It would die if its timid eyes were compelled to see blood. He conceived Nature to be a woman with a deep aversion to tragedy.

He threw a pine cone at a jovial squirrel, and he ran with chattering fear. High in a treetop he stopped, and, poking his head cautiously from behind a branch, looked down with an air of trepidation.

The youth felt triumphant at this exhibition. There was the law, he said. Nature had given him a sign. The squirrel, immediately upon recognizing danger, had taken to his legs without ado. He did not stand stolidly baring his furry belly to the missile, and die with an upward glance at the sympathetic heavens. On the contrary, he had fled as fast as his legs could carry him; and he was but an ordinary squirrel, too—doubtless no philosopher of his race. The youth wended, feeling that Nature was of his mind. She reenforced his argument with proofs that lived where the sun shone.

Once he found himself almost into a swamp. He was obliged to walk upon bog tufts and watch his feet to keep from the oily mire. Pausing at one time to look about him he saw, out at some black water, a small animal pounce in and emerge directly with a gleaming fish.

The youth went again into the deep thickets. The brushed branches made a noise that drowned the sounds of cannon. He walked on, going from obscurity into promises of a greater obscurity.

At length he reached a place where the high, arching boughs made a chapel. He softly pushed the green doors aside and entered. Pine needles were a gentle brown carpet. There was a religious half light.

Near the threshold he stopped, horror-stricken at the sight of a thing.

He was being looked at by a dead man who was seated with his back against a columnlike tree. The corpse was dressed in a uniform that once had been blue, but was now faded to a melancholy shade of green. The eyes, staring at the youth, had changed to the dull hue to be seen on the side of a dead fish. The mouth was open. Its red had changed to an appalling yellow. Over the gray skin of the face ran little ants. One was trundling some sort of a bundle along the upper lip.

The youth gave a shriek as he confronted the thing. He was for moments turned to stone before it. He remained staring into the liquid-looking eyes. The dead man and the living man exchanged a long look. Then the youth cautiously put one hand behind him and brought it against a tree. Leaning upon this he retreated, step by step, with his face still toward the thing. He feared that if he turned his back the body might spring up and stealthily pursue him.

The branches, pushing against him, threatened to throw him over upon it. His unguided feet, too, caught aggravatingly in brambles; and with it all he received a subtle suggestion to touch the corpse. As he thought of his hand upon it he shuddered profoundly.

At last he burst the bonds which had fastened him to the spot and fled, unheeding the underbrush. He was pursued by a sight of the black ants swarming greedily upon the gray face and venturing horribly near to the eyes.

After a time he paused, and, breathless and panting, listened He imagined some strange voice would come from the dead throat and squawk after him in horrible menaces.

The trees about the portal of the chapel moved soughingly in a soft wind. A sad silence was upon the little guarding edifice.

Chapter VIII

The trees began softly to sing a hymn of twilight. The sun sank until slanted bronze rays struck the forest. There was a lull in the noises of insects as if they had bowed their beaks and were making a devotional pause. There was silence save for the chanted chorus of the trees.

Then, upon this stillness, there suddenly broke a tremendous clangor of sounds. A crimson roar came from the distance.

The youth stopped. He was transfixed by this terrific medley of all noises. It was as if worlds were being rended. There was the ripping sound of musketry and the breaking crash of the artillery.

His mind flew in all directions. He conceived the two armies to be at each other panther fashion. He listened for a time. Then he began to run in the direction of the battle. He saw that it was an ironical thing for him to be running thus toward that which he had been at such pains to avoid. But he said, in substance, to himself that if the earth and the moon were about to clash, many persons would doubtless plan to get upon the roofs to witness the collision.

As he ran, he became aware that the forest had stopped its music, as if at last becoming capable of hearing the foreign sounds. The trees hushed and stood motionless. Everything seemed to be listening to the crackle and clatter and ear-shaking thunder. The chorus pealed over the still earth.

It suddenly occurred to the youth that the fight in which he had been was, after all, but perfunctory popping. In the hearing of this present din he was doubtful if he had seen real battle scenes. This uproar explained a celestial battle; it was tumbling hordes a-struggle in the air.

Reflecting, he saw a sort of a humor in the point of view of himself and his fellows during the late encounter. They had taken themselves and the enemy very seriously and had imagined that they were deciding the war. Individuals must have supposed that they were cutting the letters of their names deep into everlasting tablets of brass, or enshrining their reputations forever in the hearts of their countrymen, while, as to fact, the affair would appear in printed reports under a meek and immaterial title. But he saw that it was good, else, he said, in battle every one would surely run save forlorn hopes and their ilk.

He went rapidly on. He wished to come to the edge of the forest that he might peer out.

As he hastened, there passed through his mind pictures of stupendous conflicts. His accumulated thought upon such subjects was used to form scenes. The noise was as the voice of an eloquent being, describing.

Sometimes the brambles formed chains and tried to hold him back. Trees, confronting him, stretched out their arms and forbade him to pass. After its previous hostility this new resistance of the forest filled him with a fine bitterness. It seemed that Nature could not be quite ready to kill him.

But he obstinately took roundabout ways, and presently he was where he could see long gray walls of vapor where lay battle lines. The voices of cannon shook him. The musketry sounded in long irregular surges that played havoc with his ears. He stood regardant for a moment. His eyes had an awestruck expression. He gawked in the direction of the fight.

Presently he proceeded again on his forward way. The battle was like the grinding of an immense and terrible machine to him. Its complexities and powers, its grim processes, fascinated him. He must go close and see it produce corpses.

He came to a fence and clambered over it. On the far side, the ground was littered with clothes and guns. A newspaper, folded up, lay in the dirt. A dead soldier was stretched with his face hidden in his arm. Farther off there was a group of four or five corpses keeping mournful company. A hot sun had blazed upon the spot.

In this place the youth felt that he was an invader. This forgotten part of the battle ground was owned by the dead men, and he hurried, in the vague apprehension that one of the swollen forms would rise and tell him to begone.

He came finally to a road from which he could see in the distance dark and agitated bodies of troops, smoke-fringed. In the lane was a blood-stained crowd streaming to the rear. The wounded men were cursing, groaning, and wailing. In the air, always, was a mighty swell of sound that it seemed could sway the earth. With the courageous words of the artillery and the spiteful sentences of the musketry mingled red cheers. And from this region of noises came the steady current of the maimed.

One of the wounded men had a shoeful of blood. He hopped like a schoolboy in a game. He was laughing hysterically.

One was swearing that he had been shot in the arm through the commanding general's mismanagement of the army. One was marching with an air imitative of some sublime drum major. Upon his features was an unholy mixture of merriment and agony. As he marched he sang a bit of doggerel in a high and quavering voice:

> "Sing a song 'a vic'try,
> A pocketful 'a bullets,
> Five an' twenty dead men
> Baked in a—pie."

Parts of the procession limped and staggered to this tune.

Another had the gray seal of death already upon his face. His lips were curled in hard lines and his teeth were clinched. His hands were bloody from where he had pressed them upon his wound. He seemed to be awaiting the moment when he should pitch headlong. He stalked like the specter of a soldier, his eyes burning with the power of a stare into the unknown.

There were some who proceeded sullenly, full of anger at their wounds, and ready to turn upon anything as an obscure cause.

An officer was carried along by two privates. He was peevish. "Don't joggle so, Johnson, yeh fool," he cried. "Think m' leg is made of iron? If yeh can't carry me decent, put me down an' let some one else do it."

He bellowed at the tottering crowd who blocked the quick march of his bearers. "Say, make way there, can't yeh? Make way, dickens take it all."

They sulkily parted and went to the roadsides. As he was carried past they made pert remarks to him. When he raged in reply and threatened them, they told him to be damned.

The shoulder of one of the tramping bearers knocked heavily against the spectral soldier who was staring into the unknown.

The youth joined this crowd and marched along with it. The torn bodies expressed the awful machinery in which the men had been entangled.

Orderlies and couriers occasionally broke through the throng in the roadway, scattering wounded men right and left, galloping on followed by howls. The melancholy march was continually disturbed by the messengers, and sometimes by bustling batteries that came swinging and thumping down upon them, the officers shouting orders to clear the way.

There was a tattered man, fouled with dust, blood and powder stain from hair to shoes, who trudged quietly at the youth's side. He was listening with eagerness and much humility to the lurid descriptions of a bearded sergeant. His lean features wore an expression of awe and admiration. He was like a listener in a country store to wondrous tales told among the sugar barrels. He eyed the story-teller with unspeakable wonder. His mouth was agape in yokel fashion.

The sergeant, taking note of this, gave pause to his elaborate history while he administered a sardonic comment. "Be keerful, honey, you'll be a-ketchin' flies," he said.

The tattered man shrank back abashed.

After a time he began to sidle near to the youth, and in a diffident way try to make him a friend. His voice was gentle as a girl's voice and his eyes were pleading. The youth saw with surprise that the soldier had two wounds, one in the head, bound with a blood-soaked rag, and the other in the arm, making that member dangle like a broken bough.

After they had walked together for some time the tattered man mustered sufficient courage to speak. "Was pretty good fight, wa'n't it?" he timidly said. The youth, deep in thought, glanced up at the bloody and grim figure with its lamblike eyes. "What?"

"Was pretty good fight, wa'n't it?"

"Yes," said the youth shortly. He quickened his pace.

But the other hobbled industriously after him. There was an air of apology in his manner, but he evidently thought that he needed only to talk for a time, and the youth would perceive that he was a good fellow.

"Was pretty good fight, wa'n't it?" he began in a small voice, and then he achieved the fortitude to continue. "Dern me if I ever see fellers fight so. Laws, how they did fight! I knowed th' boys 'd like when they onct got square at it. Th' boys ain't had no fair chanct up t' now, but this time they showed what they was. I knowed it 'd turn out this way. Yeh can't lick them boys. No, sir!

They 're fighters, they be."

He breathed a deep breath of humble admiration. He had looked at the youth for encouragement several times. He received none, but gradually he seemed to get absorbed in his subject.

"I was talkin' 'cross pickets with a boy from Georgie, onct, an' that boy, he ses, 'Your fellers 'll all run like hell when they onct hearn a gun,' he ses. 'Mebbe they will,' I ses, 'but I don't b'lieve none of it,' I ses; 'an' b'jiminey,' I ses back t' 'um, 'mebbe your fellers 'll all run like hell when they onct hearn a gun,' I ses. He larfed. Well, they didn't run t' day, did they, hey? No, sir! They fit, an' fit, an' fit."

His homely face was suffused with a light of love for the army which was to him all things beautiful and powerful.

After a time he turned to the youth. "Where yeh hit, ol' boy?" he asked in a brotherly tone.

The youth felt instant panic at this question, although at first its full import was not borne in upon him.

"What?" he asked.

"Where yeh hit?" repeated the tattered man.

"Why," began the youth, "I—I—that is—why—I——"

He turned away suddenly and slid through the crowd. His brow was heavily flushed, and his fingers were picking nervously at one of his buttons. He bent his head and fastened his eyes studiously upon the button as if it were a little problem.

The tattered man looked after him in astonishment.

Chapter IX

The youth fell back in the procession until the tattered soldier was not in sight. Then he started to walk on with the others.

But he was amid wounds. The mob of men was bleeding. Because of the tattered soldier's question he now felt that his shame could be viewed. He was continually casting sidelong glances to see if the men were contemplating the letters of guilt he felt burned into his brow.

At times he regarded the wounded soldiers in an envious way. He conceived persons with torn bodies to be peculiarly happy. He wished that he, too, had a wound, a red badge of courage.

The spectral soldier was at his side like a stalking reproach. The man's eyes were still fixed in a stare into the unknown. His gray, appalling face had attracted attention in the crowd, and men, slowing to his dreary pace, were walking with him. They were discussing his plight, questioning him and giving him advice. In a dogged way he repelled them, signing to them to go on and leave him alone. The shadows of his face were deepening and his tight lips seemed holding in check the moan of great despair. There could be seen a certain stiffness in the movements of his body, as if he were taking infinite care not to arouse the passion of his wounds. As he went on, he seemed always looking for a place, like one who goes to choose a grave.

Something in the gesture of the man as he waved the bloody and pitying soldiers away made the youth start as if bitten. He yelled in horror. Tottering forward he laid a quivering hand upon the man's arm. As the latter slowly turned his waxlike features toward him, the youth screamed:

"Gawd! Jim Conklin!"

The tall soldier made a little commonplace smile. "Hello, Henry," he said.

The youth swayed on his legs and glared strangely. He stuttered and stammered. "Oh, Jim—oh, Jim—oh, Jim——"

The tall soldier held out his gory hand. There was a curious red and black combination of new blood and old blood upon it. "Where yeh been, Henry?" he asked. He continued in a monotonous voice, "I thought mebbe yeh got keeled over. There's been thunder t' pay t'-day. I was worryin' about it a good deal."

The youth still lamented. "Oh, Jim—oh, Jim—oh, Jim——"

"Yeh know," said the tall soldier, "I was out there." He made a careful gesture. "An', Lord, what a circus! An', b'jiminey, I got shot—I got shot. Yes, b'jiminey, I got shot." He reiterated this fact in a bewildered way, as if he did not know how it came about.

The youth put forth anxious arms to assist him, but the tall soldier went firmly on as if propelled. Since the youth's arrival as a guardian for his friend, the other wounded men had ceased to display much interest. They occupied themselves again in dragging their own tragedies toward the rear.

Suddenly, as the two friends marched on, the tall soldier seemed to be overcome by a terror. His face turned to a semblance of gray paste. He clutched the youth's arm and looked all about him, as if dreading to be overheard. Then he began to speak in a shaking whisper:

"I tell yeh what I'm 'fraid of, Henry—I 'll tell yeh what I 'm 'fraid of. I 'm 'fraid I 'll fall down—an' then yeh know—them damned artillery wagons—they like as not 'll run over me. That 's what I 'm 'fraid of——"

The youth cried out to him hysterically: "I 'll take care of yeh, Jim! I 'll take care of yeh! I swear t' Gawd I will!"

"Sure—will yeh, Henry?" the tall soldier beseeched.

"Yes—yes—I tell yeh—I 'll take care of yeh, Jim!" protested the youth. He could not speak accurately because of the gulpings in his throat.

But the tall soldier continued to beg in a lowly way. He now hung babelike to the youth's arm. His eyes rolled in the wildness of his terror. "I was allus a good friend t' yeh, wa'n't I, Henry? I 've allus been a pretty good feller, ain't I? An' it ain't much t' ask, is it? Jest t' pull me along outer th' road? I 'd do it fer you, wouldn't I, Henry?"

He paused in piteous anxiety to await his friend's reply.

The youth had reached an anguish where the sobs scorched him. He strove to express his loyalty, but he could only make fantastic gestures.

However, the tall soldier seemed suddenly to forget all those fears. He became again the grim, stalking specter of a soldier. He went stonily forward. The youth wished his friend to lean upon him, but the other always shook his head and strangely protested. "No—no—no—leave me be—leave me be——"

His look was fixed again upon the unknown. He moved with mysterious purpose, and all of the youth's offers he brushed aside. "No—no—leave me be—leave me be——"

The youth had to follow.

Presently the latter heard a voice talking softly near his shoulder. Turning he saw that it belonged to the tattered soldier. "Ye 'd better take 'im outa th' road, pardner. There 's a batt'ry comin' helitywhoop down th' road an' he 'll git runned over. He 's a goner anyhow in about five minutes—yeh kin see that. Ye 'd better take 'im outa th' road. Where th' blazes does he git his stren'th from?"

"Lord knows!" cried the youth. He was shaking his hands helplessly.

He ran forward presently and grasped the tall soldier by the arm. "Jim! Jim!" he coaxed, "come with me."

The tall soldier weakly tried to wrench himself free. "Huh," he said vacantly. He stared at the youth for a moment. At last he spoke as if dimly comprehending. "Oh! Inteh th' fields? Oh!"

He started blindly through the grass.

The youth turned once to look at the lashing riders and jouncing guns of the battery. He was startled from this view by a shrill outcry from the tattered man.

"Gawd! He's runnin'!"

Turning his head swiftly, the youth saw his friend running in a staggering and stumbling way toward a little clump of bushes. His heart seemed to wrench itself almost free from his body at this sight. He made a noise of pain. He and the tattered man began a pursuit. There was a singular race.

When he overtook the tall soldier he began to plead with all the words he could find. "Jim—Jim—what are you doing—what makes you do this way—you 'll hurt yerself."

The same purpose was in the tall soldier's face. He protested in a dulled way, keeping his eyes fastened on the mystic place of his intentions. "No—no—don't tech me—leave me be—leave me be——"

The youth, aghast and filled with wonder at the tall soldier, began quaveringly to question him. "Where yeh goin', Jim? What you thinking about? Where you going? Tell me, won't you, Jim?"

The tall soldier faced about as upon relentless pursuers. In his eyes there was a great appeal. "Leave me be, can't yeh? Leave me be fer a minnit."

The youth recoiled. "Why, Jim," he said, in a dazed way, "what's the matter with you?"

The tall soldier turned and, lurching dangerously, went on. The youth and the tattered soldier followed, sneaking as if whipped, feeling unable to face the stricken man if he should again confront them. They began to have thoughts of a solemn ceremony. There was something ritelike in these movements of the doomed soldier. And there was a resemblance in him to a devotee of a mad religion, blood-sucking, muscle-wrenching, bone-crushing. They were awed and afraid. They hung back lest he have at command a dreadful weapon.

At last, they saw him stop and stand motionless. Hastening up, they perceived that his face wore an expression telling that he had at last found the place for which he had struggled. His spare figure was erect; his bloody hands were quietly at his side. He was waiting with patience for something that he had come to meet. He was at the rendezvous. They paused and stood, expectant.

There was a silence.

Finally, the chest of the doomed soldier began to heave with a strained motion. It increased in violence until it was as if an animal was within and was kicking and tumbling furiously to be free.

This spectacle of gradual strangulation made the youth writhe, and once as his friend rolled his eyes, he saw something in them that made him sink wailing to the ground. He raised his voice in a last supreme call.

"Jim—Jim—Jim——"

The tall soldier opened his lips and spoke. He made a gesture. "Leave me be—don't tech me—leave me be——"

There was another silence while he waited.

Suddenly, his form stiffened and straightened. Then it was shaken by a prolonged ague. He stared into space. To the two watchers there was a curious and profound dignity in the firm lines of his awful face.

He was invaded by a creeping strangeness that slowly enveloped him. For a moment the tremor of his legs caused him to dance a sort of hideous hornpipe. His arms beat wildly about his head in expression of implike enthusiasm.

His tall figure stretched itself to its full height. There was a slight rending sound. Then it began to swing forward, slow and straight, in the manner of a falling tree. A swift muscular contortion made the left shoulder strike the ground first.

The body seemed to bounce a little way from the earth. "God!" said the tattered soldier.

The youth had watched, spellbound, this ceremony at the place of meeting. His face had been twisted into an expression of every agony he had imagined for his friend.

He now sprang to his feet and, going closer, gazed upon the pastelike face. The mouth was open and the teeth showed in a laugh.

As the flap of the blue jacket fell away from the body, he could see that the side looked as if it had been chewed by wolves.

The youth turned, with sudden, livid rage, toward the battlefield. He shook his fist. He seemed about to deliver a philippic. [6]

"Hell——"

The red sun was pasted in the sky like a wafer.

Chapter X

The tattered man stood musing.

"Well, he was reg'lar jim-dandy fer nerve, wa'n't he," said he finally in a little awestruck voice. "A reg'lar jim-dandy." He thoughtfully poked one of the docile hands with his foot. "I wonner where he got 'is stren'th from? I never seen a man do like that before. It was a funny thing. Well, he was a reg'lar jim-dandy."

The youth desired to screech out his grief. He was stabbed, but his tongue lay dead in the tomb of his mouth. He threw himself again upon the ground and began to brood.

6. A speech characterized by strong denunciation, exemplified by the *Philippics* of Demosthenes to the Athenians against the invading Philip of Macedonia.

The tattered man stood musing.

"Look-a-here, pardner," he said, after a time. He regarded the corpse as he spoke. "He 's up an' gone, ain't 'e, an' we might as well begin t' look out fer ol' number one. This here thing is all over. He 's up an' gone, ain't 'e? An' he 's all right here. Nobody won't bother 'im. An' I must say I ain't enjoying any great health m'self these days."

The youth, awakened by the tattered soldier's tone, looked quickly up. He saw that he was swinging uncertainly on his legs and that his face had turned to a shade of blue.

"Good Lord!" he cried, "you ain't goin' t'—not you, too."

The tattered man waved his hand. "Nary die," he said. "All I want is some pea soup an' a good bed. Some pea soup," he repeated dreamfully.

The youth arose from the ground. "I wonder where he came from. I left him over there." He pointed. "And now I find 'im here. And he was coming from over there, too." He indicated a new direction. They both turned toward the body as if to ask of it a question.

"Well," at length spoke the tattered man, "there ain't no use in our stayin' here an' tryin' t' ask him anything."

The youth nodded an assent wearily. They both turned to gaze for a moment at the corpse.

The youth murmured something.

"Well, he was a jim-dandy, wa'n't 'e?" said the tattered man as if in response.

They turned their backs upon it and started away. For a time they stole softly, treading with their toes. It remained laughing there in the grass.

"I'm commencin' t' feel pretty bad," said the tattered man, suddenly breaking one of his little silences. "I'm commencin' t' feel pretty damn' bad."

The youth groaned. "O Lord!" He wondered if he was to be the tortured witness of another grim encounter.

But his companion waved his hand reassuringly. "Oh, I'm not goin' t' die yit! There too much dependin' on me fer me t' die yit. No, sir! Nary die! I can't! Ye'd oughta see th' swad a' chil'ren I've got, an' all like that."

The youth glancing at his companion could see by the shadow of a smile that he was making some kind of fun.

As they plodded on the tattered soldier continued to talk. "Besides, if I died, I wouldn't die th' way that feller did. That was th' funniest thing. I'd jest flop down, I would. I never seen a feller die th' way that feller did.

"Yeh know Tom Jamison, he lives next door t' me up home. He's a nice feller, he is, an' we was allus good friends. Smart, too. Smart as a steel trap. Well, when we was a-fightin' this atternoon, all-of-a-sudden he begin t' rip up an' cuss an' beller at me. 'Yer shot, yeh blamed infernal!'—he swear horrible—he ses t' me. I put up m' hand t' m' head an' when I looked at m' fingers, I seen, sure 'nough, I was shot. I give a holler an' begin t' run, but b'fore I could git away another one hit me in th' arm an' whirl' me clean 'round. I got skeared when they was all a-shootin' b'hind me an' I run t' beat all, but I cotch it pretty bad. I've an idee I'd a' been fightin' yit, if t'was n't fer Tom Jamison."

Then he made a calm announcement: "There's two of 'em— little ones—but they 're beginnin' t' have fun with me now. I don't b'lieve I kin walk much furder."

They went slowly on in silence. "Yeh look pretty peek-ed yer- self," said the tattered man at last. "I bet yeh 've got a worser one than yeh think. Ye'd better take keer of yer hurt. It don't do t' let sech things go. It might be inside mostly, an' them plays thunder. Where is it located?" But he continued his harangue without waiting for a reply. "I see a feller git hit plum in th' head when my reg'ment was a-standin' at ease onct. An' everybody yelled out to 'im: Hurt, John? Are yeh hurt much? 'No,' ses he. He looked kinder surprised, an' he went on tellin' 'em how he felt. He sed he didn't feel nothin'. But, by dad, th' first thing that feller knowed he was dead. Yes, he was dead—stone dead. So, yeh wanta watch out. Yeh might have some queer kind 'a hurt yerself. Yeh can't never tell. Where is your'n located?"

The youth had been wriggling since the introduction of this topic. He now gave a cry of exasperation and made a furious mo- tion with his hand. "Oh, don't bother me!" he said. He was en- raged against the tattered man, and could have strangled him. His companions seemed ever to play intolerable parts. They were ever upraising the ghost of shame on the stick of their curiosity. He turned toward the tattered man as one at bay. "Now, don't bother me," he repeated with desperate menace.

"Well, Lord knows I don't wanta bother anybody," said the other. There was a little accent of despair in his voice as he replied, "Lord knows I 've gota 'nough m' own t' tend to."

The youth, who had been holding a bitter debate with himself and casting glances of hatred and contempt at the tattered man, here spoke in a hard voice. "Good-by," he said.

The tattered man looked at him in gaping amazement. "Why— why, pardner, where yeh goin'?" he asked unsteadily. The youth looking at him, could see that he, too, like that other one, was beginning to act dumb and animal-like. His thoughts seemed to be floundering about in his head. "Now—now—look—a—here, you Tom Jamison—now—I won't have this—this here won't do. Where—where yeh goin'?"

The youth pointed vaguely. "Over there," he replied.

"Well, now look—a—here—now," said the tattered man, rambling on in idiot fashion. His head was hanging forward and his words were slurred. "This thing won't do, now, Tom Jamison. It won't do. I know yeh, yeh pig-headed devil. Yeh wanta go trompin' off with a bad hurt. It ain't right—now—Tom Jamison—it ain't. Yeh wanta leave me take keer of yeh, Tom Jamison. It ain't—right —it ain't—fer yeh t' go—trompin' off—with a bad hurt—it ain't —ain't—ain't right—it ain't."

In reply the youth climbed a fence and started away. He could hear the tattered man bleating plaintively.

Once he faced about angrily. "What?"

"Look—a—here, now, Tom Jamison—now—it ain't——"

The youth went on. Turning at a distance he saw the tattered man wandering about helplessly in the field.

He now thought that he wished he was dead. He believed that he envied those men whose bodies lay strewn over the grass of the fields and on the fallen leaves of the forest.

The simple questions of the tattered man had been knife thrusts to him. They asserted a society that probes pitilessly at secrets until all is apparent. His late companion's chance persistency made him feel that he could not keep his crime concealed in his bosom. It was sure to be brought plain by one of those arrows which cloud the air and are constantly pricking, discovering, proclaiming those things which are willed to be forever hidden. He admitted that he could not defend himself against this agency. It was not within the power of vigilance.

Chapter XI

He became aware that the furnace roar of the battle was growing louder. Great brown clouds had floated to the still heights of air before him. The noise, too, was approaching. The woods filtered men and the fields became dotted.

As he rounded a hillock, he perceived that the roadway was now a crying mass of wagons, teams, and men. From the heaving tangle issued exhortations, commands, imprecations. Fear was sweeping it all along. The cracking whips bit and horses plunged and tugged. The white-topped wagons strained and stumbled in their exertions like fat sheep.

The youth felt comforted in a measure by this sight. They were all retreating. Perhaps, then, he was not so bad after all. He seated himself and watched the terror-stricken wagons. They fled like soft, ungainly animals. All the roarers and lashers served to help him to magnify the dangers and horrors of the engagement that he might try to prove to himself that the thing with which men could charge him was in truth a symmetrical act.[7] There was an amount of pleasure to him in watching the wild march of this vindication.

Presently the calm head of a forward-going column of infantry appeared in the road. It came swiftly on. Avoiding the obstructions gave it the sinuous movement of a serpent. The men at the head butted mules with their musket stocks. They prodded teamsters indifferent to all howls. The men forced their way through parts of the dense mass by strength. The blunt head of the column pushed. The raving teamsters swore many strange oaths.

The commands to make way had the ring of a great importance in them. The men were going forward to the heart of the din. They were to confront the eager rush of the enemy. They felt the pride of their onward movement when the remainder of the army seemed trying to dribble down this road. They tumbled teams about with a fine feeling that it was no matter so long as their column got to the front in time. This importance made their faces grave and stern. And the backs of the officers were very rigid.

As the youth looked at them the black weight of his woe returned to him. He felt that he was regarding a procession of chosen beings. The separation was as great to him as if they had marched with weapons of flame and banners of sunlight. He could never be like them. He could have wept in his longings.

He searched about in his mind for an adequate malediction for the indefinite cause, the thing upon which men turn the words of final blame. It—whatever it was—was responsible for him, he said. There lay the fault.

The haste of the column to reach the battle seemed to the forlorn young man to be something much finer than stout fighting. Heroes, he thought, could find excuses in that long seething lane. They could retire with perfect self-respect and make excuses to the stars.

He wondered what those men had eaten that they could be in such haste to force their way to grim chances of death. As he

7. That is, an act justified by its cause.

watched his envy grew until he thought that he wished to change lives with one of them. He would have liked to have used a tremendous force, he said, throw off himself and become a better. Swift pictures of himself, apart, yet in himself, came to him—a blue desperate figure leading lurid charges with one knee forward and a broken blade high—a blue, determined figure standing before a crimson and steel assault, getting calmly killed on a high place before the eyes of all. He thought of the magnificent pathos of his dead body.

These thoughts uplifted him. He felt the quiver of war desire. In his ears, he heard the ring of victory. He knew the frenzy of a rapid successful charge. The music of the trampling feet, the sharp voices, the clanking arms of the column near him made him soar on the red wings of war. For a few moments he was sublime.

He thought that he was about to start for the front. Indeed, he saw a picture of himself, dust-stained, haggard, panting, flying to the front at the proper moment to seize and throttle the dark, leering witch of calamity.

Then the difficulties of the thing began to drag at him. He hesitated, balancing awkwardly on one foot.

He had no rifle; he could not fight with his hands, said he resentfully to his plan. Well, rifles could be had for the picking. They were extraordinarily profuse.

Also, he continued, it would be a miracle if he found his regiment. Well, he could fight with any regiment.

He started forward slowly. He stepped as if he expected to tread upon some explosive thing. Doubts and he were struggling.

He would truly be a worm if any of his comrades should see him returning thus, the marks of his flight upon him. There was a reply that the intent fighters did not care for what happened rearward saving that no hostile bayonets appeared there. In the battle-blur his face would, in a way, be hidden, like the face of a cowled man.

But then he said that his tireless fate would bring forth, when the strife lulled for a moment, a man to ask of him an explanation. In imagination he felt the scrutiny of his companions as he painfully labored through some lies.

Eventually, his courage expended itself upon these objections. The debates drained him of his fire.

He was not cast down by this defeat of his plan, for, upon studying the affair carefully, he could not but admit that the objections were very formidable.

Furthermore, various ailments had begun to cry out. In their presence he could not persist in flying high with the wings of war;

they rendered it almost impossible for him to see himself in a heroic light. He tumbled headlong.

He discovered that he had a scorching thirst. His face was so dry and grimy that he thought he could feel his skin crackle. Each bone of his body had an ache in it, and seemingly threatened to break with each movement. His feet were like two sores. Also, his body was calling for food. It was more powerful than a direct hunger. There was a dull, weight-like feeling in his stomach, and, when he tried to walk, his head swayed and he tottered. He could not see with distinctness. Small patches of green mist floated before his vision.

While he had been tossed by many emotions, he had not been aware of ailments. Now they beset him and made clamor. As he was at last compelled to pay attention to them, his capacity for self-hate was multiplied. In despair, he declared that he was not like those others. He now conceded it to be impossible that he should ever become a hero. He was a craven loon. Those pictures of glory were piteous things. He groaned from his heart and went staggering off.

A certain mothlike quality within him kept him in the vicinity of the battle. He had a great desire to see, and to get news. He wished to know who was winning.

He told himself that, despite his unprecedented suffering, he had never lost his greed for a victory, yet, he said, in a half-apologetic manner to his conscience, he could not but know that a defeat for the army this time might mean many favorable things for him. The blows of the enemy would splinter regiments into fragments. Thus, many men of courage, he considered, would be obliged to desert the colors and scurry like chickens. He would appear as one of them. They would be sullen brothers in distress, and he could then easily believe he had not run any farther or faster than they. And if he himself could believe in his virtuous perfection, he conceived that there would be small trouble in convincing all others.

He said, as if in excuse for this hope, that previously the army had encountered great defeats and in a few months had shaken off all blood and tradition of them, emerging as bright and valiant as a new one; thrusting out of sight the memory of disaster, and appearing with the valor and confidence of unconquered legions. The shrilling voices of the people at home would pipe dismally for a time, but various generals were usually compelled to listen to these ditties. He of course felt no compunctions for proposing a general as a sacrifice. He could not tell who the chosen for the barbs might be, so he could center no direct sympathy upon him. The people were afar and he did not conceive public opinion to be accurate at long range. It was quite probable they would hit the wrong man who, after he had recovered from his amazement would perhaps spend the rest of his days in writing replies to the songs of his alleged failure. It would be very unfortunate, no doubt, but in this case a general was of no consequence to the youth.

In a defeat there would be a roundabout vindication of himself. He thought it would prove, in a manner, that he had fled early because of his superior powers of perception. A serious prophet upon predicting a flood should be the first man to climb a tree. This would demonstrate that he was indeed a seer.

A moral vindication was regarded by the youth as a very important thing. Without salve, he could not, he thought, wear the sore badge of his dishonor through life. With his heart continually assuring him that he was despicable, he could not exist without making it, through his actions, apparent to all men.

If the army had gone gloriously on he would be lost. If the din meant that now his army's flags were tilted forward he was a condemned wretch. He would be compelled to doom himself to isolation. If the men were advancing, their indifferent feet were trampling upon his chances for a successful life.

As these thoughts went rapidly through his mind, he turned upon them and tried to thrust them away. He denounced himself as a villain. He said that he was the most unutterably selfish man in existence. His mind pictured the soldiers who would place their defiant bodies before the spear of the yelling battle fiend, and as he saw their dripping corpses on an imagined field, he said that he was their murderer.

Again he thought that he wished he was dead. He believed that he envied a corpse. Thinking of the slain, he achieved a great contempt for some of them, as if they were guilty for thus becoming lifeless. They might have been killed by lucky chances, he said, before they had had opportunities to flee or before they had been really tested. Yet they would receive laurels from tradition. He cried out bitterly that their crowns were stolen and their robes of glorious memories were shams. However, he still said that it was a great pity he was not as they.

A defeat of the army had suggested itself to him as a means of escape from the consequences of his fall. He considered, now, however, that it was useless to think of such a possibility. His education had been that success for that mighty blue machine was certain; that it would make victories as a contrivance turns out buttons. He presently discarded all his speculations in the other direction. He returned to the creed of soldiers.

When he perceived again that it was not possible for the army to be defeated, he tried to bethink him of a fine tale which he could take back to his regiment, and with it turn the expected shafts of derision.

But, as he mortally feared these shafts, it became impossible for him to invent a tale he felt he could trust. He experimented with many schemes, but threw them aside one by one as flimsy. He was quick to see vulnerable places in them all.

Furthermore, he was much afraid that some arrow of scorn might lay him mentally low before he could raise his protecting tale.

He imagined the whole regiment saying: "Where's Henry Fleming? He run, didn't 'e? Oh, my!" He recalled various persons who would be quite sure to leave him no peace about it. They would doubtless question him with sneers, and laugh at his stammering hesitation. In the next engagement they would try to keep watch of him to discover when he would run.

Wherever he went in camp, he would encounter insolent and lingeringly cruel stares. As he imagined himself passing near a crowd of comrades, he could hear some one say, "There he goes!"

Then, as if the heads were moved by one muscle, all the faces were turned toward him with wide, derisive grins. He seemed to hear some one make a humorous remark in a low tone. At it the others all crowed and cackled. He was a slang phrase.

Chapter XII

The column that had butted stoutly at the obstacles in the roadway was barely out of the youth's sight before he saw dark waves of men come sweeping out of the woods and down through the fields. He knew at once that the steel fibers had been washed from their hearts. They were bursting from their coats and their equipments as from entanglements. They charged down upon him like terrified buffaloes.

Behind them blue smoke curled and clouded above the treetops, and through the thickets he could sometimes see a distant pink glare. The voices of the cannon were clamoring in interminable chorus.

The youth was horrorstricken. He stared in agony and amazement. He forgot that he was engaged in combating the universe. He threw aside his mental pamphlets on the philosophy of the retreated and rules for the guidance of the damned.

The fight was lost. The dragons were coming with invincible strides. The army, helpless in the matted thickets and blinded by the overhanging night, was going to be swallowed. War, the red animal, war, the blood-swollen god, would have bloated fill.

Within him something bade to cry out. He had the impulse to make a rallying speech, to sing a battle hymn, but he could only get his tongue to call into the air: "Why—why—what—what 's th' matter?"

Soon he was in the midst of them. They were leaping and scampering all about him. Their blanched faces shone in the dusk. They seemed, for the most part, to be very burly men. The youth turned from one to another of them as they galloped along. His incoherent questions were lost. They were heedless of his appeals. They did not seem to see him.

They sometimes gabbled insanely. One huge man was asking of the sky: "Say, where de plank road? Where de plank road!"[8] It was as if he had lost a child. He wept in his pain and dismay.

Presently, men were running hither and thither in all ways. The artillery booming, forward, rearward, and on the flanks made jumble of ideas of direction. Landmarks had vanished into the gathered gloom. The youth began to imagine that he had got into the center of the tremendous quarrel, and he could perceive no way out of it. From the mouths of the fleeing men came a thousand wild questions, but no one made answers.

The youth, after rushing about and throwing interrogations at the heedless bands of retreating infantry, finally clutched a man by the arm. They swung around face to face.

"Why—why——" stammered the youth struggling with his balking tongue.

The man screamed: "Let go me! Let go me!" His face was livid and his eyes were rolling uncontrolled. He was heaving and panting. He still grasped his rifle, perhaps having forgotten to release his hold upon it. He tugged frantically, and the youth being compelled to lean forward was dragged several paces.

"Let go me! Let go me!"

"Why—why——" stuttered the youth.

"Well, then!" bawled the man in a lurid rage. He adroitly and fiercely swung his rifle. It crushed upon the youth's head. The man ran on.

The youth's fingers had turned to paste upon the other's arm. The energy was smitten from his muscles. He saw the flaming wings of lightning flash before his vision. There was a deafening rumble of thunder within his head.

Suddenly his legs seemed to die. He sank writhing to the ground.

---

8. Crane's attempt to approximate a German accent; see Hungerford, below.

He tried to arise. In his efforts against the numbing pain he was like a man wrestling with a creature of the air.

There was a sinister struggle.

Sometimes he would achieve a position half erect, battle with the air for a moment, and then fall again, grabbing at the grass. His face was of a clammy pallor. Deep groans were wrenched from him.

At last, with a twisting movement, he got upon his hands and knees, and from thence, like a babe trying to walk, to his feet. Pressing his hands to his temples he went lurching over the grass.

He fought an intense battle with his body. His dulled senses wished him to swoon and he opposed them stubbornly, his mind portraying unknown dangers and mutilations if he should fall upon the field. He went tall soldier fashion. He imagined secluded spots where he could fall and be unmolested. To search for one he strove against the tide of his pain.

Once he put his hand to the top of his head and timidly touched the wound. The scratching pain of the contact made him draw a long breath through his clinched teeth. His fingers were dabbled with blood. He regarded them with a fixed stare.

Around him he could hear the grumble of jolted cannon as the scurrying horses were lashed toward the front. Once, a young officer on a besplashed charger nearly ran him down. He turned and watched the mass of guns, men, and horses sweeping in a wide curve toward a gap in a fence. The officer was making excited motions with a gauntleted hand. The guns followed the teams with an air of unwillingness, of being dragged by the heels.

Some officers of the scattered infantry were cursing and railing like fishwives. Their scolding voices could be heard above the din. Into the unspeakable jumble in the roadway rode a squadron of cavalry. The faded yellow of their facings[9] shone bravely. There was a mighty altercation.

The artillery were assembling as if for a conference.

The blue haze of evening was upon the field. The lines of forest were long purple shadows. One cloud lay along the western sky partly smothering the red.

As the youth left the scene behind him, he heard the guns suddenly roar out. He imagined them shaking in black rage. They belched and howled like brass devils guarding a gate. The soft air was filled with the tremendous remonstrance. With it came the shattering peal of opposing infantry. Turning to look behind him,

9. Ornamental coverings around the edges of collars, cuffs, and lapels of a military jacket.

he could see sheets of orange light illumine the shadowy distance. There were subtle and sudden lightnings in the far air. At times he thought he could see heaving masses of men.

He hurried on in the dusk. The day had faded until he could barely distinguish place for his feet. The purple darkness was filled with men who lectured and jabbered. Sometimes he could see them gesticulating against the blue and somber sky. There seemed to be a great ruck of men and munitions spread about in the forest and in the fields.

The little narrow roadway now lay lifeless. There were overturned wagons like sun-dried bowlders. The bed of the former torrent was choked with the bodies of horses and splintered parts of war machines.

It had come to pass that his wound pained him but little. He was afraid to move rapidly, however, for a dread of disturbing it. He held his head very still and took many precautions against stumbling. He was filled with anxiety, and his face was pinched and drawn in anticipation of the pain of any sudden mistake of his feet in the gloom.

His thoughts, as he walked, fixed intently upon his hurt. There was a cool, liquid feeling about it and he imagined blood moving slowly down under his hair. His head seemed swollen to a size that made him think his neck to be inadequate.

The new silence of his wound made much worriment. The little blistering voices of pain that had called out from his scalp were, he thought, definite in their expression of danger. By them he believed that he could measure his plight. But when they remained ominously silent he became frightened and imagined terrible fingers that clutched into his brain.

Amid it he began to reflect upon various incidents and conditions of the past. He bethought him of certain meals his mother had cooked at home, in which those dishes of which he was particularly fond had occupied prominent positions. He saw the spread table. The pine walls of the kitchen were glowing in the warm light from the stove. Too, he remembered how he and his companions used to go from the schoolhouse to the bank of a shaded pool. He saw his clothes in disorderly array upon the grass of the bank. He felt the swash of the fragrant water upon his body. The leaves of the overhanging maple rustled with melody in the wind of youthful summer.

He was overcome presently by a dragging weariness. His head hung forward and his shoulders were stooped as if he were bearing a great bundle. His feet shuffled along the ground.

He held continuous arguments as to whether he should lie down and sleep at some near spot, or force himself on until he reached a certain haven. He often tried to dismiss the question, but his body persisted in rebellion and his senses nagged at him like pampered babies.

At last he heard a cheery voice near his shoulder: "Yeh seem t' be in a pretty bad way, boy?"

The youth did not look up, but he assented with thick tongue. "Uh!"

The owner of the cheery voice took him firmly by the arm. "Well," he said, with a round laugh, "I'm goin' your way. Th' hull gang is goin' your way. An' I guess I kin give yeh a lift." They began to walk like a drunken man and his friend.

As they went along, the man questioned the youth and assisted him with the replies like one manipulating the mind of a child. Sometimes he interjected anecdotes. "What reg'ment do yeh b'long teh? Eh? What 's that? Th' 304th N' York? Why, what corps is that in? Oh, it is? Why, I thought they wasn't engaged t'-day—they 're 'way over in th' center. Oh, they was, eh? Well, pretty nearly everybody got their share 'a fightin' t'-day. By dad, I give myself up fer dead any number 'a times. There was shootin' here an' shootin' there, an' hollerin' here an' hollerin' there, in th' damn' darkness, until I couldn't tell t' save m' soul which side I was on. Sometimes I thought I was sure 'nough from Ohier, an' other times I could 'a swore I was from th' bitter end of Florida. It was th' most mixed up dern thing I ever see. An' these here hull woods is a reg'lar mess. It 'll be a miracle if we find our reg'ments t'-night. Pretty soon, though, we 'll meet a-plenty of guards an' provost-guards, an' one thing an' another. Ho! there they go with an off'cer, I guess. Look at his hand a-draggin'. He 's got all th' war he wants, I bet. He won't be talkin' so big about his reputation an' all when they go t' sawin' off his leg. Poor feller! My brother 's got whiskers jest like that. How did yeh git 'way over here, any-how? Your reg'ment is a long way from here, ain't it? Well, I guess we can find it. Yeh know there was a boy killed in my comp'ny t'-day that I thought th' world an' all of. Jack was a nice feller. By ginger, it hurt like thunder t' see ol' Jack jest git knocked flat. We was a-standin' purty peaceable fer a spell, 'though there was men runnin' ev'ry way all 'round us, an' while we was a-standin' like that, 'long come a big fat feller. He began t' peck at Jack's elbow, an' he ses: 'Say, where 's th' road t' th' river?' An' Jack, he never paid no attention, an' th' feller kept on a-peckin at his elbow an' sayin': 'Say, where 's th' road t' th' river?' Jack was a-lookin' ahead all th' time tryin' t' see th' Johnnies comin' through th' woods, an' he never paid no attention t' this big fat feller fer a long time, but at last he turned 'round an' he ses: "Ah, go t' hell an' find th' road t' th' river!' An' jest then a shot slapped him bang on th' side th' head. He was a sergeant, too. Them was his last words. Thunder, I wish we was sure 'a findin' our reg'ments t'-night. It's goin' t' be long huntin'. But I guess we kin do it."

In the search which followed, the man of the cheery voice seemed to the youth to possess a wand of a magic kind. He threaded the mazes of the tangled forest with a strange fortune. In encounters with guards and patrols he displayed the keenness of a detective and the valor of a gamin. Obstacles fell before him and became of assistance. The youth, with his chin still on his breast, stood woodenly by while his companion beat ways and means out of sullen things.

The forest seemed a vast hive of men buzzing about in frantic circles, but the cheery man conducted the youth without mistakes, until at last he began to chuckle with glee and self-satisfaction. "Ah, there yeh are! See that fire?"

The youth nodded stupidly.

"Well, there 's where your reg'ment is. An' now, good-by, ol' boy, good luck t' yeh."

A warm and strong hand clasped the youth's languid fingers for an instant, and then he heard a cheerful and audacious whistling as the man strode away. As he who had so befriended him was thus passing out of his life, it suddenly occurred to the youth that he had not once seen his face.

Chapter XIII

The youth went slowly toward the fire indicated by his departed friend. As he reeled, he bethought him of the welcome his comrades would give him. He had a conviction that he would soon feel in his sore heart the barbed missiles of ridicule. He had no strength to invent a tale; he would be a soft target.

He made vague plans to go off into the deeper darkness and hide, but they were all destroyed by the voices of exhaustion and pain from his body. His ailments, clamoring, forced him to seek the place of food and rest, at whatever cost.

He swung unsteadily toward the fire. He could see the forms of men throwing black shadows in the red light, and as he went nearer it became known to him in some way that the ground was strewn with sleeping men.

Of a sudden he confronted a black and monstrous figure. A rifle barrel caught some glinting beams. "Halt! halt!" He was dismayed for a moment, but he presently thought that he recognized the nervous voice. As he stood tottering before the rifle barrel, he called out: "Why, hello, Wilson, you—you here?"

The rifle was lowered to a position of caution and the loud soldier came slowly forward. He peered into the youth's face. "That you, Henry?"

"Yes, it's—it's me."

"Well, well, ol' boy," said the other, "by ginger, I'm glad t' see yeh! I give yeh up fer a goner. I thought yeh was dead sure enough." There was husky emotion in his voice.

The youth found that now he could barely stand upon his feet. There was a sudden sinking of his forces. He thought he must hasten to produce his tale to protect him from the missiles already at the lips of his redoubtable comrades. So, staggering before the loud soldier, he began: "Yes, yes. I've—I've had an awful time. I've been all over. Way over on th' right. Ter'ble fightin' over there. I had an awful time. I got separated from th' reg'ment. Over on th' right, I got shot. In th' head. I never see sech fightin'. Awful time. I don't see how I could a' got separated from th' reg'-ment. I got shot, too."

His friend had stepped forward quickly. "What? Got shot? Why didn't yeh say so first? Poor ol' boy, we must—hol' on a minnit; what am I doin'. I'll call Simpson."

Another figure at that moment loomed in the gloom. They could see that it was the corporal. "Who yeh talkin' to, Wilson?" he demanded. His voice was anger-toned. "Who yeh talkin' to? Yeh th' derndest sentinel—why—hello, Henry, you here? Why, I thought you was dead four hours ago! Great Jerusalem, they keep turnin' up every ten minutes or so! We thought we'd lost forty-two men by straight count, but if they keep on a-comin' this way, we'll git th' comp'ny all back by mornin' yit. Where was yeh?"

"Over on th' right. I got separated"—began the youth with considerable glibness.

But his friend had interrupted hastily. "Yes, an' he got shot in th' head an' he's in a fix, an' we must see t' him right away." He rested his rifle in the hollow of his left arm and his right around the youth's shoulder.

"Gee, it must hurt like thunder!" he said.

The youth leaned heavily upon his friend. "Yes, it hurts—hurts a good deal," he replied. There was a faltering in his voice.

"Oh," said the corporal. He linked his arm in the youth's and drew him forward. "Come on, Henry. I'll take keer 'a yeh."

As they went on together the loud private called out after them: "Put 'im t' sleep in my blanket, Simpson. An'—hol' on a minnit —here's my canteen. It's full 'a coffee. Look at his head by th' fire an' see how it looks. Maybe it's a pretty bad un. When I git relieved in a couple 'a minnits, I'll be over an' see t' him."

The youth's senses were so deadened that his friend's voice sounded from afar and he could scarcely feel the pressure of the corporal's arm. He submitted passively to the latter's directing strength. His head was in the old manner hanging forward upon his breast. His knees wobbled.

The corporal led him into the glare of the fire. "Now, Henry," he said, "let's have look at yer ol' head."

The youth sat down obediently and the corporal, laying aside his rifle, began to fumble in the bushy hair of his comrade. He was obliged to turn the other's head so that the full flush of the fire light would beam upon it. He puckered his mouth with a critical air. He drew back his lips and whistled through his teeth when his fingers came in contact with the splashed blood and the rare wound.

"Ah, here we are!" he said. He awkwardly made further investigations. "Jest as I thought," he added, presently. "Yeh've been grazed by a ball. It's raised a queer lump jest as if some feller had lammed yeh on th' head with a club. It stopped a-bleedin' long time ago. Th' most about it is that in th' mornin' yeh'll feel that a number ten hat wouldn't fit yeh. An' your head'll be all het up an' feel as dry as burnt pork. An' yeh may git a lot 'a other sick-nesses, too, by mornin'. Yeh can't never tell. Still, I don't much think so. It's jest a damn' good belt on th' head, an' nothin' more. Now, you jest sit here an' don't move, while I go rout out th' relief. Then I'll send Wilson t' take keer 'a yeh."

The corporal went away. The youth remained on the ground like a parcel. He stared with a vacant look into the fire.

After a time he aroused, for some part, and the things about him began to take form. He saw that the ground in the deep shadows was cluttered with men, sprawling in every conceivable posture. Glancing narrowly into the more distant darkness, he caught occasional glimpses of visages that loomed pallid and ghostly, lit with a phosphorescent glow. These faces expressed in their lines the deep stupor of the tired soldiers. They made them appear like men drunk with wine. This bit of forest might have appeared to an ethereal wanderer as a scene of the result of some frightful debauch.

On the other side of the fire the youth observed an officer asleep, seated bolt upright, with his back against a tree. There was some-thing perilous in his position. Badgered by dreams, perhaps, he swayed with little bounces and starts, like an old, toddy-stricken grandfather in a chimney corner. Dust and stains were upon his face. His lower jaw hung down as if lacking strength to assume its normal position. He was the picture of an exhausted soldier after a feast of war.

He had evidently gone to sleep with his sword in his arms. These two had slumbered in an embrace, but the weapon had been allowed in time to fall unheeded to the ground. The brass-mounted hilt lay in contact with some parts of the fire.

Within the gleam of rose and orange light from the burning sticks were other soldiers, snoring and heaving, or lying deathlike in slumber. A few pairs of legs were stuck forth, rigid and straight. The shoes displayed the mud or dust of marches and bits of rounded trousers, protruding from the blankets, showed rents and tears from hurried pitchings through the dense brambles.

The fire crackled musically. From it swelled light smoke. Over-head the foliage moved softly. The leaves, with their faces turned toward the blaze, were colored shifting hues of silver, often edged with red. Far off to the right, through a window in the forest could be seen a handful of stars lying, like glittering pebbles, on the black level of the night.

Occasionally, in this low-arched hall, a soldier would arouse and turn his body to a new position, the experience of his sleep having taught him of uneven and objectionable places upon the ground under him. Or, perhaps, he would lift himself to a sitting posture, blink at the fire for an unintelligent moment, throw a swift glance at his prostrate companion, and then cuddle down again with a grunt of sleepy content.

The youth sat in a forlorn heap until his friend the loud young soldier came, swinging two canteens by their light strings. "Well, now, Henry, ol' boy," said the latter, "we'll have yeh fixed up in jest about a minnit."

He had the bustling ways of an amateur nurse. He fussed around the fire and stirred the sticks to brilliant exertions. He made his patient drink largely from the canteen that contained the coffee. It was to the youth a delicious draught. He tilted his head afar back and held the canteen long to his lips. The cool mixture went caressingly down his blistered throat. Having finished, he sighed with comfortable delight.

The loud young soldier watched his comrade with an air of satisfaction. He later produced an extensive handkerchief from his pocket. He folded it into a manner of bandage and soused water from the other canteen upon the middle of it. This crude arrangement he bound over the youth's head, tying the ends in a queer knot at the back of the neck.

"There," he said, moving off and surveying his deed, "yeh look like th' devil, but I bet yeh feel better."

The youth contemplated his friend with grateful eyes. Upon his aching and swelling head the cold cloth was like a tender woman's hand.

"Yeh don't holler ner say nothin'," remarked his friend approvingly. "I know I'm a blacksmith at takin' keer 'a sick folks, an' yeh never squeaked. Yer a good un, Henry. Most 'a men would a' been in th' hospital long ago. A shot in th' head ain't foolin' business."

The youth made no reply, but began to fumble with the buttons of his jacket.

"Well, come, now," continued his friend, "come on. I must put yeh t' bed an' see that yeh git a good night's rest."

The other got carefully erect, and the loud young soldier led him among the sleeping forms lying in groups and rows. Presently he stooped and picked up his blankets. He spread the rubber one upon the ground and placed the woolen one about the youth's shoulders.

"There now," he said, "lie down an' git some sleep."

The youth, with his manner of doglike obedience, got carefully down like a crone stooping. He stretched out with a murmur of relief and comfort. The ground felt like the softest couch.

But of a sudden he ejaculated: "Hol' on a minnit! Where you goin' t' sleep?"

His friend waved his hand impatiently. "Right down there by yeh."

"Well, but hol' on a minnit," continued the youth. "What yeh goin' t' sleep in? I've got your——"

The loud young soldier snarled: "Shet up an' go on t' sleep. Don't be makin' a damn' fool 'a yerself," he said severely.

After the reproof the youth said no more. An exquisite drowsiness had spread through him. The warm comfort of the blanket enveloped him and made a gentle languor. His head fell forward on his crooked arm and his weighted lids went softly down over his eyes. Hearing a splatter of musketry from the distance, he wondered indifferently if those men sometimes slept. He gave a long sigh, snuggled down into his blanket, and in a moment was like his comrades.

Chapter XIV

When the youth awoke it seemed to him that he had been asleep for a thousand years, and he felt sure that he opened his eyes upon an unexpected world. Gray mists were slowly shifting before the first efforts of the sun rays. An impending splendor could be seen in the eastern sky. An icy dew had chilled his face, and immediately upon arousing he curled farther down into his blanket. He stared for a while at the leaves overhead, moving in a heraldic wind of the day.

The distance was splintering and blaring with the noise of fighting. There was in the sound an expression of a deadly persistency, as if it had not begun and was not to cease.

About him were the rows and groups of men that he had dimly seen the previous night. They were getting a last draught of sleep before the awakening. The gaunt, careworn features and dusty figures were made plain by this quaint light at the dawning, but it dressed the skin of the men in corpselike hues and made the tangled limbs appear pulseless and dead. The youth started up with a little cry when his eyes first swept over this motionless mass of men, thick-spread upon the ground, pallid, and in strange postures. His disordered mind interpreted the hall of the forest as a charnel place. He believed for an instant that he was in the house of the dead, and he did not dare to move lest these corpses start up, squalling and squawking. In a second, however, he achieved his proper mind. He swore a complicated oath at himself. He saw that this somber picture was not a fact of the present, but a mere prophecy.

He heard then the noise of a fire crackling briskly in the cold air, and, turning his head, he saw his friend pottering busily about a small blaze. A few other figures moved in the fog, and he heard the hard cracking of axe blows.

Suddenly there was a hollow rumble of drums. A distant bugle sang faintly. Similar sounds, varying in strength, came from near and far over the forest. The bugles called to each other like brazen gamecocks. The near thunder of the regimental drums rolled.

The body of men in the woods rustled. There was a general uplifting of heads. A murmuring of voices broke upon the air. In it there was much bass of grumbling oaths. Strange gods were addressed in condemnation of the early hours necessary to correct war. An officer's peremptory tenor rang out and quickened the stiffened movement of the men. The tangled limbs unraveled. The corpse-hued faces were hidden behind fists that twisted slowly in the eye sockets.

The youth sat up and gave vent to an enormous yawn. "Thunder!" he remarked petulantly. He rubbed his eyes, and then putting up his hand felt carefully of the bandage over his wound. His friend, perceiving him to be awake, came from the fire. "Well, Henry, ol' man, how do yeh feel this mornin'?" he demanded.

The youth yawned again. Then he puckered his mouth to a little pucker. His head, in truth, felt precisely like a melon, and there was an unpleasant sensation at his stomach.

"Oh, Lord, I feel pretty bad," he said.

"Thunder!" exclaimed the other. "I hoped ye'd feel all right this mornin'. Let's see th' bandage—I guess it's slipped." He began to tinker at the wound in rather a clumsy way until the youth exploded.

"Gosh-dern it!" he said in sharp irritation; "you're the hangdest man I ever saw! You wear muffs on your hands. Why in good thunderation can't you be more easy? I'd rather you'd stand off an' throw guns at it. Now, go slow, an' don't act as if you was nailing down carpet."

He glared with insolent command at his friend, but the latter answered soothingly. "Well, well, come now, an' git some grub," he said. "Then, maybe, yeh'll feel better."

At the fireside the loud young soldier watched over his comrade's wants with tenderness and care. He was very busy marshaling the little black vagabonds of tin cups and pouring into them the streaming, iron colored mixture from a small and sooty tin pail. He had some fresh meat, which he roasted hurriedly upon a stick. He sat down then and contemplated the youth's appetite with glee.

The youth took note of a remarkable change in his comrade since those days of camp life upon the river bank. He seemed no more to be continually regarding the proportions of his personal prowess. He was not furious at small words that pricked his conceits. He was no more a loud young soldier. There was about him now a fine reliance. He showed a quiet belief in his purposes and his abilities. And this inward confidence evidently enabled him to be indifferent to little words of other men aimed at him.

The youth reflected. He had been used to regarding his comrade as a blatant child with an audacity grown from his inexperience, thoughtless, headstrong, jealous, and filled with a tinsel courage. A swaggering babe accustomed to strut in his own dooryard. The youth wondered where had been born these new eyes; when his comrade had made the great discovery that there were many men who would refuse to be subjected by him. Apparently, the other had now climbed a peak of wisdom from which he could perceive himself as a very wee thing. And the youth saw that ever after it would be easier to live in his friend's neighborhood.

His comrade balanced his ebony coffee-cup on his knee. "Well,

Henry," he said, "what d'yeh think th' chances are? D'yeh think we'll wallop 'em?"

The youth considered for a moment. "Day-b'fore-yesterday," he finally replied, with boldness, "you would 'a' bet you'd lick the hull kit-an'-boodle all by yourself."

His friend looked a trifle amazed. "Would I?" he asked. He pondered. "Well, perhaps I would," he decided at last. He stared humbly at the fire.

The youth was quite disconcerted at this surprising reception of his remarks. "Oh, no, you wouldn't either," he said, hastily trying to retrace.

But the other made a deprecating gesture. "Oh, yeh needn't mind, Henry," he said. "I believe I was a pretty big fool in those days." He spoke as after a lapse of years.

There was a little pause.

"All th' officers say we've got th' rebs in a pretty tight box," said the friend, clearing his throat in a commonplace way. "They all seem t' think we've got 'em jest where we want 'em."

"I don't know about that," the youth replied. "What I seen over on th' right makes me think it was th' other way about. From where I was, it looked as if we was gettin' a good poundin' yestirday."

"D'yeh think so?" inquired the friend. "I thought we handled 'em pretty rough yestirday."

"Not a bit," said the youth. "Why, lord, man, you didn't see nothing of the fight. Why!" Then a sudden thought came to him. "Oh! Jim Conklin's dead."

His friend started. "What? Is he? Jim Conklin?"

The youth spoke slowly. "Yes. He's dead. Shot in th' side."

"Yeh don't say so. Jim Conklin. . . . poor cuss!"

All about them were other small fires surrounded by men with their little black utensils. From one of these near came sudden sharp voices in a row. It appeared that two light-footed soldiers had been teasing a huge, bearded man, causing him to spill coffee upon his blue knees. The man had gone into a rage and had sworn comprehensively. Stung by his language, his tormentors had immediately bristled at him with a great show of resenting unjust oaths. Possibly there was going to be a fight.

The friend arose and went over to them, making pacific motions with his arms. "Oh, here, now, boys, what's th' use?" he said. "We'll be at th' rebs in less'n an hour. What's th' good fightin' 'mong ourselves?"

One of the light-footed soldiers turned upon him red-faced and violent. "Yeh needn't come around here with yer preachin'. I s'pose yeh don't approve 'a fightin' since Charley Morgan licked yeh; but I don't see what business this here is 'a yours or anybody else."

"Well, it ain't," said the friend mildly. "Still I hate t' see——"
There was a tangled argument.

"Well, he——," said the two, indicating their opponent with accusative forefingers.

The huge soldier was quite purple with rage. He pointed at the two soldiers with his great hand, extended clawlike. "Well, they——"

But during this argumentative time the desire to deal blows seemed to pass, although they said much to each other. Finally the friend returned to his old seat. In a short while the three antagonists could be seen together in an amiable bunch.

"Jimmie Rogers ses I'll have t' fight him after th' battle t'-day," announced the friend as he again seated himself. "He ses he don't allow no interferin' in his business. I hate t' see th' boys fightin' 'mong themselves."

The youth laughed. "Yer changed a good bit. Yeh ain't at all like yeh was. I remember when you an' that Irish feller——" He stopped and laughed again.

"No, I didn't use t' be that way," said his friend thoughtfully. "That's true 'nough."

"Well, I didn't mean——" began the youth.

The friend made another deprecatory gesture. "Oh, yeh needn't mind, Henry."

There was another little pause.

"Th' reg'ment lost over half th' men yestirday," remarked the friend eventually. "I thought a' course they was all dead, but, laws, they kep' a-comin' back last night until it seems, after all, we didn't lose but a few. They'd been scattered all over, wanderin' around in th' woods, fightin' with other reg'ments, an' everything. Jest like you done."

"So?" said the youth.

Chapter XV

The regiment was standing at order arms at the side of a lane, waiting for the command to march, when suddenly the youth remembered the little packet enwrapped in a faded yellow envelope which the loud young soldier with lugubrious words had intrusted to him. It made him start. He uttered an exclamation and turned toward his comrade.

"Wilson!"

"What?"

His friend, at his side in the ranks, was thoughtfully staring down the road. From some cause his expression was at that moment very meek. The youth, regarding him with sidelong glances, felt impelled to change his purpose. "Oh, nothing," he said.

His friend turned his head in some surprise, "Why, what was yeh goin' t' say?"

"Oh, nothing," repeated the youth.

He resolved not to deal the little blow. It was sufficient that the fact made him glad. It was not necessary to knock his friend on the head with the misguided packet.

He had been possessed of much fear of his friend, for he saw how easily questionings could make holes in his feelings. Lately, he had assured himself that the altered comrade would not tantalize him with a persistent curiosity, but he felt certain that during the first period of leisure his friend would ask him to relate his adventures of the previous day.

He now rejoiced in the possession of a small weapon with which he could prostrate his comrade at the first signs of a cross-examination. He was master. It would now be he who could laugh and shoot the shafts of derision.

The friend had, in a weak hour, spoken with sobs of his own death. He had delivered a melancholy oration previous to his funeral, and had doubtless in the packet of letters, presented various keepsakes to relatives. But he had not died, and thus he had delivered himself into the hands of the youth.

The latter felt immensely superior to his friend, but he inclined to condescension. He adopted toward him an air of patronizing good humor.

His self-pride was now entirely restored. In the shade of its flourishing growth he stood with braced and self-confident legs, and since nothing could now be discovered he did not shrink from an encounter with the eyes of judges, and allowed no thoughts of his own to keep him from an attitude of manfulness. He had performed his mistakes in the dark, so he was still a man.

Indeed, when he remembered his fortunes of yesterday, and looked at them from a distance he began to see something fine there. He had license to be pompous and veteranlike.

His panting agonies of the past he put out of his sight.

In the present, he declared to himself that it was only the doomed and the damned who roared with sincerity at circumstance. Few but they ever did it. A man with a full stomach and the respect of his fellows had no business to scold about anything that he might think to be wrong in the ways of the universe, or even with the ways of society. Let the unfortunates rail; the others may play marbles.

He did not give a great deal of thought to these battles that lay directly before him. It was not essential that he should plan his ways in regard to them. He had been taught that many obligations of a life were easily avoided. The lessons of yesterday had been that retribution was a laggard and blind. With these facts before him he did not deem it necessary that he should become feverish over the possibilities of the ensuing twenty-four hours. He could leave much to chance. Besides, a faith in himself had secretly blossomed. There was a little flower of confidence growing within him. He was now a man of experience. He had been out among the dragons, he said, and he assured himself that they were not so hideous as he had imagined them. Also, they were inaccurate; they did not sting with precision. A stout heart often defied, and defying, escaped.

And, furthermore, how could they kill him who was the chosen of gods and doomed to greatness?

He remembered how some of the men had run from the battle. As he recalled their terror-struck faces he felt a scorn for them. They had surely been more fleet and more wild than was absolutely necessary. They were weak mortals. As for himself, he had fled with discretion and dignity.

He was aroused from this reverie by his friend, who, having hitched about nervously and blinked at the trees for a time, suddenly coughed in an introductory way, and spoke.

"Fleming!"

"What?"

The friend put his hand up to his mouth and coughed again. He fidgeted in his jacket.

"Well," he gulped, at last, "I guess yeh might as well give me back them letters." Dark, prickling blood had flushed into his cheeks and brow.

"All right, Wilson," said the youth. He loosened two buttons of his coat, thrust in his hand, and brought forth the packet. As he extended it to his friend the latter's face was turned from him.

He had been slow in the act of producing the packet because during it he had been trying to invent a remarkable comment upon the affair. He could conjure nothing of sufficient point. He was compelled to allow his friend to escape unmolested with his packet. And for this he took unto himself considerable credit. It was a generous thing.

His friend at his side seemed suffering great shame. As he contemplated him, the youth felt his heart grow more strong and stout. He had never been compelled to blush in such manner for his acts; he was an individual of extraordinary virtues.

He reflected, with condescending pity: "Too bad! Too bad! The poor devil, it makes him feel tough!"

After this incident, and as he reviewed the battle pictures he had seen, he felt quite competent to return home and make the hearts of the people glow with stories of war. He could see himself in a room of warm tints telling tales to listeners. He could exhibit laurels. They were insignificant; still, in a district where laurels were infrequent, they might shine.

He saw his gaping audience picturing him as the central figure in blazing scenes. And he imagined the consternation and the ejaculations of his mother and the young lady at the seminary as they drank his recitals. Their vague feminine formula for beloved ones doing brave deeds on the field of battle without risk of life would be destroyed.

Chapter XVI

A sputtering of musketry was always to be heard. Later, the cannon had entered the dispute. In the fog-filled air their voices made a thudding sound. The reverberations were continual. This part of the world led a strange, battleful existence.

The youth's regiment was marched to relieve a command that had lain long in some damp trenches. The men took positions behind a curving line of rifle pits that had been turned up, like a large furrow, along the line of woods. Before them was a level stretch, peopled with short, deformed stumps. From the woods beyond came the dull popping of the skirmishers and pickets, firing in the fog. From the right came the noise of a terrific fracas.

The men cuddled behind the small embankment and sat in easy attitudes awaiting their turn. Many had their backs to the firing. The youth's friend lay down, buried his face in his arms, and almost instantly, it seemed, he was in a deep sleep.

The youth leaned his breast against the brown dirt and peered over at the woods and up and down the line. Curtains of trees interfered with his ways of vision. He could see the low line of trenches but for a short distance. A few idle flags were perched on the dirt hills. Behind them were rows of dark bodies with a few heads sticking curiously over the top.

Always the noise of skirmishers came from the woods on the front and left, and the din on the right had grown to frightful proportions. The guns were roaring without an instant's pause for breath. It seemed that the cannon had come from all parts and were engaged in a stupendous wrangle. It became impossible to make a sentence heard.

The youth wished to launch a joke—a quotation from newspapers. He desired to say, "All quiet on the Rappahannock,"[1] but the guns refused to permit even a comment upon their uproar. He never successfully concluded the sentence. But at last the guns stopped, and among the men in the rifle pits rumors again flew, like birds, but they were now for the most part black creatures who flapped their wings drearily near to the ground and refused to rise on any wings of hope. The men's faces grew doleful from the interpreting of omens. Tales of hesitation and uncertainty on the part of those high in place and responsibility came to their ears. Stories of disaster were borne into their minds with many proofs. This din of musketry on the right, growing like a released genie of sound, expressed and emphasized the army's plight.

The men were disheartened and began to mutter. They made gestures expressive of the sentence: "Ah, what more can we do?" And it could always be seen that they were bewildered by the alleged news and could not fully comprehend a defeat.

Before the gray mists had been totally obliterated by the sun rays, the regiment was marching in a spread column that was retiring carefully through the woods. The disordered, hurrying lines of the enemy could sometimes be seen down through the groves and little fields. They were yelling, shrill and exultant.

At this sight the youth forgot many personal matters and became greatly enraged. He exploded in loud sentences. "B'jiminey, we're generaled by a lot 'a lunkheads."

"More than one feller has said that t'-day," observed a man.

His friend, recently aroused, was still very drowsy. He looked behind him until his mind took in the meaning of the movement. Then he sighed. "Oh, well, I s'pose we got licked," he remarked sadly.

The youth had a thought that it would not be handsome for him to freely condemn other men. He made an attempt to restrain himself, but the words upon his tongue were too bitter. He presently began a long and intricate denunciation of the commander of the forces.

1. "All quiet along the Potomac" was a phrase used by Northern newspapers during the winter of 1862-63 to satirize the inactivity of the Union forces in Virginia.

"Mebbe, it wa'n't all his fault—not all together. He did th' best he knowed. It's our luck t' git licked often," said his friend in a weary tone. He was trudging along with stooped shoulders and shifting eyes like a man who has been caned and kicked.

"Well, don't we fight like the devil? Don't we do all that men can?" demanded the youth loudly.

He was secretly dumfounded at this sentiment when it came from his lips. For a moment his face lost its valor and he looked guiltily about him. But no one questioned his right to deal in such words, and presently he recovered his air of courage. He went on to repeat a statement he had heard going from group to group at the camp that morning. "The brigadier said he never saw a new reg'-ment fight the way we fought yestirday, didn't he? And we didn't do better than many another reg'ment, did we? Well, then, you can't say it's th' army's fault, can you?"

In his reply, the friend's voice was stern. "'A course not," he said. "No man dare say we don't fight like th' devil. No man will ever dare say it. Th' boys fight like hell-roosters. But still—still, we don't have no luck."

"Well, then, if we fight like the devil an' don't ever whip, it must be the general's fault," said the youth grandly and decisively. "And I don't see any sense in fighting and fighting and fighting, yet always losing through some derned old lunkhead of a general."

A sarcastic man who was tramping at the youth's side, then spoke lazily. "Mebbe yeh think yeh fit th' hull battle yestirday, Fleming," he remarked.

The speech pierced the youth. Inwardly he was reduced to an abject pulp by these chance words. His legs quaked privately. He cast a frightened glance at the sarcastic man.

"Why, no," he hastened to say in a conciliating voice, "I don't think I fought the whole battle yesterday."

But the other seemed innocent of any deeper meaning. Apparently, he had no information. It was merely his habit. "Oh!" he replied in the same tone of calm derision.

The youth, nevertheless, felt a threat. His mind shrank from going near to the danger, and thereafter he was silent. The signifi-cance of the sarcastic man's words took from him all loud moods that would make him appear prominent. He became suddenly a modest person.

There was low-toned talk among the troops. The officers were impatient and snappy, their countenances clouded with the tales of misfortune. The troops, sifting through the forest, were sullen. In the youth's company once a man's laugh rang out. A dozen soldiers turned their faces quickly toward him and frowned with vague displeasure.

The noise of firing dogged their footsteps. Sometimes, it seemed to be driven a little way, but it always returned again with increased insolence. The men muttered and cursed, throwing black looks in its direction.

In a clear space the troops were at last halted. Regiments and brigades, broken and detached through their encounters with thickets, grew together again and lines were faced toward the pursuing bark of the enemy's infantry.

This noise, following like the yelpings of eager, metallic hounds, increased to a loud and joyous burst, and then, as the sun went serenely up the sky, throwing illuminating rays into the gloomy thickets, it broke forth into prolonged pealings. The woods began to crackle as if afire.

"Whoop-a-dadee," said a man, "here we are! Everybody fightin'. Blood an' destruction."

"I was willin' t' bet they'd attack as soon as th' sun got fairly up," savagely asserted the lieutenant who commanded the youth's company. He jerked without mercy at his little mustache. He strode to and fro with dark dignity in the rear of his men, who were lying down behind whatever protection they had collected.

A battery had trundled into position in the rear and was thoughtfully shelling the distance. The regiment, unmolested as yet, awaited the moment when the gray shadows of the woods before them should be slashed by the lines of flame. There was much growling and swearing.

"Good Gawd," the youth grumbled, "we're always being chased around like rats! It makes me sick. Nobody seems to know where we go or why we go. We just get fired around from pillar to post and get licked here and get licked there, and nobody knows what it's done for. It makes a man feel like a damn' kitten in a bag. Now, I'd like to know what the eternal thunders we was marched into these woods for anyhow, unless it was to give the rebs a regular pot shot at us. We came in here and got our legs all tangled up in these cussed briers, and then we begin to fight and the rebs had an easy time of it. Don't tell me it's just luck! I know better. It's this derned old——"

The friend seemed jaded, but he interrupted his comrade with a voice of calm confidence. "It'll turn out all right in th' end," he said.

"Oh, the devil it will! You always talk like a dog-hanged parson. Don't tell me! I know——"

At this time there was an interposition by the savage-minded lieutenant, who was obliged to vent some of his inward dissatisfaction upon his men. "You boys shut right up! There no need 'a your wastin' your breath in long-winded arguments about this an' that an' th' other. You've been jawin' like a lot 'a old hens. All you've got t' do is to fight, an' you'll get plenty 'a that t' do in about ten minutes. Less talkin' an' more fightin' is what's best for you boys. I never saw sech gabbling jackasses."

He paused, ready to pounce upon any man who might have the temerity to reply. No words being said, he resumed his dignified pacing.

"There's too much chin music an' too little fightin' in this war, anyhow," he said to them, turning his head for a final remark.

The day had grown more white, until the sun shed his full radiance upon the thronged forest. A sort of a gust of battle came sweeping toward that part of the line where lay the youth's regiment. The front shifted a trifle to meet it squarely. There was a wait. In this part of the field there passed slowly the intense moments that precede the tempest.

A single rifle flashed in a thicket before the regiment. In an instant it was joined by many others. There was a mighty song of clashes and crashes that went sweeping through the woods. The guns in the rear, aroused and enraged by shells that had been thrown burrlike at them, suddenly involved themselves in a hideous altercation with another band of guns. The battle roar settled to a rolling thunder, which was a single, long explosion.

In the regiment there was a peculiar kind of hesitation denoted in the attitudes of the men. They were worn, exhausted, having slept but little and labored much. They rolled their eyes toward the advancing battle as they stood awaiting the shock. Some shrank and flinched. They stood as men tied to stakes.

Chapter XVII

This advance of the enemy had seemed to the youth like a ruthless hunting. He began to fume with rage and exasperation. He beat his foot upon the ground, and scowled with hate at the swirling smoke that was approaching like a phantom flood. There was a maddening quality in this seeming resolution of the foe to give him no rest, to give him no time to sit down and think. Yesterday he had fought and had fled rapidly. There had been many adventures. For to-day he felt that he had earned opportunities for contemplative repose. He could have enjoyed portraying to uninitiated listeners various scenes at which he had been a witness or ably discussing the processes of war with other proved men. Too it was important that he should have time for physical recuperation. He was sore and stiff from his experiences. He had received his fill of all exertions, and he wished to rest.

But those other men seemed never to grow weary; they were fighting with their old speed. He had a wild hate for the relentless foe. Yesterday, when he had imagined the universe to be against him, he had hated it, little gods and big gods; to-day he hated the army of the foe with the same great hatred. He was not going to be badgered of his life, like a kitten chased by boys, he said. It was not well to drive men into final corners; at those moments they could all develop teeth and claws.

He leaned and spoke into his friend's ear. He menaced the words with a gesture. "If they keep on chasing us, by Gawd, they'd better watch out. Can't stand *too* much."

The friend twisted his head and made a calm reply. "If they keep on a-chasin' us they'll drive us all inteh th' river."

The youth cried out savagely at this statement. He crouched behind a little tree, with his eyes burning hatefully and his teeth set in a cur-like snarl. The awkward bandage was still about his head, and upon it, over his wound, there was a spot of dry blood. His hair was wondrously tousled, and some straggling, moving locks hung over the cloth of the bandage down toward his forehead. His jacket and shirt were open at the throat, and exposed his young bronzed neck. There could be seen spasmodic gulpings at his throat.

His fingers twined nervously about his rifle. He wished that it was an engine of annihilating power. He felt that he and his companions were being taunted and derided from sincere convictions that they were poor and puny. His knowledge of his inability to take vengeance for it made his rage into a dark and stormy specter, that possessed him and made him dream of abominable cruelties. The tormentors were flies sucking insolently at his blood, and he thought that he would have given his life for a revenge of seeing their faces in pitiful plights.

The winds of battle had swept all about the regiment, until the one rifle, instantly followed by brothers, flashed in its front. A moment later the regiment roared forth its sudden and valiant retort. A dense wall of smoke settled slowly down. It was furiously slit and slashed by the knifelike fire from the rifles.

To the youth the fighters resembled animals tossed for a death struggle into a dark pit. There was a sensation that he and his fellows, at bay, were pushing back, always pushing fierce onslaughts of creatures who were slippery. Their beams of crimson seemed to get no purchase upon the bodies of their foes; the latter seemed to evade them with ease, and come through, between, around, and about with unopposed skill.

When, in a dream, it occurred to the youth that his rifle was an impotent stick, he lost sense of everything but his hate, his desire to smash into pulp the glittering smile of victory which he could feel upon the faces of his enemies.

The blue smoke-swallowed line curled and writhed like a snake stepped upon. It swung its ends to and fro in an agony of fear and rage.

The youth was not conscious that he was erect upon his feet. He did not know the direction of the ground. Indeed, once he even lost the habit of balance and fell heavily. He was up again immediately. One thought went through the chaos of his brain at the time. He wondered if he had fallen because he had been shot. But the suspicion flew away at once. He did not think more of it.

He had taken up a first position behind the little tree, with a direct determination to hold it against the world. He had not deemed it possible that his army could that day succeed, and from this he felt the ability to fight harder. But the throng had surged in all ways, until he lost directions and locations, save that he knew where lay the enemy.

The flames bit him, and the hot smoke broiled his skin. His rifle barrel grew so hot that ordinarily he could not have borne it upon his palms; but he kept on stuffing cartridges into it, and pounding them with his clanking, bending ramrod. If he aimed at some changing form through the smoke, he pulled his trigger with a fierce grunt, as if he were dealing a blow of the fist with all his strength.

When the enemy seemed falling back before him and his fellows, he went instantly forward, like a dog who, seeing his foes lagging, turns and insists upon being pursued. And when he was compelled to retire again, he did it slowly, sullenly, taking steps of wrathful despair.

Once he, in his intent hate, was almost alone, and was firing, when all those near him had ceased. He was so engrossed in his occupation that he was not aware of a lull.

He was recalled by a hoarse laugh and a sentence that came to his ears in a voice of contempt and amazement. "Yeh infernal fool, don't yeh know enough t' quit when there ain't anything t' shoot at? Good Gawd!"

He turned then and, pausing with his rifle thrown half into position, looked at the blue line of his comrades. During this moment of leisure they seemed all to be engaged in staring with astonishment at him. They had become spectators. Turning to the front again he saw, under the lifted smoke, a deserted ground.

He looked bewildered for a moment. Then there appeared upon the glazed vacancy of his eyes a diamond point of intelligence. "Oh," he said, comprehending.

He returned to his comrades and threw himself upon the ground. He sprawled like a man who had been thrashed. His flesh seemed strangely on fire, and the sounds of the battle continued in his ears. He groped blindly for his canteen.

The lieutenant was crowing. He seemed drunk with fighting. He called out to the youth: "By heavens, if I had ten thousand wild cats like you I could tear th' stomach outa this war in less'n a week!" He puffed out his chest with large dignity as he said it.

Some of the men muttered and looked at the youth in awe-struck ways. It was plain that as he had gone on loading and firing and cursing without the proper intermission, they had found time to regard him. And they now looked upon him as a war devil.

The friend came staggering to him. There was some fright and dismay in his voice. "Are yeh all right, Fleming? Do yeh feel all right? There ain't nothin' th' matter with yeh, Henry, is there?"

"No," said the youth with difficulty. His throat seemed full of knobs and burrs.

These incidents made the youth ponder. It was revealed to him that he had been a barbarian, a beast. He had fought like a pagan who defends his religion. Regarding it, he saw that it was fine, wild, and, in some ways, easy. He had been a tremendous figure, no doubt. By this struggle he had overcome obstacles which he had admitted to be mountains. They had fallen like paper peaks, and he was now what he called a hero. And he had not been aware of the process. He had slept and, awakening, found himself a knight.

He lay and basked in the occasional stares of his comrades. Their faces were varied in degrees of blackness from the burned powder. Some were utterly smudged. They were reeking with perspiration, and their breaths came hard and wheezing. And from these soiled expanses they peered at him.

"Hot work! Hot work!" cried the lieutenant deliriously. He walked up and down, restless and eager. Sometimes his voice could be heard in a wild, incomprehensible laugh.

When he had a particularly profound thought upon the science of war he always unconsciously addressed himself to the youth.

There was some grim rejoicing by the men. "By thunder, I bet this army'll never see another new reg'ment like us!"

"You bet!"

"A dog, a woman, an' a walnut tree,
Th' more yeh beat 'em, th' better they be!

That's like us."

"Lost a piler men, they did. If an ol' woman swep' up th' woods she'd git a dustpanful."

"Yes, an' if she'll come around ag'in in'bout an hour she'll git a pile more."

The forest still bore its burden of clamor. From off under the trees came the rolling clatter of the musketry. Each distant thicket seemed a strange porcupine with quills of flame. A cloud of dark smoke, as from smoldering ruins, went up toward the sun now bright and gay in the blue, enameled sky.

Chapter XVIII

The ragged line had respite for some minutes, but during its pause the struggle in the forest became magnified until the trees seemed to quiver from the firing and the ground to shake from the rushing of the men. The voices of the cannon were mingled in a long and interminable row. It seemed difficult to live in such an atmosphere. The chests of the men strained for a bit of freshness, and their throats craved water.

There was one shot through the body, who raised a cry of bitter lamentation when came this lull. Perhaps he had been calling out during the fighting also, but at that time no one had heard him. But now the men turned at the woeful complaints of him upon the ground.

"Who is it? Who is it?"

"It's Jimmie Rogers. Jimmie Rogers."

When their eyes first encountered him there was a sudden halt, as if they feared to go near. He was thrashing about in the grass, twisting his shuddering body into many strange postures. He was screaming loudly. This instant's hesitation seemed to fill him with a tremendous, fantastic contempt, and he damned them in shrieked sentences.

The youth's friend had a geographical illusion concerning a stream, and he obtained permission to go for some water. Immediately canteens were showered upon him. "Fill mine, will yeh?" "Bring me some, too." "And me, too." He departed, ladened. The youth went with his friend, feeling a desire to throw his heated body into the stream and, soaking there, drink quarts.

They made a hurried search for the supposed stream, but did not find it. "No water here," said the youth. They turned without delay and began to retrace their steps.

From their position as they again faced toward the place of the fighting, they could of course comprehend a greater amount of the battle than when their visions had been blurred by the hurling smoke of the line. They could see dark stretches winding along the land, and on one cleared space there was a row of guns making gray clouds, which were filled with large flashes of orange-colored flame. Over some foliage they could see the roof of a house. One window, glowing a deep murder red, shone squarely through the leaves. From the edifice a tall leaning tower of smoke went far into the sky.

Looking over their own troops, they saw mixed masses slowly getting into regular form. The sunlight made twinkling points of the bright steel. To the rear there was a glimpse of a distant roadway as it curved over a slope. It was crowded with retreating infantry. From all the interwoven forest arose the smoke and bluster of the battle. The air was always occupied by a blaring.

Near where they stood shells were flip-flapping and hooting. Occasional bullets buzzed in the air and spanged into tree trunks. Wounded men and other stragglers were slinking through the woods.

Looking down an aisle of the grove, the youth and his companion saw a jangling general and his staff almost ride upon a wounded man, who was crawling on his hands and knees. The general reined strongly at his charger's opened and foamy mouth and guided it with dexterous horsemanship past the man. The latter scrambled in wild and torturing haste. His strength evidently failed him as he reached a place of safety. One of his arms suddenly weakened, and he fell, sliding over upon his back. He lay stretched out, breathing gently.

A moment later the small, creaking cavalcade was directly in front of the two soldiers. Another officer, riding with the skillful abandon of a cowboy, galloped his horse to a position directly before the general. The two unnoticed foot soldiers made a little show of going on, but they lingered near in the desire to overhear the conversation. Perhaps, they thought, some great inner historical things would be said.

The general, whom the boys knew as the commander of their division, looked at the other officer and spoke coolly, as if he were criticising his clothes. "Th' enemy's formin' over there for another charge," he said. "It'll be directed against Whiterside, an' I fear they'll break through there unless we work like thunder t' stop them."

The other swore at his restive horse, and then cleared his throat. He made a gesture toward his cap. "It'll be hell t' pay stoppin' them," he said shortly.

"I presume so," remarked the general. Then he began to talk rapidly and in a lower tone. He frequently illustrated his words with a pointing finger. The two infantrymen could hear nothing until finally he asked: "What troops can you spare?"

The officer who rode like a cowboy reflected for an instant. "Well," he said, "I had to order in th' 12th to help th' 76th, an' I haven't really got any. But there's th' 304th. They fight like a lot 'a mule drivers. I can spare them best of any."

The youth and his friend exchanged glances of astonishment.

The general spoke sharply. "Get 'em ready, then. I'll watch developments from here, an' send you word when t' start them. It'll happen in five minutes."

As the other officer tossed his fingers toward his cap and wheeling his horse, started away, the general called out to him in a sober voice: "I don't believe many of your mule drivers will get back."

The other shouted something in reply. He smiled.

With scared faces, the youth and his companion hurried back to the line.

These happenings had occupied an incredibly short time, yet the youth felt that in them he had been made aged. New eyes were given to him. And the most startling thing was to learn suddenly that he was very insignificant. The officer spoke of the regiment as if he referred to a broom. Some part of the woods needed sweeping, perhaps, and he merely indicated a broom in a tone properly indifferent to its fate. It was war, no doubt, but it appeared strange.

As the two boys approached the line, the lieutenant perceived them and swelled with wrath. "Fleming—Wilson—how long does it take yeh to git water, anyhow—where yeh been to."

But his oration ceased as he saw their eyes, which were large with great tales. "We're goin' t' charge—we're goin' t' charge!" cried the youth's friend, hastening with his news.

"Charge?" said the lieutenant. "Charge? Well, b'Gawd! Now, this is real fightin'." Over his soiled countenance there went a boastful smile. "Charge? Well, b'Gawd!"

A little group of soldiers surrounded the two youths. "Are we, sure 'nough? Well, I'll be derned! Charge? What fer? What at? Wilson, you're lyin'."

"I hope to die," said the youth, pitching his tones to the key of angry remonstrance. "Sure as shooting, I tell you."

And his friend spoke in re-enforcement. "Not by a blame sight, he ain't lyin'. We heard 'em talkin'."

They caught sight of two mounted figures a short distance from them. One was the colonel of the regiment and the other was the officer who had received orders from the commander of the division. They were gesticulating at each other. The soldier, pointing at them, interpreted the scene.

One man had a final objection: "How could yeh hear 'em talkin'?" But the men, for a large part, nodded, admitting that previously the two friends had spoken truth.

They settled back into reposeful attitudes with airs of having accepted the matter. And they mused upon it, with a hundred varieties of expression. It was an engrossing thing to think about. Many tightened their belts carefully and hitched at their trousers.

A moment later the officers began to bustle among the men, pushing them into a more compact mass and into a better alignment. They chased those that straggled and fumed at a few men who seemed to show by their attitudes that they had decided to remain at that spot. They were like critical shepherds struggling with sheep.

Presently, the regiment seemed to draw itself up and heave a deep breath. None of the men's faces were mirrors of large thoughts. The soldiers were bended and stooped like sprinters before a signal. Many pairs of glinting eyes peered from the grimy faces toward the curtains of the deeper woods. They seemed to be engaged in deep calculations of time and distance.

They were surrounded by the noises of the monstrous altercation between the two armies. The world was fully interested in other matters. Apparently, the regiment had its small affair to itself.

The youth, turning, shot a quick, inquiring glance at his friend. The latter returned to him the same manner of look. They were the only ones who possessed an inner knowledge. "Mule drivers—hell t' pay—don't believe many will get back." It was an ironical secret. Still, they saw no hesitation in each other's faces, and they nodded a mute and unprotesting assent when a shaggy man near them said in a meek voice: "We'll git swallowed."

Chapter XIX

The youth stared at the land in front of him. Its foliages now seemed to veil powers and horrors. He was unaware of the machinery of orders that started the charge, although from the corners of his eyes he saw an officer, who looked like a boy a-horseback, come galloping, waving his hat. Suddenly he felt a straining and heaving among the men. The line fell slowly forward like a toppling wall, and, with a convulsive gasp that was intended for a cheer, the regiment began its journey. The youth was pushed and jostled for a moment before he understood the movement at all, but directly he lunged ahead and began to run.

He fixed his eye upon a distant and prominent clump of trees where he had concluded the enemy were to be met, and he ran toward it as toward a goal. He had believed throughout that it was a mere question of getting over an unpleasant matter as quickly as possible, and he ran desperately, as if pursued for a murder. His face was drawn hard and tight with the stress of his endeavor. His eyes were fixed in a lurid glare. And with his soiled and disordered dress, his red and inflamed features surmounted by the dingy rag with its spot of blood, his wildly swinging rifle and banging accouterments, he looked to be an insane soldier.

As the regiment swung from its position out into a cleared space the woods and thickets before it awakened. Yellow flames leaped toward it from many directions. The forest made a tremendous objection.

The line lurched straight for a moment. Then the right wing swung forward; it in turn was surpassed by the left. Afterward the center careered to the front until the regiment was a wedge-shaped mass, but an instant later the opposition of the bushes, trees, and uneven places on the ground split the command and scattered it into detached clusters.

The youth, light-footed, was unconsciously in advance. His eyes still kept note of the clump of trees. From all places near it the clannish yell of the enemy could be heard. The little flames of rifles leaped from it. The song of the bullets was in the air and shells snarled among the treetops. One tumbled directly into the middle of a hurrying group and exploded in crimson fury. There was an instant's spectacle of a man, almost over it, throwing up his hands to shield his eyes.

Other men, punched by bullets, fell in grotesque agonies. The regiment left a coherent trail of bodies.

They had passed into a clearer atmosphere. There was an effect like a revelation in the new appearance of the landscape. Some men working madly at a battery were plain to them, and the opposing infantry's lines were defined by the gray walls and fringes of smoke.

It seemed to the youth that he saw everything. Each blade of the green grass was bold and clear. He thought that he was aware of every change in the thin, transparent vapor that floated idly in

sheets. The brown or gray trunks of the trees showed each rough-
ness of their surfaces. And the men of the regiment, with their
starting eyes and sweating faces, running madly, or falling, as if
thrown headlong, to queer, heaped-up corpses—all were comprehended. His mind took a mechanical but firm impression, so that
afterward everything was pictured and explained to him, save why
he himself was there.

But there was a frenzy made from this furious rush. The men,
pitching forward insanely, had burst into cheerings, moblike and
barbaric, but tuned in strange keys that can arouse the dullard
and the stoic. It made a mad enthusiasm that, it seemed, would be
incapable of checking itself before granite and brass. There was the
delirium that encounters despair and death, and is heedless and
blind to the odds. It is a temporary but sublime absence of selfishness. And because it was of this order was the reason, perhaps, why
the youth wondered, afterward, what reasons he could have had for
being there.

Presently the straining pace ate up the energies of the men. As
if by agreement, the leaders began to slacken their speed. The
volleys directed against them had had a seeming windlike effect.
The regiment snorted and blew. Among some stolid trees it began
to falter and hesitate. The men, staring intently, began to wait for
some of the distant walls of smoke to move and disclose to them
the scene. Since much of their strength and their breath had vanished, they returned to caution. They were become men again.

The youth had a vague belief that he had run miles, and he
thought, in a way, that he was now in some new and unknown land.

The moment the regiment ceased its advance the protesting
splutter of musketry became a steadied roar. Long and accurate
fringes of smoke spread out. From the top of a small hill came level
belchings of yellow flame that caused an inhuman whistling in the
air.

The men, halted, had opportunity to see some of their comrades
dropping with moans and shrieks. A few lay under foot, still or
wailing. And now for an instant the men stood, their rifles slack
in their hands, and watched the regiment dwindle. They appeared
dazed and stupid. This spectacle seemed to paralyze them, overcome them with a fatal fascination. They stared woodenly at the
sights, and, lowering their eyes, looked from face to face. It was a
strange pause, and a strange silence.

Then, above the sounds of the outside commotion, arose the
roar of the lieutenant. He strode suddenly forth, his infantile features black with rage.

"Come on, yeh fools!" he bellowed. "Come on! Yeh can't stay here. Yeh must come on." He said more, but much of it could not be understood.

He started rapidly forward, with his head turned toward the men. "Come on," he was shouting. The men stared with blank and yokel-like eyes at him. He was obliged to halt and retrace his steps. He stood then with his back to the enemy and delivered gigantic curses into the faces of the men. His body vibrated from the weight and force of his imprecations. And he could string oaths with the facility of a maiden who strings beads.

The friend of the youth aroused. Lurching suddenly forward and dropping to his knees, he fired an angry shot at the persistent woods. This action awakened the men. They huddled no more like sheep. They seemed suddenly to bethink them of their weapons, and at once commenced firing. Belabored by their officers, they began to move forward. The regiment, involved like a cart involved in mud and muddle, started unevenly with many jolts and jerks. The men stopped now every few paces to fire and load, and in this manner moved slowly on from trees to trees.

The flaming opposition in their front grew with their advance until it seemed that all forward ways were barred by the thin leaping tongues, and off to the right an ominous demonstration could sometimes be dimly discerned. The smoke lately generated was in confusing clouds that made it difficult for the regiment to proceed with intelligence. As he passed through each curling mass the youth wondered what would confront him on the farther side.

The command went painfully forward until an open space interposed between them and the lurid lines. Here, crouching and cowering behind some trees, the men clung with desperation, as if threatened by a wave. They looked wild-eyed, and as if amazed at this furious disturbance they had stirred. In the storm there was an ironical expression of their importance. The faces of the men, too, showed a lack of a certain feeling of responsibility for being there. It was as if they had been driven. It was the dominant animal failing to remember in the supreme moments the forceful causes of various superficial qualities. The whole affair seemed incomprehensible to many of them.

As they halted thus the lieutenant again began to bellow profanely. Regardless of the vindictive threats of the bullets, he went about coaxing, berating, and bedamning. His lips, that were habitually in a soft and childlike curve, were now writhed into unholy contortions. He swore by all possible deities.

Once he grabbed the youth by the arm. "Come on, yeh lunkhead!" he roared. "Come on! We'll all git killed if we stay here.

We've on'y got t' go across that lot. An' then"—the remainder of his idea disappeared in a blue haze of curses.

The youth stretched forth his arm. "Cross there?" His mouth was puckered in doubt and awe.

"Certainly. Jest 'cross th' lot! We can't stay here," screamed the lieutenant. He poked his face close to the youth and waved his bandaged hand. "Come on!" Presently he grappled with him as if for a wrestling bout. It was as if he planned to drag the youth by the ear on to the assault.

The private felt a sudden unspeakable indignation against his officer. He wrenched fiercely and shook him off.

"Come on yerself, then," he yelled. There was a bitter challenge in his voice.

They galloped together down the regimental front. The friend scrambled after them. In front of the colors the three men began to bawl: "Come on! come on!" They danced and gyrated like tortured savages.

The flag, obedient to these appeals, bended its glittering form and swept toward them. The men wavered in indecision for a moment, and then with a long, wailful cry the dilapidated regiment surged forward and began its new journey.

Over the field went the scurrying mass. It was a handful of men splattered into the faces of the enemy. Toward it instantly sprang the yellow tongues. A vast quantity of blue smoke hung before them. A mighty banging made ears valueless.

The youth ran like a madman to reach the woods before a bullet could discover him. He ducked his head low, like a football player. In his haste his eyes almost closed, and the scene was a wild blur. Pulsating saliva stood at the corners of his mouth.

Within him, as he hurled himself forward, was born a love, a despairing fondness for this flag which was near him. It was a creation of beauty and invulnerability. It was a goddess, radiant, that bended its form with an imperious gesture to him. It was a woman, red and white, hating and loving, that called him with the voice of his hopes. Because no harm could come to it he endowed it with power. He kept near, as if it could be a saver of lives, and an imploring cry went from his mind.

In the mad scramble he was aware that the color sergeant flinched suddenly, as if struck by a bludgeon. He faltered, and then became motionless, save for his quivering knees.

He made a spring and a clutch at the pole. At the same instant his friend grabbed it from the other side. They jerked at it, stout and furious, but the color sergeant was dead, and the corpse would not relinquish its trust. For a moment there was a grim encounter.

The dead man, swinging with bended back, seemed to be obstinately tugging, in ludicrous and awful ways, for the possession of the flag.

It was past in an instant of time. They wrenched the flag furiously from the dead man, and, as they turned again, the corpse swayed forward with bowed head. One arm swung high, and the curved hand fell with heavy protest on the friend's unheeding shoulder.

Chapter XX

When the two youths turned with the flag they saw that much of the regiment had crumbled away, and the dejected remnant was coming slowly back. The men, having hurled themselves in projectile fashion, had presently expended their forces. They slowly retreated, with their faces still toward the spluttering woods, and their hot rifles still replying to the din. Several officers were giving orders, their voices keyed to screams.

"Where in hell yeh goin'?" the lieutenant was asking in a sarcastic howl. And a red-bearded officer, whose voice of triple brass could plainly be heard, was commanding: "Shoot into 'em! Shoot into 'em, Gawd damn their souls!" There was a *melée* of screeches, in which the men were ordered to do conflicting and impossible things.

The youth and his friend had a small scuffle over the flag. "Give it t' me!" "No, let me keep it!" Each felt satisfied with the other's possession of it, but each felt bound to declare, by an offer to carry the emblem, his willingness to further risk himself. The youth roughly pushed his friend away.

The regiment fell back to the stolid trees. There it halted for a moment to blaze at some dark forms that had begun to steal upon its track. Presently it resumed its march again, curving among the tree trunks. By the time the depleted regiment had again reached the first open space they were receiving a fast and merciless fire. There seemed to be mobs all about them.

The greater part of the men, discouraged, their spirits worn by the turmoil, acted as if stunned. They accepted the pelting of the bullets with bowed and weary heads. It was of no purpose to strive against walls. It was of no use to batter themselves against granite. And from this consciousness that they had attempted to conquer an unconquerable thing there seemed to arise a feeling that they had been betrayed. They glowered with bent brows, but dangerously, upon some of the officers, more particularly upon the red-bearded one with the voice of triple brass.

However, the rear of the regiment was fringed with men, who continued to shoot irritably at the advancing foes. They seemed resolved to make every trouble. The youthful lieutenant was perhaps the last man in the disordered mass. His forgotten back was toward the enemy. He had been shot in the arm. It hung straight and rigid. Occasionally he would cease to remember it, and be about to emphasize an oath with a sweeping gesture. The multiplied pain caused him to swear with incredible power.

The youth went along with slipping, uncertain feet. He kept watchful eyes rearward. A scowl of mortification and rage was upon his face. He had thought of a fine revenge upon the officer who had referred to him and his fellows as mule drivers. But he saw that it could not come to pass. His dreams had collapsed when the mule drivers, dwindling rapidly, had wavered and hesitated on the little clearing, and then had recoiled. And now the retreat of the mule drivers was a march of shame to him.

A dagger-pointed gaze from without his blackened face was held toward the enemy, but his greater hatred was riveted upon the man, who, not knowing him, had called him a mule driver.

When he knew that he and his comrades had failed to do anything in successful ways that might bring the little pangs of a kind of remorse upon the officer, the youth allowed the rage of the baffled to possess him. This cold officer upon a monument, who dropped epithets unconcernedly down, would be finer as a dead man, he thought. So grievous did he think it that he could never possess the secret right to taunt truly in answer.

He had pictured red letters of curious revenge. "We *are* mule drivers, are we?" And now he was compelled to throw them away.

He presently wrapped his heart in the cloak of his pride and kept the flag erect. He harangued his fellows, pushing against their chests with his free hand. To those he knew well he made frantic appeals, beseeching them by name. Between him and the lieutenant, scolding and near to losing his mind with rage, there was felt a subtle fellowship and equality. They supported each other in all manner of hoarse, howling protests.

But the regiment was a machine run down. The two men babbled at a forceless thing. The soldiers who had heart to go slowly were continually shaken in their resolves by a knowledge that comrades were slipping with speed back to the lines. It was difficult to think of reputation when others were thinking of skins. Wounded men were left crying on this black journey.

The smoke fringes and flames blustered always. The youth, peering once through a sudden rift in a cloud, saw a brown mass of troops, interwoven and magnified until they appeared to be thousands. A fierce-hued flag flashed before his vision.

Immediately, as if the uplifting of the smoke had been prearranged, the discovered troops burst into a rasping yell, and a hundred flames jetted toward the retreating band. A rolling gray cloud again interposed as the regiment doggedly replied. The youth had to depend again upon his misused ears, which were trembling and buzzing from the *melée* of musketry and yells.

The way seemed eternal. In the clouded haze men became panicstricken with the thought that the regiment had lost its path, and was proceeding in a perilous direction. Once the men who headed the wild procession turned and came pushing back against their comrades, screaming that they were being fired upon from points which they had considered to be toward their own lines. At this cry a hysterical fear and dismay beset the troops. A soldier, who heretofore had been ambitious to make the regiment into a wise little band that would proceed calmly amid the huge-appearing difficulties, suddenly sank down and buried his face in his arms with an air of bowing to a doom. From another a shrill lamentation rang out filled with profane allusions to a general. Men ran hither and thither, seeking with their eyes roads of escape. With serene regularity, as if controlled by a schedule, bullets buffed into men.

The youth walked stolidly into the midst of the mob, and with his flag in his hands took a stand as if he expected an attempt to push him to the ground. He unconsciously assumed the attitude of the color bearer in the fight of the preceding day. He passed over his brow a hand that trembled. His breath did not come freely. He was choking during this small wait for the crisis.

His friend came to him. "Well, Henry, I guess this is good-by-John."[2]

"Oh, shut up, you damned fool!" replied the youth, and he would not look at the other.

The officers labored like politicians to beat the mass into a proper circle to face the menaces. The ground was uneven and torn. The men curled into depressions and fitted themselves snugly behind whatever would frustrate a bullet.

The youth noted with vague surprise that the lieutenant was standing mutely with his legs far apart and his sword held in the manner of a cane. The youth wondered what had happened to his vocal organs that he no more cursed.

There was something curious in this little intent pause of the lieutenant. He was like a babe which, having wept its fill, raises its eyes and fixes upon a distant joy. He was engrossed in this contem-

2. Apparently a proverbial expression for "farewell."

plation, and the soft under lip quivered from self-whispered words.

Some lazy and ignorant smoke curled slowly. The men, hiding from the bullets, waited anxiously for it to lift and disclose the plight of the regiment.

The silent ranks were suddenly thrilled by the eager voice of the youthful lieutenant bawling out: "Here they come! Right onto us, b'Gawd!" His further words were lost in a roar of wicked thunder from the men's rifles.

The youth's eyes had instantly turned in the direction indicated by the awakened and agitated lieutenant, and he had seen the haze of treachery disclosing a body of soldiers of the enemy. They were so near that he could see their features. There was a recognition as he looked at the types of faces. Also he perceived with dim amazement that their uniforms were rather gay in effect, being light gray, accented with a brilliant-hued facing. Too, the clothes seemed new.

These troops had apparently been going forward with caution, their rifles held in readiness, when the youthful lieutenant had discovered them and their movement had been interrupted by the volley from the blue regiment. From the moment's glimpse, it was derived that they had been unaware of the proximity of their dark-suited foes or had mistaken the direction. Almost instantly they were shut utterly from the youth's sight by the smoke from the energetic rifles of his companions. He strained his vision to learn the accomplishment of the volley, but the smoke hung before him.

The two bodies of troops exchanged blows in the manner of a pair of boxers. The fast angry firings went back and forth. The men in blue were intent with the despair of their circumstances and they seized upon the revenge to be had at close range. Their thunder swelled loud and valiant. Their curving front bristled with flashes and the place resounded with the clangor of their ramrods. The youth ducked and dodged for a time and achieved a few unsatisfactory views of the enemy. There appeared to be many of them and they were replying swiftly. They seemed moving toward the blue regiment, step by step. He seated himself gloomily on the ground with his flag between his knees.

As he noted the vicious, wolflike temper of his comrades he had a sweet thought that if the enemy was about to swallow the regimental broom as a large prisoner, it could at least have the consolation of going down with bristles forward.

But the blows of the antagonist began to grow more weak. Fewer bullets ripped the air, and finally, when the men slackened to learn of the fight, they could see only dark, floating smoke. The regiment lay still and gazed. Presently some chance whim came to the pestering blur, and it began to coil heavily away. The men saw a ground vacant of fighters. It would have been an empty stage if it were not for a few corpses that lay thrown and twisted into fantastic shapes upon the sward.

At sight of this tableau, many of the men in blue sprang from behind their covers and made an ungainly dance of joy. Their eyes burned and a hoarse cheer of elation broke from their dry lips.

It had begun to seem to them that events were trying to prove that they were impotent. These little battles had evidently endeavored to demonstrate that the men could not fight well. When on the verge of submission to these opinions, the small duel had showed them that the proportions were not impossible, and by it they had revenged themselves upon their misgivings and upon the foe.

The impetus of enthusiasm was theirs again. They gazed about them with looks of uplifted pride, feeling new trust in the grim, always confident weapons in their hands. And they were men.

Chapter XXI

Presently they knew that no firing threatened them. All ways seemed once more opened to them. The dusty blue lines of their friends were disclosed a short distance away. In the distance there were many colossal noises, but in all this part of the field there was a sudden stillness.

They perceived that they were free. The depleted band drew a long breath of relief and gathered itself into a bunch to complete its trip.

In this last length of journey the men began to show strange emotions. They hurried with nervous fear. Some who had been dark and unfaltering in the grimmest moments now could not conceal an anxiety that made them frantic. It was perhaps that they dreaded to be killed in insignificant ways after the times for proper military deaths had passed. Or, perhaps, they thought it would be too ironical to get killed at the portals of safety. With backward looks of perturbation, they hastened.

As they approached their own lines there was some sarcasm exhibited on the part of a gaunt and bronzed regiment that lay resting in the shade of trees. Questions were wafted to them.

"Where th' hell yeh been?"

"What yeh comin' back fer?"

"Why didn't yeh stay there?"

"Was it warm out there, sonny?"

"Goin' home now, boys?"

One shouted in taunting mimicry: "Oh, mother, come quick an' look at th' sojers!"

There was no reply from the bruised and battered regiment, save that one man made broadcast challenges to fist fights and the red-bearded officer walked rather near and glared in great swashbuckler style at a tall captain in the other regiment. But the lieutenant suppressed the man who wished to fist fight, and the tall captain, flushing at the little fanfare of the red-bearded one, was obliged to look intently at some trees.

The youth's tender flesh was deeply stung by these remarks. From under his creased brows he glowered with hate at the mockers. He meditated upon a few revenges. Still, many in the regiment hung their heads in criminal fashion, so that it came to pass that the men trudged with sudden heaviness, as if they bore upon their bended shoulders the coffin of their honor. And the youthful lieutenant, recollecting himself, began to mutter softly in black curses.

They turned when they arrived at their old position to regard the ground over which they had charged.

The youth in this contemplation was smitten with a large astonishment. He discovered that the distances, as compared with the brilliant measurings of his mind, were trivial and ridiculous. The stolid trees, where much had taken place, seemed incredibly near. The time, too, now that he reflected, he saw to have been short. He wondered at the number of emotions and events that had been crowded into such little spaces. Elfin thoughts must have exaggerated and enlarged everything, he said.

It seemed, then, that there was bitter justice in the speeches of the gaunt and bronzed veterans. He veiled a glance of disdain at his fellows who strewed the ground, choking with dust, red from perspiration, misty-eyed, disheveled.

They were gulping at their canteens, fierce to wring every mite of water from them, and they polished at their swollen and watery features with coat sleeves and bunches of grass.

However, to the youth there was a considerable joy in musing upon his performances during the charge. He had had very little time previously in which to appreciate himself, so that there was now much satisfaction in quietly thinking of his actions. He recalled bits of color that in the flurry had stamped themselves unawares upon his engaged senses.

As the regiment lay heaving from its hot exertions the officer who had named them as mule drivers came galloping along the line. He had lost his cap. His tousled hair streamed wildly, and his face was dark with vexation and wrath. His temper was displayed with more clearness by the way in which he managed his horse. He jerked and wrenched savagely at his bridle, stopping the hard-breathing animal with a furious pull near the colonel of the regiment. He immediately exploded in reproaches which came unbidden to the ears of the men. They were suddenly alert, being always curious about black words between officers.

"Oh, thunder, MacChesnay, what an awful bull you made of this thing!" began the officer. He attempted low tones, but his indignation caused certain of the men to learn the sense of his words. "What an awful mess you made! Good Lord, man, you stopped about a hundred feet this side of a very pretty success! If your men had gone a hundred feet farther you would have made a great charge, but as it is—what a lot of mud diggers you've got anyway!"

The men, listening with bated breath, now turned their curious eyes upon the colonel. They had a ragamuffin interest in this affair.

The colonel was seen to straighten his form and put one hand forth in oratorical fashion. He wore an injured air; it was as if a deacon had been accused of stealing. The men were wiggling in an ecstasy of excitement.

But of a sudden the colonel's manner changed from that of a deacon to that of a Frenchman. He shrugged his shoulders. "Oh, well, general, we went as far as we could," he said calmly.

" 'As far as you could?' Did you, b'Gawd?" snorted the other. "Well, that wasn't very far, was it?" he added, with a glance of cold contempt into the other's eyes. "Not very far, I think. You were intended to make a diversion in favor of Whiterside. How well you succeeded your own ears can now tell you." He wheeled his horse and rode stiffly away.

The colonel, bidden to hear the jarring noises of an engagement in the woods to the left, broke out in vague damnations.

The lieutenant, who had listened with an air of impotent rage to the interview, spoke suddenly in firm and undaunted tones. "I don't care what a man is—whether he is a general or what—if he says th' boys didn't put up a good fight out there he's a damned fool."

"Lieutenant," began the colonel, severely, "this is my own affair, and I'll trouble you——"

The lieutenant made an obedient gesture. "All right, colonel, all right," he said. He sat down with an air of being content with himself.

The news that the regiment had been reproached went along the line. For a time the men were bewildered by it. "Good thunder!" they ejaculated, staring at the vanishing form of the general. They conceived it to be a huge mistake.

Presently, however, they began to believe that in truth their efforts had been called light. The youth could see this conviction
weigh upon the entire regiment until the men were liked cuffed and
cursed animals, but withal rebellious.

The friend, with a grievance in his eye, went to the youth. "I
wonder what he does want," he said. "He must think we went out
there an' played marbles! I never see sech a man!"

The youth developed a tranquil philosophy for these moments
of irritation. "Oh, well," he rejoined, "he probably didn't see nothing of it at all and got mad as blazes, and concluded we were a lot
of sheep, just because we didn't do what he wanted done. It's a
pity old Grandpa Henderson got killed yestirday—he'd have known
that we did our best and fought good. It's just our awful luck, that's
what."

"I should say so," replied the friend. He seemed to be deeply
wounded at an injustice. "I should say we did have awful luck!
There's no fun in fightin' fer people when everything yeh do—no
matter what—ain't done right. I have a notion t' stay behind next
time an' let 'em take their ol' charge an' go t' th' devil with it."

The youth spoke soothingly to his comrade. "Well, we both did
good. I'd like to see the fool what'd say we both didn't do as good
as we could!"

"Of course we did," declared the friend stoutly. "An' I'd break
th' feller's neck if he was as big as a church. But we're all right,
anyhow, for I heard one feller say that we two fit th' best in th'
reg'ment, an' they had a great argument 'bout it. Another feller,
'a course, he had t' up an' say it was a lie—he seen all what was
goin' on an' he never seen us from th' beginnin' t' th' end. An' a
lot more struck in an' ses it wasn't a lie—we did fight like thunder,
an' they give us quite a send-off. But this is what I can't stand—
these everlastin' ol' soldiers, titterin' an' laughin', an' then that
general, he's crazy."

The youth exclaimed with sudden exasperation: "He's a lunkhead! He makes me mad. I wish he'd come along next time. We'd
show 'im what——"

He ceased because several men had come hurrying up. Their
faces expressed a bringing of great news.

"O Flem, yeh jest oughta heard!" cried one, eagerly.

"Heard what?" said the youth.

"Yeh jest oughta heard!" repeated the other, and he arranged
himself to tell his tidings. The others made an excited circle. "Well,
sir, th' colonel met your lieutenant right by us—it was damned-
est thing I ever heard—an' he ses: 'Ahem! ahem!' he ses. 'Mr.

Hasbrouck!' he ses, 'by th' way, who was that lad what carried th' flag?' he ses. There, Flemin', what d' yeh think 'a that? 'Who was th' lad what carried th' flag?' he ses, an' th' lieutenant, he speaks up right away: 'That's Flemin', an' he's a jimhickey,' he ses, right away. What? I say he did. 'A jimhickey,' he ses—those 'r his words. He did, too. I say he did. If you kin tell this story better than I kin, go ahead an' tell it. Well, then, keep yer mouth shet. Th' lieutenant, he ses: 'He's a jimhickey,' an' th' colonel, he ses: 'Ahem! ahem! he is, indeed, a very good man t' have, ahem! He kep' th' flag 'way t' th' front. I saw 'im. He's a good un,' ses th' colonel. 'You bet,' ses th' lieutenant, 'he an' a feller named Wilson was at th' head 'a th' charge, an' howlin' like Indians all th' time,' he ses. 'Head 'a th' charge all th' time,' he ses. 'A feller named Wilson,' he ses. There, Wilson, m'boy, put that in a letter an' send it hum t' yer mother, hay? 'A feller named Wilson,' he ses. An' the colonel, he ses: 'Were they, indeed? Ahem! ahem! My sakes!' he ses. 'At th' head 'a th' reg'ment?' he ses. 'They were,' ses th' lieutenant. 'My sakes!' ses th' colonel. He ses: 'Well, well, well,' he ses, 'those two babies?' 'They were,' ses th' lieutenant. 'Well, well,' ses th' colonel, 'they deserve t' be major generals,' he ses. 'They deserve t' be major-generals.' "

The youth and his friend had said: "Huh!" "Yer lyin', Thompson." "Oh, go t' blazes!" "He never sed it." "Oh, what a lie!" "Huh!" But despite these youthful scoffings and embarrassments, they knew that their faces were deeply flushing from thrills of pleasure. They exchanged a secret glance of joy and congratulation.

They speedily forgot many things. The past held no pictures of error and disappointment. They were very happy, and their hearts swelled with grateful affection for the colonel and the youthful lieutenant.

Chapter XXII

When the woods again began to pour forth the dark-hued masses of the enemy the youth felt serene self-confidence. He smiled briefly when he saw men dodge and duck at the long screechings of shells that were thrown in giant handfuls over them. He stood, erect and tranquil, watching the attack begin against a part of the line that made a blue curve along the side of an adjacent hill. His vision being unmolested by smoke from the rifles of his companions, he had opportunities to see parts of the hard fight. It was a relief to perceive at last from whence came some of these noises which had been roared into his ears.

Off a short way he saw two regiments fighting a little separate battle with two other regiments. It was in a cleared space, wearing a set-apart look. They were blazing as if upon a wager, giving and taking tremendous blows. The firings were incredibly fierce and rapid. These intent regiments apparently were oblivious of all larger purposes of war, and were slugging each other as if at a matched game.

In another direction he saw a magnificent brigade going with the evident intention of driving the enemy from a wood. They passed in out of sight and presently there was a most awe-inspiring racket in the wood. The noise was unspeakable. Having stirred this prodigious uproar, and, apparently, finding it too prodigious, the brigade, after a little time, came marching airily out again with its fine formation in nowise disturbed. There were no traces of speed in its movements. The brigade was jaunty and seemed to point a proud thumb at the yelling wood.

On a slope to the left there was a long row of guns, gruff and maddened, denouncing the enemy, who, down through the woods, were forming for another attack in the pitiless monotony of conflicts. The round red discharges from the guns made a crimson flare and a high, thick smoke. Occasional glimpses could be caught of groups of the toiling artillerymen. In the rear of this row of guns stood a house, calm and white, amid bursting shells. A congregation of horses, tied to a long railing, were tugging frenziedly at their bridles. Men were running hither and thither.

The detached battle between the four regiments lasted for some time. There chanced to be no interference, and they settled their dispute by themselves. They struck savagely and powerfully at each other for a period of minutes, and then the lighter-hued regiments faltered and drew back, leaving the dark-blue lines shouting. The youth could see the two flags shaking with laughter amid the smoke remnants.

Presently there was a stillness, pregnant with meaning. The blue lines shifted and changed a trifle and stared expectantly at the silent woods and fields before them. The hush was solemn and churchlike, save for a distant battery that, evidently unable to remain quiet, sent a faint rolling thunder over the ground. It irritated, like the noises of unimpressed boys. The men imagined that it would prevent their perched ears from hearing the first words of the new battle.

Of a sudden the guns on the slope roared out a message of warning. A spluttering sound had begun in the woods. It swelled with amazing speed to a profound clamor that involved the earth in noises. The splitting crashes swept along the lines until an interminable roar was developed. To those in the midst of it it became a din fitted to the universe. It was the whirring and thumping of gigantic machinery, complications among the smaller stars. The youth's ears were filled cups. They were incapable of hearing more.

On an incline over which a road wound he saw wild and desperate rushes of men perpetually backward and forward in riotous surges. These parts of the opposing armies were two long waves that pitched upon each other madly at dictated points. To and fro they swelled. Sometimes, one side by its yells and cheers would proclaim decisive blows, but a moment later the other side would be all yells and cheers. Once the youth saw a spray of light forms go in houndlike leaps toward the waving blue lines. There was much howling, and presently it went away with a vast mouthful of prisoners. Again, he saw a blue wave dash with such thunderous force against a gray obstruction that it seemed to clear the earth of it and leave nothing but trampled sod. And always in their swift and deadly rushes to and fro the men screamed and yelled like maniacs.

Particular pieces of fence or secure positions behind collections of trees were wrangled over, as gold thrones or pearl bedsteads. There were desperate lunges at these chosen spots seemingly every instant, and most of them were bandied like light toys between the contending forces. The youth could not tell from the battle flags flying like crimson foam in many directions which color of cloth was winning.

His emaciated regiment bustled forth with undiminished fierceness when its time came. When assaulted again by bullets, the men burst out in a barbaric cry of rage and pain. They bent their heads in aims of intent hatred behind the projected hammers of their guns. Their ramrods clanged loud with fury as their eager arms pounded the cartridges into the rifle barrels. The front of the regiment was a smoke-wall penetrated by the flashing points of yellow and red.

Wallowing in the fight, they were in an astonishingly short time resmudged. They surpassed in stain and dirt all their previous appearances. Moving to and fro with strained exertion, jabbering the while, they were, with their swaying bodies, black faces, and glowing eyes, like strange and ugly fiends jigging heavily in the smoke.

The lieutenant, returning from a tour after a bandage, produced from a hidden receptacle of his mind new and portentous oaths suited to the emergency. Strings of expletives he swung lashlike over the backs of his men, and it was evident that his previous efforts had in nowise impaired his resources.

The youth, still the bearer of the colors, did not feel his idleness. He was deeply absorbed as a spectator. The crash and swing of the great drama made him lean forward, intent-eyed, his face working in small contortions. Sometimes he prattled, words coming unconsciously from him in grotesque exclamations. He did not know that he breathed; that the flag hung silently over him, so absorbed was he.

A formidable line of the enemy came within dangerous range. They could be seen plainly—tall, gaunt men with excited faces running with long strides toward a wandering fence.

At sight of this danger the men suddenly ceased their cursing monotone. There was an instant of strained silence before they threw up their rifles and fired a plumping volley at the foes. There had been no order given; the men, upon recognizing the menace, had immediately let drive their flock of bullets without waiting for word of command.

But the enemy were quick to gain the protection of the wandering line of fence. They slid down behind it with remarkable celerity, and from this position they began briskly to slice up the blue men.

These latter braced their energies for a great struggle. Often, white clinched teeth shone from the dusky faces. Many heads surged to and fro, floating upon a pale sea of smoke. Those behind the fence frequently shouted and yelped in taunts and gibe-like cries, but the regiment maintained a stressed silence. Perhaps, at this new assault the men recalled the fact that they had been named mud diggers, and it made their situation thrice bitter. They were breathlessly intent upon keeping the ground and thrusting away the rejoicing body of the enemy. They fought swiftly and with a despairing savageness denoted in their expressions.

The youth had resolved not to budge whatever should happen. Some arrows of scorn that had buried themselves in his heart had generated strange and unspeakable hatred. It was clear to him that his final and absolute revenge was to be achieved by his dead body lying, torn and gluttering,[3] upon the field. This was to be a poignant retaliation upon the officer who had said "mule drivers," and later "mud diggers," for in all the wild graspings of his mind for a unit responsible for his sufferings and commotions he always seized upon the man who had dubbed him wrongly. And it was his idea, vaguely formulated, that his corpse would be for those eyes a great

3. Also in the manuscript; perhaps an error either for "glittering" or for "gut- tering," the dropping of melted wax from a candle.

and salt reproach.

The regiment bled extravagantly. Grunting bundles of blue began to drop. The orderly sergeant of the youth's company was shot through the cheeks. Its supports being injured, his jaw hung afar down, disclosing in the wide cavern of his mouth a pulsing mass of blood and teeth. And with it all he made attempts to cry out. In his endeavor there was a dreadful earnestness, as if he conceived that one great shriek would make him well.

The youth saw him presently go rearward. His strength seemed in nowise impaired. He ran swiftly, casting wild glances for succor.

Others fell down about the feet of their companions. Some of the wounded crawled out and away, but many lay still, their bodies twisted into impossible shapes.

The youth looked once for his friend. He saw a vehement young man, powder-smeared and frowzled, whom he knew to be him. The lieutenant, also, was unscathed in his position at the rear. He had continued to curse, but it was now with the air of a man who was using his last box of oaths.

For the fire of the regiment had begun to wane and drip. The robust voice, that had come strangely from the thin ranks, was growing rapidly weak.

Chapter XXIII

The colonel came running along back of the line. There were other officers following him. "We must charge 'm!" they shouted. "We must charge 'm!" they cried with resentful voices, as if anticipating a rebellion against this plan by the men.

The youth, upon hearing the shouts, began to study the distance between him and the enemy. He made vague calculations. He saw that to be firm soldiers they must go forward. It would be death to stay in the present place, and with all the circumstances to go backward would exalt too many others. Their hope was to push the galling foes away from the fence.

He expected that his companions, weary and stiffened, would have to be driven to this assault, but as he turned toward them he perceived with a certain surprise that they were giving quick and unqualified expressions of assent. There was an ominous, clanging overture to the charge when the shafts of the bayonets rattled upon the rifle barrels. At the yelled words of command the soldiers sprang forward in eager leaps. There was new and unexpected force in the movement of the regiment. A knowledge of its faded and jaded condition made the charge appear like a paroxysm, a display of the strength that comes before a final feebleness. The men scampered in insane fever of haste, racing as if to achieve a sudden success before an exhilarating fluid should leave them. It was a blind and despairing rush by the collection of men in dusty and tattered blue, over a green sward and under a sapphire sky, toward a fence, dimly outlined in smoke, from behind which spluttered the fierce rifles of enemies.

The youth kept the bright colors to the front. He was waving his free arm in furious circles, the while shrieking mad calls and appeals, urging on those that did not need to be urged, for it seemed that the mob of blue men hurling themselves on the dangerous group of rifles were again grown suddenly wild with an enthusiasm of unselfishness. From the many firings starting toward them, it looked as if they would merely succeed in making a great sprinkling of corpses on the grass between their former position and the fence. But they were in a state of frenzy, perhaps because of forgotten vanities, and it made an exhibition of sublime recklessness. There was no obvious questioning, nor figurings, nor diagrams. There was, apparently, no considered loopholes. It appeared that the swift wings of their desires would have shattered against the iron gates of the impossible.

He himself felt the daring spirit of a savage, religion-mad. He was capable of profound sacrifices, a tremendous death. He had no time for dissections, but he knew that he thought of the bullets only as things that could prevent him from reaching the place of his endeavor. There were subtle flashings of joy within him that thus should be his mind.

He strained all his strength. His eyesight was shaken and dazzled by the tension of thought and muscle. He did not see anything excepting the mist of smoke gashed by the little knives of fire, but he knew that in it lay the aged fence of a vanished farmer protecting the snuggled bodies of the gray men.

As he ran a thought of the shock of contact gleamed in his mind. He expected a great concussion when the two bodies of troops crashed together. This became a part of his wild battle madness. He could feel the onward swing of the regiment about him and he conceived of a thunderous, crushing blow that would prostrate the resistance and spread consternation and amazement for miles. The flying regiment was going to have a catapultian effect. This dream made him run faster among his comrades, who were giving vent to hoarse and frantic cheers.

But presently he could see that many of the men in gray did not intend to abide the blow. The smoke, rolling, disclosed men who ran, their faces still turned. These grew to a crowd, who retired stubbornly. Individuals wheeled frequently to send a bullet at the blue wave.

But at one part of the line there was a grim and obdurate group that made no movement. They were settled firmly down behind posts and rails. A flag, ruffled and fierce, waved over them and their rifles dinned fiercely.

The blue whirl of men got very near, until it seemed that in truth there would be a close and frightful scuffle. There was an expressed disdain in the opposition of the little group, that changed the meaning of the cheers of the men in blue. They became yells of wrath, directed, personal. The cries of the two parties were now in sound an interchange of scathing insults.

They in blue showed their teeth; their eyes shone all white. They launched themselves as at the throats of those who stood resisting. The space between dwindled to an insignificant distance.

The youth had centered the gaze of his soul upon that other flag. Its possession would be high pride. It would express bloody minglings, near blows. He had a gigantic hatred for those who made great difficulties and complications. They caused it to be as a craved treasure of mythology, hung amid tasks and contrivances of danger.

He plunged like a mad horse at it. He was resolved it should not escape if wild blows and darings of blows could seize it. His own emblem, quivering and aflare, was winging toward the other. It seemed there would shortly be an encounter of strange beaks and claws, as of eagles.

The swirling body of blue men came to a sudden halt at close and disastrous range and roared a swift volley. The group in gray was split and broken by this fire, but its riddled body still fought. The men in blue yelled again and rushed in upon it.

The youth, in his leapings, saw, as through a mist, a picture of four or five men stretched upon the ground or writhing upon their knees with bowed heads as if they had been stricken by bolts from the sky. Tottering among them was the rival color bearer, whom the youth saw had been bitten vitally by the bullets of the last formidable volley. He perceived this man fighting a last struggle, the struggle of one whose legs are grasped by demons. It was a ghastly battle. Over his face was the bleach of death, but set upon it was the dark and hard lines of desperate purpose. With this terrible grin of resolution he hugged his precious flag to him and was stumbling and staggering in his design to go the way that led to safety for it.

But his wounds always made it seem that his feet were retarded, held, and he fought a grim fight, as with invisible ghouls fastened greedily upon his limbs. Those in advance of the scampering blue men, howling cheers, leaped at the fence. The despair of the lost was in his eyes as he glanced back at them.

The youth's friend went over the obstruction in a tumbling heap and sprang at the flag as a panther at prey. He pulled at it and, wrenching it free, swung up its red brilliancy with a mad cry of exultation even as the color bearer, gasping, lurched over in a final throe and, stiffening convulsively, turned his dead face to the ground. There was much blood upon the grass blades.

At the place of success there began more wild clamorings of cheers. The men gesticulated and bellowed in an ecstasy. When they spoke it was as if they considered their listener to be a mile away. What hats and caps were left to them they often slung high in the air.

At one part of the line four men had been swooped upon, and they now sat as prisoners. Some blue men were about them in an eager and curious circle. The soldiers had trapped strange birds, and there was an examination. A flurry of fast questions was in the air.

One of the prisoners was nursing a superficial wound in the foot. He cuddled it, baby-wise, but he looked up from it often to curse with an astonishing utter abandon straight at the noses of his captors. He consigned them to red regions; he called upon the pestilential wrath of strange gods. And with it all he was singularly free from recognition of the finer points of the conduct of prisoners of war. It was as if a clumsy clod had trod upon his toe and he conceived it to be his privilege, his duty, to use deep, resentful oaths.

Another, who was a boy in years, took his plight with great calmness and apparent good nature. He conversed with the men in blue, studying their faces with his bright and keen eyes. They spoke of battles and conditions. There was an acute interest in all their faces during this exchange of view points. It seemed a great satisfaction to hear voices from where all had been darkness and speculation.

The third captive sat with a morose countenance. He preserved a stoical and cold attitude. To all advances he made one reply without variation, "Ah, go t' hell!"

The last of the four was always silent and, for the most part, kept his face turned in unmolested directions. From the views the youth received he seemed to be in a state of absolute dejection. Shame was upon him, and with it profound regret that he was, perhaps, no more to be counted in the ranks of his fellows. The youth could detect no expression that would allow him to believe that the other was giving a thought to his narrowed future, the pictured dungeons, perhaps, and starvations and brutalities, liable to the imagination. All to be seen was shame for captivity and regret for the right to antagonize.

After the men had celebrated sufficiently they settled down behind the old rail fence, on the opposite side to the one from which their foes had been driven. A few shot perfunctorily at distant marks.

There was some long grass. The youth nestled in it and rested, making a convenient rail support the flag. His friend, jubilant and glorified, holding his treasure with vanity, came to him there. They sat side by side and congratulated each other.

Chapter XXIV

The roarings that had stretched in a long line of sound across the face of the forest began to grow intermittent and weaker. The stentorian speeches of the artillery continued in some distant encounter, but the crashes of the musketry had almost ceased. The youth and his friend of a sudden looked up, feeling a deadened form of distress at the waning of these noises, which had become a part of life. They could see changes going on among the troops. There were marchings this way and that way. A battery wheeled leisurely. On the crest of a small hill was the thick gleam of many departing muskets.

The youth arose. "Well, what now, I wonder?" he said. By his tone he seemed to be preparing to resent some new monstrosity in the way of dins and smashes. He shaded his eyes with his grimy hand and gazed over the field.

His friend also arose and stared. "I bet we're goin' t' git along out of this an' back over th' river," said he.

"Well, I swan!" said the youth.

They waited, watching. Within a little while the regiment received orders to retrace its way. The men got up grunting from the grass, regretting the soft repose. They jerked their stiffened legs, and stretched their arms over their heads. One man swore as he rubbed his eyes. They all groaned "O Lord!" They had as many objections to this change as they would have had to a proposal for a new battle.

They trampled slowly back over the field across which they had run in a mad scamper.

The regiment marched until it had joined its fellows. The reformed brigade, in column, aimed through a wood at the road. Directly they were in a mass of dust-covered troops, and were trudging along in a way parallel to the enemy's lines as these had been defined by the previous turmoil.

They passed within view of a stolid white house, and saw in front of it groups of their comrades lying in wait behind a neat breast-work. A row of guns were booming at a distant enemy. Shells thrown in reply were raising clouds of dust and splinters. Horsemen dashed along the line of intrenchments.

At this point of its march the division curved away from the field and went winding off in the direction of the river. When the significance of this movement had impressed itself upon the youth he turned his head and looked over his shoulder toward the trampled and *débris*-strewed ground. He breathed a breath of new satisfaction. He finally nudged his friend. "Well, it's all over," he said to him.

His friend gazed backward. "B'Gawd, it is," he assented. They mused.

For a time the youth was obliged to reflect in a puzzled and uncertain way. His mind was undergoing a subtle change. It took moments for it to cast off its battleful ways and resume its accustomed course of thought. Gradually his brain emerged from the clogged clouds, and at last he was enabled to more closely comprehend himself and circumstance.

He understood then that the existence of shot and counter-shot was in the past. He had dwelt in a land of strange, squalling upheavals and had come forth. He had been where there was red of blood and black of passion, and he was escaped. His first thoughts were given to rejoicings at this fact.

Later he began to study his deeds, his failures, and his achievements. Thus, fresh from scenes where many of his usual machines of reflection had been idle, from where he had proceeded sheeplike, he struggled to marshal all his acts.

At last they marched before him clearly. From this present view point he was enabled to look upon them in spectator fashion and to criticise them with some correctness, for his new condition had already defeated certain sympathies.

Regarding his procession of memory he felt gleeful and unregretting, for in it his public deeds were paraded in great and shining prominence. Those performances which had been witnessed by his fellows marched now in wide purple and gold, having various deflections. They went gayly with music. It was pleasure to watch these things. He spent delightful minutes viewing the gilded images of memory.

He saw that he was good. He recalled with a thrill of joy the respectful comments of his fellows upon his conduct.

Nevertheless, the ghost of his flight from the first engagement appeared to him and danced. There were small shoutings in his brain about these matters. For a moment he blushed, and the light of his soul flickered with shame.

A specter of reproach came to him. There loomed the dogging memory of the tattered soldier—he who, gored by bullets and faint for blood, had fretted concerning an imagined wound in another; he who had loaned his last of strength and intellect for the tall soldier; he who, blind with weariness and pain, had been deserted in the field.

For an instant a wretched chill of sweat was upon him at the thought that he might be detected in the thing. As he stood persistently before his vision, he gave vent to a cry of sharp irritation and agony.

His friend turned. "What's the matter, Henry?" he demanded. The youth's reply was an outburst of crimson oaths.

As he marched along the little branch-hung roadway among his prattling companions this vision of cruelty brooded over him. It clung near him always and darkened his view of these deeds in purple and gold. Whichever way his thoughts turned they were followed by the somber phantom of the desertion in the fields. He looked stealthily at his companions, feeling sure that they must discern in his face evidences of this pursuit. But they were plodding in ragged array, discussing with quick tongues the accomplishments of the late battle.

"Oh, if a man should come up an' ask me, I'd say we got a dum good lickin'."

"Lickin'—in yer eye! We ain't licked, sonny. We're goin' down here aways, swing aroun', an' come in behint 'em."

"Oh, hush, with your comin' in behint 'em. I've seen all 'a that I wanta. Don't tell me about comin' in behint——"

"Bill Smithers, he ses he'd rather been in ten hundred battles than been in that heluva hospital. He ses they got shootin' in th' night-time, an' shells dropped plum among 'em in th' hospital. He ses sech hollerin' he never see."

"Hasbrouck? He's th' best off'cer in this here reg'ment. He's a whale."

"Didn't I tell yeh we'd come aroun' in behint 'em? Didn't I tell yeh so? We——"

"Oh, shet yeh mouth!"

For a time this pursuing recollection of the tattered man took all elation from the youth's veins. He saw his vivid error, and he was afraid that it would stand before him all his life. He took no share in the chatter of his comrades, nor did he look at them or know them, save when he felt sudden suspicion that they were seeing his thoughts and scrutinizing each detail of the scene with the tattered soldier.

Yet gradually he mustered force to put the sin at a distance. And at last his eyes seemed to open to some new ways. He found that he could look back upon the brass and bombast of his earlier gospels and see them truly. He was gleeful when he discovered that he now despised them.

With this conviction came a store of assurance. He felt a quiet manhood, nonassertive but of sturdy and strong blood. He knew that he would no more quail before his guides wherever they should point. He had been to touch the great death, and found that, after all, it was but the great death. He was a man.

So it came to pass that as he trudged from the place of blood and wrath his soul changed. He came from hot plowshares[4] to prospects of clover tranquilly, and it was as if hot plowshares were not. Scars faded as flowers.

It rained. The procession of weary soldiers became a bedraggled train, despondent and muttering, marching with churning effort in a trough of liquid brown mud under a low, wretched sky. Yet the youth smiled, for he saw that the world was a world for him, though many discovered it to be made of oaths and walking sticks.[5] He had rid himself of the red sickness of battle. The sultry nightmare was in the past. He had been an animal blistered and sweating in the heat and pain of war. He turned now with a lover's thirst to images of tranquil skies, fresh meadows, cool brooks—an existence of soft and eternal peace.

Over the river a golden ray of sun came through the hosts of leaden rain clouds.

---

4. That is, swords or weapons; from Isaiah, ii:4, "They shall beat their swords into plowshares."

5. Crane wrote "The End" after this sentence in his manuscript. Later, he crossed out "The End" and added the remainder of the paragraph. The concluding sentence of the novel does not appear in the manuscript.

Textual Appendix

EMENDATIONS

Emendations are noted by page and line numbers. The following abbreviations are used:

1895: *The Red Badge of Courage* (New York: D. Appleton & Co., 1895).

MS: *The Red Badge of Courage: A Facsimile of the Manuscript*, ed. Fredson Bowers (Washington, D.C.: NCR/Microcard Edition, 1972).

6.37	1895/bank; MS/bunk
17.5	1895/blatant; MS/loud ("blatant") is lightly canceled and "loud" lightly substituted, a revision apparently missed by the typist)
18.22	1895/good!"; MS/good."
26.2	1895/would; MS/could
27.7	1895/cammand; MS/command
27.25	1895/Se; MS/So
29.36	1895/knitting; MS/knotting
31.12	1895/thought; MS/thoughts
34.3	1895/emblem; MS/emblems
35.33	1895/gate; MS/grate
39.10	1895/aid; MS/aide
40.19	1895/guilt and; MS/guilt little and
41.6	1895/a air; MS/an air
45.22–23	1895/different; MS/diffident
48.24	1895/shoulders; MS/shoulder
52.20	1895/'a feller; MS/a feller
55.32	1895/would, in a way be; MS/would, in a way, be
56.8	1895/weight like; MS/weight-like
64.3	1895/recognzied; MS/recognized
65.17	1895/draw; MS/drew
68.9	1895/began; MS/began
71.29	1895/a course; MS/a course
74.22	1895/continued; MS/continual
75.27	1895/somtimes; MS/sometimes
77.11	1895/yellings; MS/yelpings
78.24	1895/burlike; MS/burr-like
79.36	1895/others; MS/brothers
81.22	1895/burs; MS/burrs
82.4	1895/an'; MS/an'
82.6	1895/an' hour; MS/an' hour
82.38	1895/onto; MS/into
92.19	1895/allusions; MS/illusions
92.28–29	1895/good-by—John; MS/good-by-John
96.22	1895/"As far as you could?; MS/" 'As far as you could'?
97.31	1895/laughin,'; MS/laughin',
98.21	1895/major-generals.'; MS/major-generals.'
100.5	1895/up; MS/cups
100.40	1895/friends; MS/fiends
103.21	1895/savage religion mad; MS/savage, religion-mad

THE MANUSCRIPT OF *THE RED BADGE OF COURAGE*: UNCANCELED PASSAGES AND THE DISCARDED CHAPTER XII

The long version or final manuscript of *The Red Badge of Courage*, now available in a facsimile edition prepared by Fredson Bowers (see Selected Bibliography, below), reveals a number of striking characteristics of the process by which Crane worked his way toward the published version of the novel. Among these are: his consistent change of proper names (Fleming, Wilson, Conklin) to attributive names(the youth, the loud soldier, the tall soldier, etc.); his fore-shortening of a number of chapters by cutting major sections from their conclusions (most of these cut passages do not survive); his discarding of all of Chapter XII after he had completed the draft; his partial and inconsistent revision of dialect, generally toward a lessening of dialect; and his inclusion of numerous passages which he did not cancel in the manuscript but which do not appear in the published novel.

Crane cut Chapter XII in manuscript and later cut other passages in typescript or proof either because he believed this material slowed the narrative pace of the novel or because he found some of its themes incongruous in relation to his final estimate of his protagonist. Or perhaps he had some combination of these motives. Although this material clearly has no place in the text of *The Red Badge* (see "A Note on the Text," preceding the text of the novel), it is of considerable interest to the student of the novel, as is revealed by its extensive use by such critics as Mordecai Marcus and Edwin Cady in the essays included in this edition.

The text of the uncanceled passages is that of R. W. Stallman's reproduction of them in his *Stephen Crane: An Omnibus*, silently corrected by collation with the facsimile of the *Red Badge* manuscript. Chapter XII, manuscript pages 98–103, survives in a fragment of pp. 98–99, 101–2. Its text is that of the facsimile of the *Red Badge* manuscript.

Uncanceled but Unpublished Passages

For each entry, page and line numbers are followed by the phrase which precedes the uncanceled but unpublished passage. Crane's errors in spelling are left uncorrected and unnoted.

6:26–27 care a hang.
I tell yeh what I know an' yeh kin take it er leave it. Suit yerselves. It dont make no difference t' me.

9:7 about right.

Young fellers in the army get awful careless in their ways, Henry. They're away f'm home and they don't have nobody to look after 'em. I'm 'feared fer yeh about that. Yeh ain't never been used to doing fer yerself. So yeh must keep writing to me how yer clothes are lasting.

9:16 us all.

Don't fergit to send yer socks to me the minute they git holes in 'em and here's a little bible I want yeh to take along with yeh, Henry. I don't presume yeh'll be a-setting reading it all day long, child, ner nothin' like that. Many a time, yeh'll fergit yeh got it, I don't doubt. But there'll be many a time, too, Henry, when yeh'll be wanting advice, boy, and all like that, and there'll be nobody round, perhaps, to tell yeh things. Then if yeh take it out, boy, yeh'll find wisdom in it—wisdom in it, Henry—with little or no searching.

16:21 perception.

"I told you so, did't I?"

27:27 He's a funny feller.

"Hear that what th' ol' colonel ses, boys. He ses he'll shoot th' first man what'll turn an' run."

"He'd better try it. I'd like t' see him shoot at *me*."

"He wants t' look fer his *own*self. *He* don't wanta go 'round talkin' big."

"They say Perrey's division's a-givin'em thunder."

"Ed Williams over in Company A, he ses th' rebs'll all drop their guns an' run an' holler if we onct give 'em one good lickin'."

"Oh, thunder, Ed Williams, what does he know? Ever since he got shot at on picket, he's been runnin' the war."

"Well, he—"

"Hear th' news, boys? Corkright's crushed the hull rebel right an' captured two hull divisions. We'll be back in winter quarters by a short cut t'-morrah."

"I tell yeh I've been all over that there kentry where th' rebel right is an it's th' nastiest part th' rebel line. It's all mussed up with hills an' little damn creeks. I'll bet m' shirt Corkright never harmed 'em down there."

"Well he's a fighter an' if they could be licked, he'd lick'em."

40:20 no words.

who, through his suffering, thinks that he peers into the core of things and see that the judgment of man is thistle-down in wind.

49:25 bone-crushing.

They could not understand.

52:5 blamed infernal.
tooty-tooty-tooty-too

58:38 of the damned.
He lost concern for himself.

68:39–40 eye sockets.
It was the soldier's bath.

72:40 his sight.
The long tirades against nature he now believed to be foolish compositions born of his condition. He did not altogether repudiate them because he did not remember all that he had said. He was inclined to regard his past rebellions with an indulgent smile. They were all right in their hour, perhaps.

73:4 play marbles.
Since he was comfortable and contented, he had no desire to set things straight. Indeed, he no more contended that they were not straight. How could they be crooked when he was restored to a requisite amount of happiness. There was a slowly developeing conviction that in all his red speeches he had been ridiculously mistaken. Nature was a fine thing moving with a magnificent justice. The world was fair and wide and glorious. The sky was kind, and smiled tenderly, full of encouragement, upon him.

Some poets now received his scorn. Yesterday, in his misery, he had thought of certain persons who had written. Their remembered words, broken and detached, had come piece-meal to him. For these people he had then felt a glowing, brotherly regard. They had wandered in paths of pain and they had made pictures of the black landscape that others might enjoy it with them. He had, at that time, been sure that their wise, contemplating spirits had been in sympathy with him, had shed tears from the clouds. He had walked alone, but there had been pity, made before a reason for it.

But he was now, in a measure, a successful man and he could no longer tolerate in himself a spirit of fellowship for poets. He abandoned them. Their songs about black landscapes were of no importance to him since his new eyes said that his landscape was not black. People who called landscapes black were idiots.

He achieved a mighty scorn for such a snivelling race.

He felt that he was the child of the powers. Through the peace of his heart, he saw the earth to be a garden in which grew no weeds of agony. Or, perhaps, if there did grow a few, it was in obscure corners where no one was obliged to encounter them unless a ridiculous search was made. And, at any rate, they were tiny ones.

He returned to his old belief in the ultimate, astonishing success of his life. He, as usual, did not trouble about processes. It was ordained, because he was a fine creation. He saw plainly that he was the chosen of some gods. By fearful and wonderful roads he was to be led to a crown. He was, of course, satisfied that he deserved it.

106:36 a mad scamper.
The fence, deserted, resumed with its careening posts and disjointed bars, an air of quiet rural depravity. Beyond it, there lay spread a few corpses. Conspicuous, was the contorted body of the color-bearer in grey whose flag the youth's friend was now bearing away.

107:5 line of intrenchments.
As they passed near other commands, men of the delapidated regiment procured the captured flag from Wilson and, tossing it high into the air cheered tumultuously as it turned, with apparent reluctance, slowly over and over.

107:33 certain sympathies.
His friend, too, seemed engaged with some retrospection for he suddenly gestured and said: "Good Lord!"
"What?" asked the youth.
"Good Lord!" repeated his friend. "Yeh know Jimmie Rogers? Well, he—gosh, when he was hurt I started t' git some water fer 'im an', thunder, I ain't seen 'im from that time 'til this. I clean forgot what I—say, has anybody seen Jimmie Rogers?"
"Seen 'im? No! He's dead," they told him.
His friend swore.
But the youth, regarding his procession of memory, felt

107:42 his conduct.
He said to himself again the sentence of the insane lieutenant: "If I had ten thousand wild-cats like you, I could tear th' stomach outa this war in less'n a week." It was a little coronation.

107:44 danced.
Echoes of his terrible combat with the arrayed forces of the universe came to his ears.

108:2 with shame.
However, he presently procured an explanation and an apology. He said that those tempestuous moments were of the wild mistakes and ravings of a novice who did not comprehend. He had been a mere man railing at a condition but now he was out of it and could see that it had been very proper and just. It had been neces-

sary for him to swallow swords that he might have a better throat for grapes. Fate had in truth been kind to him; she had stabbed him with benign purpose and diligently cudgeled him for his own sake. In his rebellion, he had been very portentious, no doubt, and sincere, and anxious for humanity, but now that he stood safe, with no lack of blood, it was suddenly clear to him that he had been wrong not to kiss the knife and bow to the cudgel. He had foolishly squirmed.

But the sky would forget. It was true, he admitted, that in the world it was the habit to cry devil at persons who refused to trust what they could not trust, but he thought that perhaps the stars dealt differently. The imperturbable sun shines on insult and worship.

As Fleming was thus fraternizing again with nature, a spectre

108:39   yer mouth!"
"You make me sick."
"G' home, yeh fool."

109:3   at a distance.
And then he regarded it with what he thought to be great calmness. At last, he concluded that he saw in it quaint uses. He exclaimed that its importance in the aftertime would be great to him if it even succeeded in hindering the workings of his egotism. It would make a sobering balance. It would become a good part of him. He would have upon him often the consciousness of a great mistake. And he would be taught to deal gently and with care. He would be a man.

This plan for the utilization of a sin did not give him complete joy but it was the best sentiment he could formulate under the circumstances and when it was combined with his successes, or public deeds, he knew that he was quite contented.

109:7   despised them.
He was emerged from his struggles, with a large sympathy for the machinery of the universe. With his new eyes, he could see that the secret and open blows which were being dealt about the world with such heavenly lavishness were in truth blessings. It was a diety laying about him with the bludgeon of correction.

His loud mouth against these things had been lost as the storm ceased. He would no more stand upon places high and false, and denounce the distant planets. He beheld that he was tiny but not inconsequent to the sun. In the space-wide whirl of events no grain like him would be lost.

109:12   it was but the great death.
and was for others.

CHAPTER XII†

It was always clear to the youth that he was entirely different from other men, that his mind had been cast in a unique mold. Hence laws that might be just to the ordinary man, were, when applied to him, peculiar and galling outrages. Minds, he said, were not made all with one stamp and colored green. He was of no general pattern. It was not right to measure his acts by a world-wide standard. The laws of the world were wrong because through, the vain spectacles of their makers, he appeared, with all men, as of a common size and of a green color. There was no justice on the earth when justice was meant. Men were too puny and prattling to know anything of it. If there was a justice, it must be in the hands of a God.

He regarded his sufferings as unprecedented. No man had ever achieved such misery. There was a melancholy grandeur in the isolation of his experiences. He saw that he was a speck raising his minute arms against all possible forces and fates which were swelling down upon him in black tempests. He could derive some consolation from viewing the sublimity of the odds.

As he went on, he began to feel that nature, for her part, would not blame him for his rebellion. He still distinctly felt that he was arrayed against the universe but he believed now that there was no malice in the vast breasts of his space-filling foes. It was merely law, not merciful to the individual; but just, to a system. Nature had provided the creations with various defenses and ways of escape that they might fight or flee, and she had limited dangers in powers of attack and pursuit that the things might resist or hide with a security proportionate to their strength and wisdom. It was cruel but it was war. Nature fought for her system; individuals fought for liberty to breathe. The animals had the previlege of using their legs and their brains. It was all the same old philosophy. He could not omit a small grunt of satisfaction as he saw with what brilliancy he had reasoned it out.

He now said that, if, as he supposed, his life was being relentlessly pursued, it was not his duty to bow to the approaching death. Nature did not expect submission. On the contrary, it was his business to kick and bite and give blows as a stripling in the hands of a murderer. The law was that he should fight. He would be saved according to the importance of his strength.

His egotism made him feel safe, for a time, from the iron hands.

It being in his mind that he had solved these matters, he eagerly

† From *The Red Badge of Courage: A Facsimile Edition of the Manuscript.* Reprinted from NCR/Microcard Editions (Washington, D.C., 1972), vol. II, pp. 181–84, by permission of Information Handling Services. © 1975 by Indian Head, Inc.

applied his findings to the incident of his flight from the battle. It was not a fault, a shameful thing; it was an act obedient to a law. It was—

But he was aware that when he had erected a vindicating structure of great principles, it was the clam toes of tradition that kicked it all down about his ears. He immediately antagonized then this devotion to the by-gone; this universal adoration of the past. From the bitter pinnacle of his wisdom he saw that mankind not only worshipped the gods of the ashes but that the gods of the ashes were worshipped because they were the gods of the ashes. He percieved with anger the present state of affairs in it's bearing upon his case. And he resolved to reform it all.

He had, presently, a feeling that he was the growing prophet of a world-reconstruction. Far down in the untouched depths of his being, among the hidden currents of his soul, he saw born a voice. He concieved a new world modelled by the pain of his life, and in which no old shadows fell blighting upon the temple of thought. And there were many personal advantages in it.

* * *

He saw himself chasing a thought-phantom across the sky before the assembled eyes of mankind. He could say to them that it was an angel whose possession was existence perfected; they would declare it to be a greased pig. He had no desire to devote his life to proclaiming the angel, when he could plainly percieve that mankind would hold, from generation to generation, to the theory of the greased pig.

It would be pleasure to reform a docile race. But he saw that there were none and he did not intend to raise his voice against the hooting of continents.

Thus he abandoned the world to it's devices. He felt that many men must have so abandoned it, but he saw how they could be reconciled to it and agree to accept the stone idols and the greased pigs, when they contemplated the opportunities for plunder.

For himself, however, he saw no salve, no reconciling opportunities. He was entangled in the errors. He began to rage anew against circumstances which he did not name and against processes of which he knew only the name. He felt that he was being grinded beneath stone feet which he despised. The detached bits of truth which formed the knowledge of the world could not save him. There was a dreadful, unwritten martyrdom in his state.

He made a little search for some thing upon which to concentrate the hate of his despair; he fumbled in his mangled intellect to find the Great Responsibility.

He again hit upon nature. He again saw her grim dogs upon his trail. There were unswerving, merciless and would overtake him at the appointed time. His mind pictured the death of Jim Conklin and in the scene, he saw the shadows of his fate. Dread words had been said from star to star. An event had been penned by the implacable forces.

He was of the unfit, then. He did not come into the scheme of further life. His tiny part had been done and he must go. There was no room for him. On all the vast lands there was not a foot-hold. He must be thrust out to make room for the more important.

Regarding himself as one of the unfit, he believed that nothing could accede for misery, a perception of this fact. He thought that he measured with his falling heart, tossed in like a pebble by his supreme and awful foe, the most profound depths of pain. It was a barbarous process with [no?] affection for the man and the oak, and no sympathy for the rabbit and the weed. He thought of his own capacity for pity and there was an infinite irony in it.

He desired to revenge himself upon the universe. Feeling in his body all spears of pain, he would have capsized, if possible, the world and made chaos. Much cruelty lay in the fact that he was a babe.

Admitting that he was powerless and at the will of law, he yet planned to escape; menaced by fatality he schemed to avoid it. He thought of various places in the world where he imagined that he would be safe. He remembered hiding once in an empty flour-barrel that sat in his mother's pantry. His playmates, hunting the bandit-chief, had thundered on the barrel with their fierce sticks but he had lain snug and undetected. They had searched the house. He now created in thought a secure spot where an all-powerful eye would fail to percieve him; where an all-powerful stick would fail to bruise his life.

There was in him a creed of freedom which no contemplation of inexorable law could destroy. He saw himself living in watchfulness, frustrating the plans of the unchangeable, making of fate a fool. He had ways, he thought, of working out his * * *

Backgrounds and Sources

Stephen Crane: An Introduction

FREDERICK C. CREWS

[Crane's Life and Times]†

1. *Biography*

Stephen Crane's life was short and bizarre. Born in 1871 in Newark, New Jersey, he was the fourteenth and last child of two devout Methodists. The family atmosphere was generous ("mother was always more of a Christian than a Methodist") and wholesomely innocent; the Reverend Jonathan Crane seemed not to have heard of blacker sins than smoking, dancing, and playing billiards. Crane, as a son of Methodists, was steeped in hymn-singing and Bible-reading, but as a fourteenth child he was more or less free from close supervision. "Stevie is like the wind in Scripture," observed his mother uneasily. "He bloweth whither he listeth." In view of the significance of the childhood world in his writings, we should like to know much more than we do about his early years. Except for a few details that suggest his peculiarly hard-boiled genius, such as his losing a tooth in defense of the view that Tennyson's poems were "swill," the information that survives is suggestive of a normal, restless, but somewhat reticent boy. By the time he was fifteen, his consuming ambition was to be a professional baseball player, and somewhat later he was remembered for having tried to balance a pool cue on the end of his nose. He was noted for his casual skepticism, his kindliness, and his devotion to animals and sports. As for the Methodist view of things, that fell an early victim to his premature worldly wisdom. "I used to like church and prayer meetings when I was a kid," Crane recalled, "but that cooled off and when I was thirteen or about that, my brother Will told me not to believe in Hell after my uncle had been boring me about the lake of fire and the rest of the sideshows." The voice here, to say nothing of the spiritual development reported, is almost that of Huckleberry Finn.

In his formal education, Crane continued to play the role of bad boy. At Claverack College, an advanced preparatory school, he con-

† From *The Red Badge of Courage* by Stephen Crane, edited by Frederick C. Crews (Indianapolis: Bobbs-Merrill, 1964), pp. vii–xiv. Copyright © 1964 by The Bobbs-Merrill Company, Inc. Reprinted by permission of the publisher.

123

centrated on baseball, pool, and poker, while his summers were given over to loafing and to newspaper work for his brother Townley in Asbury Park, New Jersey. At Lafayette College he was asked to leave after one semester, and at Syracuse University the story was much the same: one semester of sports and dissipations; miscellaneous reading and writing; but little attention to the academic curriculum. "Humanity was a more interesting study," as he commented later, and so he set out, in June of 1891, to "recover from college."

At this point Crane's life seems to quicken its pace. He had already done some reporting for the *New York Tribune*, and now he went off to immerse himself in the low life of the City. Intermittent newspaper work provided him with a bare subsistence, enabling him to conduct a systematic private exploration of the Bowery. He felt that to get beneath the surface he must actually live the life of the poor; like Kipling's Dick Heldar in *The Light That Failed*, which has been suggested as a direct influence upon him, he hoped to gain artistic authenticity by imposing the conditions of suffering on his own body. Curiously, however, his imagination always ran ahead of his actual experience. His Bowery novel, *Maggie: A Girl of the Streets*, apparently had been largely drawn up in his college room at Syracuse, just as *The Red Badge* was to be written before he had observed his first military battle.

The first edition of *Maggie*, published pseudonymously in 1893, was overlooked, but Crane was not quite unknown when *The Red Badge of Courage* appeared as a book in the fall of 1895. Both William Dean Howells and Hamlin Garland had seen the signs of power in *Maggie* and had encouraged Crane to persevere; Garland, in fact, gave Crane the money to retrieve the second half of *The Red Badge* from a typist. There was also a small notoriety attaching to Crane's weird, cryptic poems, which were collected in *The Black Riders and Other Lines*, 1895. The poems may owe something to Emily Dickinson, but they can hardly be called derivative. For metrical flatness, abruptness, private allegory, and mordancy of idea, they remain unique in our language, though their merit is debatable.

The Red Badge of Courage made Crane a famous man. It had created a minor stir in a shortened, serialized form in various newspapers during December of 1894, but as a book it was an unprecedented success. English reviewers in particular hailed Crane as a great genius (though it was suspected they were merely gleeful over an American book that seemed to belittle the American Army), and when Crane's age and inexperience were known he was transformed into the *enfant terrible* of American letters. The transformation was not altogether for the best. From now on Crane was expected to produce masterpieces while simultaneously turning out an incessant stream of journalism, mostly on war. Furthermore, though he was usually shy and chivalrous with women, was almost never drunk, and disapproved of narcotics, in the mass-fantasy of the American public he was cast as a remarkable profligate. Crane soon became so exasperated with American philistinism that he began to seek ways of remaining outside the country altogether.

Many critics have detected a general falling-off in Crane's art after *The Red Badge*. *The Third Violet* (1897) and *Active Service* (1899) showed an inaptitude for either relaxed, discursive realism or satire, and many of Crane's short stories were too obviously hack work written for cash. *The O'Ruddy*, which he failed to complete before his death, was another misguided attempt at popularity, this time in the form of a whimsical romance. The war sketches in *Wounds in the Rain*, published posthumously, reveal more humor, common sense, and political awareness than his earlier work; but with the increased factual detail there is sometimes a loss of vitality in language. And yet there were notable exceptions to the downward trend. The title poem of Crane's second book of verse, *War Is Kind* (1899), is certainly his finest poem, while his three most deservedly famous stories, "The Open Boat," "The Bride Comes to Yellow Sky," and "The Blue Hotel," were written in 1897 and 1898. Crane's genius evidently deserted him only when he tried to be a more optimistic and "public" writer than he naturally was.

The last few years of Crane's life were colorful in the extreme. His commissioned travels as a reporter took him to the West and to Mexico, where he was nearly murdered; to Greece, where he tried with modest success to see the Greco-Turkish War; and to Cuba and Puerto Rico, where he observed the Spanish-American War at such close range and with such debonair bravery as to suggest an unconscious longing for death or mutilation. Earlier, before dawn on January 2, 1897, another assignment to cover a Cuban insurrection had resulted in the sinking of his steamer, possibly through sabotage, and his exposure to the sea in a ten-foot dinghy for more than a full day. This incident was the most terrifying one of his life, though the other survivors attested to his calm heroism; it may also have initiated the permanent waning of his health. Yet in introducing him personally to the cruel natural forces of which he had frequently written, often with bombast, Crane's ordeal presented him with a concrete image for his deepest feelings about the precarious life of man. "The Open Boat" is almost a factual account of Crane's experience, but it is also a work of art whose place among the best American short stories is secure.

The Crane legend is appropriately completed by his brief parody of the life of an English squire. In Florida he had fallen in love with Cora Howorth Stewart (or Cora Taylor), estranged wife of a British soldier and mistress of the Hotel de Dream, one of Jacksonville's more elegant bawdy houses. This was the most extraordinary of Crane's much-disputed "rescues" of low women—though the rescue was incomplete, for Cora went back into business after his death. In the meantime, however, she and Crane made a well-suited couple, sharing frank conversation and literary tastes. Though they probably were not legally married, they succeeded in creating such an impression of respectability that at one time Cora entertained hopes of being presented at the British Court. After Crane's return from Cuba in 1899, they had settled in a decaying fourteenth-century manor in Sussex called Brede Place, haunted, so the servants claimed, by "the bloody shade of old Sir Goddard Oxenbridge." We may never know what prompted Crane to buy this immense ruin, with its bats, its one primitive toilet, and its doors that would never close; if he wanted solitude, he was to be disappointed. Henry James, who lived nearby in more consistently baronial style, was a frequent visitor, as were Conrad, H. G. Wells, and less sympathetic people who wanted to see the legend in action. Since the more malicious guests expected a show, Crane obliged by playing the cowboy or the hereditary nobleman; but he was very ill and was writing frantically in an effort to wipe out his debts. One day in March 1900 he leaned over to pat a dog and found that his mouth had filled with blood. Three months later, rushed to a sanatorium in Germany, Crane was dead of tuberculosis.

II. The Red Badge *as a Work of the 1890's*

Crane's masterpiece was published in the middle of the decade that many historians regard as the watershed of American history. The America of the past had been rural, individualistic, self-confident, and expansionary; that of our own century was to be urban, industrial, and increasingly sensitive to the precariousness of our role as a world power. The nineties, we may say, witnessed the birth pangs of the new order; the official values of the nation were still those of an optimistic agrarian democracy, while a minority of writers and reformers were beginning to grasp the implications of sweatshops and slums, class struggle, and a boom-and-bust economy. The bland rural life that Henry Fleming leaves behind to go to war could no longer be regarded seriously as the heart of the American experience; war itself, as Herbert Spencer argued and as Henry temporarily learns, now seemed a better image of reality. Crane's America gave him ample cause to mock Henry's first notion of glorious, Homeric possibilities. The widening chasm between rich and poor, the blind worship of money, and the use of military force for economic imperialism were teaching Crane and others that the meek were not about to inherit the earth. The meek of Europe were arriving at Ellis Island, which had just opened to "process" them, and were passing into the huge, hostile cities, where they would be lucky to earn a subsistence. This was the age that saw the Homestead Steel Strike, the financial panic of 1893, the Antitrust Act, and the formation of the Populist Party—all of which Crane might have noted in the years just prior to the publication of *The Red Badge*. And Crane, we remember, was at this time a curious young journalist who was studying the very poor in New York, the center of discontent. It is impossible to doubt that the prevailing climate (at least among the have-nots) of desperate cynicism about national and social ideals had an effect on the tone of *The Red Badge*. Someone who passes his time exploring the Bowery need not read Zola to get a sense of the ways in which men can be victimized by circumstance and their own failings. Nor need he go to Marx to understand that the privates and the generals in any war are there for different reasons. Nor, indeed, must he read through Nietzsche to grasp the idea that no providential God is watching over the fate of the green infantryman who hopes to be the next Achilles.

In a sense, therefore, *The Red Badge* is a faithful, though oblique, reflection of the era in which it was written; it expresses certain doubts about the meaning of individual virtue in a world that has become suddenly cruel and mechanical. For this very reason, however, Crane's novel fails to typify the literary tastes of the nineties. Most Americans still regarded literature as an amusing diversion from life rather than an honest image of it, and the most popular writers, such as Thomas Bailey Aldrich, Francis Marion Crawford, and James Whitcomb Riley, were usually the most socially innocuous. More serious novelists like James and Howells strove to be realistic, but they did nothing to deny the prevailing belief that fiction should be refined, unsensational, and concerned with ethical ideals. The canons of genteel taste, formulated by such respected critics as George E. Woodberry. William C. Brownell, Edmund C. Stedman, and Charles Dudley Warner, demanded a lofty tone and a high moral purposefulness. *The Red Badge of Courage* does not simply fail to meet such expectations, it deliberately flouts them; and we may fix one element of Crane's relation to his times by saying that he self-consciously tried to break all the rules of the Genteel Tradition. His inscription in a friend's copy of *Maggie* epitomizes his cockiness: "This work is a mud-puddle, I am told on the best authority. Wade in and have a swim."

This side of Crane suggests his affinity with naturalism, the literary movement that Zola had been leading for some time and that was making its first tentative impact on America in the work of Hamlin Garland, Frank Norris, and Crane himself. The extent of Crane's acquaintance with Zola, Flaubert, Turgenev, and other Continental naturalists has not been satisfactorily determined, but it is certain that, somehow or other, he came to share their view that fiction should be "scientific" in its anatomy of causes and circumstances. As Crane affirmed in a letter, he intended simply to offer "a slice out of life; and if there is any moral or lesson in it, I do not try to point it out." His taste for violence, his choice of trapped and defeated characters rather than traditional heroes, and his refusal to soften their misery with hints of eternal reward typified the naturalistic program.

It would be unwise, however, to paste the label of one literary school or another on Crane. He was quite as friendly with Howells and James as with the budding naturalists, and there was nothing imitative in his nature. Where he chiefly differed from the naturalists was in his abrupt metaphorical style and his radical conciseness. The ideal of naturalism was laborious documentation—to omit nothing from the demonstration of environment's sway over individuals. Crane, as Norris put it, "knew when to shut up." His contemporaries recognized, and Crane freely acknowledged, that he was attempting in words what the Impressionists were doing with paint: to capture discrete moments in sudden flashes of illumination, to record life's impact on the senses before reason has intervened to give everything a familiar name. In pursuing his elegant and sometimes strained metaphors, Crane verges on self-conscious dandyism —another trait common to many writers of the nineties—but the general effect of his style is to make us undergo the experience of his characters with vivid immediacy. A power of this kind cannot be learned from any source, and ultimately we must conclude that the origin of Crane's art is his own genius. Yet we can recognize that the tendency of that art is suggestive of various social and literary developments in his day. From the hindsight of our own age Crane's intentions and devices appear as part of a broad movement away from moral abstractions to sensuous impressions, from hackneyed romance to a poetic investigation of life in its meaner predicaments.

* * *

STEPHEN CRANE

Letters: A Selection†

18. To Dr. Lucius L. Button

[Inscribed on a copy of *Maggie*]   [March, 1893?]
It is inevitable that you will be greatly shocked by the book but continue, please, with all possible courage, to the end. For it tries to

† From *Stephen Crane: Letters*, ed. R. W. Stallman and Lillian Gilkes (New York: New York University Press, 1960), pp. 14, 31–32, 108–110, 158–59. Copyright © 1960 by New York University. Reprinted by permission.

show that environment is a tremendous thing in the world and frequently shapes lives regardless. If one proves that theory one makes room in Heaven for all sorts of souls, notably an occasional street girl, who are not confidently expected to be there by many excellent people.

It is probable that the reader of this small thing may consider the author to be a bad man; but obviously that is a matter of small consequence to   *The Author*

34. To Lily Brandon Munroe

143 East 23rd St. N.Y./Care, Vosburg[h]/[March, 1894?] Dearest: Truly, I feel that I have decieved [*sic*] you by not starting for Europe today or to-morrow but as a matter of fact, I had postponed it for two reasons. One was because my literary fathers —Howells and Garland—objected to it, and the other was because you had not answered my letter. I did not intend starting for Europe or anywheres else until I had given you sufficient opportunity to reply. It would have been a lonely business—to go so far without a word from you.

To speak, to tell you of my success, dear, is rather more difficult. My career has been more of a battle than a journey. You know, when I left you [in 1892], I renounced the clever school in literature. It seemed to me that there must be something more in life than to sit and cudgel one's brains for clever and witty expedients. So I developed all alone a little creed of art which I thought was a good one. Later I discovered that my creed was identical with the one of Howells and Garland and in this way I became involved in the beautiful war between those who say that art is man's substitute for nature and we are the most successful in art when we approach the nearest to nature and truth, and those who say—well, I don't know what they say. They don't, they can't say much but they fight villianously [*sic*] and keep Garland and I out of the big magazines. Howells, of course, is too powerful for them.

If I had kept to my clever, Rudyard-Kipling style, the road might have been shorter but, ah, it wouldn't be the true road. The two years of fighting have been well-spent. And now I am almost at the end of it. This winter fixes me firmly. We have proved too formidable for them, confound them. * * *

137. To John Northern Hilliard

[January, 1896?] . . . As far as myself and my own meagre success are concerned, I began the battle of life with no talent, no equipment, but with an ardent admiration and desire. I did little work at school, but con-

fined my abilities, such as they were, to the diamond. Not that I
disliked books, but the cut-and-dried curriculum of the college did
not appeal to me. Humanity was a much more interesting study.
When I ought to have been at recitations I was studying faces on
the streets, and when I ought to have been studying my next day's
lessons I was watching the trains roll in and out of the Central Station. So, you see, I had, first of all, to recover from college. I had to
build up, so to speak. And my chiefest desire was to write plainly
and unmistakably, so that all men (and some women) might read
and understand. That to my mind is good writing. There is a great
deal of labor connected with literature. I think that is the hardest
thing about it. There is nothing to respect in art save one's own
opinion of it. . . .

The one thing that deeply pleases me in my literary life—brief
and inglorious as it is—is the fact that men of sense believe me to
be sincere. "Maggie," published in paper covers, made me the
friendship of Hamlin Garland and W. D. Howells, and the one
thing that makes my life worth living in the midst of all this abuse
and ridicule is the consciousness that never for an instant have
those friendships at all diminished. Personally I am aware that my
work does not amount to a string of dried beans—I always calmly
admit it. But I also know that I do the best that is in me, without
regard to cheers or damnation. When I was the mark for every
humorist in the country I went ahead, and now, when I am the
mark for only 50 per cent of the humorists of the country, I go
ahead, for I understand that a man is born into the world with his
own pair of eyes, and he is not at all responsible for his vision—he
is merely responsible for his quality of personal honesty. To keep
close to this personal honesty is my supreme ambition. There is a
sublime egotism in talking of honesty. I, however, do not say that I
am honest. I merely say that I am as nearly honest as a weak
mental machinery will allow. This aim in life struck me as being
the only thing worth while. A man is sure to fail at it, but there is
something in the failure.

216. To John Northern Hilliard

[Ravensbrook, 1897?]
. . . I have only one pride—and may it be forgiven me. This single
pride is that the English edition of "The Red Badge" has been
received with praise by the English reviewers. Mr. George Wyndham, Under Secretary for War in the British Government, says, in
an essay, that the book challenges comparison with the most vivid
scenes of Tolstoi's 'War and Peace" or of Zola's "Downfall"; and
the big reviews here praise it for just what I intended it to be, a psy-

chological portrayal of fear. They all insist that I am a veteran of
the civil war, whereas the fact is, as you know, I never smelled even
the powder of a sham battle. I know what the psychologists say,
that a fellow can't comprehend a condition that he has never experienced, and I argued that many times with the Professor. Of
course, I have never been in a battle, but I believe that I got my
sense of the rage of conflict on the football field, or else fighting is a
hereditary instinct, and I wrote intuitively; for the Cranes were a
family of fighters in the old days, and in the Revolution every
member did his duty. But be that as it may, I endeavored to express
myself in the simplest and most concise way. If I failed, the fault is
not mine. I have been very careful not to let any theories or pet
ideas of my own creep into my work. Preaching is fatal to art in literature. I try to give to readers a slice out of life; and if there is any
moral or lesson in it, I do not try to point it out. I let the reader
find it for himself. The result is more satisfactory to both the reader
and myself. As Emerson said, "There should be a long logic
beneath the story, but it should be kept carefully out of sight."
Before "The Red Badge of Courage" was published, I found it difficult to make both ends meet. The book was written during this
period. It was an effort born of pain, and I believe that it was beneficial to it as a piece of literature. It seems a pity that this should be
so—that art should be a child of suffering; and yet such seems to be
the case. * * *

JAMES B. COLVERT

The Origins of Stephen Crane's Literary Creed†

Literary source hunters have experienced little difficulty in sug-
gesting influences upon Stephen Crane's early novels and stories.
But where such study should ideally throw light upon the genesis
and processes of Crane's art, too often the claims and surmises
about his literary origins are so general or so tenuous that they serve
more to endarken than enlighten. Spiller, in the *Literary History of
the United States*, fairly states the whole case:

> The appearance of an original artist, springing without ante-
> cedent into life, is always illusion, but the sources of Crane's phi-
> losophy and art are as yet undeciphered. Neither the cold-
> blooded determinism of his belief nor the sensuous awareness of
> his writing can be without source, but nowhere in the scant
> record he has left is there evidence that he, like Garland, read

† From *University of Texas Studies in English*, XXXIV, 179–88. Copyright © 1955 by the University of Texas Press. Reprinted by permission.

widely in the current books on biological science. A direct influence of Darwin, Spencer, Haeckel, or their American popularizers cannot be established. Rather he seems to have absorbed these influences at second hand through Russian and French writers.[1] The problem of the "cold-blooded determinism of his belief" aside for the moment, how can the literary historian account for the "illusion" of Crane's appearance as an "original" artist and the amazing rapidity of his apparently untutored growth? In the spring of 1891 he was a Sophomore at Syracuse University, ambitiously planning to end his college career in order to become a writer; by the fall of 1892 he had already formulated the creed of art by which he was to be guided for the remaining eight years of his life and was presumably writing his first novel; by the spring of 1893 the author of *Maggie: A Girl of the Streets*[2] had won the attentions of two of the most influential literary men of his time, Hamlin Garland and William Dean Howells.

Two theories are commonly advanced to explain this phenomenal literary development. First is the popular and persistent notion, perhaps inevitable in view of his unusual literary rise, that Crane had no origins at all, that he was a "natural" genius who had no need for a literary situation in which to develop. An informed contemporary, Howells, could only say that the young author of *Maggie* "sprang into life fully armed,"[3] and Garland, Crane's patron for a time after 1893, propagated for almost twenty years the idea that his protégé was an inexplicable genius, a sort of unconscious recorder of whatever came to him from the outer reaches of a ghostly world. This belief is commonly found in history and criticism even today. He was, a critic wrote in 1941, "an artist who was really not conscious at all. He arrived . . . fully equipped. He had no need to improve."[4] And as late as 1952 a historian asserted that Crane was an artist of "amazing, almost miraculous prescience," and thus "that despair of the academic critic, a highly 'original' writer."[5]

The other view, accepted in part at least by Spiller in the *Literary History of the United States*, is that Crane sprang directly from the tradition of the French and Russian naturalists, a thesis extensively argued in Lars Ahnebrink's study of *The Beginnings of Naturalism in American Fiction*.[6] Ahnebrink attributes Crane's basic concept of fiction and the writer to the European naturalists, particularly Zola, whose *L'Assommoir* and *La Débâcle* he regards as important

1. Robert E. Spiller and others, eds., *Literary History of the United States* (3 vols., New York, 1948), II, 1021.
2. The book, Spiller writes (*ibid.*, 1022), with which "modern American fiction was born."
3. Thomas Beer, *Stephen Crane: A Study in American Letters* (New York, 1923), 96.
4. H. E. Bates, *The Modern Short Story* (New York, 1941), 65.
5. Edward Wagenknecht, *The Cavalcade of the American Novel* (New York, 1952), 212.
6. University of Uppsala, *Essays and Studies on American Language and Literature*, IX (1950).

sources for Crane's first three novels, *Maggie, George's Mother*, and *The Red Badge of Courage*. Turgenev's *Fathers and Sons*, Ahne-brink thinks, probably influenced *George's Mother*, and Ibsen's *An Enemy of the People* perhaps suggested Crane's novelette, *The Monster*.

But there are serious objections to both of these views. The notion that Crane had no literary antecedents contradicts the fundamental principle that every writer is at first dependent upon his times and its traditions, however widely he may later deviate from them in the process of creating something new out of the old. Nor is the second theory much more acceptable. The chief difficulty with the idea that Crane adopted the doctrines and methods of the naturalists is that it assumes, without much evidence, that he read and imitated the writers of this school, an assumption which does not at all square with the fact that Crane's work and the naturalists' differ in many important respects. There are reasons to doubt seriously that the American ever read Zola or the Russians. When Ahnebrink asserts that "even before the composition of *Maggie*, he [Crane] was familiar with some of Zola's work," he ignores the fact that Crane read *Nana*—the only novel by Zola he ever commented on—more than five years after he started writing *Maggie*.[7] No evidence exists that he ever read *L'Assommoir*, and *La Débâcle* he threw aside, according to Thomas Beer, after reading only a few pages.[8] There is no external—and no convincing internal—evidence that he knew either Turgenev or Ibsen.

On the contrary, there is good reason to believe that Crane was unusually ill-read. John Barry, the editor of *The Forum* who read Crane's *The Black Riders* in manuscript in 1894, referred to the young poet as "woefully ignorant of books,"[9] and Berryman, who thinks Crane's reading has been underestimated, can nevertheless assert that "it is not easy to think of another important prose-writer or poet so ignorant of traditional literature in English as Stephen Crane was and remained."[1] All his life he denied, sometimes with considerable irritation, any connection with the naturalists. "They stand me against walls," he complained about his English acquaintances to James Huneker in 1897, "with a teacup in my hand and tell me how I have stolen all my things from de Maupassant, Zola, Loti, and the bloke who wrote—I forgot the name."[2] Except for a reference to the brief period in 1891 when, as a student at Syracuse, he was studying intensely with a view to forming his style, there is little evidence that he ever read much at all, an omission he once

7. Beer, *Stephen Crane: A Study in American Letters*, 148.
8. *Ibid.*, 97.
9. John D. Barry, "A Note on Stephen Crane," *The Bookman*, XIII (1901), 148.

1. John Berryman, *Stephen Crane* (New York, 1950), 24.
2. Robert W. Stallman, ed., *Stephen Crane: An Omnibus* (New York, 1952), 674. All references to Crane's letters are to this source.

defended on the ground that in this way he avoided the risk of unconscious imitation.[3] Unlike Frank Norris, who once referred to himself as "Mr. Norris, Esq. (The Boy Zola)!" Crane seems to owe little, if anything, to nineteenth-century French and Russian naturalism.[4]

How, then, can the literary beginnings of this precocious (but, one supposes, hardly supernatural) young writer be accounted for? "Here came a boy," Beer wrote of the twenty-year-old ex-college student who went into the East Side slums in the spring of 1891 for material for *Maggie*, "whose visual sense was unique in American writing and whose mind by some inner process had stripped itself of all respect for these prevalent theories which have cursed the national fiction. He was already an ironist, already able to plant his impressions with force and reckless of the consequent shock to a public softened by long nursing at the hands of limited men."[5] But what had stimulated to action his natural rebelliousness and what were the "inner processes" that turned him to slums for the subject of his painfully realistic *Maggie*? From whom had he learned the use of irony, and to whom was he indebted for his interest in painting and his characteristic use of color imagery? What was the origin of his belief that direct personal experience is the only valid material for the writer, and what led him to emphasize so strongly his belief that absolute honesty is a prime virtue of the artist? These questions, it would seem, define the problem of Crane's literary origins and the answers are to be found in the period of his almost incredibly brief apprenticeship to the craft of fiction in the years 1891–92.

Crane left one of the most important clues to his artistic origins in a letter of 1896 to Lily Brandon Munro, a lady he was once in love with in his Syracuse student days. "You know," he wrote, "when I left you [in the fall of 1892] I renounced the clever school in literature. It seemed to me that there must be something more in life than to sit and cudgel one's brains for clever and witty expedients. So I developed all alone a little creed of art which I thought was a good one. . . . If I had kept to my clever Rudyard-Kipling style, the road might have been shorter, but, ah, it wouldn't be the true road."[6] The significant point here is not so much Crane's rejection of Kipling as a literary mentor as his implicit admission

3. Barry, "A Note on Stephen Crane," 148.
4. This view is in harmony with that of Albert J. Salvan, a student of Zola who concludes in his study of the naturalist's influence in the United States: "Dans la question toujours délicate d'etablir un rapport d'influence définie entre Zola et Stephen Crane, nous sommes forcés de rester sur une note evasive. Il n'est guère douteux que l'auteur de Maggie manquait d'une connaissance très entendue de la littérature française du XIXᵉ siecle en général." *Zola aux Etats-Unis* (Providence, 1943), 163.
5. Beer, *Stephen Crane: A Study in American Letters*, 77.
6. Stallman, *Stephen Crane: An Omnibus*, 648.

that the Englishmen had served him as a model sometime between 1891 and 1892. It seems more than likely that the young American owed to Kipling the basic principles of his artistic beliefs, for Crane's theory of literature matches precisely the esthetic credo of Dick Heldar, the young artist-hero of Kipling's *The Light That Failed*, a novel Crane read sometime before 1892, probably during the spring semester of 1891 at Syracuse University.

Few young writers in a rebellious mood were likely to escape the attraction of Kipling in the first years of the nineties. At the time *The Light That Failed* was appearing in *Lippincott's Magazine* in January of 1891, Kipling was already a best-selling author whose fiction was considered new and unorthodox. His amazing popularity had in fact become a subject for reviewer's verse:

> No matter where I go, I hear
> The same old tale of wonder;
> It's some delusion wild, I fear,
> The world is laboring under.
> Why every friend I've met today
> (I couldn't help but note it)
> Has asked me "Have you read 'Mulvaney'
> Rudyard Kipling wrote it."[7]

Immediately following this is a review of *The Light That Failed* which emphasizes the unorthodoxy of his realistic tale of an artist's adventures as a war correspondent and suggests something of the appeal it must have had for the youthful Crane, then a cub reporter for his brother Townley's Asbury Park news agency: "Bohemian and unconventional as the characters are," the reviewer states, "no one who has seen much of the two classes whence they are chiefly drawn—newspaper correspondents and lady art students—can say they are grossly exaggerated."[8]

There is convincing evidence that Crane not only knew this novel before 1892, but that it indeed made a profound impression upon him. S. C. Osborn notes that Crane's famous image at the end of Chapter IX in *The Red Badge of Courage*, "The sun was pasted against the sky like a wafer," occurs in Kipling's *The Light That Failed* and concludes that the younger writer unconsciously incorporated the idea into *The Red Badge*.[9] There are strong reflections, moreover, of Kipling's early manner—the impressionistic

7. "The Light That Failed," *The Literary News*, XII (1891), 29.
8. *Ibid.*, 19.
9. Scott C. Osborn, "Stephen Crane's Imagery: 'Pasted Like a Wafer,'" *AL*, XXIII (1951), 362. Osborn notes only one occurrence: "The fog was driven apart for a moment, and the sun shone, a blood-red wafer, on the water." *The Writings in Prose and Verse of Rudyard Kipling* (New York, 1897), IX, 63. The image occurs in variations twice more: "A puddle far across the mud caught the last rays of the sun and turned it into a wrathful red disc" (p. 13), and again: "The sun caught the steel and turned it into a savage red disc" (p. 31). See the final note in this essay.

"modern" imagery, the sententious, often flippant, dialogue, and a keen sense of the ironic—in Crane's earliest fiction, *The Sullivan County Sketches*, written in the summers of 1891 and 1892. In these pieces, which comprise all that may be properly called apprentice work, if the first drafts of *Maggie* and a story published in the Syracuse school paper are excepted, Crane put into practice the basic theories of Dick Heldar, the rebellious and unorthodox artist in *The Light That Failed*.

Dick Heldar must have been the apotheosis of all that the nineteen-year-old Crane hoped to become. Dick is an Impressionist painter in revolt against the canons of nineteenth-century respectability. He chooses Bohemian life for the freedom it gives him in his enthusiastic pursuit of fame, and with great determination he seeks the truth about life in the slums of London and on the battlegrounds of remote deserts. He is proud, independent, and free in the expression of iconoclastic opinions.

Crane's orientation was remarkably similar. As a boy he was in perpetual revolt against the respectability of his conventional, middle-class Methodist home life, and at Claverack College, Lafayette, and Syracuse, an indifferent student at all three places, he incurred the displeasure of the faculty for expressing "angular" opinions. He was asked to withdraw from Lafayette at the end of his first semester for refusing to conform to academic regimen. "Away with literary fads and canons," he exclaimed to a friend in the late spring of 1891,[1] and about the same time he began making trips to New York to study life on the Bowery and in the slums. In the fall of 1892, after he was dismissed from the *Tribune* for writing an ironic account of an Asbury Park labor parade, Crane moved into the East Side more or less permanently, where he remained, observing and writing in wretched poverty for more than two years.

This way of life he led by choice like Kipling's Dick Heldar, from whom he probably got the idea that this privation was valuable, perhaps even indispensable, to his development as an artist. "There are few things more edifying unto Art than the actual belly-pinch of hunger," Kipling explains when he puts Dick into the London slums to starve and paint within walking distance of an affluent friend. "I never knew," Dick says in explaining the value of his experience with poverty, "what I had to learn about the human face before."[2] When he is at last paid for some art work, Dick calls upon his friend and explains that he could not have asked for help because "I had a sort of superstitution that this temporary starvation—that's what it was, and it hurt—would bring me more luck

1. Arthur Oliver, "Jersey Memories— Stephen Crane," *New Jersey Historical Society Proceedings*, n.s., XVI (1931), 454–55.

2. Rudyard Kipling, *The Light That Failed*, in *The Writings in Prose and Verse of Rudyard Kipling* (New York, 1897), IX, 41.

later."[3] Crane, as his way of life during this period shows, was of the same belief. One of his nieces, recalling her uncle's misery in the New York slums, was puzzled by his conduct: "We still wonder why he went through such experiences when he was always so very welcome at both our house and Uncle Edmund's. Perhaps he was seeking his own 'Experience in Misery' . . . altho doubtless it came also through his desire to make his own way independently."[4] To these views Crane himself assented, but a more significant explanation lies in his persistent notion that great art is born of the "belly-pinch of hunger":

> It was during this period [he wrote to the editor of Leslie's Weekly about November, 1895] that I wrote "The Red Badge of Courage." It was an effort born of pain—despair, almost; and I believe that this made it a better piece of literature than it otherwise would have been. It seems a pity that art should be a child of pain, and yet I think it is. Of course we have fine writers who are prosperous and contented, but in my opinion their work would be greater if this were not so. It lacks the sting it would have if written under the spur of a great need.[5]

The remarkable kinship in temperament and attitude between Kipling's protagonist and Crane strongly suggests that Dick's ideas about art deeply impressed the young writer. Dick may have inspired Crane in the use of color images for special effects, a stylistic feature which blazes forth in the Sullivan County tales of 1892. For *The Light That Failed* bristles with artist talk about color. Heldar exclaims with sensuous enthusiasm about the scenery of Sudan: "What color that was! Opal and amber and claret and brick-red and sulphur—cockatoo-crest sulphur—against brown, with a nigger black rock sticking up in the middle of it all, and a decorative frieze of camels festooning in front of a pure pale turquoise sky."[6] Crane's interest in painting, it is true, probably originated in his associations with his sister, Mary Helen, who taught art in Asbury Park in the late eighties and early nineties, and with Phebe English, a young art student with whom he fell in love when he was a student at Claverack College.[7] But in *The Light That Failed* he had before him not only an enthusiastic apreciation of the expressive potentialities of color, but also a striking example, in Kipling's "wrathful red disk" images, of how color could be used by the writer to evoke mood and emotional atmosphere.

More important in Crane's literary credo, though, are the princi-

3. *Loc. cit.*
4. Edna Crane Sidbury, "My Uncle, Stephen Crane, as I Knew Him," *Literary Digest International Book Review*, IV (1926), 249.
5. Stallman, *Stephen Crane: An Omni-*

bus, 591.
6. *The Light That Failed*, 53.
7. Joseph J. Kwiat, "Stephen Crane and Painting," *The American Quarterly*, IV (1952), 331.

ples governing the selection of materials, their treatment, and the attitude of the artist toward them. In *The Light That Failed* Kipling advances and defends the position that real life furnishes the only valid materials for art. "How can you do anything," his hero exclaims, "until you have seen everything, or as much as you can?[8] Like the blind and ruined Heldar, who met his death following wars to the far corners of the earth, Crane, ill with tuberculosis, wandered away his energies—in the West, Mexico, the Florida swamps, Greece, and Cuba—in quest of experience in the world of action. "I decided," he wrote once in reference to his literary creed of 1892, "that the nearer a writer gets to life the greater he becomes as an artist,"[9] and in 1897, when his career was drawing to a close, he wrote from England to his brother William: "I am a wanderer now and I must see enough."[1] Both Crane and Kipling's hero expressed and acted upon the firm belief that the artist's material is necessarily drawn from personal experience.

Important corollaries for the realist are the convictions that all experience, ugly and unpleasant though it may be, must be faithfully and truthfully reported if the artist is to maintain his integrity. Around this idea Kipling builds one of the key scenes in *The Light That Failed*. Heldar, disappointed because one of his realistic war sketches has been rejected by all the magazines, decides to alter it to conform to the conventional idea of what the soldier is like:

> I lured my model, a beautiful rifleman, up here with drink. . . . I made him a flushed dishevelled, bedevilled scallawag, with his helmet at the back of his head, and the living fear of death in his eye, and the blood ozzing out of a cut over his ankle-bone. He wasn't pretty, but he was all soldier and very much man. . . . The art-manager of that abandoned paper said that his subscribers wouldn't like it. It was brutal and coarse and violent. . . . I took my "Last Shot" back. . . . I put him into a lovely red coat without a speck on it. That is Art. I cleaned his rifle—rifles are always clean on service—because that is Art. . . . I shaved his chin, I washed his hands, and gave him an air of fatted peace. . . . Price, thank Heaven! twice as much as for the first sketch.[2]

"If you try to give these people the thing as God gave it," Dick argues when his friend Torpenhow reprimands him for this practice, "keyed down to their comprehension and according to the powers he has given you . . . half a dozen epicene young pagans who haven't even been to Algiers will tell you, first that your notion is borrowed and, secondly, that it isn't Art!"[3] But Torpenhow destroys the repainted picture and delivers Dick an impassioned lec-

8. *The Light That Failed*, 105.
9. Stallman, *Stephen Crane: An Omnibus*, 627.
1. *Ibid.*, 663.
2. *The Light That Failed*, 55–56.
3. *Ibid.*, 49.

ture on truth and integrity in the practice of art, after which the penitent Heldar concludes, "You're so abominably reasonable!"[4]

This idea Crane was expounding as early as the spring of 1891, about the time he read Kipling's novel. "I became involved," he wrote again in reference to his creed of 1892, "in the beautiful war between those who say that art is man's substitute for nature and we are the most successful in art when we approach the nearest to nature and truth, and those who say—well, I don't know what they say. Then they can't say much but they fight villainously."[5] On another occasion he stated Dick's idea more explicitly: "I cannot see why people hate ugliness in art. Ugliness is just a matter of treatment. The scene of Hamlet and his mother and old Polonius behind the curtain is ugly, if you heard it in a police court, Hamlet treats his mother like a drunken carter and his words when he has killed Polonius are disgusting. But who cares?"[6]

Writing in 1898 about his literary aims, Crane reasserted his belief in this principle and showed how largely it had figured in his career: "The one thing that deeply pleases me in my literary life— brief and inglorious as it is—is the fact that men of sense believe me to be sincere. . . . I do the best that is in me, without regard to cheers or damnation."[7] This echoes the principle oratorically preached to Dick upon the occasion of his moral lapse: "For work done without conviction, for power wasted in trivialities, for labor expended with levity for the deliberate purpose of winning the easy applause of a fashion-driven public, there remains but one end,— the oblivion that is preceded by toleration and cenotaphed with contempt."[8]

These striking parallels in the artistic aims and attitudes of Dick Heldar and Crane strongly suggest that Kipling's novel provided the young American with his basic conception of the art of fiction. Since the evidence for the influence of the naturalists upon Crane's literary theory is unconvincing, and since he knew neither Howells nor Garland's theories of realism and veritism until after 1892, before which time he had read *The Light That Failed*, it seems likely indeed that Kipling is Crane's chief literary ancestor. This belief is further strengthened by the fact that Crane read Kipling's book at the most impressionable period of his literary life. As a rank novice, rebellious against social and literary conventions and search-ing for a rationale for a new fiction, Crane must have found Kip-ling's ideas immensely stimulating. "For short, scattered periods Crane read curiously," Berryman states, "and instinct or luck or fate led him early to what mattered."[9] Later, it is true, he found sup-

4. *Ibid.*, 56.
5. Stallman, *Stephen Crane: An Omni-bus*, 648.
6. Berryman, *Stephen Crane*, 21.
7. Stallman, *Stephen Crane: An Omni-bus*, 679–80.
8. *The Light That Failed*, 67.
9. Berryman, *Stephen Crane*, 24.

port for his creed in the ideas of Howells, Garland, and the Impressionist painters with whom he was in constant association during his Bohemian New York period. But the book which laid the basic principle was *The Light That Failed*. Here is developed explicitly a whole literary credo which exactly parallels Crane's. In advocating and following closely the principles that art is grounded in actual experience, that absolute honesty in the artist is an indispensable virtue, that all experience, including the ugly and the unpleasant, is material for the artist, Crane, through Kipling, anticipated the "cult of experience" in American fiction which reached its full development in the literary renaissance of the twenties.[1]

DONALD PIZER

Stephen Crane: The Naturalist as Romantic Individualist†

For the past thirty years or more it has been customary to begin any consideration of Stephen Crane with an account of the critical neglect of his work. This complaint is no longer justified, for there has been of late much critical interest in both Crane's biography and his work. From the initial treatment of Crane as an inexplicable genius, as a literary "natural," there has evolved a conception of him as a conscious and subtle craftsman and artist. From being considered as a bright but short-lived and uninfluential meteor in the literary firmament, he is now thought, somewhat exaggeratedly to be sure, to have innovated the "two main technical movements of modern fiction—realism and symbolism."[1]

My concern here, however, is not with the meaning or technique of Crane's writing, but rather with the quality of mind and literary self-confidence which led him to that writing. This self-confidence took two literary forms—a choice of material which would shock, as in *Maggie* (1893); and a willingness to trust his imagination in dealing with material about which he knew little, as in *The Red Badge of Courage* (1895). The story of a prostitute who was both a

1. When this article was in page proof, I saw R. W. Stallman's "The Scholar's Net: Literary Sources," *College English*, XVII (1955), 20–27, in which Mr. Stallman states that Scott C. Osborn, who first pointed out the similarity between Kipling and Crane's wafer image, "failed to explore the related images for what they mean and how they are used. . . . Nor is there any other point of correspondence between *The Light That Failed* and *The Red Badge of Courage*—only this

single image" (p. 20).
† From *Realism and Naturalism in Nineteenth-Century American Literature* (Carbondale: Southern Illinois University Press, 1966), pp. 94–98. Copyright 1966 by Donald Pizer. Other views of Crane's impressionism can be found in the essays by Edwin Cady and Sergio Perosa, below.
1. *Stephen Crane: An Omnibus*, ed. R. W. Stallman (New York, 1952), p. xix.

product and a victim of her environment was perhaps not as contemporaneously shocking as it was once thought to be, but to Crane, a young and comparatively unread writer, it appeared so.[2] He inscribed several copies of *Maggie* with the admonition that "It is inevitable that you will be greatly shocked by the book but continue, please, with all possible courage, to the end."[3] A serious author who will knowingly shock his readers is an author confident of the correctness of his vision of life, despite its being out of joint with conventional morality. And an author who will—as Crane did in *The Red Badge*—trust his imaginative conception of war and of its effects on men is just as confident of the validity of his personal vision.

One reason for Crane's self-confidence suggests itself immediately. Both *Maggie* and *The Red Badge* were written before Crane was twenty-three. In Crane's case, however, the self-confidence of a youthful and temperamentally cocky personality was reinforced and given an explicit rhetoric by the acceptance of an impressionistic critical doctrine. A clue to the source of this doctrine lies in Crane's lifelong sense of debt toward Hamlin Garland and William Dean Howells. This sense of debt was undoubtedly derived in part from Garland's and Howells's early aiding and championing of Crane. But it also derived, it appears, from Crane's early adoption and use of a particular critical idea of Garland's and Howells's.

In 1891, when Crane was nineteen and had as yet written little, he spent the summer helping his brother report New Jersey shore news for the *New York Tribune*. One of his assignments was to cover a series of "Lecture Studies in American Literature and Expressive Art" which Hamlin Garland was giving at the Avon-by-the-Sea Seaside Assembly.[4] Garland, at this time, was an enthusiastic advocate of impressionism in painting and literature and was formulating and writing the essays which would comprise *Crumbling Idols*. On August 17, Garland gave a lecture on Howells which Crane reported for the *Tribune*. Garland, in discussing Howells's work and ideas, placed him squarely in his own evolutionary, impressionistic critical system. Howells, Crane reported Garland, believed in " 'the progress of ideas, the relative in art.' " He therefore " 'does not insist upon any special material, but only that the novelist be true to himself and to things as he sees them.' "[5] On

2. See Marcus Cunliffe, "Stephen Crane and the American Background of *Maggie*," *American Quarterly*, VII (Spring, 1955), 31–44.

3. *Stephen Crane: Letters*, ed. R. W. Stallman and Lillian Gilkes (New York, 1960), p. 14; hereafter referred to as *Letters*.

4. The program for the full schedule of lectures has been published by Lars Ahnebrink, *The Beginnings of Naturalism in American Fiction* (Cambridge, Mass., 1950), pp. 442–43.

5. "Howells Discussed at Avon-by-the-Sea," *New York Tribune*, August 18, 1891, p. 5. Republished by Donald Pizer, "Crane Reports Garland on Howells," *Modern Language Notes*, LXX (January, 1955), 37–39.

the surface, it would appear that these remarks would make little impression on a listener. But Crane not only heard them, he reported them. Moreover, he immediately became acquainted with Garland and spent some time with him at Avon that summer and the next, when Garland again gave a lecture series and Crane again reported shore news.

In 1895 Crane inscribed a copy of *The Red Badge* to Howells as a token of the "veneration and gratitude of Stephen Crane for many things he has learned of the common man and, above all, for a certain readjustment of his point of view victoriously concluded some time in 1892."[6] About a year earlier he had written in a letter than in 1892 he had renounced the "clever school in literature" and had "developed all alone a little creed of art which I thought was a good one. Later I discovered that my creed was identical with the one of Howells and Garland. . . ."[7] The important elements in these two statements of literary indebtedness are Crane's realization of a debt to Howells and his further realization of the similarity of his "little creed" with the critical ideas of Garland and Howells. Whether Crane discovered his creed "all alone" and merely received confirmation from Garland and Howells, or whether he "'victoriously concluded" his acceptance of the creed after being introduced to it by Garland's statement of Howells's belief, is perhaps not too important. Important, rather, is Crane's derivation in 1892 of a concept of personal honesty and vision similar to both Garland's idea—which Garland saw exemplified in Howells—that " 'the novelist [must] be true to himself and to things as he sees them' " and Howells's own statement that the novelist should above all "remember that there is no greatness, no beauty, which does not come from truth to your own knowledge of things."[8] Crane distinctly parallels these statements in several of his sparsely recorded critical remarks. In 1896, for example, he wrote: "I had no other purpose in writing 'Maggie' than to show people to people as they seem to me. If that be evil, make the most of it."[9] Earlier that year he had stated this idea even more elaborately: ". . . I understand that a man is born into the world with his own pair of eyes, and he is not at all responsible for his vision—he is merely responsible for his quality of personal honesty."[1]

Crane, then, entered the literary arena armed with a powerful weapon—a belief in the primacy of his personal vision. On a superficial level, this faith led him to exploit and defend the unconventional and forbidden in *Maggie*, confident of the validity of

6. *Letters*, p. 62.
7. To Lily B. Munroe, March, 1894; *ibid.*, p. 31.
8. William Dean Howells, *Criticism and Fiction* (New York, 1891), p. 145.

9. Letter to Miss Catherine Harris, November 12, 1896; *Letters*, p. 133.
1. Letter to John N. Hilliard, January, 1896; *ibid.*, p. 110.

showing "people to people as they seem to me." On a level of greater depth and significance, his faith in his own vision led him to exploit his inner eye, his imaginative conception of war and its effects. In both, Crane—like Garland—was revealing an acceptance of the strain of romantic individualism which demands that the artist above all be independent and self-reliant, that he be confident that within himself lies the touchstone of artistic truth.

DONALD PIZER

[Crane and *The Red Badge of Courage*: A Guide to Criticism]†

I have sought to note all major work containing general critical estimates of Crane and interpretations of *The Red Badge of Courage* through 1969. For biographies of Crane and for significant studies published since 1969, see the Bibliography at the end of this edition.

General Estimates and Interpretations of Crane

Some of the early estimates of Crane remain among the best general introductions to his work. George Wyndham's "A Remarkable Book" (*New Review*, Jan., 1896); Edward Garnett's "Mr. Stephen Crane: An Appreciation" (*Academy*, 17 December 1898; reprinted, with additions, in Garnett's *Friday Nights*, New York, 1922); and H. G. Wells's "Stephen Crane: From an English Standpoint" (*North American Review*, Aug., 1900; reprinted in *The Shock of Recognition*, ed. Edmund Wilson, New York, 1943) helped to establish such permanent areas of critical interest as Crane's irony and psychological realism, the canon of his best work, and the relationship of his technique and form to painting. Vincent Starrett's "Stephen Crane: An Estimate" (*Sewanee Review*, July, 1920; reprinted in Starrett's *Buried Caesars*, Chicago. 1923) played an important role in the "rediscovery" of Crane and continues to have intrinsic value. Alfred Kazin's pages on Crane in *On Native Grounds* (New York, 1942) and Grant C. Knight's section in *The Critical Period in American Literature* (Chapel Hill, N.C., 1951) have not weathered as well as the essays by Garnett and Wells. The best recent general estimates, most of which combine biographical

† From "Stephen Crane," in *Fifteen American Authors Before 1900: Bibliographical Essays on Research and Criticism*, ed. Robert A. Rees and Earl Harbert (Madison: University of Wisconsin Press, 1971), pp. 111–18, 121–27. Copyright 1971 by University of Wisconsin Press. Reprinted by permission.

and critical interpretation, are by Warner Berthoff, *The Ferment of Realism* (New York, 1965); Larzer Ziff, *The American 1890s* (New York, 1966); Jay Martin, *Harvests of Change* (Englewood Cliffs, N.J., 1967); and Jean Cazemajou, *Stephen Crane* (University of Minnesota Pamphlets on American Writers, 1969).

I will now discuss, more or less in chronological order, the major critical approaches to Crane's work. My classification is, of course, in part arbitrary, but some classification is necessary if the basic tendencies in Crane criticism are to be made discernible.

In Crane's own day it was common to call him an impressionist and to associate his techniques with those of the studio. Garnett and Wells stressed this aspect of Crane, as did Ford Madox Ford in his later and influential article "Techniques" (*Southern Review*, July, 1935). Impressionism, however, has often served merely as a vague description of Crane's color sense and of his highly distinctive narrative technique and prose style. More recent critics who are absorbed in the possibility of discussing Crane as an impressionist have refined their use of the term in several ways. One group has sought to define his impressionism by locating its source in Crane's contemporary world. Joseph J. Kwiat, in "Stephen Crane and Painting" (*American Quarterly*, Winter, 1952), builds valiantly on a base of scanty evidence to claim that Crane's association with various minor illustrators during 1891–93 led to his acceptance of impressionistic ideas and techniques. On the whole, it has been less difficult to find literary sources for Crane's impressionistic aesthetic. James B. Colvert, in "The Origins of Stephen Crane's Literary Creed" (*University of Texas Studies in English*, 1955), persuasively contends that Crane's voiced literary ideals ("I understand that a man is born into the world with his own pair of eyes," etc.) parallel those of the artist Dick Heldar in Kipling's *The Light That Failed*. Donald Pizer, in "Romantic Individualism in Garland, Norris, and Crane " (*American Quarterly*, Winter, 1958), and Stanley Wertheim, in "Crane and Garland: The Education of an Impressionist" (*North Dakota Quarterly*, Winter, 1967), stress the impact of Garland's impressionistic beliefs on Crane during the vital 1892–93 period. Even Crane's color sense has been associated with a literary source, by Robert L. Hough, in "Crane and Goethe: A Forgotten Relationship" (*Nineteenth-Century Fiction*, Sept., 1962).

The difficult task of attempting to pinpoint what is meant by Crane's stylistic impressionism was first undertaken at any length by R. W. Stallman in his 1952 *Omnibus* volume. Stallman's belief that Crane's style is "prose pointillism" suffers from the inevitable fuzziness that results from the translation of brush and canvas terminology into literary practice and effect. Much more useful are the recent and important articles by Sergio Perosa, "Stephen Crane fra naturalismo e impressionismo" (*Annali de Ca' Fascari* [Venezia], 1964; translated and reprinted in *Stephen Crane: A Collection of Critical Essays*, ed. Maurice Bassan), and by Orm Øverland, "The Impressionism of Stephen Crane," in *Americana Norvegica*, edited by Sigmund Skard and Henry H. Wasser (Philadelphia, 1966). Both writers closely examine Crane's point-of-view technique, his episodic structure, his imagery and symbolism, and his syntax and diction. Although their essays are major contributions to our understanding of Crane's prose style and fictional technique, their critical insights are ultimately of value in spite of rather than because of their consideration of Crane as an impressionist. In short, the term "impressionist" has been useful as a way of placing Crane in a particular historical context, but it is of less worth as a means of describing the particulars of his style because of the obfuscating associations attached to the term.

A significant variation in the interpretation of Crane as an impressionist was first introduced by Charles C. Walcutt in *American Literary Naturalism, A Divided Stream* (Minneapolis. Minn., 1956) and pursued at greater length by David R. Weimer in *The City as Metaphor* (New York, 1966). Walcutt's remark that Crane is probably closer to expressionism than impressionism is fully and brilliantly explored by Weimer, who concludes that Crane's fragmentation and stylization of experience are less related to the eye of the impressionist painter than to the intellect of the expressionist playwright.

Although Crane's fellow writers have tended to consider him principally as an impressionist, academic criticism, with its ideological bent, has more frequently approached him as a naturalist. Much of this criticism straitjacketed Crane in an abstract definition of naturalism ("pessimistic determinism" or the like) and served little purpose except to pigeonhole him neatly. Two influential studies of this kind are Oscar Cargill's *Intellectual America* (New York, 1941) and Malcolm Cowley's " 'Not Men': A Natural History of American Naturalism"(*Kenyon Review*, Summer, 1947; reprinted in *Critiques and Essays on Modern Fiction*, 1920–51, ed. John W. Aldridge, New York, 1952). This simplistic view of Crane persists even in such otherwise sophisticated works as Desmond Maxwell's *American Fiction: The Intellectual Background* (New York, 1963) and Edward Stone's *Voices of Despair* (Athens, Ohio, 1966). Occasionally it appears in somewhat disguised form, as in Gordon O. Taylor's *The Passages of Thought: Psychological Representation in the American Novel, 1870–1900* (New York, 1969), but is essentially the same old naturalistic wolf.

The three most important studies of Crane as naturalist are Lars Ahnebrink, *The Beginnings of Naturalism in American Fiction*

(Uppsala, 1950); Charles C. Walcutt, *American Literary Natural-ism*; and Donald Pizer, "Late Nineteenth-Century American Naturalism: An Essay in Definition" (*Bucknell Review*, Fall, 1965). Ahnebrink seeks to place Crane fully in the European naturalistic tradition, particularly that of Zola. His critical method consists largely of the examination of parallel passages and themes in the work of Crane and such writers as Zola, Tolstoy, Turgenev, and Ibsen. His parallels, however, reveal primarily that descriptions of a slum tenement, for example, will often include odors, noise, and violence. They do not cast light on the distinctive qualities of mind that produced works as different as *Maggie* and *L'Assommoir*. Nevertheless, Ahnebrink's voluminous documentation convincingly establishes the pervasiveness of such subjects as alcoholism and slum conditions in the late nineteenth-century social and literary consciousness of both Europe and America. Walcutt's study of Crane as a naturalist appears to work at cross-purposes with his general thesis that American naturalism is a divided stream—that is, that the nineteenth-century currents of intuitional idealism and mechanistic determinism reach an uneasy and inconsistent union in the naturalistic novel. To Walcutt, Crane is the one major example in American naturalism of a complete and coherent determinist. Walcutt successfully discusses *Maggie* as a deterministic novel, but in his analyses of Crane's later work, including *The Red Badge*, he overemphasizes deterministic threads in a complex pattern of themes. Paradoxically, Walcutt's greatest impact on Crane criticism has probably been less his discussion of Crane than his general thesis in *American Literary Naturalism*. For since 1956 many critics have accepted his belief that American naturalism—including the work of Crane—must be approached as a complex literary phenomenon rather than as merely a weak-minded illustration of a particular philosophical doctrine. Pizer's article follows in the path blazed by Walcutt with two major differences. What Walcutt views as thematically and artistically inept (particularly the mixing of philosophical attitudes), Pizer views as a source of depth and power. And Pizer places Crane in a definition of naturalism which derives from the practice rather than the theory of late nineteenth-century American fiction and which therefore refuses to consider deviations from Zolaesque or other concepts of naturalism as aesthetically or thematically significant.

I have already noted the Freudian aspects of the biographies by Beer and Berryman. Maxwell Geismar, in *Rebels and Ancestors* (Boston, 1953); Daniel G. Hoffman, in *The Poetry of Stephen Crane*; and Stanley Wertheim, in "Stephen Crane and the Wrath of Jehovah" (*Literary Review*, Summer, 1964), also view Crane as a classic Oedipal case. Geismar in particular vigorously searches out

Oedipal symbols in most of Crane's work. Hoffman, however, adopts this angle of approach as one of several critical methods, and Wertheim explores less blatantly than most Freudian critics the theme of guilt in Crane. Inevitably, *George's Mother* has attracted the greatest attention from Freudian-minded critics. Often, a Freudian reading of this novel is awkwardly applied to other major works by Crane, as in Norman Lavers' "Order in *The Red Badge of Courage*" (*University Review*, Summer, 1966). Jungian readings of Crane tend to concentrate on *The Red Badge* and Crane's concept of the hero. John E. Hart's "*The Red Badge of Courage* as Myth and Symbol (*University of Kansas City Review*, Summer, 1953) remains the best of such studies. Donald B. Gibson's *The Fiction of Stephen Crane* (Carbondale, Ill., 1968) is ostensibly a study of Crane in relation to Erich Neumann's Jungian *The Origins and History of Consciousness*. In fact, it is an amateurish reading of Crane in which the author mechanically applies a free will-determinism formula to the interpretation of work after work. Gibson lacks any "feel" for his subject (he can ask of the phrase "squat ignorant stables" in *Maggie*, "What are 'ignorant' stables?") and his book is best forgotten.

Crane's social themes are often mentioned in discussions of his New York slum writing, but there is little full-scale discussion of him as a critic of his society. (He appears only briefly, for example, in W. F. Taylor's standard *The Economic Novel in America*.) Two exceptions, both of which discover a strong sense of the reality of the class struggle in his work, are Russel B. Nye's "Stephen Crane as Social Critic" (*Modern Quarterly*, Summer, 1940) and M. Solomon's "Stephen Crane: A Critical Study" (*Masses & Mainstream*, Jan., 1956). Neither study is entirely persuasive, primarily because of the difficulty in separating Crane's social attitudes from other, more prominent aspects of his thought—his views of God and nature, for example. Moreover, it is obvious that his social ideas cannot be adequately described by summarizing the plots of his fiction, as Robert W. Schneider does in *Five Novelists of the Progressive Era* (New York, 1965). Crane's idea of society is no doubt a significant element in his thought (most full-length studies of his work inevitably touch upon it), but a meaningful discussion of that idea awaits a critic who is willing to confront the full complexity of Crane's themes and techniques in pursuit of his subject.

Studies of Crane as religious symbolist tend to concentrate on *The Red Badge* and on his poetry. Since examination of religious themes in his poetry usually occurs within full-scale discussions of his poetic art, I will reserve commenting on these themes until later. More pertinent at this point is the controversial reading of *The Red Badge* by R. W. Stallman, a reading which implies that

Christian symbolism is at the heart of all of Crane's work. Stallman's interpretation of *The Red Badge* as a story of Christian redemption first appeared in his 1951 Modern Library edition of the novel. Since then he has repeated it many times (with occasional variations in emphasis), most notably in his "Stephen Crane: A Revaluation," in *Critiques and Essays on Modern Fiction, 1920–51*, edited by John W. Aldridge, in his 1952 *Omnibus* volume, in his essays on Crane in *The Houses That James Built* (East Lansing, Mich., 1961), and in his Crane biography. Few readers of Crane would deny that Christian symbols and themes pervade his work, but most would probably echo Isaac Rosenfeld's early comment in "Stephen Crane as Symbolist" (*Kenyon Review*, Spring, 1953) that Stallman "is working his poor horse to death." I shall take up Stallman's reading of *The Red Badge* at greater length later, but it is appropriate at this time to note such major negative responses to his methods and thesis as Philip Rahv, "Fiction and the Criticism of Fiction" (*Kenyon Review*, Spring, 1956); Norman Friedman, "Criticism and the Novel" (*Antioch Review*, Fall, 1958); and, in particular, Stanley B. Greenfield, "The Unmistakable Stephen Crane" (*PMLA*, Dec., 1958). The general import of these responses is that Stallman has woven a disparate group of images into a theme which is extraneous to or contradicted by the themes present in the plot and characterization of the novel. This debate on the validity of a predominantly Christian symbolist reading of Crane occurred primarily during the 1950s, when both New Criticism analyses of fiction and Christian myth interpretations of all literature were much in vogue. Except for Stallman, critics of the 1960s have turned to other interests, which suggests that an emphasis upon Crane as a Christian symbolist has had its day.

A more recent critical tendency has been to attempt to define Crane's moral position without recourse to the absolutes of pessimistic determinism or Christian redemption. In a series of closely reasoned articles which usually draw upon Crane's best work, a number of critics have discussed Crane's cosmic vision as a complex entity that defies easy classification. The first such writer was John W. Shroeder, in "Stephen Crane Embattled" (*University of Kansas City Review*, Winter, 1950); followed by Greenfield; by James B. Colvert, in "Style and Meaning in Stephen Crane's 'The Open Boat'" (*University of Texas Studies in English*, 1958) and "Structure and Theme in Stephen Crane's Fiction" (*Modern Fiction Studies*, Autumn, 1959); by George W. Johnson, in "Stephen Crane's Metaphor of Decorum" (*PMLA*, June, 1963); and by Max Westbrook, in "Stephen Crane: The Pattern of Affirmation" (*Nineteenth-Century Fiction*, Dec., 1959), "Stephen Crane and the Personal Universal" (*Modern Fiction Studies*, Winter, 1962–

63), and "Stephen Crane's Social Ethic" (*American Quarterly*, Winter, 1962). Most of these critics accept Greenfield's view that Crane's work exhibits a "balance between the deterministic and volitional views of life." Each, however, asserts this position somewhat differently. Colvert, for example, stresses Crane's ironic relationship to his characters, Johnson their role-playing, and Westbrook their ethical limitations yet ultimate responsibility. With the exception of Shroeder's early, tentative article, all are major efforts. Perhaps the essays of Colvert and Johnson will have the most influence on Crane criticism, since their study of Crane's technique as a means of describing his ethic avoids the usual hazards of attempting to apply such philosophically absolute terms as "free will" and "determinism" directly to the complex reality of a literary construct.

Our greater knowledge of Crane's life and times and the recent growth of American Studies as a discipline have encouraged critical studies which stress the American roots of his subjects and themes. A pioneer "Americanist" study of Crane was Marcus Cunliffe's "Stephen Crane and the American Background of *Maggie*" (*American Quarterly*, Spring, 1955). Cunliffe ably demonstrates that the sources of Crane's story are less attributable to Zola then to American social reform tracts of the 1880s and 1890s. In other attempts to dispel the notion that Crane was a "sport" on the American scene, Donald Pizer, in "Romantic Individualism in Garland, Norris, and Crane," notes the similarity between Crane's aesthetic beliefs and an Emersonian faith in the artist's private vision, and Daniel G. Hoffman, in *The Poetry of Stephen Crane*, locates the specific sources of Crane's symbolic technique in an Emersonian aesthetic. Edwin H. Cady has opened up two rich areas of interest of Crane in an American context: Crane and the American enthusiasm for sports, in "Stephen Crane and the Strenuous Life" (*ELH*, Dec., 1961), and Crane and the code of the Christian gentleman, in *Stephen Crane* (New York, 1962). And Crane has belatedly and unconvincingly been discussed by David W. Noble in connection with an American Edenic myth, in *The Eternal Adam and the New World Garden* (New York, 1968).

Perhaps the most important study of Crane in relation to his American setting is Eric Solomon's *Stephen Crane: From Parody to Realism* (Cambridge, Mass., 1966). Solomon believes that many of Crane's themes have their origin in his conscious parody of late nineteenth-century popular literary formulas and subjects—slum reform and temperance writing, romantic war fiction, the dime western, and children's stories. His book is both the best study of the literary origins of Crane's fiction and one of the few full-length studies of Crane which discusses the various major divisions in his work with a coherent and acceptable analytical device, that of

Crane as parodist. Nevertheless, this device is also the source of some of the book's weaknesses. Least significant of these is Solomon's neglect of his thesis when he is confronted by an essentially nonparodic work, such as "The Open Boat." More vital are his bypassing of a theoretical discussion of parody as a literary mode and his fuzzy and limited concept of "realism." For Solomon, realism seems to be merely the opposite of what Crane is parodying in particular works, and he concludes that most of Crane's major fiction moves from a parody half to a realistic half. In short, Solomon is often formulistic and he is weak on theory. But no student of Crane can neglect his discussion of the relationship between Crane's writing and the literature of his time.

Finally, Crane has come within the compass of the recent critical movement which finds most major writers to be existentialists. Two articles which adopt this view toward his work are William B. Stein's "Stephen Crane's *Homo Absurdus*" (*Bucknell Review*, May, 1959) and Florence Leaver's "Isolation in the Work of Stephen Crane" (*South Atlantic Quarterly*, Autumn 1962). Both critics find that Crane's work exhibits the existential themes of the absurdity of ethical values and the isolation of man in an amoral, Godless universe. Although these are by no means novel conclusions, both writers state their case persuasively.

* * *

The best general introductions to *The Red Badge of Courage* are those by Richard Chase and Frederick C. Crews in their editions of the novel (Boston, 1960, and Indianapolis, Ind., 1964) and by Edwin H. Cady in his *Stephen Crane*. A useful collection of criticism is *Stephen Crane's "The Red Badge of Courage": Text and Criticism*, edited by Richard Lettis et al. (New York, 1960). I have already discussed general textual studies of *The Red Badge*, but I should note at this point textual commentary which bears significantly on interpretation of the novel. Both Olov W. Fryckstedt, in "Henry Fleming's Tupenny Fury: Cosmic Pessimism in Stephen Crane's *The Red Badge of Courage*" (*Studia Neophilologica*, 1961), and Edwin H. Cady (in his *Stephen Crane*) take up the thematic implications of the omission from the 1895 edition of several uncanceled passages which are present in the long version manuscript. Both agree that the passages are heavy-handed, ironic accounts of Henry's attempt to find a naturalistic explanation for his actions and that their omission is therefore an improvement. Joseph Katz, in his introductions to the facsimile edition of the December 9, 1894, *New York Press* syndicated version of *The Red Badge* (Gainesville, Fla., 1967) and to the facsimile edition of the 1895 Appleton text (Columbus, Ohio, 1969), seeks to demonstrate that Crane's preparation of an abridged text for syndication represents a major and beneficial revision of his manuscript, since the syndicated text contains a number of important passages not in the long version but present in the 1895 edition. Until there is evidence, however, that Crane participated in the preparation of his novel for its December 1894 syndication, it can be maintained with equal probability that his revision of the long version occurred at some unknown time before late 1894.

At one stage in the history of Crane scholarship, *The Red Badge* was an active field for source hunters. Crane's reading of Zola and Tolstoy, his acquaintance with Civil War veterans, his knowledge of various Civil War novels and historical works—all were pursued with vigor and often with the intent of establishing a major source. Today, the tendency in general accounts of *The Red Badge* is to deemphasize the importance of sources and to acknowledge the existence of several different threads of influence without stressing one or the other. Nevertheless, some kinds of source study have undoubtedly been more fruitful than others, with the search for literary antecedents perhaps among the less productive because the least demonstrable.

Lars Ahnebrink's *The Beginnings of Naturalism in American Fiction* is the definitive study of Crane's possible debts to Zola's *La Débâcle* and to Tolstoy's war fiction. On the whole, however, V. S. Pritchett's comment in *The Living Novel* (New York, 1947) that the influence of European war novels on Crane was general rather than specific is more persuasive than Ahnebrink's detailed analogies. Crane's Homeric parallels have been discussed by Warren D. Anderson, in "Homer and Stephen Crane" (*Nineteenth-Century Fiction*, June, 1964), and Robert Dusenberg, in "The Homeric Mood in *The Red Badge of Courage*" (*Pacific Coast Philology*, Apr., 1968). A group of Civil War novels are offered as sources by H. T. Webster, "Wilbur F. Hinman's *Corporal Si Klegg* and Stephen Crane's *The Red Badge of Courage*" (*American Literature*, Nov., 1939); Thomas F. O'Donnell, "De Forest, Van Petten, and Stephen Crane" (*American Literature*, Jan., 1956) (*Miss Ravenel's Conversion*); and Eric Solomon, "Another Analogue for *The Red Badge of Courage*" (*Nineteenth-Century Fiction*, June, 1958) (Joseph Kirkland's *The Captain of Company K*). Recently, several critics have cited essays which contain ideas about war that appear to resemble Crane's. Eric Solomon, in "Yet Another Source for *The Red Badge of Courage*" (*English Language Notes*, Mar., 1965), suggests Horace Porter's "The Philosophy of Courage," and Neal J. Osborn, in "William Ellery Channing and *The Red Badge of Courage*" (*Bulletin of the New York Public Library*. Mar., 1965), offers Channing's sermon on "War."

A much more profitable vein of source hunting is that which con-

cerns Crane's use of Civil War material. Lyndon U. Pratt, in "A
Possible Source of·*The Red Badge of Courage*" (*American Literature*,
Mar., 1939), and Thomas F. O'Donnell, in "John B. Van Petten:
Stephen Crane's History Teacher" (*American Literature*, May,
1955), note Crane's association with the Union veteran General
Van Petten, his history teacher at Claverack. The most important
study of this kind is Harold R. Hungerford's " 'That Was at Chancellorsville': The Factual Framework of *The Red Badge of Courage*" (*American Literature*, Jan., 1963). Hungerford demonstrates
beyond doubt that Henry's "Various Battles" are those of Chancellorsville and that Crane's source was principally *Battles and Leaders
of the Civil War*. Frederick C. Crews, in his edition of *The Red
Badge of Courage*, supplements Hungerford's article by supplying
several maps of the battle and by textual annotation which notes
references and allusions to the Chancellorsville campaign.

R. W. Stallman's well-known discussion of the wafer image at
the close of Chapter Nine has stimulated interest in the source of
the image. Scott C. Osborn, in "Stephen Crane's Imagery: 'Pasted
Like a Wafer' " (*American Literature*, Nov., 1951), locates the
image in Kipling's *The Light that Failed* and believes that both
Kipling and Crane intended a sealing wax rather than a communion
allusion. Stallman came to the rescue of his reading in "The Scholar's Net: Literary Sources" (*College English*, Oct., 1955) but was
answered in turn by Edward Stone, in "The Many Suns of *The
Red Badge of Courage*" (*American Literature*, Nov., 1957), and by
Eric W. Carlson, in "Crane's *The Red Badge of Courage*" (*Explicator*, Mar., 1958). In "Stephen Crane's 'Fierce Red Wafer' "
(*English Language Notes*, Dec., 1963), Cecil D. Eby, Jr., indirectly
defends Stallman when he claims that the presence of "fierce" in
the manuscript does not invalidate a religious allusion. And
undoubtedly we shall be hearing again about this "two-handed
engine" of American scholarship.

Criticism of *The Red Badge* has been so varied in focus and
method that it is difficult to shape a discussion of its major tendencies. One problem in particular, however, which has occupied
almost all critics is that of Crane's relationship to Henry Fleming at
the close of the novel. Does Crane wish us to accept at face value
Henry's estimation of himself as a "man"; or is Crane once again
ironically depicting Henry's capacity for self-delusion; or is his characterization of Henry consciously or unconsciously ambivalent? To
emphasize this particular crux in the interpretation of *The Red
Badge* is to oversimplify some critical discussions and to reorient the
principal direction of others, but it is perhaps the only way to bring
some order in brief compass to a large body of work.

The position that Crane is ruthlessly ironic toward Henry

throughout the novel and that the book is therefore a study of
man's ability to delude himself under any circumstances is best represented by Charles C. Walcutt in his *American Literary Naturalism, A Divided Stream*. With the principal exception of Jay Martin,
in *Harvests of Change*, most critics have not accepted such an
extreme view of Crane's attitude toward Fleming. They argue that
evidence both within the novel and in such works as "The Open
Boat" reveals Crane's belief that men can become "interpreters" of
their experience. A position directly opposed to that of Walcutt can
be closely identified with two schools of criticism—the religious and
the mythic. If Henry undergoes a sacramental experience in the
novel (either in connection with Jim Conklin or in relation to
battle in general) or if he is initiated into manhood in any one of
several mythic patterns, his final self-evaluation is lent authority,
since it is the product of his maturation. The religious interpretation of *The Red Badge*—in particular the interpretation of Jim
Conklin's death as a redemption experience—is of course closely
associated with the work of R. W. Stallman, from the introduction
to his Modern Library edition in 1951 to his 1968 biography. (It
would be an interesting exercise, by the way, to trace the permuta-
tions in the tone of Stallman's discussions of the redemption theme
in *The Red Badge*, from the certainty of the early 1950s to the willingness to hedge in 1968. But major critics, like major writers,
should not be held to a foolish consistency, and the religious center
of the novel has always been the principal focus of Stallman's interpretation.) The fullest endorsement of Stallman's redemption reading is by Daniel G. Hoffman in his introduction to *The Red Badge
of Courage and Other Stories* (New York, 1957). The most elaborate and successful interpretation of the novel as an initiation myth
is by John E. Hart, in "*The Red Badge of Courage* as Myth and
Symbol." A rather weak echo of Hart's thesis can be found in
David L. Evans, "Henry's Hell: The Night Journey in *The Red
Badge of Courage*" (*Proceedings of the Utah Academy of Sciences,
Arts & Letters*, 1967).

In other "affirmative" readings of *The Red Badge*, however, there
is less of a sense that a particular critical method, such as symbolic
imagery or myth criticism, has produced a predictable interpreta-
tion. A sizable number of critics have had the "felt response" that
Crane wished to affirm some aspect of experience in his depiction of
Henry and they have struggled manfully in order to define the
nature of this theme. So James B. Colvert, Eric Solomon, and John
Fraser—in "Structure and Theme in Stephen Crane's Fiction";
"The Structure of *The Red Badge of Courage*" (*Modern Fiction
Studies*, Autumn, 1959); and "Crime and Forgiveness: *The Red
Badge of Courage* in Time of War" (*Criticism*, Summer, 1967)—

contend that Fleming matures during the novel in his understanding of social and moral reality and that this maturity takes the fictional configuration of his movement from isolation to group acceptance, loyalty, and duty. Other critics, though they also stress some growth on Henry's part, see his development in less positive terms. James T. Cox, in "The Imagery of *The Red Badge of Courage*" (*Modern Fiction Studies*, Autumn, 1959), and Marston La France, in "Stephen Crane's *Private Fleming: His Various Battles*," in *Patterns of Commitment in American Literature*, edted by Marston La France (Toronto, 1967), argue persuasively that Henry progresses from a romantic vision of the world to an awareness that man lives in a hostile and godless universe. A third group of critics often adopts Freudian ideas to maintain that Henry's maturity stems from his ability to exorcise the specter of fear in its various guises. Perhaps the best of such readings is Daniel Weiss's "*The Red Badge of Courage*" (*Pyschoanalytic Review*, Summer, Fall, 1965), though the articles by Bernard Weisberger, "*The Red Badge of Courage*," in *Twelve Original Essays on Great American Novels*, edited by Charles Shapiro (Detroit, Mich., 1958), and Kermit Vanderbilt and Daniel Weiss, "From Rifleman to Flagbearer: Henry Fleming's Separate Peace in *The Red Badge of Courage*" (*Modern Fiction Studies*, Winter, 1965–66), should also be noted.

The critical approach which stresses that purposeful ambivalence is the key to the close of the novel stems largely from Stanley B. Greenfield's influential article "The Unmistakable Stephen Crane." Greenfield argues that Crane portrays life as an experience in which the individual can both learn and remain deluded. Henry, for example, has gained from his experiences but he is nevertheless deluded in his understanding of what he has gained. Thus, Crane's tone is the mixed one of sympathetic identification and of irony. Ralph Ellison states this view of the novel succinctly in *Shadow and Act* (New York, 1964), when he writes that "although Henry has been initiated into the battle of life, he has by no means finished with illusion—but that, too, is part of the human condition." Further support of Greenfield's thesis can be found in Frederick C. Crews's introduction to *The Red Badge*; Donald Pizer, "Late Nineteenth-Century American Naturalism: An Essay in Definition"; Larzer Ziff, *The American 1890s*; and John J. McDermott, "Symbolism and Psychological Realism in *The Red Badge of Courage*" (*Nineteenth-Century Fiction*, Dec., 1968).

To some critics, however, the ambivalences (or ambiguities) at the close of the novel constitute major weaknesses either in Henry or in Crane's artistry. William B. Dillingham, in "Insensibility in *The Red Badge of Courage*" (*College English*, Dec., 1963), and John W. Rathbun, in "Structure and Meaning in *The Red Badge*

of Courage" (*Ball State University Forum*, Winter, 1969), believe
that Henry's movement from introspective self-analysis to instinctive participation in group action is necessary and triumphant but
that it also represents the loss of a distinctively human form of sensitivity. And Clark Griffith, in "Stephen Crane and the Ironic Last
Word" (*Philological Quarterly*, Jan., 1968), holds that Crane's
belief that life is an insoluble puzzle led him to undermine, with a
final ironic touch, our acceptance of any meaning which his characters think they have gained from experience. Griffith's position is
not far from the view that the insoluble ambiguities at the close of
The Red Badge stem from Crane's conscious or unconscious confusion. John Berryman writes more frankly than most readers who
hold this view when he comments, in "Stephen Crane, *The Red
Badge of Courage*," in *The American Novel*, edited by Wallace
Stegner (New York, 1965), "I do not know what Crane intended.
Perhaps he intended to have his cake and eat it too—irony at the
end, but heroism too." Mordecai Marcus, in "The Unity of *The
Red Badge of Courage*," in *Stephen Crane's "The Red Badge of
Courage": Text and Criticism*, edited by Richard Lettis et al., and
James B. Colvert, in "Stephen Crane's Magic Mountain," in *Stephen Crane: A Collection of Critical Essays*, edited by Maurice
Bassan, also adopt this position. Marcus asserts that Crane could
not make up his mind whether Henry had matured or was deluded,
while Colvert, in a probing and provocative essay, finds that Crane's
joining of sentimental solipsism and ironic deflation in his own self-
evaluation is the underlying source of the novel's flawed conclusion.
    Studies of the form of *The Red Badge* have tended to concen-
trate on its imagery and symbolism, with Stallman's religious reading often serving as a starting point. Stallman's interpretation of the
imagery and symbolism of *The Red Badge* (as well as his reply to
critics of this approach) can best be found in *The Houses That
James Built*. Edwin H. Cady states the position of those critics who
reject Stallman's thesis when he writes in his *Stephen Crane*: "The
decisive difficulties with the Christian-symbolist reading of *The Red
Badge*, it seems, are that there appears to be no way to make a coherent account of the symbol as referential to Christian doctrine
and then to match that with what happens in the novel." A
number of critics other than Stallman have pursued various threads
of imagery in the novel with less ambitious aims but often with
more productive results. Among these are Claudia C. Wogan,
"Crane's Use of Color in *The Red Badge of Courage*" (*Modern
Fiction Studies*, Summer, 1960) (a simple listing); Mordecai and
Erin Marcus, "Animal Imagery in *The Red Badge of Courage*"
(*Modern Language Notes*, Feb., 1959); James W. Tuttleton, "The
Imagery of *The Red Badge of Courage*" (*Modern Fiction Studies*,

Winter, 1962-63) (pagan religious imagery); William J. Free, "Smoke Imagery in *The Red Badge of Courage*" (*College Language Association Journal*, Dec., 1963); and John J. McDermott, "Symbolism and Psychological Realism in *The Red Badge of Courage*" (wound symbolism). Other than Stallman, the major reading of *The Red Badge* as a work in which theme and form arise out of a complex interaction of image patterns is James T. Cox's "The Imagery of *The Red Badge of Courage*." Cox's brilliant commentary on various imagistic threads (particularly those involving the sun) is a high point in the application of New Criticism techniques to *The Red Badge*. That is, his argument is persuasive but it is occasionally difficult to recall that he is writing about *The Red Badge*.

A secondary area of formalistic analysis has been the overall structure of the novel. R. W. Stallman has often called the form of *The Red Badge* "a repetitive alternation of contradictory moods." Thomas M. Lorch, in "The Cyclical Structure of *The Red Badge of Courage*"(*College Language Association Journal*, Mar. 1967), also stresses repetitive change, though that of action and of Henry's thought rather than of mood. On the other hand, Eric Solomon, in "The Structure of *The Red Badge of Courage*," and John M. Rathbun, in "Structure and Meaning in *The Red Badge of Courage*," suggest that the key to the novel's form is its developmental structure. A good many of the significant aspects of the form and technique of *The Red Badge* have either been totally neglected or only tentatively sketched, perhaps because critical preoccupation with the imagery of the novel has obscured the need to examine other formalistic problems. However, Robert L. Hough, in "Crane's Henry Fleming: Speech and Vision" (*Forum* [Houston], Winter, 1961), comments briefly on Crane's shifts in levels of diction; Mordecai Marcus, in "The Unity of *The Red Badge of Courage*," in *Stephen Crane's "The Red Badge of Courage": Text and Criticism*, edited by Robert Lettis et al., attempts to define the various kinds of irony in the novel; and Edwin H. Cady (in his *Stephen Crane*) and Robert C. Albrecht, in "Content and Style in *The Red Badge of Courage*" (*College English*, Mar., 1966), try to come to grips with the complex problem of Crane's point-of-view technique. Finally, Donald Pizer, in "A Primer of Fictional Aesthetics" (*College English*, Mar., 1968), uses *The Red Badge* to illustrate a number of ways in which formalistic analysis can be brought to bear upon a complex work of fiction.

Sources

HAROLD R. HUNGERFORD

"That Was at Chancellorsville": The Factual Framework of *The Red Badge of Courage*†

The name of the battle in which Henry Fleming achieved his manhood is never given in *The Red Badge of Courage*. Scholars have not agreed that the battle even ought to have a name; some have implied that it is a potpourri of episodes from a number of battles.[1] Yet an examination of the evidence leads to the conclusion that the battle does have a name—Chancellorsville. Throughout the book, it can be demonstrated, Crane consistently used the time, the place, and the actions of Chancellorsville as a factual framework within which to represent the perplexities of his young hero.[2]

I

Evidence of two sorts makes the initial hypothesis that Crane used Chancellorsville probable. In the first place, Crane said so in his short story "The Veteran," which was published less than a year after *The Red Badge*. In this story he represented an elderly Henry Fleming as telling about his fear and flight in his first battle. "That was at Chancellorsville," Henry said. His brief account is consistent in every respect with the more extended account in *The Red Badge*; old Henry's motives for flight were those of the young Henry, and he referred to Jim Conklin in a way which made it clear that Jim was long since dead.

This brief reference in "The Veteran" is, so far as I know, the

† *American Literature*, XXXIV (January, 1963), 520–31. Copyright 1963 by Duke University Press. Reprinted by permission.

1. Lyndon Upson Pratt, in "A Possible Source for *The Red Badge of Courage*," *American Literature*, XI, 1–10 (March, 1939), suggests that the battle is partially based upon Antietam. Lars Ahnebrink denies his arguments and favors elements from Tolstoi and Zola in *The Beginnings of Naturalism in American Fiction*, "Upsala Essays and Studies in American Language and Literature," IX (Upsala, 1950). Both argue from a handful of parallel incidents of the sort which seem to me the common property of any war; neither makes any pretense of accounting for all the realistic framework of the novel.

2. This study developed from a class project in English 208 at the University of California (Berkeley) in the spring 1958 and 1959. I am grateful to those who worked with Crane in these courses; and I am particularly grateful to George R. Stewart, who was unfailingly helpful to me in many ways and to whose scholarly acumen and knowledge of the Civil War I am deeply indebted.

only direct indication Crane ever gave that the battle in *The Red Badge* was Chancellorsville. He appears never to have mentioned the matter in his letters, and his biographers recount no references to it. Such evidence as that cited above must be used with discretion; Crane might conceivably have changed his mind. But there is no good reason why he should have done so; and in any case, the clue given us by "The Veteran" can be thoroughly corroborated by a second kind of evidence, that of time and place.

No one questions that *The Red Badge* is about the Civil War; the references to Yanks and Johnnies, to blue uniforms on one side and to gray and butternut on the other clearly establish this fact. If we turn now to military history, we find that the evidence of place and time points directly to Chancellorsville.

Only three actual place-names are used in the book: Washington, Richmond, and the Rappahannock River.[3] Henry Fleming and his fellow-soldiers had come through Washington to their winter quarters near the Rappahannock River, and their army was close enough to Richmond that cavalry could move against that city. Such a combination points to northern Virginia, through which the Rappahannock flows, to which Union soldiers would come through Washington, and from which Richmond would be readily accessible. Chancellorsville was fought in northern Virginia.

Furthermore, the battle was the first major engagement of the year, occurring when the spring rains were nearly over. The year cannot be 1861; the war began in April, and soldiers would not have spent the winter in camp. Nor can it be 1862; the first eastern battle of 1862, part of McClellan's Peninsular Campaign, in no way resembled that in the book and was far removed from the Rappahannock. It cannot be 1864; the Battle of the Wilderness was fought near the Rappahannock but did not end in a Union defeat. Its strategy was in any case significantly different from that of the battle in *The Red Badge*. Finally, 1865 is ruled out; Lee had surrendered by the time the spring rains ended.

If we are to select any actual conflict at all, a *reductio ad absurdum* indicates the first eastern battle of 1863, and that battle was Chancellorsville. Moreover, 1863 marked the turning-point in the Union fortunes; before Gettysburg the South had, as Wilson remarked in *The Red Badge*, licked the North "about every clip." After Gettysburg no Union soldier would have been likely to make such a statement; and Gettysburg was the next major battle after Chancellorsville.

3. For Washington, see p. 10; for Richmond, p. 12; for the Rappahannock, p. 75. Henry's reference to the Rappahannock may be an ironic twist on a journalist's cliché, but the twist itself—the original was Potomac—seems to me to be the result of conscious intent on Crane's part.

Like the evidence of "The Veteran," the evidence of time and place points to Chancellorsville, and it is therefore at least a tenable hypothesis that Chancellorsville and *The Red Badge* are closely connected. In the next three sections I shall present independent proof of that hypothesis by showing that the battle in Crane's novel is closely and continuously parallel to the historical Chancellorsville.[4]

II

The events preceding the battle occupy the first two chapters and part of the third (pp.5–21). The opening chapter establishes the situation of the Union army. As winter passed into spring, that army was resting in winter camp across a river from a Confederate army. It had been there for some time—long enough for soldiers to build huts with chimneys, long enough for a new recruit to have been encamped for some months without seeing action. " . . . there had come months of monotonous life in a camp. . . . since his regiment had come to the field the army had done little but sit still and try to keep warm" (p. 10). Such was the situation of the Army of the Potomac in April, 1863; it had spent a cold, wet winter encamped at Falmouth, Virginia, on the north bank of the Rappahannock River opposite the Confederate army. The army had been inactive since mid-December; its men had dug themselves into just such huts, covered with folded tents and furnished with clay chimneys, as Crane describes (pp. 6–7). Furthermore, the arrival of a new Union commander, General Joseph Hooker, had meant hour after hour of drill and review for the soldiers; and Henry was "drilled and drilled and reviewed, and drilled and drilled and reviewed" (p. 10).

To this monotony the "tall soldier"—Jim Conklin—brought the news that 'The cavalry started this morning. . . . They say there ain't hardly any cavalry left in camp. They're going to Richmond, or some place, while we fight all the Johnnies. It's some dodge like that" (p. 12). He had earlier announced, "We're goin't' move t'-morrah—sure. . . . We're goin' 'way up th' river, cut across, an' come around in behint 'em" (p. 5). Of course Jim was "the fast-flying messenger of a mistake," but the mistake was solely one of dates; the infantry did not move at once. Many soldiers at Falmouth

4. The literature on Chancellorsville is substantial. The most useful short study is Edward J. Stackpole, *Chancellorsville: Lee's Greatest Battle* (Harrisburg, Pa., 1958). The definitive analysis is John Bigelow, Jr., *The Campaign of Chancellorsville: A Strategic and Tactical Study* (New Haven, 1910). Orders, correspondence, and reports are available in *The War of the Rebellion: A Compilation of the Official Records of the Union and Confederate Armies*, ser. 1, vol. XXV, parts 1 and 2 (Washington, D.C., 1889). See also *Battles and Leaders of the Civil War* (New York, 1884), III, 152–243. The parallels presented below are drawn from these; all are in substantial agreement.

jumped to Jim's conclusion when eleven thousand cavalrymen left camp April 13 for a raid on the Confederate railroad lines near Richmond. No one in the book denied that the cavalry had left; and Jim's analysis of the flank movement was to be confirmed at the end of the book when another soldier said, "Didn't I tell yeh we'd come aroun' in behint 'em? Didn't I tell yeh so?" (p. 108). The strategy Jim had predicted was precisely that of Chancellorsville.

The Union army at Falmouth did not leave camp for two weeks after the departure of the cavalry, and such a period accords with the time represented in the book; "for days" after the cavalry left, Henry fretted about whether or not he would run (pp. 13–14).

Finally Henry's regiment, the 304th New York, was assembled, and it began to march before dawn. When the sun rose, "the river was not in view" (p. 16). Since the rising sun was at the backs of the marching men, they were going west. The eager soldiers "expressed commiseration for that part of the army which had been left upon the river bank" (p. 16) That night the regiment encamped; tents were pitched and fires lighted. "When another night came" (p. 20), the men crossed a river on *two* pontoon bridges and continued unmolested to a camping place.

This description fits aptly the march of the Second Corps. Many of its regiments were mustered before dawn on April 28, and then marched west and away from the Rappahannock. The Second, unlike the other corps marching to Chancellorsville, was ordered not to make any special secret of its whereabouts and was allowed fires when it camped. The Second crossed the Rappahannock on *two* pontoon bridges the evening of April 30 and camped safely near Chancellorsville that night; all the other corps had to ford at least one river, without the convenience of bridges. Furthermore, by no means all of the army moved at once; two full corps and one division of the Second Corps were left behind at Falmouth to conduct a holding action against Lee.

It is clear from the text that at least one day intervened between the evening on which Henry's regiment crossed the bridges and the morning of its first day of fighting (pp. 20–21). If Crane was following the chronology of Chancellorsville, this intervening day of pensive rest was May 1, on which only the Fifth and Twelfth Corps saw fighting.

III

Action began early for Henry's regiment the next day, the events of which parallel those at Chancellorsville on May 2. The statements (pp. 21–37) about what Henry and his regiment did are clear enough. He was rudely awakened at dawn, ran down a wood road, and crossed a little stream. His regiment was moved three times before the noon meal, and then moved again; one of these movements took Henry and his companions back, for in the afternoon they proceeded over the same ground they had taken that morning and then into new territory. By early afternoon, then, Henry had seen no fighting. At least a brigade ahead of them went into action; it was routed and fled, leaving the reserves, of which Henry's regiment was a part, to withstand the enemy. The regiment successfully resisted the first charge, but when the enemy re-attacked, Henry fled.

It might seem that tracing the path of Henry and his regiment before his flight would not be impossible, but it has proved to be so. The regimental movements which Crane describes loosely parallel the movements of many regiments at Chancellorsville; they directly parallel the movements of none.[5] Nevertheless, broad parallels do exist. Many regiments of the Second Corps moved southeast from Chancellorsville on May 2; many of them first encountered the enemy in midafternoon.

Furthermore, it can be demonstrated that the 304th, like the regiments of the Second Corps, was near the center of the Union line. In the first place, the "cheery man" tells Henry, and us, so (p. 62). His testimony deserves some credence; anyone who can so unerringly find a regiment in the dark should know what he is talking about. Moreover, the conversation of the soldiers before the assault (pp. 26–27) makes it clear that they were not facing the rebel right, which would have been opposite the Union left. Nor were they far to the Union right, as I shall show later.

The evidence given us by the terrain Henry crossed also points to a position at about the center of the Union line. During the morning and early afternoon he crossed several streams and passed into and out of cleared fields and dense woods. The land was gently rolling; there were occasional fences and now and then a house. Such topographical features, in 1863, characterized the area south and east of Chancellorsville itself. Further east, in the area held by the Union left, the terrain opened up and the dense second-growth forest thinned out; further west the forest was very thick indeed, with few fields or other open areas. But southeast of Chancellorsville, where the Union center was located, the land was cultivated to a degree; fields had been cleared and cut off from the forest by fences. Topography so conditioned action at Chancellorsville that

5. So flat a statement deserves explanation. I have read with great care all of the 307 reports of unit commanders in the *Official Records.* I have also studied more than a dozen histories of regiments which first saw action at Chancellorsville. Many show general parallels; none show parallels with the novel which I consider close enough to be satisfactory.

every historian of the battle perforce described the terrain; if Crane knew the battle as well as I suggest he did, he must have known its topography.

Topography also gives us our only clue to the untraceable path of Henry's flight. At one point he "found himself almost into a swamp. He was obliged to walk upon bog tufts, and watch his feet to keep from the oily mire" (p. 41). A man fleeing west from the center of the Union line would have encountered swamps after a few miles of flight. The detail is perhaps minor, but it corroborates the path Henry had to follow to reach the place where he received his "red badge of courage." He went west, toward the Union right held by the Eleventh Corps.

Henry's flight led him to the path of the retreating wounded soldiers, among them Jim Conklin. The scene of Jim's death (pp. 47–51) contains no localizing evidence, for Crane was concentrating upon the men, not their surroundings. Nevertheless, it is appropriate to Chancellorsville; the roads leading to the river were clogged with retreating Union wounded in the late afternoon of May 2. There were no ambulances near the battle lines, and many wounded men died as they walked.

By contrast, the scene of Henry's wound can be readily fixed. He received it in the middle of the most-discussed single action of the battle, an action which cost Stonewall Jackson his life and a major general his command, almost surely won the battle for Lee, and generated thirty-five years of acrimonious debate. Even today, to mention Chancellorsville is inevitably to bring up the rout of the Eleventh Corps.

About sunset on May 2, 1863, Stonewall Jackson's crack troops attacked the predominantly German Eleventh Corps. The Eleventh, which was on the extreme right of the Union line and far from the fighting, was taken wholly by surprise, and many soldiers turned and ran in terrified disorder. The result was near-catastrophe for the Union; now that Jackson's men had turned the flank, the path lay open for an assault on the entire unprotected rear of the Union army.

Appropriately enough for such a battle, Jackson's men were halted by one of history's more extraordinary military maneuvers. For in a battle in which hardly any cavalry were used, a small detachment of cavalrymen held Jackson's corps off long enough to enable artillery to be dragged into place and charged with canister. The cavalrymen could do so because the dense woods confined Jackson's men to the road. The small detachment was the Eighth Pennsylvania Cavalry; the time was between 6:30 and 7 P.M. Theirs was the only cavalry charge at Chancellorsville, and it became famous not only because it had saved the Union army—perhaps even the Union—but also because no two observers could agree on its

details; any historian is therefore obliged to give the charge considerable attention.

All these elements fit the time and place of Henry's wounding.
Night was falling fast after his long afternoon of flight; "landmarks
had vanished into the gathered gloom" (p. 59). All about Henry
"very burly men" were fleeing from the enemy. "They sometimes
gabbled insanely. One huge man was asking of the sky, 'Say, where
de plank road? Where de plank road?' " A popular stereotype holds
that all Germans are burly, and an unsympathetic listener could
regard rapidly-spoken German as "gabbling." Certainly the replacement of *th* by *d* fits the pattern of Germans; Crane's Swede in
"The Veteran" also lacks *th*. These might be vulgar errors, but they
identified a German pretty readily in the heyday of dialect stories.
Furthermore, plank roads were rare in northern Virginia; but a
plank road ran through the Union lines toward the Rappahannock.

One of these fleeing Germans hit Henry on the head; and after
he received his wound, while he was still dazed, Henry saw the
arrival of the calvary and of the artillery:

> Around him he could hear the grumble of jolted cannon as the
> scurrying horses were lashed toward the front. . . . He turned and
> watched the mass of guns, men, and horses sweeping in a wide
> curve toward a gap in a fence. . . . Into the unspeakable jumble
> in the roadway rode a squadron of cavalry. The faded yellow of
> their facings shone bravely. There was a mighty altercation (p.
> 60).

As Henry fled the scene, he could hear the guns fire and the opposing infantry fire back. "There seemed to be a great ruck of men and
munitions spread about in the forest and in the fields" (p. 61).

Every element of the scene is consistent with contemporary
descriptions of the rout of the Eleventh Corps. The time is appropriate; May 2 was the first real day of battle at Chancellorsville as it
was the first day for Henry. The place is appropriate; if Henry had
begun the day in the Union center and then had fled west through
the swamps, he would have come toward the right of the Union
line, where the men of the Eleventh Corps were fleeing in rout.
The conclusion is unavoidable: Crane's use of the factual framework of Chancellorsville led him to place his hero in the middle of
that battle's most important single action.

The first day of battle in *The Red Badge* ended at last when the
cheery man found Henry, dazed and wandering, and led him back
to his regiment by complicated and untraceable paths.

IV

The second day of battle, like the first, began early. Henry's regiment was sent out "to relieve a command that had lain long in

some damp trenches" (p. 74). From these trenches could be heard the noise of skirmishers in the woods to the front and left, and the din of battle to the right was tremendous. Again, such a location fits well enough the notion of a center regiment; the din on the right, in the small hours of May 3, would have come from Jackson's men trying to re-establish their connection with the main body of Lee's army.

Soon, however, Henry's regiment was withdrawn and began to retreat from an exultant enemy; Hooker began such a withdrawal about 7:30 A.M. on May 3. Finally the retreat stopped and almost immediately thereafter Henry's regiment was sent on a suicidal charge designed to prevent the enemy from breaking the Union lines. This charge significantly resembles that of the 124th New York, a regiment raised principally in the county which contains Port Jervis, Crane's hometown; and the time of this charge of the 124th—about 8:30 A.M.—fits the time-scheme of *The Red Badge* perfectly.[6]

The next episode (pp. 98–101) can be very precisely located; Crane's description is almost photographically accurate. Henry was about a quarter of a mile south of Fairview, the "slope on the left" from which the "long row of guns, gruff and maddened, denounc[ed] the enemy" (p. 99). Moreover, "in the rear of this row of guns stood a house, calm and white, amid bursting shells. A congregation of horses, tied to a railing, were tugging frenziedly at their bridles. Men were running hither and thither" (p. 99). This is a good impression of the Chancellor House, which was used as the commanding general's headquarters and which alone, in a battle at which almost no cavalry were present, had many horses belonging to the officers and orderlies tied near it.

The second charge of the 304th, just before the general retreat was ordered, is as untraceable as the first. It has, however, its parallel at Chancellorsville: several regiments of the Second Corps were ordered to charge the enemy about 10 A.M. on May 3 to give the main body of the army time to withdraw the artillery and to begin its retreat.

The two days of battle came to an end for Henry Fleming when his regiment was ordered to "retrace its way" and rejoined first its brigade and then its division on the way back toward the river. Such a retreat, in good order and relatively free from harassment by an exhausted enemy, began at Chancellorsville about 10 A.M. on May 3. Heavy rains again were beginning to make the roads into bogs; these rains prevented the Union soldiers from actually recrossing the river for two days, for the water was up to the level of several of

6. See Cornelius Weygandt, *History of the 124th New York* (Newburgh, N.Y., 1877).

the bridges. "It rained" in the penultimate paragraph of *The Red Badge*; and the battle was over for Henry Fleming as for thousands of Union soldiers at Chancellorsville.

V

This long recitation of parallels, I believe, demonstrates that Crane used Chancellorsville as a factual framework for his novel. We have reliable external evidence that Crane studied *Battles and Leaders of the Civil War* in preparation for *The Red Badge* because he was concerned with the accuracy of his novel.[7] He could have found in the ninety pages *Battles and Leaders* devotes to Chancellorsville all the information he needed on strategy, tactics, and topography. A substantial part of these ninety pages is devoted to the rout of the Eleventh Corps and the charge of the Eighth Pennsylvania Cavalry. These pages also contain what someone so visually minded as Crane could hardly have overlooked: numerous illustrations, many from battlefield sketches. The illustrations depict, among other subjects, the huts at Falmouth; men marching in two parallel columns;[8] pontoon bridges; the Chancellor House during and after the battle; and the rout of the Eleventh. With these Crane could have buttressed the unemotional but authoritative reports of Union and Confederate officers which he found in *Battles and Leaders*.

If it is unfashionable to regard Crane as a man concerned with facts, we ought to remember that late in his life he wrote *Great Battles of the World*[9]—hack work, to be sure, but scrupulously accurate in its selection of incident and detail and in its analysis of strategy. One can do far worse than to learn about Bunker Hill from Crane.

VI

Two questions remain unanswered. First, why did Crane not identify the battle in *The Red Badge* as he did in "The Veteran"? One answer is fairly simple: no one called the battle Chancellorsville in the book because no one would have known it was Chancellorsville. No impression is more powerful to the reader of Civil War

7. Thomas Beer, *Stephen Crane* (New York, 1923), pp. 97–98. Corwin Knapp Linson, *My Stephen Crane*, ed. Edwin H. Cady (Syracuse, 1959), pp. 37–38, corroborates Beer's account.
8. Here the illustration seems to explain the otherwise inexplicable description in the novel (p. 16); Civil War soldiers rarely marched thus.
9. Philadelphia, 1901. *Great Battles* is not in the collected edition, *The Work of Stephen Crane*, 12 vols. (New York, 1925–1926), and apparently has never been discussed by scholars. It includes no Civil War battles, although Crane at one time considered an article on Fredericksburg, the battle immediately preceding Chancellorsville; see *Stephen Crane: Letters*, ed. R. W. Stallman and Lillian Gilkes (New York, 1960), p. 98.

reports and memoirs than that officers and men seldom knew where they were. They did not know the names of hills, of streams, or even of villages. Probably not more than a few hundred of the 130,000 Union men at Chancellorsville knew until long afterwards the name of the four corners around which the battle raged. A private soldier knew his own experiences, but not names or strategy; we have been able to reconstruct the strategy and the name because Crane used a factual framework for his novel; and the anonymity of the battle is the result of that framework.

Of course the anonymity is part of Crane's artistic technique as well. We do not learn Henry Fleming's full name until Chapter 11; we never learn Wilson's first name. Crane sought to give only so much detail as was necessary to the integrity of the book. He was not, like Zola and Tolstoi, concerned with the panorama of history and the fate of nations, but with the mind and actions of a youth unaccustomed to war. For such purposes, the name of the battle, like the names of men, did not matter; in fact, if Crane had named the battle he might have evoked in the minds of his readers reactions irrelevant to his purpose, reactions which might have set the battle in its larger social and historical framework. It would have been a loss of control.

Why, with the whole Civil War available, should Crane have chosen Chancellorsville? Surely, in the first place, because he knew a good deal about it. Perhaps he had learned from his brother, "an expert in the strategy of Gettysburg and Chancellorsville."[1] More probably he had heard old soldiers talk about their war experiences while he was growing up. Many middle-aged men in Port Jervis had served in the 124th New York; Chancellorsville had been their first battle, and first impressions are likely to be the most vivid. It is hard to believe that men in an isolated small town could have resisted telling a hero-worshiping small boy about a great adventure in their lives.

Moreover, Chancellorsville surely appealed to Crane's sense of the ironic and the colorful. The battle's great charges, its moments of heroism, went only to salvage a losing cause; the South lost the war and gained only time from Chancellorsville; the North, through an incredible series of blunders, lost a battle it had no business losing. The dead, as always, lost the most. And when the battle ended, North and South were just where they had been when it began. There is a tragic futility about Chancellorsville just as there is a tragic futility to The Red Badge.

Finally, Chancellorsville served Crane's artistic purposes. It was the first battle of the year and the first battle for many regiments. It was therefore an appropriate introduction to war for a green soldier in an untried regiment.

1. Thomas Beer, Stephen Crane, p. 47.

The evidence of this study surely indicates that Crane was not merely a dreamer spinning fantasies out of his imagination; on the contrary, he was capable of using real events for his own fictional purposes with controlled sureness. Knowledge of the ways in which he did so is, I should think, useful to criticism. For various cogent reasons, Crane chose Chancellorsville as a factual framework within which to represent the dilemma of young Henry Fleming. Many details of the novel are clearly drawn from that battle; none are inconsistent with it. Old Henry Fleming was a truthful man: "that was at Chancellorsville."

ERIC SOLOMON

A Definition of the War Novel†

A man said to the universe:
"Sir, I exist!"
"However," replied the universe,
"The fact has not created in me
A sense of obligation."
—Crane, *War Is Kind*, xxi

The Red Badge of Courage (1895) stands by itself in nine-teenth-century English and American war fiction. Indeed, it is still the masterwork in English among the abundance of war novels that two world conflicts and dozens of smaller wars have produced. Stephen Crane's novel is the first work of any length in English fiction purely dedicated to an artistic reproduction of war, and it has rarely been approached in craft or intensity. The novel became part of the literary heritage of the twentieth century, and whether or not a modern war writer consciously recalls Crane's performance in the genre, *The Red Badge of Courage* remains, in Matthew Arnold's term, a touchstone for modern war fiction. Crane gave the war novel its classic form.

Of course, in writing about war, Crane drew on a form of fiction that was more traditional than any of the other genres in which he worked.[1] In the nineteenth century, war novels of one kind or

† From *Stephen Crane: From Parody to Realism* (Cambridge: Harvard University Press, 1966), pp. 68–77. Copyright © 1966 by the President and Fellows of Harvard College. Reprinted by permission of the publishers. For further discussions of the relationship of the *Red Badge* to traditional war fiction, see the essays by George Wyndham, Joseph Conrad, and John Berryman, below.

1. According to Harry Levin, "War is the test-case for realistic fiction. No other subject can be so obscured by the ivy of tradition, the crystallization of legend, the conventions of epic and romance." Harry Levin, *The Gates of Horn* (New York, 1963), p. 137. Crane establishes a new type of war fiction through criticism of these traditions and conventions. In the same manner as Thackeray, Crane exposes the delusions expressed in the aristic conventions themselves, "the sequence of idealized poses or poeticized fantasies, the literary modes associated with social or psychological artifice." See John Loofbourow, *Thackeray and The Form of Fiction* (Princeton, 1964), p. 15.

another appeared from such authors of historical romances as Sir Walter Scott, James Fenimore Cooper, and William Gilmore Simms, whose books resounded with battle scenes, thrilling chases, valiant heroes. All these novelists had in common a predilection for abstract terminology and a custom of interspersing the combat scenes among Gothic or other domestic plot episodes. Other writers like the Englishman George Gleig or the Irishman Charles Lever wrote of battle as a rollicking adventure. William Makepeace Thackeray dealt with war only obliquely while avoiding combat scenes—but did savagely mock the concept of military heroism—and later in the century Rudyard Kipling, in a rather embarrassed manner, glorified the joys and brutalities of military life.[2]

By the time American novelists began writing about the Civil War, a European tradition of irony and realism, and a motif of the development, through war, from innocence to maturity, had been established through the war fiction of De Vigny, Stendhal, Zola, and Tolstoy. For the most part, however, American war fiction was hardly realistic. There were some fine individual scenes of combat imbedded among the sentimental and dashing effusions of George Cary Eggleston, George Washington Cable, Harold Frederic, Charles King, and Thomas Nelson Page, among many others, but generally all these authors wrote what can be roughly categorized as war adventure or romance. The Civil War was usually a background for a stirring love story often complicated by the Northern versus Southern brother theme. One of Charles King's novels describes its hero as "an ardent patriot, an enthusiastic soldier, a born calvaryman."[3] These three phrases might delineate the viewpoint of the great mass of Civil War potboilers, romances, and dime novels; the patriotic element provided the controlling theme, battle was spirited and chivalric, and the hero was a born soldier who needed to undergo no tempering process through war. The battle settings appeared in heightened or rhetorical terms. Even a realist like Harold Frederic leans on heavily overwrought description: "The clouds hung thick and close above, as if to keep the stars from beholding this repellent sample of earth's titanic beast, *Man*, at his worst. An Egyptian blackness was over it all. At intervals a lighting flash from the crest of the uttermost knoll tore this evil pall of darkness asunder, and then, with a roar and a scream, a spluttering line of vivid flame would arch its sinister way across the sky . . ."[4] Occasionally these novelists sketched the war background in a more realistic manner, but then the romantic posturing of the hero seemed to clash with the grim mood of war, and the adventures did not

2. For a fuller survey, see my unpublished dissertation, "Studies in Nineteenth-Century War Fiction," Harvard University, 1958.
3. Charles King, *Between the Lines* (New York, 1888), p. 17.
4. Harold Frederic, *Marsena and Other Stories of the Wartime* (New York, 1894), p. 80.

seem appropriate to the background of death and misery. The war novels of John Esten Cooke provide perhaps the best examples of this mélange of carefully documented battle plans, maneuvers, mass combats with darkly picturesque figures, evil intrigues, solitary horsemen, suspense, multitudes of secret sins, and themes of love, honor, revenge. In *Mohun* (1869), war as history mixes with melodrama and elegy, nostalgia for the dear days of cavalry glamor and the lost cause. Sidney Lanier's *Tiger-Lilies* (1867) has a few bits of irony and realism, but the novel as a whole is poetic and philosophic rant. Throughout the nineteenth century war was, in popular fiction—with some exceptions—not a serious metaphor for life. If there was a norm for war fiction, it was the flashing-sword and magnolia-blossom novels of Cooke and his followers. Perhaps the plot of an anonymous tale that appeared in the New York *Daily Tribune* on July 19, 1891, will exemplify the traditions against which Stephen Crane was reacting when he conceived his war novel. "Thompson of Ours" is the jolly account of a noble young officer who saves his comrades by riding like the wind to bring aid, though concealing a serious wound. Among his many heroics, this generous act of hiding his wound earns the lovable daredevil the Victoria Cross. Crane, by writing of a hero who reverses the romantic ideal and pretends to have a wound where he actually received none, parodied the heroic and set a pattern of antiheroics.

It should be stressed that Stephen Crane was not the first to write realistically about the Civil War. Three predecessors, Joseph Kirkland, John William De Forest, and Ambrose Bierce, expressed in a realistic, ironic mode the emotional impact of combat. Despite its heavy overlay of genteel love story, Kirkland's *The Captain of Company K* (1891) is a genuine antiwar polemic, with many realistic touches and descriptions of infantry engagements. And the novel displays a hero who runs in panic during his baptism of fire, and later lies about a wound received while in flight.[5] While J. W. De Forest's *Miss Ravenel's Conversion from Secession to Loyalty* (1867) is similar to the work of Scott and Thackeray in its main plot, the combat scenes are without doubt more realistic in grim detail than are the comparatively impressionistic renderings in Crane's novel. Unfortunately, De Forest never fully integrates these combat descriptions, drawn from his own experiences as he recorded them in his notebooks, letters, and articles, into the development of character; the novel is both real and improbable.

Surely the finest war fiction before *The Red Badge of Courage* appears in the vignettes of cosmic irony brought together in Ambrose Bierce's very short stories of war, in *Tales of Soldiers and*

5. I have discussed Kirkland's novel as a possible source in "Another Analogue for *The Red Badge of Courage*," *Nineteenth-Century Fiction*, 13 (1958–59), 63–67.

Civilians (1891). Despite flat characters, Bierce expertly invokes, by superb selection of detail and response, war's paradoxes and enigmatic agonies. More than any other writer, Bierce resembles Crane in technique—in the treatment of time, nature, religion, and the theme of growth through combat. And Bierce's best tale, "Chickamauga," parodies reality by reflecting war through the mimicking actions of a small boy, just as Crane would do in one of his finest war stories, "Death and the Child." But Stephen Crane's more aambitious fiction surpasses Bierce's bitter portraits of combat.[6]

The contribution of Crane to the genre of war fiction was twofold. First, he defined in his novel the form that deals with war and its effect upon the sensitive individual who is inextricably involved; he uses war as a fictional test of mind and spirit in a situation of great tension. Also he constructed a book that still stands as the technical masterpiece in the field.

Crane accomplishes in the longer form of the novel what Bierce attained in the short story. *The Red Badge of Courage* creates a single world, a unique atmosphere where war is the background and the foreground. Without resorting to the props of counterplots dealing with romance and intrigue employed by every novelist who wrote of war from Scott to Kipling (with the possible exception of Tolstoy of *Sebastopol*—but *not* of the Crane of *Active Service*), Crane works within a tightly restricted area. He writes a kind of grammar in which war is the subject, the verb, and the object of every sentence. Like the painters of the Italian Renaissance who conceived the *tondo*, a form that forced the artist to choose and manipulate his subject matter to fit a small circular canvas, Crane chose to restrict his novel to war and its impact upon his hero. There is no mention of the causes or motives of the war or of any battle; Crane's war is universal, extricated from any specific historical situation. We may gain an impression of how a literary artist makes a *tondo* of war by an analysis of the structure of *The Red Badge of Courage*. For Crane approached the subject of war as an artist, picking his materials for their fictional value. He was not reliving an experience but creating one. As for the conception of the novel, "It was an effort born of pain," states the author.[7] *The Red Badge of Courage* employs previous assumptions about heroic sol-

---

6. For a more extended treatment of Crane's predecessors in Civil War fiction, see my *The Faded Banners* (New York, 1960).

7. Crane, letter to an editor of *Leslie's Weekly*, about Nov. 1895, in *Stephen Crane: Letters*, ed. R. W. Stallman and Lillian Gilkes (New York: New York University Press, 1960), p. 78. Crane goes on to mention his admiration for Tolstoy. Impressive as Crane's achievement in war fiction is, his novel does not approach *War and Peace*. If Crane created a *tondo*, then Tolstoy fashioned a fresco. To shift the metaphor, the one wrote a lyric, the other a symphony. Crane does not attempt to deal with Tolstoy's vast theme of war *and* peace. Women, politics, history, even logistics and strategy, are outside of Crane's stark realm. *War and Peace* might best be called a synthesis, an epic rather than a war novel.

diers that informed almost all popular Civil War fiction before the rise of realism in the 1890's in order to reject them. He parodies, then, an approach to war rather than a body of war fiction; thus his book survives long after the immediate occasion for its germination is forgotten, survives as creative art, not as critical comment.[8] Crane synthesizes parody with reality, integrates parodic, realistic, and, of course, imaginative visions into a unity. He subtly distorts the traditions rather than creating a new inverted form; his method is allusive satire rather than direct travesty.

Unlike many of his other novels where Crane starts with direct burlesque of a traditional form, *The Red Badge of Courage* uses parody obliquely. By making his hero anonymous for much of the novel and by investing him with cowardly instincts, Crane does away with the traditional cliché of war fiction, the bravery of the hero. As we have noticed, earlier nineteenth-century war fiction, with the exception of Bierce's short pieces, leaned on either a love story or a historical framework. Crane glances at this custom by having Henry immediately imagine a briefly seen dark-haired girl to be in love with his heroic person. This tiny scene, early in the novel, is Crane's deliberately brief bow to the usual materials of war fiction, for the girl is never spoken of again. Only war can define Crane's protagonist: "He finally concluded that the only way to prove himself was to go into the blaze . . ." (p. 14).

From start to finish Crane's war novel is shot through with mockery of the common views of war that marked the bulk of the century's war fiction. Like Henry Fleming himself, Crane commits many "crimes against the gods of tradition" (p. 15). Most obviously, his hero is no familiar hero: he is a coward, a deserter, a liar. And, like Cervantes' mocked knight, Henry has rooted his warlike dreams in reading about "vague and bloody conflicts that had thrilled him with their sweep and fire . . . a Greeklike struggle . . . distinctly Homeric. . . . He had read of marches, seiges, conflicts. . . . His busy mind had drawn for him large pictures extravagant in color, lurid with breathless deeds" (p. 7).

Crane parodies war fiction in three ways: through direct depiction of the reversal of Henry's romantic stereotypes; through the indirect characterization of Henry as a fallible, egocentric antihero; and, as always in Crane's best fiction, through the sense of reality —which by its denial of romantic illusions convinced many contem-

8. "Some novels might be fairly described as ruined parodies. The little dolls whittled in fun escape the author's derision and take on life. . . . Cervantes' masterpiece lives not because it succeeds as parody but because it immensely fails. Setting out to demonstrate the folly of romantic aspirations, Cervantes ends by locating in just this folly, this futility, such aspirations' grandeur and so provides . . . an adjective and a metaphor for the new human condition." John Updike, *Assorted Prose* (New York, 1965), pp. 247–48.

porary reviewers that the author must have been himself a war veteran. The three approaches are not distinct. They reflect back on each other and often work together. For example, when Henry overhears a general, he expects a Napoleonic phrase, but the reality refers to a box of cigars (p. 15). Later he expects another general to request information from the private—for that is the way it is in dime novels. And the lesson that fictional generalizations are invalid is one element of the youth's wartime education. Those men are absurd who "supposed that they were cutting the letters of their names deep into the everlasting tablets of brass" (p. 43). As we shall see, Henry's dreams of sublime heroism are slow to die; halfway through the novel he sees himself as a hero out of Scott or Cooke, "a blue desperate figure leading lurid charges with one knee forward and a broken blade high . . . getting calmly killed on a high place before the eyes of all" (p. 55). The fact that his dreams come true in part, that he does stand out heroically in the regiment's final charge, keeps the novel from any rigid, black and white contrast between dream and reality. When Henry earns his red badge, it is in an episode that travesties heroic action. But Crane's artistic and moral vision allows him to move through travesty and mock heroics to reality and genuine courage. Yet the clichés of war fiction—the past flashing before the eyes of a dying man, the return to the regiment, the educational process of the baptism of fire—are alternately mocked and used in *The Red Badge of Courage*, while the realities of combat blast literary preconceptions, the "vague feminine formula for beloved ones doing brave deeds on the field of battle without risk of life" (p. 74). Although Crane clearly admires Henry's ultimate combat heroism, the parodic insight protects the author from hero worship. For all his eventual success as a warrior, Henry rejects the romantic tradition. He cannot (because of his bodily aches) "persist in flying high with the wings of war; they rendered it almost impossible for him to see himself in a heroic light" (p. 55–56).

Perhaps *The Red Badge of Courage* should be termed an impressionistic-naturalistic novel. Certainly Crane uses both manners throughout. The combining of a vivid, swift montage of combat impressions with a harsh, overwhelming naturalistic view of the individuals trapped in the war machine is Crane's method of fitting the combat world into fiction. The seminal character of Crane's novel is evident when one considers that Barbusse, Remarque, Aldington, and many other portrayers of the incredible butchery of World War I turn to a similar use of impressionism for the overall battlefield picture and naturalism for the detail and characterizations.

The form of *The Red Badge of Courage* represents Crane's fundamental parodic strategy. While many readers have noted the double movement of the plot, few have accepted the second half of the novel as other than repetition or a sellout to expected standards of heroism. Yet his war novel is not broken-backed. The first half focuses in a parodic manner on Henry Fleming, the antihero, isolated in his romantic literary fancies of what war should be. The second half portrays in a realistic mode the experiences of the larger body of men who muddle through. Henry is as egocentric and emotional in his bravery as in his cowardice, but Crane shows the young soldier's later action in the context of the regiment's dogged behavior. Thus the rhythm of the novel's two parts reflects the author's basic approach to fiction: the movement from parody to realism. And Henry's later heroism is not inconsistent with the first part's parodic mode; reality is not only the reverse of romance but in some ways a verification of the truths that lie behind the idealized conventions.

* * *

SCOTT C. OSBORN

Stephen Crane's Imagery: "Pasted Like a Wafer"†

Probably the most famous of Stephen Crane's "revolutionary" impressionistic images concludes Chapter IX of *The Red Badge of Courage* (1895): "The red sun was pasted in the sky like a wafer." Such images, critics have said, marked the beginning of "modernism" in American prose fiction. Yet no one, so far as I know, has pointed out the resemblance of Crane's image to one in Kipling's *The Light That Failed* (1891): "The fog was driven apart for a moment, and the sun shone, a blood-red wafer, on the water."[1] The images seem nearly identical, and in both the sun seems compared to a red wafer of wax used to seal an envelope.[2] Kipling's figure is as "impressionistic" as Crane's, but no one, so far as I have found, has called Kipling an impressionist or a "colorist."

† *American Literature*, XXIII (November, 1951), 362. Reprinted by permission. For other articles devoted to the wafer image, see "Crane and *The Red Badge*: A Guide to Criticism," above, and the Bibliography at the end of this edition. Many of the essays in the Criticism section contain extended discussions of the image.
1. *The Writings in Prose and Verse of Rudyard Kipling*, 14 vols. (New York, 1897), IX, 63, first published in the United States in *Lippincott's Magazine*, Jan., 1891, as a complete novel, with the "wafer" image on p. 29.
2. Robert W. Stallman thinks Crane's metaphorical wafer to be that used in the communion, by which Crane symbolizes Henry Fleming's absolution and salvation; see the Modern Library edition of *The Red Badge of Courage*, (New York, 1951), Introduction, pp. xxxiv–xxxv. More likely the wafer or seal—both "red" and "pasted"—indicates the ironically enigmatic indifference of heaven to the youth's blasphemy against war.

In view of Crane's known enthusiasm for Kipling in the early nineties[3] and his interest early and late in war, it seems altogether probable that he read *The Light That Failed* before writing *The Red Badge of Courage*. He was not plagiarizing Kipling, but perhaps unconsciously using a figure or an impression (though impressed by a literary evocation instead of by a direct observation) which he had felt to be striking and apt when he first saw it. Simple coincidence seems incredible in this case. In any event, Kipling, not Crane, should be credited with first using the "revolutionary" wafer image.

3. John Berryman, *Stephen Crane* (New York, 1951), pp. 24, 97, 248.

Criticism

Early Estimates

STEPHEN CRANE

The Veteran†

Out of the low window could be seen three hickory trees placed irregularly in a meadow that was resplendent in springtime green. Farther away, the old, dismal belfry of the village church loomed over the pines. A horse meditating in the shade of one of the hickories lazily swished his tail. The warm sunshine made an oblong of vivid yellow on the floor of the grocery.

"Could you see the whites of their eyes?" said the man who was seated on a soap-box.

"Nothing of the kind," replied old Henry warmly. "Just a lot of flitting figures, and I let go at where they 'peared to be the thickest. Bang!"

"Mr. Fleming," said the grocer—his deferential voice expressed somehow the old man's exact social weight—"Mr. Fleming, you never was frightened much in them battles, was you?"

The veteran looked down and grinned. Observing his manner, the entire group tittered. "Well, I guess I was," he answered finally. "Pretty well scared, sometimes. Why, in my first battle I thought the sky was falling down. I thought the world was coming to an end. You bet I was scared."

Every one laughed. Perhaps it seemed strange and rather wonderful to them that a man should admit the thing, and in the tone of their laughter there was probably more admiration than if old Fleming had declared that he had always been a lion. Moreover, they knew that he had ranked as an orderly sergeant, and so their opinion of his heroism was fixed. None, to be sure, knew how an orderly sergeant ranked, but then it was understood to be somewhere just shy of a major-general's stars. So when old Henry admitted that he had been frightened, there was a laugh.

"The trouble was," said the old man, "I thought they were all shooting at me. Yes, sir, I thought every man in the other army was aiming at me in particular, and only me. And it seemed so darned unreasonable, you know. I wanted to explain to 'em what an

† *McClure's*, VII (August, 1896), 222–24.

almighty good fellow I was, because I thought then they might quit all trying to hit me. But I couldn't explain, and they kept on being unreasonable—blim!—blam!—bang! So I run!"

Two little triangles of wrinkles appeared at the corners of his eyes. Evidently he appreciated some comedy in this recital. Down near his feet, however, little Jim, his grandson, was visibly horror-stricken. His hands were clasped nervously, and his eyes were wide with astonishment at this terrible scandal, his most magnificent grandfather telling such a thing.

"That was at Chancellorsville. Of course, afterward I got kind of used to it. A man does. Lots of men, though, seem to feel all right from the start. I did, as soon as I 'got on to it,' as they say now; but at first I was pretty flustered. Now, there was young Jim Conklin, old Si Conklin's son—that used to keep the tannery—you none of you recollect him—well, he went into it from the start just as if he was born to it. But with me it was different. I had to get used to it."

When little Jim walked with his grandfather he was in the habit of skipping along on the stone pavement in front of the three stores and the hotel of the town and betting that he could avoid the cracks. But upon this day he walked soberly, with his hand gripping two of his grandfather's fingers. Sometimes he kicked abstractedly at dandelions that curved over the walk. Any one could see that he was much troubled.

"There's Sickles's colt over in the medder, Jimmie," said the old man. "Don't you wish you owned one like him?"

"Um," said the boy, with a strange lack of interest. He continued his reflections. Then finally he ventured: "Grandpa—now—was that true what you was telling those men?"

"What?" asked the grandfather. "What was I telling them?"

"Oh, about your running."

"Why, yes, that was true enough, Jimmie. It was my first fight, and there was an awful lot of noise, you know."

Jimmie seemed dazed that this idol, of its own will, should so totter. His stout boyish idealism was injured.

Presently the grandfather said. "Sickles's colt is going for a drink. Don't you wish you owned Sickles's colt, Jimmie?"

The boy merely answered: "He ain't as nice as our'n." He lapsed then into another moody silence.

One of the hired men, a Swede, desired to drive to the county-seat for purposes of his own. The old man loaned a horse and an unwashed buggy. It appeared later that one of the purposes of the Swede was to get drunk.

After quelling some boisterous frolic of the farm-hands and boys in the garret, the old man had that night gone peacefully to sleep, when he was aroused by clamoring at the kitchen door. He grabbed his trousers, and they waved out behind as he dashed forward. He could hear the voice of the Swede, screaming and blubbering. He pushed the wooden button, and, as the door flew open, the Swede, a maniac, stumbled inward, chattering, weeping, still screaming. "De barn fire! Fire! Fire! De barn fire! Fire! Fire! Fire!"

There was a swift and indescribable change in the old man. His face ceased instantly to be a face; it became a mask, a gray thing, with horror written about the mouth and eyes. He hoarsely shouted at the foot of the little rickety stairs, and immediately, it seemed, there came down an avalanche of men. No one knew that during this time the old lady had been standing in her night-clothes at the bed-room door, yelling: "What's th' matter? What's th' matter? What's th' matter?"

When they dashed toward the barn it presented to their eyes its usual appearance, solemn, rather mystic in the black night. The Swede's lantern was overturned at a point some yards in front of the barn doors. It contained a wild little conflagration of its own, and even in their excitement some of those who ran felt a gentle secondary vibration of the thrifty part of their minds at sight of this overturned lantern. Under ordinary circumstances it would have been a calamity.

But the cattle in the barn were trampling, trampling, trampling, and above this noise could be heard a humming like the song of innumerable bees. The old man hurled aside the great doors, and a yellow flame leaped out at one corner and sped and wavered frantically up the old gray wall. It was glad, terrible, this single flame, like the wild banner of deadly and triumphant foes.

The motley crowd from the garret had come with all the pails of the farm. They flung themselves upon the well. It was a leisurely old machine, long dwelling in indolence. It was in the habit of giving out water with a sort of reluctance. The men stormed at it, cursed it; but it continued to allow the buckets to be filled only after the wheezy windlass had howled many protests at the mad-handed men.

With his opened knife in his hand old Fleming himself had gone headlong into the barn, where the stifling smoke swirled with the air-currents, and where could be heard in its fulness the terrible chorus of the flames, laden with tones of hate and death, a hymn of wonderful ferocity.

He flung a blanket over an old mare's head, cut the halter close to the manger, led the mare to the door, and fairly kicked her out to safety. He returned with the same blanket, and rescued one of the workhorses. He took five horses out, and then came out himself.

with his clothes bravely on fire. He had no whiskers, and very little hair on his head. They soused five pailfuls of water on him. His eldest son made a clean miss with the sixth pailful, because the old man had turned and was running down the decline and around to the basement of the barn, where were the stanchions of the cows. Some one noticed at the time that he ran very lamely, as if one of the frenzied horses had smashed his hip.

The cows, with their heads held in the heavy stanchions, had thrown themselves, strangled themselves, tangled themselves: done everything which the ingenuity of their exuberant fear could suggest to them.

Here, as at the well, the same thing happened to every man save one. Their hands went mad. They became incapable of everything save the power to rush into dangerous situations.

The old man released the cow nearest the door, and she, blind drunk with terror, crashed into the Swede. The Swede had been running to and fro babbling. He carried an empty milk-pail, to which he clung with an unconscious, fierce enthusiasm. He shrieked like one lost as he went under the cow's hoofs, and the milk-pail, rolling across the floor, made a flash of silver in the gloom.

Old Fleming took a fork, beat off the cow, and dragged the paralyzed Swede to the open air. When they had rescued all the cows save one, which had so fastened herself that she could not be moved an inch, they returned to the front of the barn and stood sadly, breathing like men who had reached the final point of human effort.

Many people had come running. Someone had even gone to the church, and now, from the distance, rang the tocsin note of the old bell. There was a long flare of crimson on the sky, which made remote people speculate as to the whereabouts of the fire.

The long flames sang their drumming chorus in the voices of the heaviest bass. The wind whirled clouds of smoke and cinders into the faces of the spectators. The form of the old barn was outlined in black amid these masses of orange-hued flames.

And then came this Swede again, crying as one who is the weapon of the sinister fates. "De colts! De colts! You have forgot de colts!"

Old Fleming staggered. It was true; they had forgotten the two colts in the box-stalls at the back of the barn. "Boys," he said, "I must try to get 'em out." They clamored about him then, afraid for him, afraid of what they should see. Then they talked wildly each to each. "Why, it's sure death!" "He would never get out!" "Why, it's suicide for a man go in there!" Old Fleming stared absentmindedly at the open doors. "The poor little things," he said. He rushed into the barn.

When the roof fell in, a great funnel of smoke swarmed toward the sky, as if the old man's mighty spirit, released from its body—a little bottle—had swelled like the genie of fable. The smoke was tinted rose-hue from the flames, and perhaps the unutterable midnights of the universe will have no power to daunt the color of this soul.

GEORGE WYNDHAM

A Remarkable Book†

* * *

Mr. Stephen Crane, the author of *The Red Badge of Courage* (London: Heinemann), is a great artist, with something new to say, and consequently, with a new way of saying it. His theme, indeed, is an old one, but old themes re-handled anew in the light of novel experience, are the stuff out of which masterpieces are made, and in *The Red Badge of Courage* Mr. Crane has surely contrived a masterpiece. He writes of war—the ominous and alluring possibility for every man, since the heir of all the ages has won and must keep his inheritance by secular combat. The conditions of the age-long contention have changed and will change, but its certainty is coeval with progress: so long as there are things worth fighting for fighting will last, and the fashion of fighting will change under the reciprocal stresses of rival inventions. Hence its double interest of abiding necessity and ceaseless variation. Of all these variations the most marked has followed, within the memory of most of us, upon the adoption of long-range weapons of precision, and continues to develop, under our eyes, with the development of rapidity in firing. And yet, with the exception of Zola's *la Débâcle*, no considerable attempt has been made to portray war under its new conditions. The old stories are less trustworthy than ever as guides to the experiences which a man may expect in battle and to the emotions which those experiences are likely to arouse. No doubt the prime factors in the personal problem—the chances of death and mutilation—continue to be about the same. In these respects it matters little whether you are pierced by a bullet at two thousand yards or stabbed at hands' play with a dagger. We know that the most appalling death-rolls of recent campaigns have been more than equalled in ancient warfare; and, apart from history, it is clear that, unless one side runs away, neither can win save by the infliction of decisive losses. But although these personal risks continue to be

† *New Review*, XIV (January, 1896), 32–40.

essentially the same, the picturesque and emotional aspects of war are completely altered by every change in the shape and circumstance of imminent death. And these are the fit materials for literature—the things which even dull men remember with the undying imagination of poets, but which, for lack of the writer's art, they cannot communicate. The sights flashed indelibly on the retina of the eye; the sounds that after long silences suddenly cypher; the stenches that sicken in after-life at any chance allusion to decay; or, stirred by these, the storms of passions that force yells of defiance out of inarticulate clowns; the winds of fear that sweep by night along prostrate ranks, with the acceleration of trains and the noise as of a whole town waking from nightmare with stertorous, indrawn gasps—these colossal facts of the senses and the soul are the only colours in which the very image of war can be painted. Mr. Crane has composed his palette with these colours, and has painted a picture that challenges comparison with the most vivid scenes of Tolstoï's *la Guerre et la Paix* or of Zola's *la Débâcle*. This is unstinted praise, but I feel bound to give it after reading the book twice and comparing it with Zola's *Sédan* and Tolstoï's account of Rostow's squadron for the first time under fire. Indeed, I think that Mr. Crane's picture of war is more complete than Tolstoï's, more true than Zola's. Rostow's sensations are conveyed by Tolstoï with touches more subtile than any to be found even in his *Sébastopol*, but they make but a brief passage in a long book, much else of which is devoted to the theory that Napoleon and his marshals were mere waifs on a tide of humanity or to the analysis of divers characters exposed to civilian experiences. Zola, on the other hand, compiles an accurate catalogue of almost all that is terrible and nauseating in war; but it is his own catalogue of facts made in cold blood, and not the procession of flashing images shot through the senses into one brain and fluctuating there with its rhythm of exaltation and fatigue. *La Débâcle* gives the whole truth, the truth of science, as it is observed by a shrewd intellect, but not the truth of experience as it is felt in fragments magnified or diminished in accordance with the patient's mood. The terrible things in war are not always terrible; the nauseating things do not always sicken. On the contrary, it is even these which sometimes lift the soul to heights from which they become invisible. And, again, at other times, it is the little miseries of most ignoble insignificance which fret through the last fibres of endurance.

Mr. Crane, for his distinction, has hit on a new device, or at least on one which has never been used before with such consistency and effect. In order to show the features of modern war, he takes a subject—a youth with a peculiar temperament, capable of exaltation and yet morbidly sensitive. Then he traces the successive impressions made on such a temperament, from minute to minute, during two days of heavy fighting. He stages the drama of war, so to speak, within the mind of one man, and then admits you as to a theatre. You may, if you please, object that his youth is unlike most other young men who serve in the ranks, and that the same events would have impressed the average man differently; but you are convinced that this man's soul is truly drawn, and that the impressions made in it are faithfully rendered. The youth's temperament is merely the medium which the artist has chosen: that it is exceptionally plastic makes but for the deeper incision of his work. It follows from Mr. Crane's method that he creates by his art even such a first-hand report of war as we seek in vain among the journals and letters of soldiers. But the book is not written in the form of an autobiography: the author narrates. He is therefore at liberty to give scenery and action, down to the slightest gestures and outward signs of inward elation or suffering, and he does this with the vigour and terseness of a master. Had he put his descriptions of scenery and his atmospheric effects, or his reports of overheard conversations, into the mouth of his youth, their very excellence would have belied all likelihood. Yet in all his descriptions and all his reports he confines himself only to such things as that youth heard and saw, and, of these, only to such as influenced his emotions. By this compromise he combines the strength and truth of a monodrama with the directness and colour of the best narrative prose. The monodrama suffices for the lyrical emotion of Tennyson's *Maud*; but in Browning's *Martin Relf* you feel the constraint of a form which in his *Ring and the Book* entails repetition often intolerable.

Mr. Crane discovers his youth, Henry Fleming, in a phase of disillusion. It is some monotonous months since boyish "visions of broken-bladed glory" impelled him to enlist in the Northern Army towards the mddle of the American war. That impulse is admirably given:—"One night as he lay in bed, the winds had carried to him the clangouring of the church bells, as some enthusiast jerked the rope frantically to tell the twisted news of a great battle. This voice of the people rejoicing in the night had made him shiver in a prolonged ecstasy of excitement. Later he had gone down to his mother's room, and had spoken thus: 'Ma, I'm going to enlist.' 'Henry, don't you be a fool,' his mother had replied. She had then covered her face with the quilt. There was an end to the matter for that night." But the next morning he enlists. He is impatient of the homely injunctions given him in place of the heroic speech he expects in accordance with a tawdry convention, and so departs, with a "vague feeling of relief." But, looking back from the gate, he sees his mother "kneeling among the potato parings. Her brown face upraised and stained with tears, her spare form quivering." Since then the army has done "little but sit still and try to keep warm" till he has "grown to regard himself merely as a part of a vast blue demonstration." In the sick langour of this waiting, he begins to suspect his courage and lies awake by night through hours of morbid introspection. He tries "to prove to himself mathematically that he would not run from a battle"; he constantly leads the conversation round to the problem of courage in order to gauge the confidence of his messmates.

"How do you know you won't run when the time comes?" asked the youth. "Run?" said the loud one, "run?—of course not!" He laughed. "Well," continued the youth, "lots of good-a-'nough men have thought they were going to do great things before the fight, but when the time come they skedaddled." "Oh, that's all true, I s'pose," replied the other, "but I'm not going to skedaddle. The man that bets on my running will lose his money, that's all." He nodded confidently.

The youth is a "mental outcast" among his comrades, "wrestling with his personal problem," and sweating as he listens to the muttered scoring of a card game, his eyes fixed on the "red, shivering reflection of a fire." Every day they drill; every night they watch the red campfires of the enemy on the far shore of a river, eating their hearts out. At last they march:—"In the gloom before the break of the day their uniforms glowed a deep purple blue. From across the river the red eyes were still peering. In the eastern sky there was a yellow patch, like a rug laid for the feet of the coming sun; and against it, black and pattern-like, loomed the gigantic figure of the colonel on a gigantic horse." The book is full of such vivid impressions, half of sense and half of imagination:—The columns as they marched "were like two serpents crawling from the cavern of night." But the march, which, in his boyish imagination, should have led forthwith into melodramatic action is but the precursor of other marches. After days of weariness and nights of discomfort, at last, as in life, without preface, and in a lull of the mind's anxiety, the long-dreaded and long-expected is suddenly and smoothly in process of accomplishment:—"One grey morning he was kicked on the leg by the tall soldier, and then, before he was entirely awake, he found himself running down a wood road in the midst of men who were panting with the first effects of speed. His canteen banged rhythmically upon his thigh, and his haversack bobbed softly. His musket bounced a trifle from his shoulder at each stride and made his cap feel uncertain upon his head." From this moment, reached on the thirtieth page, the drama races through another hundred and sixty pages to the end of the book, and to read those pages is in itself an experience of breathless, lambent, detonating life. So brilliant and detached are the images evoked that, like illuminated bodies actually seen, they leave their fever-bright phantasms floating before the brain. You may shut the book, but you still see the battle-flags "jerked about madly in the smoke," or sinking with "dying gestures of despair," the men "dropping here and there like bundles"; the captain shot dead with "an astonished and sorrowful look as if he thought some friend had done him an ill-turn"; and the litter of corpses, "twisted in fantastic contortions," as if "they had fallen from some great height, dumped out upon the ground from the sky." The book is full of sensuous impressions that leap out from the picture: of gestures, attitudes, grimaces, that flash into portentous definition, like faces from the climbing clouds of nightmare. It leaves the imagination bounded with a "dense wall of smoke, furiously slit and slashed by the knife-like fire from the rifles." It leaves, in short, such indelible traces as are left by the actual experience of war. The picture shows grisly shadows and vermilion splashes, but, as in the vast drama it reflects so truly, these features, though insistent, are small in size, and are lost in the immensity of the theatre. The tranquil forest stands around; the "fairy-blue of the sky" is over it all. And, as in the actual experience of war, the impressions which these startling features inflict, though acute, are localised and not too deep: are as it were mere pin-pricks, or, at worst, clean cuts from a lancet in a body thrilled with currents of physical excitement and sopped with anaesthetics of emotion. Here is the author's description of a forlorn hope:—

As the regiment swung from its position out into a cleared space the woods and thickets before it awakened. Yellow flames leaped toward it from many directions. The line swung straight for a moment. Then the right wing swung forward; it in turn was surpassed by the left. Afterward the centre careered to the front until the regiment was a wedge-shaped mass . . . the men. pitching forward insanely, had burst into cheerings, mob-like and barbaric, but tuned in strange keys that can arouse the dullard and the stoic. . . . There was the delirium that encounters despair and death, and is heedless and blind to odds. . . . Presently the straining pace ate up the energies of the men. As if by agreement, the leaders began to slacken their speed. The volleys directed against them had a seeming wind-like effect. The regiment snorted and blew. Among some stolid trees it began to falter and hesitate. . . . The youth had a vague belief that he had run miles, and he thought, in a way, that he was now in some new and unknown land. . . .

The charge withers away, and the lieutenant, the youth, and his friend run forward to rally the regiment.

In front of the colours three men began to bawl, "Come on! Come on!" They danced and gyrated like tortured savages. The flag, obedient to these appeals, bended its glittering form and swept toward them. The men wavered in indecision for a moment, and then with a long wailful cry the dilapidated regiment surged forward and began its new journey. Over the field went the scurrying mass. It was a handful of men splattered into the faces of the enemy. Toward it instantly sprang the yellow tongues. A vast quantity of blue smoke hung before them. A mighty banging made ears valueless. The youth ran like a madman to reach the woods before a bullet could discover him. He ducked his head low, like a football player. In his haste his eyes almost closed, and the scene was a wild blur. Pulsating saliva stood at the corner of his mouth. Within him, as he hurled forward, was born a love, a despairing fondness for this flag that was near him. It was a creation of beauty and invulnerability. It was a goddess radiant, that bended its form with an imperious gesture to him. It was a woman, red and white, hating and loving. that called him with the voice of his hopes. Because no harm could come to it he endowed it with power. He kept near, as if it could be a saver of lives, and an imploring cry went from his mind.

This passage directly challenges comparison with Zola's scene, in which the lieutenant and the old tradition, of an invincible Frenchman over-running the world "between his bottle and his girl," expire together among the morsels of a bullet-eaten flag. Mr. Crane has probably read *la Débâcle*, and wittingly threw down his glove. One can only say that he is justified of his courage.

Mr. Crane's method, when dealing with things seen and heard, is akin to Zola's: he omits nothing and extenuates nothing, save the actual blasphemy and obscenity of a soldier's oaths. These he indicates, sufficiently for any purpose of art, by brief allusions to their vigour and variety. Even Zola has rarely surpassed the appalling realism of Jim Conklin's death in Chapter X. Indeed, there is little to criticise in Mr. Crane's observation, except an undue subordination of the shrill cry of bullets to the sharp crashing of rifles. He omits the long chromatic whine defining its invisible arc in the air, and the fretful snatch a few feet from the listener's head. In addition to this gift of observation, Mr. Crane has at command the imaginative phrase. The firing follows a retreat as with "yellings of eager metallic hounds"; the men at their mechanic loading and firing are like "fiends jigging heavily in the smoke"; in a lull before the attack "there passed slowly the intense moments that precede the tempst"; then, after single shots, "the battle roar settled to a rolling thunder, which was a single long explosion." And, as I have said, when Mr. Crane deals with things felt he gives a truer report than Zola. He postulates his hero's temperament—a day-dreamer given over to morbid self-analysis who enlists, not from any deep-seated belief in the holiness of fighting for his country, but in hasty pursuit of a vanishing ambition. This choice enables Mr. Crane to double his picturesque advantage with an ethical advantage equally great. Not only is his youth, like the sufferer in *The Fall of the House of Usher*, super-sensitive to every pin-prick of sensation: he is also a delicate meter of emotion and fancy. In such a nature the waves of feeling take exaggerated curves, and hallucination haunts the brain. Thus, when awaiting the first attack, his mind is thronged with vivid images of a circus he had seen as a boy: it is there in definite detail, even as the Apothecary's shop usurps Romeo's mind at the crisis of his fate. And thus also, like Herodotus' Aristodemus, he vacillates between cowardice and heroism. Nothing could well be more subtile than his self-deception and that sudden enlightenment which leads him to "throw aside his mental pamphlets on the philosophy of the retreated and rules for the guidance of the damned." His soul is that kind which, "sick with self-love," can only be saved "so as by fire"; and it is saved when the battlebond of brotherhood is born within it, and is found plainly of deeper import that the cause for which he and his comrades fight, even as that cause is loftier than his personal ambition. By his choice of a hero Mr. Crane displays in the same work a pageant of the senses and a tragedy of the soul.

But he does not obtrude his moral. The "tall soldier" and the lieutenant are brave and content throughout, the one by custom as a veteran, the other by constitution as a hero. But the two boys, the youth and his friend, "the loud soldier," are at first querulous braggarts, but at the last they are transmuted by danger until either might truly say:—

> We have proved we have hearts in a cause, we are noble still,
> And myself have awaked, as it seems, to the better mind;
> It is better to fight for the good than to rail at the ill;
> I have felt with my native land, I am one with my kind,
> I embrace the purpose of God, and the doom assigned.

Let no man cast a stone of contempt at these two lads during their earlier weakness until he has fully gauged the jarring discordance of battle. To be jostled on a platform when you have lost your luggage and missed your train on an errand of vital importance gives a truer pre-taste of war than any field-day; yet many a well-disciplined man will denounce the universe upon slighter provocation. It is enough that these two were boys and that they became men.

Yet must it be said that this youth's emotional experience was singular. In a battle there are a few physical cowards, abjects born with defective circulations, who literally turn blue at the approach of danger, and a few on whom danger acts like the keen, rare atmosphere of snow-clad peaks. But between these extremes come many to whom danger is as strong wine, with the multitude which gladly accepts the "iron laws of tradition" and finds welcome support in "a moving box." To this youth, as the cool dawn of his first day's fighting changed by infinitesimal gradations to a feverish noon, the whole evolution pointed to "a trap"; but I have seen another youth under like circumstances toss a pumpkin into the air and spit it on his sword. To this youth the very landscape was filled with "the stealthy approach of death." You are convinced by the author's art that it was so to this man. But to others, as the clamour increases, it is as if the serenity of the morning had taken refuge in their brains. This man "stumbles over the stones as he runs breathlessly forward"; another realises for the first time how right it is to be adroit even in running. The movement of his body becomes an art, which is not self-conscious, since its whole intention is to impress others within the limits of modest decroum. We know that both love and courage teach this mastery over the details of living. You can tell from the way one woman, out of all the myriads, walks down Piccadilly, that she is at last aware of love. And you can tell from the way a man enters a surgery or runs toward a firing-line that he, too, realises how wholly the justification of any one life lies in its perfect adjustment to others. The woman in love, the man in battle, may each say, for their moment, with the artist, "I was made perfect too." They also are the few to whom "God whispers in the ear."

But had Mr. Crane taken an average man he would have written an ordinary story, whereas he has written one which is certain to last. It is glorious to see his youth discover courage in the bed-rock of primeval antagonism after the collapse of his tinsel bravado; it is something higher to see him raise upon that rock the temple of resignation. Mr. Crane, as an artist, achieves by his singleness of purpose a truer and completer picture of war than either Tolstoï, bent also upon proving the insignificance of heroes, or Zola, bent also upon prophesying the regeneration of France. That is much; but it is more that his work of art, when completed, chimes with the universal experience of mankind; that his heroes find in their extreme danger, if not confidence in their leaders and conviction in their cause, at least the conviction that most men do what they can or, at most, what they must. We have few good accounts of battles—many of shipwrecks; and we know that, just as the storm rises, so does the commonplace captain show as a god, and the hysterical passenger as a cheerful heroine.

It is but a further step to recognise all life for a battle and this earth for a vessel lost in space. We may then infer that virtues easy in moments of distress may be useful also in everyday experience.

FRANK NORRIS
The Green Stone of Unrest†

A Mere Boy stood on a pile of blue stones.[1] His attitude was regardant. The day was seal brown. There was a vermillion valley containing a church. The church's steeple aspired strenuously in a direction tangent to the earth's center. A pale wind mentioned tremendous facts under its breath with certain effort at concealment to seven not-dwarfed poplars on an un-distant mauve hilltop.

The Mere Boy was a brilliant blue color. The effect of the scene was not un-kaleidoscopic.

After a certain appreciable duration of time the Mere Boy abandoned his regardant demeanor. The strenuously aspiring church steeple no longer projected itself upon his consciousness. He found means to remove himself from the pile of blue stones. He set his face valleyward. He proceeded.

The road was raw umber. There were in it wagon ruts. There were in it pebbles, Naples yellow in color. One was green. The Mere Boy allowed the idea of the green pebble to nick itself into the sharp edge of the disc of his Perception.

"Ah," he said, "a green pebble."

The rather pallid wind communicated another Incomprehensible Fact to the paranthine trees. It would appear that the poplars understood.

"Ah," repeated the Mere Boy, "a Green Pebble."

"Sho-o," remarked the wind.

The Mere Boy moved appreciably forward. If there were a thousand men in a procession and nine hundred and ninety-nine should suddenly expire, the one man who was remnant would assume the responsibility of the procession.

The Mere Boy was an abbreviated procession.

The blue Mere Boy transported himself diagonally athwart the larger landscape, printed in four colors, like a poster.

On the uplands were chequered squares made by fields, tilled and otherwise. Cloud-shadows moved from square to square. It was as if the Sky and Earth was playing a tremendous game of chess.

By and by the Mere Boy observed an Army of a Million Men. Certain cannon, like voluble but noncommittal toads with hunched backs, fulminated vast hiccoughs at unimpassioned intervals. Their own invulnerableness was offensive.

An officer of blue serge waved a sword, like a picture in a school

† From "Perverted Tales," San Francisco *Wave*, XVI (December 18, 1897), 5–7; text from *The Literary Criticism of Frank Norris*, ed. Donald Pizer (Austin: University of Texas Press, 1964), pp. 172–74.

1. The first sentence of this parody recalls the opening of *Maggie*, but the rest of the piece satirizes *The Red Badge of Courage*.

history. The non-committal toads pullulated with brief red pimples and swiftly relapsed to impassivity.

The line of the Army of a Million Men obnubilated itself in whiteness as a line of writing is blotted with a new blotter.

"Go teh blazes b'Jimminey," remarked the Mere Boy. "What yeh's shooting fur. They might be people in that field."

He was terrific in his denunciation of such negligence. He debated the question of his ir-removability.

"If I'm goin' teh be shot," he observed; "If I'm goin' teh be shot, b'Jimminy—"

A Thing lay in the little hollow.

The little hollow was green.

The Thing was pulpy white. Its eyes were white. It had blackish-yellow lips. It was beautifully spotted with red, like tomato stains on a rolled napkin.

The yellow sun was dropping on the green plain of the earth, like a twenty-dollar gold piece falling on the baize cloth of a gaming table.

The blue serge officer abruptly discovered the punctured Thing in the Hollow. He was struck with the ir-remediableness of the business.

"Gee," he murmured with interest. "Gee, it's a Mere Boy."

The Mere Boy had been struck with seventy-seven rifle bullets. Seventy had struck him in the chest, seven in the head. He bore close resemblance to the top of a pepper castor.

He was dead.

He was obsolete.

As the blue serge officer bent over him he became aware of a something in the Thing's hand.

It was a green pebble.

"Gee," exclaimed the blue serge officer. "A green pebble, gee."

The large Wind evolved a threnody with reference to the seven undistant poplars.

JOSEPH CONRAD

His War Book†

A Preface to Stephen Crane's *The Red Badge of Courage*

One of the most enduring memories of my literary life is the sensation produced by the appearance in 1895 of Crane's *Red Badge of Courage* in a small volume belonging to Mr. Heinemann's Pioneer

† From *Last Essays* (Garden City, N.Y.: Doubleday, Page, 1926), pp. 119–24.   Reprinted by permission of Withers, London.

Series of Modern Fiction—very modern fiction of that time, and upon the whole not devoid of merit. I have an idea the series was meant to give us shocks, and as far as my recollection goes there were, to use a term made familiar to all by another war, no "duds" in that small and lively bombardment. But Crane's work detonated on the mild din of that attack on our literary sensibilities with the impact and force of a twelve-inch shell charged with a very high explosive. Unexpected it fell amongst us; and its fall was followed by a great outcry.

Not of consternation, however. The energy of that projectile hurt nothing and no one (such was its good fortune), and delighted a good many. It delighted soldiers, men of letters, men in the street; it was welcomed by all lovers of personal expression as a genuine revelation, satisfying the curiosity of a world in which war and love have been subjects of song and story ever since the beginning of articulate speech.

Here we had an artist, a man not of experience but a man inspired, a seer with a gift for rendering the significant on the surface of things and with an incomparable insight into primitive emotions, who, in order to give us the image of war, had looked profoundly into his own breast. We welcomed him. As if the whole vocabulary of praise had been blown up sky-high by this missile from across the Atlantic, a rain of words descended on our heads, words well or ill chosen, chunks of pedantic praise and warm appreciation, clever words, and words of real understanding, platitudes, and felicities of criticism, but all as sincere in their response as the striking piece of work which set so many critical pens scurrying over the paper.

One of the most interesting, if not the most valuable, of printed criticisms was perhaps that of Mr. George Wyndham, soldier, man of the world, and in a sense a man of letters. He went into the whole question of war literature, at any rate during the nineteenth century, evoking comparisons with the *Mémoires of* General Marbot and the famous *Diary of a Cavalry Officer* as records of a personal experience. He rendered justice to the interest of what soldiers themselves could tell us, but confessed that to gratify the curiosity of the potential combatant who lurks in most men as to the picturesque aspects and emotional reactions of a battle we must go to the artist with his Heaven-given faculty of words at the service of his divination as to what the truth of things is and must be. He comes to the conclusion that;

"Mr. Crane has contrived a masterpiece."

"Contrived"—that word of disparaging sound is the last word I would have used in connection with any piece of work by Stephen Crane, who in his art (as indeed in his private life) was the least "contriving" of men. But as to "masterpiece," there is no doubt that *The Red Badge of Courage* is that, if only because of the marvellous accord of the vivid impressionistic description of action on that woodland battlefield, and the imaged style of the analysis of the emotions in the inward moral struggle going on in the breast of one individual—the Young Soldier of the book, the protagonist of the monodrama presented to us in an effortless succession of graphic and coloured phrases.

Stephen Crane places his Young Soldier in an untried regiment. And this is well contrived—if any contrivance there be in a spontaneous piece of work which seems to spurt and flow like a tapped stream from the depths of the writer's being. In order that the revelation should be complete, the Young Soldier has to be deprived of the moral support which he would have found in a tried body of men matured in achievement to the consciousness of its worth. His regiment had been tried by nothing but days of waiting for the order to move; so many days that it and the Youth within it have come to think of themselves as merely "a part of a vast blue demonstration." The army had been lying camped near a river, idle and fretting, till the moment when Stephen Crane lays hold of it at dawn with masterly simplicity: "The cold passed reluctantly from the earth. . . ." These are the first words of the war book which was to give him his crumb of fame.

The whole of that opening paragraph is wonderful in the homely dignity of the indicated lines of the landscape, and the shivering awakening of the army at the break of the day before the battle. In the next, with a most effective change to racy colloquialism of narrative, the action which motivates, sustains and feeds the inner drama forming the subject of the book, begins with the Tall Soldier going down to the river to wash his shirt. He returns waving his garment above his head. He had heard at fifth-hand from somebody that the army is going to move to-morrow. The only immediate effect of this piece of news is that a Negro teamster, who had been dancing a jig on a wooden box in a ring of laughing soldiers, finds himself suddenly deserted. He sits down mournfully. For the rest, the Tall Soldier's excitement is met by blank disbelief, profane grumbling, an invincible incredulity. But the regiment is somehow sobered. One feels it, though no symptoms can be noticed. It does not know what a battle is, neither does the Young Soldier. He retires from the babbling throng into what seems a rather comfortable dugout and lies down with his hands over his eyes to think. Thus the drama begins.

He perceives suddenly that he had looked upon wars as historical phenomenons of the past. He had never believed in war in his own country. It had been a sort of play affair. He had been drilled, inspected, marched for months, till he has despaired "of ever seeing a Greek-like struggle. Such were no more. Men were better or more timid. Secular and religious education had effaced the throat-grappling instinct, or else firm finance held in check the passions."

Very modern this touch. We can remember thoughts like these round about the year 1914. That Young Soldier is representative of mankind in more ways than one, and first of all in his ignorance. His regiment had listened to the tales of veterans, "tales of gray bewhisk-ered hordes chewing tobacco with unspeakable valour and sweep-ing along like the Huns." Still, he cannot put his faith in veterans' tales. Recruits were their prey. They talked of blood, fire, and sudden death, but much of it might have been lies. They were in no wise to be trusted. And the question arises before him whether he will or will not "run from a battle"? He does not know. He cannot know. A little panic fear enters his mind. He jumps up and asks himself aloud. "Good Lord, what's the matter with me?" This is the first time his words are quoted, on this day before the battle. He dreads not danger, but fear itself. He stands before the unknown. He would like to prove to himself by some reasoning process that he will not "run from the battle." And in his unblooded regiment he can find no help. He is alone with the prob-lem of courage.

In this he stands for the symbol of all untried men.

Some critics have estimated him a morbid case. I cannot agree to that. The abnormal cases are of the extremes; of those who crumple up at the first sight of danger, and of those of whom their fellows say "He doesn't know what fear is." Neither will I forget the rare favourites of the gods whose fiery spirit is only soothed by the fury and clamour of a battle. Of such was General Picton of Peninsular fame. But the lot of the mass of mankind is to know fear, the decent fear of disgrace. Of such is the Young Soldier of *The Red Badge of Courage*. He only seems exceptional because he has got inside of him Stephen Crane's imagination, and is presented to us with the insight and the power of expression of an artist whom a just and severe critic, on a review of all his work, has called the fore-most impressionist of his time; as Sterne was the greatest impres-sionist, but in a different way, of his age.

This is a generalized, fundamental judgment. More superficially both Zola's "La Débâcle" and Tolstoi's "War and Peace" were mentioned by critics in connection with Crane's war book. But Zola's main concern was with the downfall of the imperial régime he fancied he was portraying; and in Tolstoi's book the subtle pre-sentation of Rostov's squadron under fire for the first time is a mere episode lost in a mass of other matter, like a handful of pebbles in a heap of sand. I could not see the relevancy. Crane was concerned with elemental truth only; and in any case I think that as an artist he is non-comparable. He dealt with what is enduring, and was the most detached of men.

That is why his book is short. Not quite two hundred pages. Gems are small. The monodrama, which happy inspiration or unerring instinct has led him to put before us in narrative form, is contained between the opening words I have already quoted and a phrase on page 194 of the English edition, which runs: "He had been to touch the great death, and found that, after all, it was but the great death. He was a man."

On these words the action ends. We are only given one glimpse of the victorious army at dusk, under the falling rain, "a procession of weary soldiers became a bedraggled train, despondent and muttering, marching with churning effort in a trough of liquid brown mud under a low wretched sky . . .", while the last ray of the sun falls on the river through a break in the leaden clouds.

This war book, so virile and so full of gentle sympathy, in which not a single declamatory sentiment defaces the genuine verbal felicity, welding analysis and description in a continuous fascination of individual style, had been hailed by the critics as the herald of a brilliant career. Crane himself very seldom alluded to it, and always with a wistful smile. Perhaps he was conscious that, like the mortally wounded Tall Soldier of his book, who, snatching at the air, staggers out into a field to meet his appointed death on the first day of battle—while the terrified Youth and the kind Tattered Soldier stand by silent, watching with awe "these ceremonies at the place of meeting"—it was his fate, too, to fall early in the fray.

The Modern Critical Revival

R. W. STALLMAN

Stephen Crane: A Revaluation†

* * *

Crane's style has been likened to a unique instrument which no one after his death has ever been able to play. *The Red Badge of Courage* seems unprecedented and noncomparable. But Chekhov, who was almost of an age with Crane, and a little later Katherine Mansfield, who adopted the method of Chekhov, were both masters of the same instrument. In its episodic structure and impressionistic style Chekhov's *The Cherry Orchard* suggests a legitimate parallel to *The Red Badge of Courage*. All three artists had essentially the same literary aim and method: intensity of vision and objectivity in rendering it. All three aimed at a depersonalization of art: they aimed to get outside themselves completely in order "to find the greatest truth of the idea" and "see the thing as it really is"; to keep themselves aloof from their characters, not to become emotionally involved with their subjects, and to comment on them not by statement but by evocation picture and tone ("sentiment is the devil," said Crane, and in this he was echoing Flaubert).

Crane stands also in close kinship to Conrad and Henry James, the masters of the impressionist school. All these writers aimed to create (to use Henry James's phrase) "a direct impression of life." Their credo is voiced by Conrad in his celebrated Preface to *The Nigger of the "Narcissus"*—it is "by the power of the written word, to make you hear, to make you feel—it is, before all, to make you *see*." Their aim was to immerse the reader in the created experience, so that its impact on the reader would occur simultaneously with the discovery of it by the characters themselves. Instead of panoramic views of a battlefield, Crane paints not the whole scene but disconnected segments of it, which, accurately enough, is all

† From *Critiques and Essays on Modern Fiction, 1920–1951*, edited by John W. Aldridge (New York: Ronald Press, 1952), pp. 251–54, 262–69. Copyright 1952 The Ronald Press Company, New York. Reprinted by permission. From the Introduction, by R. W. Stallman, to the Modern Library Edition of *The Red Badge of Courage*. Copyright 1951 by Random House, Inc. Reprinted by permission. For major responses to Stallman's discussion of the Christian symbolism of *The Red Badge*, see the essays by Stanley Greenfield and Edwin Cady, below.

that a participant in an action or a spectator of a scene can possibly take into his view at any one moment. "None of them knew the colour of the sky"—that famous opening sentence of "The Open Boat"—defines the restricted point of view of the four men in the wave-tossed dinghy, their line of vision being shut off by the menacing walls of angry water. Busy at the oars, they knew the color of the sky only by the color of the sea and "they knew it was broad day because the colour of the sea changed from slate to emerald-green, streaked with amber lights, and the foam was like tumbling snow." Everything is keyed in a state of tension—even their speech, which is abrupt and composed of "disjointed sentences." Crane's style is iself composed of disjointed sentences, disconnected sense-impressions, chromatic vignettes by which the reality of the adventure is evoked in all its point-present immediacy.

Crane anticipated the French Post-Impressionist painters. *His style is*, in brief, *prose pointillism*. It is composed of disconnected images which, like the blobs of color in a French Impressionist painting, coalesce one with another, every word-group having a cross-reference relationship, every seemingly disconnected detail having interrelationship to the configurated pattern of the whole. The intensity of a Crane tale is due to this patterned coalescence of disconnected things, everything at once fluid and precise.

A striking analogy is established between Crane's use of colors and the method employed by the Impressonists and the Neo-Impressionists or Divisionists, and it is as if he had known about their theory of contrasts and composed his own prose painting by the same principle. It is the principle, as defined by the scientist Chevreul in his *Laws of Simultaneous Contrast*, that "Each plane of shade creates around itself a sort of aura of light, and each luminous plane creates around itself a zone of shade. In a similar way a coloured area communicates its 'complimentary' to the neighbouring colour, or heightens it if it is complimentary.' "[1] In almost every battle scene Crane paints in *The Red Badge of Courage*, the perspective is blurred by smoke or by the darkness of night. Here is one example of the former contrast, namely dark masses circled by light, and of the latter contrast, namely a luminous spot circled by darkness.

> The clouds were tinged an earthlike yellow in the sunrays and in the shadow were a sorry blue. The flag was sometimes eaten and lost in this mass of vapor, but more often it projected, suntouched, resplendent.

Crane's perspectives, almost without exception, are fashioned by contrasts—black masses juxtaposed against brightness, colored light

1. Cited in *Painting in France: 1895–1949*, by G. Di San Lazzaro (1949), p. 28, fnt.

set against gray mists. At dawn the army glows with a purple hue, and "In the eastern sky there was a yellow patch like a rug laid for the feet of the coming sun; and against it, *black and pattern-like*, loomed the gigantic figure of the colonel on a gigantic horse." Black is juxtaposed against yellow, or against red. Smoke wreathes around a square of white light and a path of yellow shade. Smoke dimly outlines a distance filled with *blue* uniforms, a *green* sward, and a *sapphire* sky. Further examples of color-contrast, particularly white *versus* black, occur throughout "The Open Boat," and blue is used symbolically in The Blue Hotel." Crane had an extraordinary predilection for blue, which Hamlin Garland took to be the sign manual of the Impressionists. It seems likely that Crane read Garland's *Crumbling Idols*, but in any case he wrote a novel about an impressionistic painter—the hero of *The Third Violet*. And in one of his sketches he wrote:

> The flash of the impression was like light, and for this instant it illumined all the dark recesses of one's remotest idea of sacrilege, ghastly and wanton. I bring this to you merely as *an effect of mental light and shade*, something done in thought, *similar to that which the French Impressionists do in color*, something meaningless and at the same time overwhelming, crushing, monstrous. (*The Work of Stephen Crane*, vol. IX, p. 246.)

Crane paints in words exactly as the French Impressionists paint in pigments: both use pure colors and contrasts of colors. Dark clouds or dark smoke or masses of mist and vapor are surrounded by a luminous zone; or *conversely*, specks of prismatic color are enclosed by a zone of shade. Shifting gray mists open out before the splendor of the sunrays. Or *conversely*, billowing smoke is "filled with horizontal flashes"; "the mist of smoke [is] gashed by the little knives of fire. . . " Inside the surrounding darkness the waters of the river appear wine-tinted, and campfires "shining upon the moving masses of troops, brought forth here and there sudden gleams of silver and gold. Upon the other shore a dark and mysterious range of hills was curved against the sky." Cleared atmospheres, unimpeded vision of perspective, are rarely delineated, and where they occur the precision of vision is equated, symbolically, with revelation or spiritual insight. Dark mists and vapors represent the haze of Henry's unenlightened mind ("He, the enlightened man who looks afar in the dark, had fled because of his superior perceptions and knowledge"). Darkness and smoke serve as symbols of concealment and deception, vapors masking the light of truth. Sunlight and changing colors signify spiritual insight and rebirth. Henry is a color-bearer, but it is not until he recognizes the truth of his self-deception that the youth keeps "the bright colors to the front." In the celebrated impression of the red sun "pasted in the sky like a wafer" Crane is at once an Impressionist painter and a symbolic artist. But more of that later. Meanwhile an important point about Crane's technique deserves mentioning in this brief discussion of Impressionism. The point is that Crane is a master craftsman in creating his illusions of reality by means of a fixed point of view, through a specifically located observer.

> *From their position* as they again faced toward the place of fighting, they could of course comprehend a greater amount of battle than when their visions had been blurred by the hurling smoke of the line. *They could see* dark stretches winding along the land, and on one cleared space there was a row of guns making *gray clouds, which were filled with large flashes of orange-colored flame.*

Crane presents his pictures from a fixed plane of vision, and his perspectives seem based upon the same principle of contrast as the Impressionists employed:—Darkness pierced by brilliant color (as in the above), or darkness tinged "with a phosphorescent glow."

* * *

V

That Crane is incapable of architectonics has been the critical consensus that has prevailed for over half a century; "his work is a mass of fragments"; "he can only string together a series of loosely cohering incidents"; *The Red Badge of Courage* is not constructed. Edward Garnett, the first English critic to appraise Crane's work, aptly pointed out that Crane lacks the great artist's arrangement of complex effects, which is certainly true. We look to Conrad and Henry James for "exquisite grouping of devices"; Crane's figure in the carpet is a much simpler one. What it consists of is the very thing Garnett failed to detect—a schemework of striking contrasts, alternations of contradictory moods. Crane once defined a novel as a "succession of . . . sharply-outlined pictures, which pass before the reader like a panorama, leaving each its definite impression." His own novel, nonetheless, is not simply a succession of pictures. It is a sustained structural whole. Every Crane critic concurs in this mistaken notion that *The Red Badge of Courage* is nothing more than "a series of episodic scenes," but not one critic has yet undertaken an analysis of Crane's work to see *how* the sequence of tableaux is constructed. Critical analysis of Crane's unique art is practically nonexistent. Probably no American author, unless it is Mark Twain, stands today in more imperative need of critical revaluation.

The Red Badge of Courage begins with the army immobilized— with restless men waiting for orders to move—and with Henry, because the army has done nothing, disillusioned by his first days as a recruit. In the first picture we get of Henry, he is lying on his army cot—resting on an idea. Or rather, he is wrestling with the personal problem it poses. The idea is a thirdhand rumor that tomorrow, at last, the army goes into action. When the tall soldier first announced it, he waved a shirt which he had just washed in a muddy brook, waved it in banner-like fashion to summon the men around the flag of his colorful rumor. It was a call to the colors—he shook it out and spread it about for the men to admire. But Jim Conklin's prophecy of hope meets with disbelief. "It's a lie!" shouts the loud soldier. "I don't believe the derned old army's ever going to move." No disciples rally around the red and gold flag of the herald. The skeptical soldiers think the tall soldier is telling just a tall tale; a furious altercation ensues. Meanwhile Henry in his hut engages in a spiritual debate with himself; whether to believe or disbelieve the word of his friend, whom he has known since childhood. It is the gospel truth, but Henry is one of the doubting apostles.

The opening scene thus sets going the structural pattern of the whole book. Hope and faith (paragraphs 1–3) shift to despair or disbelief (4–7). The counter-movement of opposition begins in paragraph 4, in the small detail of the Negro teamster who stops his dancing, when the men desert him to wrangle over Jim Conklin's rumor. "He sat mournfully down." This image of motion and change (the motion ceasing and the joy turning to gloom) presents the dominant leitmotiv and the form of the whole book in miniature. (Another striking instance of emblematic form occurs in Chapter VI, where Crane pictures a terror-stricken lad who throws down his gun and runs: "A lad whose face had borne an expression of exalted courage, the majesty of he who dares give his life, was, at an instant, smitten abject.") In Chapter I the opening prologue ends in a coda (paragraph 7) with theme and anti-theme here interjoined. It is the picture of the corporal—his uncertainties (whether to repair his house) and his shifting attitudes of trust and distrust (whether the army is going to move) parallel the skeptical outlook of the wrangling men. The same anti-theme of distrust is dramatized in the episode which follows this coda, and every subsequent episode in the sequence is designed similarly by one contrast pattern or another.

Change and motion begin the book. The army, which lies resting upon the hills, is first revealed to us by "the retiring fogs," and as the weather changes so the landscape changes, the brown hills turning into a new green. Now as nature stirs so the army stirs too. Nature and man are in psychic affinity; even the weather changes as though in sympathetic accord with man's plight. In the final scene it is raining but the leaden rain clouds shine with "a golden ray" as though to reflect Henry's own bright serenity, his own tranquillity of mind. But now at the beginning, and throughout the book, Henry's mind is in a "tumult of agony and despair." This psychological tumult began when Henry heard the church bell announce the gospel truth that a great battle had been fought. Noise begins the whole mental melee. The clanging church bell and then the noise of rumors disorder his mind by stirring up legendary visions of heroic selfhood. The noisy world that first colored his mind with myths now clamors to Henry to become absorbed into the solidarity of self-forgetful comradeship, but Henry resists this challenge of the "mysterious fraternity born of the smoke and danger of death," and withdraws again and again from the din of the affray to indulge in self-contemplative moods and magic reveries. The walls of the forest insulate him from the noise of battle. In seeking retreat there to absolve his shame and guilt, Henry, renouncing manhood, is "seeking dark and intricate places." It is as though he were seeking return to the womb. Nature, that "woman with a deep aversion to tragedy," is Mother Nature, and the human equation for the forest is of course Henry's own mother. Henry's flight from the forest-sanctuary represents his momentary rejection of womb-like innocence; periodically he rejects Mother Nature with her sheltering arms and her "religion of peace," and his flight from Mother Nature is symbolic of his initiation into the truth of the world he must measure up to. He is the deceived youth, for death lurks even in the forest-sanctuary. In the pond a gleaming fish is killed by one of the forest creatures, and in the forest Henry meets a rotted corpse, a man whose eyes stare like a dead fish, with ants scurrying over the face. The treachery of this forest retreat, where nothing is as it seems, symbolizes the treachery of ideals—the illusions by which we are all betrayed.

Henry's mind is in constant flux. Henry's self-combat is symbolized by the conflict among the men and between the armies, their altercation being a duplication of his own. Like the regiment that marches and countermarches over the same ground, so Henry's mind traverses the same ideas over and over again. As the cheery-voiced soldier says about the battle, "It's th' most mixed up dern thing I ever see." Mental commotion, confusion, and change are externalized in the "mighty altercation" of men and guns and nature herself. Everything becomes activated, even the dead. That corpse Henry meets on the battlefield, "the *invulnerable* dead man," cannot stay still—he "*forced* a way for himself" through the ranks. And guns throb too, "restless guns." Back and forth the stage-scenery shifts from dreams to "jolted dreams" and grim fact. Henry's illusions collapse, dreams pinpricked by reality.

Throughout the whole book *withdrawals* alternate with *engage-*

ments, with scenes of entanglement and tumult, but the same nightmarish atmosphere of upheaval and disorder pervades both the inner and the outer realms. The paradox is that when Henry becomes activated in the "vast blue demonstration" and is thereby reduced to anonymity he is then most a man, and conversely, when he affects self-dramatizing picture-postcard poses of himself as hero he is then least a man and not at all heroic. He is then innocent as a child. When disengaged from the external tumult, Henry's mind recollects former domestic scenes. Pictures of childhood and nursery imagery of babes recur at almost every interval of withdrawal. Childhood innocence and withdrawal are thus equated. The nursery limerick which the wounded soldiers sing as they retreat from the battlefront is at once a travesty of their own plight and a mockery of Henry's mythical innocence.

> Sing a song 'a vic'try
> A pocketful 'a bullets,
> Five an' twenty dead men
> Baked in a—pie.

Everything goes awry; nothing turns out as Henry had expected. Battles turn out to be "an immense and terrible machine to him" (the awful machinery of his own mind). At his battle task Henry, we are told, "was like a carpenter who has made many boxes, making still another box, only there was furious haste in his movements." Henry, "frustrated by hateful circumstances," pictures himself as boxed in by fate, by the regiment, and by the "iron laws of tradition and law on four sides. He was in a moving box." And furthermore there are those purely theoretical boxes by which he is shut in from reality—his romantic dreams, legendary visions of heroic selfhood, illusions which the vainglorious machinery of his own mind has manufactured.

The youth who had envisioned himself in Homeric poses, the legendary hero of a Greeklike struggle, has his pretty illusion shattered as soon as he announces his enlistment to his mother. "I've knet yeh eight pair of socks, Henry. . . ." His mother is busy peeling potatoes, and, madonna-like, she kneels among the parings. They are the scraps of his romantic dreams. The youthful private imagines armies to be monsters, "redoubtable dragons," but then he sees the real thing—the colonel who strokes his mustache and shouts over his shoulder, "Don't forget that box of cigars!"

The Red Badge of Courage probes a state of mind under the incessant pinpricks and bombardments of life. The theme is that man's salvation lies in change, in spiritual growth. It is only by immersion in the flux of experience that man becomes disciplined and develops in character, conscience, or soul. Potentialities for change are at their greatest in battle—a battle represents life at its most intense flux. Crane's book is not about the combat of armies; it is about the self-combat of a youth who fears and stubbornly resists change, and the actual battle is symbolic of this spiritual warfare against change and growth. To say that the book is a study in fear is as shallow an interpretation as to say that it is a narrative of the Civil War. It is the standard reading of all Crane's writings, the reading of fear into everything he wrote, and for this misleading diagnosis Thomas Beer's biography of 1923 is almost solely responsible.[2] It is this Handbook of Fear that accounts for the neglect of all critics to attempt any other reading. Beer's thesis is that all the works from the first story to the last dissect fear and that *as* they deal exclusively with fear *so* fear was the motivating passion of Crane's life. "That newspaper feller was a nervy man," said the cook of the ill-fated *Commodore*. "*He didn't seem to know what fear was.*" Yet in his art there is fear, little more than that, and in "The Blue Hotel"—so the *Literary History of the United States* tells us—the premonition of the Swede is nothing "but the manifestation of Crane's own intense fear." This equation of Crane's works with his life, however seemingly plausible, is critically fallacious, and the resultant reading is a grossly oversimplified one. Fear is only one of the many passions that comprise *The Red Badge of Courage*; they include not alone fear but rage, elation, and the equally telltale passions of pride and shame. What was Crane afraid of? If Crane was at all afraid, he was afraid of time and change. Throughout Crane's works, as in his life, there is the conflict between ideals and reality.

Our critical concern is with the plight of his hero: Henry Fleming recognizes the necessity for change and development, but he wars against it. The youth develops into the veteran—"*So it came to pass . . . his soul changed.*" Significantly enough, in thus stating what his book is about Crane intones Biblical phrasing.

Spiritual change, *that* is Henry Fleming's red badge. *His red badge is his conscience reborn and purified.* Whereas Jim Conklin's red badge of courage is the literal one, the wound of which he dies, Henry's is the psychological badge, the wound of conscience. Internal wounds are more painful than external ones. It is fitting that Henry should receive a head wound, a bump that jolts him with a severe headache! But what "salve" is there to ease the pain of his internal wound of dishonor? This is Henry's "headache"! It is the ache of his conscience that he has been honored by the regiment he has dishonored. Just as Jim runs into the fields to hide his true

2. "Let it be stated," says Beer, "that the mistress of this boy's mind was fear. His search in aesthetic was governed by terror as that of tamer men is governed by the desire of women." A very pretty analogy!

wound from Henry, so Henry runs into the fields to hide his false wound, his false badge of courage, from the tattered man who asks him where he is wounded. "It might be inside mostly, an' them plays thunder. Where is it located?" The men, so Henry feels, are perpetually probing his guilt-wound, "ever upraising the ghost of shame on the stick of their curiosity." The unmistakable implication here is of a flag, and the actual flag which Henry carries in battle is the symbol of his conscience. Conscience is also symbolized by the forest, the cathedral-forest where Henry retreats to nurse his guilt-wound and be consoled by the benedictions which nature sympathetically bestows upon him. Here in this forest-chapel there is a churchlike silence as insects "bow their beaks" while Henry bows his head in shame; they make a "devotional pause" while the trees chant a soft hymn to comfort him. But Henry is troubled; he cannot "conciliate the forest." Nor can he conciliate the flag. The flag registers the commotion of his mind, and it registers the restless movements of the nervous regiment—it flutters when the men expect battle. And when the regiment runs from the battle, the flag sinks down "as if dying. Its motion as it fell was a gesture of despair." Henry dishonors the flag not when he flees from battle but when he flees from himself, and he redeems it when he redeems his conscience.[3]

Redemption begins in confession, in absolution—in change of heart. Henry's wounded conscience is not healed until he confesses to himself the truth and opens his eyes to new ways; not until he strips his enemy heart of "the brass and bombast of his earlier gospels," the vainglorious illusions he had fabricated into a cloak of pride and self-vindication; not until he puts on new garments of humility and loving kindness for his fellow-men. Redemption begins in humility—Henry's example is the loud soldier who becomes the humble soldier. The loud soldier admits the folly of his former ways. Henry's spiritual change is a prolonged process, but it is signalized in moments when he loses his soul in the flux of things; *then* he courageously deserts himself instead of his fellow-men; then fearlessly plunging into battle, charging the enemy like "a pagan who defends his religion," he becomes swept up in a delirium of selflessness and feels himself "capable of profound sacrifices." The brave new Henry, "new bearer of the colors," triumphs over the former one. The enemy flag is wrenched from the hands of "the

3. Henry's plight is identical with the Reverend Dimmesdale's plight in Hawthorne's psychological novel, *The Scarlet Letter*, with which *The Red Badge of Courage* has bondship by the similitude of the theme of redemption through self-confession and, even more strikingly, by the symbol of the forest to signify conscience. The mythology of the scarlet letter is much the same as the mythology of the red badge: each is the emblem of moral guilt and salvation. The red badge is the scarlet letter of dishonor transferred from the bosom of Hester, the social outcast, to the mind of Henry Fleming, the "mental outcast."

rival color bearer," the symbol of Henry's own other self, and as this rival color bearer dies Henry is reborn.

Henry's regeneration is brought about by the death of Jim Conklin, the friend whom Henry had known since childhood. He goes under various names. He is sometimes called the spectral soldier (his face is a pasty gray) and sometimes the tall soldier (he is taller than all other men), but there are unmistakable hints—in such descriptive details about him as his wound in the side, his torn body and his gory hand, and even in the initials of his name, Jim Conklin—that he is intended to represent Jesus Christ. We are told that there is "a resemblance in him to a devotee of a mad religion," and among his followers the doomed man stirs up "thoughts of a solemn ceremony." When he dies, the heavens signify his death— the red sun bleeds with the passion of his wounds:

The red sun was pasted in the sky like a wafer.

This grotesque image, the most notorious metaphor in American literature, has been much debated and roundly damned by Crane's critics (e.g., Pattee, Quinn, Cargill, and a dozen others) as downright bad writing, a false, melodramatic and nonfunctional figure. Joseph Hergesheimer, Willa Cather, and Conrad admired it, but no one ventured to explain it. The other camp took potshots at it without attempting to understand what it is really all about. It is, in fact, the key to the symbolism of the whole novel, particularly the religious symbolism which radiates outwards from Jim Conklin. Like any image, it has to be related to the structure of meaning in which it functions; when lifted out of its context is bound to seem artificial and irrelevant or, on the other hand, merely "a superb piece of imagery." I do not think it can be doubted that Crane intended to suggest here the sacrificial death celebrated in communion.

Henry and the tattered soldier consecrate the death of the spectral soldier in "a solemn ceremony." Henry partakes of the sacramental blood and body of Christ, and the process of his spiritual rebirth begins at this moment when the wafer-like sun appears in the sky. It is a symbol of salvation through death. Henry, we are made to feel, recognizes in the lifeless sun his own lifeless conscience, his dead and as yet unregenerated selfhood or conscience, and that is why he blasphemes against it. His moral salvation and triumph are prepared for (1) by this ritual of purification and religious devotion and, at the very start of the book (2), by the ritual of absolution which Jim Conklin performs in the opening scene. It was the tall soldier who first "developed virtues" and showed the boys how to cleanse a flag. The way is to wash it in the muddy river. Only by experiencing life, the muddy river, can the soul be cleansed. In "The Open Boat" it is the black sea, and the whiteness of the waves as they pace to and fro in the moonlight, signifies the spiritual purification which the men win from their contest against the terrible water. The ritual of domestic comforts bestowed upon the saved men by the people on the shore, "all the remedies sacred to their minds," is a shallow thing, devoid of spiritual value. The sea offers the only true remedy, though it costs a "terrible grace." The way is to immerse oneself in the destructive element!

Kurtz, in Conrad's "Heart of Darkness," washed his soul in the Congo, and Marlow, because he had become a part of Kurtz, redeemed the heart of darkness by the same token. Conrad, like Crane, had himself experienced his own theme, but Crane was the first to produce a work based upon it. Crane's influence on Conrad is apparent in *Lord Jim*, which makes use of the same religious symbolism as *The Red Badge of Courage*. When Lord Jim goes to his death, you recall, there is an awful sunset. Conrad's "enormous sun" was suggested by Crane's grotesque symbol and paradox image of the red sun that was pasted wafer-like in the sky when Jim Conklin died. For the other Jim, "The sky over Patusan was blood-red, immense, streaming like an open vein."

Like Flaubert and James and Conrad, Crane is a great stylist. Theme and style in *The Red Badge* and in "The Open Boat" are organically conceived, the theme of change conjoined with the fluid style by which it is evoked. The deliberately disconnected and apparently disordered style is calculated to create confused impressions of change and motion. Fluidity characterizes the whole book. Crane interjects disjointed details, one nonsequitur melting into another. Scenes and objects are felt as blurred, they appear under a haze or vapor or cloud. Yet everything has relationship and is manipulated into contrapuntal patterns of color and cross-references of meaning.

Like Conrad, Crane puts language to poetic uses, which, to define it, is to use language reflexively and to use language symbolically. It is the works which employ this reflexive and symbolic use of language that constitute what is permanent of Crane.

It is the language of symbol and paradox: the wafer-like sun, in *The Red Badge*; or in "The Open Boat" the paradox of "cold, comfortable sea-water," an image which calls to mind the poetry of W. B. Yeats with its fusion of contradictory emotions. This single image evokes the sensation of the whole experience of the men in the dinghy, but it suggests furthermore another telltale significance, one that is applicable to Stephen Crane. What is readily recognizable in this paradox of "cold, comfortable sea-water" is that irony of opposites which constituted the personality of the man who wrote it. It is the subjective correlative of his own plight. The enigma of the man is symbolized in his enigmatic style.

JOHN E. HART

The Red Badge of Courage as Myth and Symbol†

When Stephen Crane published *The Red Badge of Courage* in 1895, the book created an almost immediate sensation. Crane had had no experience in war, but in portraying the reactions of a young soldier in battle, he had written with amazing accuracy. As one way of re-examining *The Red Badge of Courage*, we would want to read it as myth and symbolic action. Clearly, the construction of the story, its moral and meaning, its reliance on symbol follow in detail the traditional formula of myth.[1] Crane's main theme is the discovery of self, that unconscious self, which, when identified with the inexhaustible energies of the group, enables man to understand the "deep forces that have shaped man's destiny."[2] The progressive movement of the hero, as in all myth, is that of separation, initiation, and return.[3] Within this general framework, Crane plots his story with individual variation. Henry Fleming, a Youth, ventures forth from his known environment into a region of naturalistic, if not super-naturalistic wonder; he encounters the monstrous forces of war and death; he is transformed through a series of rites and revelations into a hero; he returns to identify this new self with the deeper communal forces of the group and to bestow the blessings of his findings on his fellow comrades.

Whatever its "realistic" style, much of the novel's meaning is revealed through the use of metaphor and symbol. The names of characters, for example, suggest both particular attributes and general qualities: the Tall Soldier, whose courage and confidence enable him to measure up to the vicissitudes of war and life; the Loud Soldier, the braggart, the over-confident, whose personality is, like Henry's, transformed in war; the Tattered Soldier, whose clothes signify his lowly and exhausted plight; the Cheery Man, whose keenness and valor prevent his falling into despair. Likewise, the use of color helps to clarify and extend the meaning. Red, traditionally associated with blood and fire, suggests courage, flag, life-energy, desire, ambition. Black, traditionally associated with death, implies "great unknown," darkness, forests, and, by extension, entombment and psychological death. The whole paraphernalia of myth-religious and sacrificial rites—the ceremonial dancing, the dragons with fiery eyes, the menacing landscape, the entombment, the sudden appearance of a guide, those symbols so profoundly

† *University of Kansas City Review*, XIX (Summer, 1953), 249–56. By permission of the author and the *University of Kansas City Review*.
1. See Joseph Campbell, *The Hero with a Thousand Faces* (New York, 1949), p. 3. Campbell defines myth as "the secret opening through which the inexhaustible energies of the cosmos pour into human cultural manifestation."
2. *Ibid.*, p. 256.
3. *Ibid.*, p. 30.

familiar to the unconscious and so frightening to the conscious personality—give new dimensions of meaning to the novel.

What prompts Henry to leave his known environment is his unconscious longing to become a hero. In a state of conscious reflection, he looks on war with distrust. Battles belonged to the past. Had not "secular and religious education" effaced the "throat grappling instinct" and "firm finance" "held in check the passions"? But in dreams, he has thrilled to the "sweep and fire" of "vague and bloody conflicts"; he has "imagined people secure in the shadow of his eagle-eyed prowess." As the wind brings the noise of the ringing church bells, he listens to their summons as a proclamation from the "voice of the people." Shivering in his bed in a "prolonged ecstasy of excitement," he determines to enlist. If the call has come in an unconscious dream-like state where the associations of wind, church bells, ecstasy, heroism, glory are identified with the "voice" of the "group," Henry, fully "awake," insists on his decision. Although his mother, motivated apparently by "deep conviction" and impregnable ethical motives, tries to dissuade his ardor, she actually helps him in the initial step of his journey. She prepares his equipment: "eight pairs of socks," "yer best shirts," "a cup of blackberry jam." She advises him to watch the company he keeps and to do as he is told. Underlining the very nature of the problem, she warns that he will be "jest one little fellow amongst a hull lot of others."

It is this conflict between unconscious desire and conscious fear that prevents Henry from coming to terms with his new environments. Consciously concerned with thoughts of rumored battle, he crawls into his hut "through an intricate hole that served it as a door," where he can be "alone with some new thoughts that had lately come to him." Although his apparent concern is over fear of battle, his real anxiety is that of his individuation. As far as his relationship to war is concerned, he knows "nothing of himself." He has always "taken certain things for granted, never challenging his belief in ultimate success, and bothering little about means and roads." Now, he is an "unknown quantity." If his problems merge into that of whether he will or will not run from an "environment" that threatens to "swallow" his very identity, he sees that it cannot be solved by "mental slate and pencil." Action—"blaze, blood, and danger"—is the only test.

In giving artistic conception to Henry's conflict, Crane relies on a pattern of darkness and light, but adapts such traditional machinery to his particular purpose. As we have seen, Henry achieves courage and strength in the "darkness" of his tent, where his unconscious mind faces the problems of his new surroundings openly and bravely. As he peers into the "ominous distance" and ponders "upon the mystic gloom" in the morning twilight, he is eager to settle his "great problem" with the "red eyes across the river"—eyes like "orbs of a row of dragons advancing." Coming from the darkness towards the dawn, he watches "the gigantic figure of the colonel on a gigantic horse." They loom "black and pattern like" against the yellow sky. As the "black rider," the messenger of death lifts "his gigantic arm and calmly stroke[s] his mustache," Henry can hardly breathe. Then, with the hazy light of day, he feels the consciousness of growing fear. It seems ironic that his comrades, especially the Tall Soldier, should be filled with ardor, even song— just as he was in the darkness of his room at home. With the "developing day," the "two long, thin, black columns" have become "two serpents crawling from the cavern of night." These columns, monsters themselves, move from darkness to light with little fear, for they move, not as so many individuals, but as group units. Clearly, if Henry is to achieve his ambitions, he must "see" and "face" the enemy in the light of day without fear, as well as "perceive" his relationship to the group, which is, in a sense, a "monster" itself.

Henry's growing concern is not for his comrades, but for himself. Although he must march along with them, he feels caught "by the iron laws of tradition." He considers himself "separated from the others." At night, when the campfires dot the landscape "like red peculiar blossoms (as communal fires which impregnate the landscape with "life" and "vitality," they suggest the life energy of the group), Henry remains a "few paces in the gloom," a "mental outcast." He is "alone in space," where only the "mood of darkness" seems to sympathize with him. He concludes that no other person is "wrestling with such a terrific personal problem." But even in the darkness of his tent he cannot escape: the "red, shivering reflection of a fire" shines through the canvas. He sees "visions of a thousand-tongued fear that would babble at his back and cause him to flee." His "fine mind" can no more face the monster war than it can cope with the "brute minds" of his comrades.

Next day as Henry, with sudden "impulse of curiosity," stares at the "woven red" against the "soft greens and browns," the harmony of landscape is broken when the line of men stumble onto a dead soldier in their path. Henry pauses and tries to "read in the dead eyes the answer to the Question." What irony it is that the ranks open "to avoid the corpse," as if, invulnerable, death forces a way itself. He notes that the wind strokes the dead man's beard, just as the black rider had stroked his mustache. Probing his sensations, he feels no ardor for battle. His soldier's clothes do not fit, for he is not a "real" soldier. His "fine mind" enables him to see what the "brute minds" of his comrades do not: the landscape threatens to engulf them. Their ardor is not heroism. They are merely going to a sacrifice, going "to look at war, the red animal—war the blood-swollen god." Even if he warned them, they would not listen. Misunderstood, he can only "look to the grave for comprehension." His feeling is prophetic, for it anticipates the death and transformation of personality that is about to occur.

Before he actually runs from battle, Henry experiences a moment of true realization. Impatient to know whether he is a "man of traditional courage," he suddenly loses "concern for himself," and becomes "not a man but a member." "Welded into a common personality" and "dominated by a single desire," he feels the "red rage" and "battle brotherhood"—that "mysterious fraternity born of the smoke and danger of death." He is carried along in a kind of "battle sleep." He rushes at the "black phantoms" like a "pestered animal." Then, awakening to the awareness of a second attack, he feels weak and bloodless. "Like the man who lost his legs at the approach of the red and green monster," he seems "to shut his eyes and wait to be gobbled." He has a revelation. Throwing down his gun, he flees like a "blind man." His vision of "selflessness" disappears; in this "blindness" his fears are magnified. "Death about to thrust him between the shoulder blades [is] far more dreadful than death about to smite him between the eyes." Impotent and blind (without gun and "vision"), he runs into the forest "as if resolved to bury himself." He is both physically and psychologically isolated from the group and hence from the very source of food and energy, both material and spiritual, that impels heroic achievement.

In the language of myth Henry's inability to face the monsters of battle in the "light," to identify himself with his comrades (both acts are, in a sense, identical), and thus to give up his individual self, which is sustained only in "darkness" and in isolation, so that his full self can be realized in the light of communal identification symbolize a loss of spirital, moral, and physical power, which only a rebirth of identity can solve. Only by being reborn can he come to understand that man's courage springs from the self-realization that he must participate harmoniously as a member of the group. Only then can he understand the "deep forces" from which his individual energy and vitality spring. Thus, Henry's entombment in the forest is only preliminary to the resurrection that will follow. Without his full powers, his transformation cannot be effected by himself, but requires the necessity of ritualistic lessons and the aid of outside forces or agents. His own attempts to expiate his feeling of guilt by logic only leave him lost and confused in the labyrinth of his limitations.

After the burial of himself in the forest, it is his unconscious awareness of the nature of death that restores the strength and energy he had felt in his dreams at home. As he pushes on, going from "obscurity into promises of a greater obscurity," he comes face to face with the very "act" from which he is running. It is a dead soldier covered with "black" ants. As he recoils in terror, the branches of the forest hold him firm. In a moment of blind fear, he imagines that "some strange voice . . . from the dead throat" will squawk after him in "horrible menaces," but he hears, almost unconsciously, only a soft wind, which sings a "hymn of twilight." This aura of tranquility, produced in a "religious half light"—the boughs are arched like a chapel—transfixes Henry. He hears a "terrific medley of all noises." It is ironic that he should be fleeing from the black rider only to encounter death and "black ants." His ego is deflated. Did he ever imagine that he and his comrades could decide the war as if they were "cutting the letters of their names deep into everlasting tablets of brass?" Actually, the "affair" would receive only a "meek and immaterial title." With this thought and the song of the wind comes a certain faith. "Pictures of stupendous conflicts" pass through his mind. As he hears the "red cheers" of marching men, he is determined: he runs in the direction of the "crimson roar" of battle.

Although Henry's old fears have not been completely overcome, his meeting with the Tattered Man clarifies the need and method of atoning for his guilt. Having joined the marching soldiers, Henry is envious of this mob of "bleeding men." He walks beside the twice-wounded Tattered Man, whose face is "suffused with a light of love for the army which [is] to him all things beautiful and powerful." Moving in the "light of love," the Man speaks in a voice as "gentle as a girl's." "Where yeh hit?" he repeatedly asks Henry. "Letters of guilt" burn on the Youth's brow. How can he defend himself against an agency which so pitilessly reveals man's secrets? How can he atone for his guilt? His wish that "he, too, had a wound, a red badge of courage" is only preliminary to the fulfillment of atonement, just as in the rites of some primitive tribes or as in Christ's crucifixion on the cross, "blood" plays an essential part in the act of atonement and in the process of transformation.

If the Tattered Man's questioning reveals the need and nature of atonement, meeting the Tall Soldier shows the quality of character needed to make the sacrifice. Justifying the "tall" of his name by his "supreme unconcern" for battle, Conklin accepts his role as part of the group with coolness and humility. Because he realizes the insignificance of self, he has no fear of a threatening landscape. Sleeping, eating, and drinking afford him greatest satisfaction. During meal time, he is "quiet and contented," as if his spirit were "communing with viands." Now, fatally wounded, he is at his rendezvous with death; his actions are ceremonial, "rite-like." He moves with "mysterious purpose," like "the devotee of a mad religion, blood-sucking, muscle-wrenching, bone-crushing." His chest heaves "as if an animal was within," his "arms beat wildly," "his tall figure [stretches] itself to its full height" and falls to the ground—dead. His side looks "as if it had been chewed by wolves," as if the monster war had eaten him and then swallowed his life. This "ceremony at the place of meeting," this sacrificial ritual of placating the monster has enabled him to find the ultimate answer to the Question, but it has consumed its victim in the process.

It is the receiving of the wound, a kind of "magic" touch, whatever its irony of being false, that actually enables Henry to effect atonement. As the army itself retreats, he is truly "at one" with the group ("at one" and atone have similar functions as the very words imply), for both are running from battle. Actually, Henry is not "conscious" of what has happened. Clutching boldly at a retreating man's arm, he begs for an answer. Desperate at being restrained, the man strikes the Youth with his rifle. Henry falls. His legs seem "to die." In a ritual not unlike that of Conklin's dying (it is Henry's "youth," his immature self dying), he grabs at the grass, he twists and lurches, he fights "an intense battle with his body." Then, he goes "tall soldier fashion." In his exaltation, he is afraid to touch his head lest he distrub his "red badge of courage." He relishes "the cool, liquid feeling," which evokes the memory of "certain meals his mother had cooked," "the bank of a shaded pool," "the melody in the wind of youthful summer." The association of blood with that of food suggests the identical function of each. Just as food is nourishment to the body, so blood is nourishment to his spiritual and moral self. Because the monster has "eaten" of him and thus destroyed his fears, he has achieved a moral and spiritual maturity, even, as his going "tall" implies, sexual potency. He feels the tranquility and harmony that has always characterized his dream state. But his wound is an actual fact, and the achieved atonement is not quite the same as in a "pure" dream state. Yet it is still achieved under the aegis of "dusk," and can only be fully realized in the full "light" of group identification.

Henry is further assisted in his transformation by an "unseen guide." Wandering in the darkness, he is overtaken by the Cheery Man, whose voice, possessing a "wand of a magic kind," guides him to his regiment. Thinking of him later, Henry recalls that "he had not once seen his face."

It is important to note here what part food and eating play in Henry's atonement and rebirth. As we have seen, food has both physical and spiritual significance. From the first, Henry has observed that "eating" was of greatest importance to the soldiers. After the Tall Soldier's death, he has speculated on "what those men had eaten that they could be in such haste to force their way to grim chances of death." Now, he discovers that he has "a scorching thirst," a hunger that is "more powerful than a direct hunger." He is desperately tired. He cannot see distinctly. He feels the need "of food and rest, at whatever cost." On seeing his comrades again, he goes directly towards the "red light"—symbol of group energy. They fuss over his wound and give him a canteen of coffee. As he swallows the "delicious draught," the mixture feels as cool to him as did the wound. He feels like an "exhausted soldier after a feast of war." He has tasted of and been eaten by the great monster. By the wound (the being eaten), he has atoned for his guilt with blood. In eating and drinking with his comrades (the communal feasting), he has achieved both literal and spiritual identification with the group. Through his initiation, he has returned as a "member," not an isolated individual. By "swallowing or being swallowed," he has, through atonement and rebirth, come to be master of himself and, henceforth, to be master of others. The Loud Soldier gives up his blankets, and Henry is, in sleep, soon "like his comrades."

In the language of myth, Henry has become a hero. When he awakes next morning from a "thousand years' " sleep, he finds, like Rip Van Winkle, a new "unexpected world." What he discovers has happened to the Loud Soldier is actually the same change that has come over him. For the first time, Henry is aware that others have been wrestling with problems not unlike his own. If the Loud Soldier is now a man of reliance, a man of "purpose and abilities," Henry perceives in imagery that recalls the "blossoming campfires" of his comrades that

> a faith in himself had secretly blossomed. There was a little flower of confidence growing within him. He was a man of experience.

Again like the Loud Soldier, he has at last

> overcome obstacles which he admitted to be mountainous. They had fallen like paper peaks, and he was now what he called a hero. He had not been aware of the process. He had slept and, awakening, found himself a knight.

Having overcome the obstacle of self, Henry has at last discovered that the dragon war is, after all, only a gigantic guard of the great death.

If the hero is to fulfill the total requirements of his role, he must bring back into the normal world of day the wisdom that he has acquired during his transformation. Like the "knight" that he is, Henry is now able to face the red and black dragons on the "clear" field of battle. He performs like a "pagan who defends his religion," a "barbarian," "a beast." As the regiment moves forward, Henry is "unconsciously in advance." Although many men shield their eyes, he looks squarely ahead. What he sees "in the new appearance of the landscape" is like "a revelation." There is both a clarity of vision and of perception: the darkness of the landscape has vanished; the blindness of his mental insight has passed. As with the wound and the coffee, he feels the "delirium that encounters despair and death." He has, perhaps, in this "temporary but sublime absence of selfishness," found the reason for being there after all. As the pace quickly "eats up the energies of the men," they dance and gyrate "like savages." Without regard for self, Henry spurs them forward towards the colors.

In the language of myth, it is woman who represents the totality of what can be known. As "life," she embodies both love and hate. To accept her is to be king, the incarnate god, of her created world. As knower (one who recognizes her), the hero is master. Meeting the goddess and winning her is the final test of the hero's talent. Curiously, it is the flag that occupies the position of goddess in the story. The flag is the lure, the beautiful maiden of the configuration, whose capture is necessary if Henry is to fulfill his role as hero. Crane writes:

> With [Henry], as he hurled himself forward, was born a love, a despairing fondness of this flag which was near him. It was a creation of beauty and invulnerability. It was a goddess, radiant, that bended its form with an imperious gesture to him. It was a woman, red and white, hating and loving, that called him with the voice of his hope. Because no harm could come to it he endowed it with power. He kept near, as if it could be a saver of lives, and an imploring cry went from his mind.

As Henry and his comrade wrench the pole from the dead bearer, they both acquire an invincible wand of hope and power. Taking it roughly from his friend, Henry has, indeed, reached heroic proportions.

In his role as hero, Henry stands "erect and tranquil" in face of the great monster. Having "rid himself of the red sickness of battle," having overcome his fear of losing individual identity, he now despises the "brass and bombast of his earlier gospels." Because he is at-one with his comrades, he has acquired their "daring spirit of a savage religion-mad," their "brute" strength to endure the violence of a violent world, the "red of blood and black of passion." His individual strength is their collective strength, that strength of the totality which the flag symbolizes. As Crane says:

> He felt a quiet manhood, nonassertive but of sturdy and strong blood. He knew that he would no more quail before his guides wherever they should point. He had been to touch the great

death, and found that, after all, it was but the great death. He was a man.

At last he has put the "somber phantom" of his desertion at a distance. Having emerged into the "golden ray of sun," Henry feels a "store of assurance."

Following the general pattern of myth with peculiar individual variations, Crane has shown how the moral and spiritual strength of the individual springs from the group, and how, through the identification of self with group, the individual can be "reborn in identity with the whole meaning of the universe." Just as his would-be hero was able to overcome his fears and achieve a new moral and spiritual existence, so all men can come to face life, face it as calmly and as coolly as one faces the terrors, the odd beings, the deluding images of dreams. If it is, as Campbell points out, the "unconscious" which supplies the "keys that open the whole realm of the desired and feared adventures of the discovery of self," then man, to discover self, must translate his dreams into actuality. To say that Henry accomplishes his purpose is not to imply that Crane himself achieved the same kind of integration. Whatever the final irony implied, he certainly saw that the discovery of self was essential to building the "bolder, cleaner, more spacious, and fully human life."

CHARLES C. WALCUTT

[Stephen Crane: Naturalist and Impressionist]†

* * *

My thesis is that naturalism is the offspring of transcendentalism. American transcendentalism asserts the unity of Spirit and Nature and affirms that intuition (by which the mind discovers its affiliation with Spirit) and scientific investigation (by which it masters Nature, the symbol of Spirit) are equally rewarding and valid approaches to reality. When this mainstream of transcendentalism divides, as it does toward the end of the nineteenth century, it produces two rivers of thought. One, the approach to Spirit through intuition, nourishes idealism, progressivism, and social radicalism. The other, the approach to Nature through science, plunges into the dark canyon of mechanistic determinism. The one is rebellious,

† From *American Literary Naturalism, A Divided Stream* (Minneapolis: University of Minnesota Press, 1956), pp. vii, viii, 66–67, 74–82. Copyright 1956 by the University of Minnesota. Reprinted by permission. The naturalism of *The Red Badge* is also the subject of Donald Pizer's "Late-Nineteenth-Century American Naturalism," below. In other essays in this edition, Marston LaFrance rejects the notion that Crane was a naturalist, while Robert Rechnitz extends Walcutt's reading of the conclusion of the novel.

the other pessimistic; the one ardent, the other fatal; the one acknowledges will, the other denies it. Thus "naturalism," flowing in both streams, is partly defying Nature and partly submitting to it; and it is in this area of tension that my investigation lies, its immediate subject being the forms which the novel assumes as one stream or the other, and sometimes both, flow through it. The problem, as will appear, is an epitome of the central problems of twentieth-century thought.

* * *

The works of Stephen Crane (1871–1900) are an early and unique flowering of pure naturalism. It is naturalism in a restricted and special sense, and it contains many non-naturalistic elements, but it is nevertheless entirely consistent and coherent. It marks the first entry, in America, of a deterministic philosophy not confused with ethical motivation into the structure of the novel. Ethical judgment there is, in plenty. To define Crane's naturalism is to understand one of the few perfect and successful embodiments of the theory in the American novel. It illustrates the old truth that literary trends often achieve their finest expressions very early in their histories. *Mutatis mutandis,* Crane is the Christopher Marlowe of American naturalism—and we have had no Shakespeare.

Crane's naturalism is to be found, first, in his attitude toward received values, which he continually assails through his naturalistic method of showing that the traditional concepts of our social morality are shams and the motivations presumably controlled by them are pretenses; second, in his impressionism, which fractures experiences into disordered sensation in a way that shatters the old moral "order" along with the old orderly processes of reward and punishment; third, in his obvious interest in a scientific or deterministic accounting for events, although he does not pretend or attempt to be scientific in either the tone or the management of his fables. Crane's naturalism does not suffer from the problem of the divided stream because each of his works is so concretely developed that it does not have a meaning apart from what happens in it. The meaning is always the action; there is no wandering into theory that runs counter to what happens in the action; and nowhere does a character operate as a genuinely free ethical agent in defiance of the author's intentions. Crane's success is a triumph of style: manner and meaning are one.

* * *

Crane's naturalism is descriptive: he does not pretend to set forth a proof, like a chemical demonstration, that what happened must have happened, inevitably. This is what Zola was forever saying he did, and it is for these pretensions of scientific demonstration and proof that he has been chided by later critics. Crane simply shows how a sequence of events takes place quite independently of the wills and judgments of the people involved. The reader is convinced that it happened that way, and he sees that the ordinary moral sentiments do not adequately judge or account for these happenings. The writer does not have to argue that he has proved anything about causation or determinism: he has absolutely shown that men's wills do not control their destinies.

The Red Badge of Courage (1895), Crane's Civil War story, is the most controversial piece in his canon. It has been much discussed and most variously interpreted, and the interpretations range about as widely as they could. Is it a Christian story of redemption? Is it a demonstration that man is a beast with illusions? Or is it, between these extremes, the story of a man who goes through the fire, discovers himself, and with the self-knowledge that he is able to attain comes to terms with the problem of life insofar as an imperfect man can come to terms with an imperfect world? It is tempting to take the middle road between the intemperate extremes; but let us see what happens before we come to the paragraphs at the end that are invoked to prove each of the explanations:

> He felt a quiet manhood, non-assertive but of sturdy and strong blood. He knew that he would no more quail before his guides wherever they should point. He had been to touch the great death, and found that, after all, it was but the great death. He was a man.
>
> So it came to pass that as he trudged from the place of blood and wrath his soul changed. He came from hot plowshares to prospects of clover tranquilly, and it was as if hot plowshares were not. Scars faded as flowers.
>
> . . . He had rid himself of the red sickness of battle. The sultry nightmare was in the past. He had been an animal blistered and sweating in the heat and pain of war. He turned now with a lover's thirst to images of tranquil skies, fresh meadows, cool brooks.

It is not obvious whether the young man who thinks these thoughts is deluding himself or not. To judge the quality of his self-analysis we must look in some detail at what he has been through. The book opens with a scene at a Union emcampment in which the uniformed arguments of the soldiers are described in a manner that recalls the mockery of "infantile orations" in Maggie. The phrase pictures a squalling child colorfully, while it conveys the author's private amusement at the image of a shouting politician. In The Red Badge there is continually a tone of mockery and sardonic imitation of men who are boisterous, crafty, arrogant, resentful, or suspicious always in an excess that makes them comical, and the author seems to delight in rendering the flavor of their extravagances. An element of the fantastic is always present, the quality apparently representing the author's feeling for the war, the situations in it, the continual and enormous incongruities between intention and execution, between a man's estimate of himself and the way he appears to others, between the motivations acknowledged to the world and those which prevail in the heart. It is with these last that the book is centrally concerned—with the problem of courage —and it is here that the meaning is most confusingly entangled with the tone.

In the opening scene the men are excited over a rumor that the troop is about to move, for the first time in months, and immediately the tone of mockery appears. A certain tall soldier "developed virtues and went resolutely to wash a shirt. He came flying back. . . . He was swelled with a tale he had heard from a reliable friend, who had heard it from a truthful cavalryman, who had heard it from his trustworthy brother. . . . He adopted the important air of a herald in red and gold." Another soldier takes the report "as an affront," and the tall soldier "felt compelled upon to defend the truth of a rumor he had himself introduced. He and the loud one came near to fighting over it." A corporal swears furiously because he has just put a floor under his tent; the men argue about strategies, clamoring at each other, "numbers making futile bids for the popular attention."

From the outer excitement we turn to the excitement in the heart of the youth who is to be the hero of the tale. He has crept off to his tent to commune with himself and particularly to wonder how he will act when he confronts the enemy. He has "dreamed of battles all his life—of vague and bloody conflicts that had thrilled him with their sweep and fire. . . . He had imagined peoples secure in the shadow of his eagle-eyed prowess." He had burned to enlist, but had been deterred by his mother's arguments that he was more important on the farm until—the point is sardonically emphasized —the newspapers carried accounts of great battles in which the North was victor. "Almost every day the newspapers printed accounts of a decisive victory." When he enlists, his mother makes a long speech to him—which is presented by Crane with no trace of mockery—but he is impatient and irritated. As he departs, there is a tableau described, for almost the only time in the book, with unqualified feeling:

> Still, when he had looked back from the gate, he had seen his mother kneeling among the potato parings. Her brown face, upraised, was stained with tears, and her spare form was quivering. He bowed his head and went on, feeling suddenly ashamed of his purposes.

Vanity amid dreams of Homeric glory occupy him thenceforth—until battle is imminent. Then he wonders whether he will run or stand; and he does not dare confide his fears to the other men because they all seem so sure of themselves and because both they and he are constantly diverted from the question by inferior concerns. When the first rumor proves false, its carrier, the tall soldier, in defense of his honor, "fought with a man from Chatfield Corners and beat him severely." (This tall soldier, whose name is Jim Conklin, has been identified symbolically with Jesus Christ by some critics.) In a similar instance, "A man fell down, and as he reached for his rifle a comrade, unseeing, trod upon his hand. He of the injured fingers swore bitterly and aloud. A low tittering laugh went among his fellows." This petty reaction alienates the boy. The tall soldier offers more theories, is challenged, and there are endless debates: "The blatant soldier often convulsed whole files by his biting sarcasms aimed at the tall one." Another soldier tries to steal a horse, is defied by the girl who owns it, and precipitates wild cheers from the men, who "entered whole-souled upon the side of the maiden. . . . They jeered the piratical private, and called attention to various defects in his personal appearance; and they were wildly enthusiastic in support of the young girl."

Approaching the first engagement, the youth perceives with terror that he is "in a moving box" of soldiers from which it would be impossible to escape, and "it occurred to him that he had never wished to come to the war . . . He had been dragged by the merciless government." He is further startled when the loud soldier, a braggart, announces with a sob that he is going to be killed, and gives the youth a packet of letters for his family. The engagement is described with terms of confusion: the youth feels "a red rage," and then "acute exasperation"; he "fought frantically" for air; the other men are cursing, babbling, and querulous; their equipment bobs "idiotically" on their backs, and they move like puppets. The assault is turned back, and the men leer at each other with dirty smiles; but just as the youth is responding in "an ecstasy of self-satisfaction" at having passed "the supreme trial," there comes a second charge from which he flees in blind panic: "He ran like a blind man. Two or three times he fell down. Once he knocked his shoulder so heavily against a tree that he went headlong." As he runs, his fear increases, and he rages at the suicidal folly of those who have stayed behind to be killed.

Just as he reaches the zone of safety, he learns that the line has held and the enemy's charge been repulsed. Instantly he "felt that he had been wronged," and begins to find reasons for the wisdom of his flight. "It was all plain that he had proceeded according to very correct and commendable rules. His actions had been sagacious things. They had been full of strategy. . . . He, the enlightened man who looks afar in the dark, had fled because of his superior perceptions and knowledge. He felt a great anger against his comrades. He knew it could be proved that they had been fools." He pities himself; he feels rebellious, agonized, and despairing. It is here that he sees a squirrel and throws a pine cone at it; when it runs he finds a triumphant exhibition in nature of the law of self-preservation. "Nature had given him a sign." The irony of this sequence is abundantly apparent. It increases when, a moment later, the youth enters a place where the "arching boughs made a chapel" and finds a horrible corpse, upright against a tree, crawling with ants and staring straight at him.

From this he flees in renewed panic, and then there is a strange turn. A din of battle breaks out, such a "tremendous clangor of sounds" as to make the engagement from which he ran seem trivial, and he runs back to watch because for such a spectacle curiosity becomes stronger than fear. He joins a ghastly procession of wounded from this battle, among whom he finds Jim Conklin, his friend, gray with the mark of death, and watches him die in throes that "caused him to dance a sort of hideous hornpipe." The guilt he feels among these frightfully wounded men, in this chapter which comes precisely in the middle of the book, should be enough to make him realize his brotherhood, his indebtedness, his duty; but his reaction as he watches the retreat swell is to justify his early flight—until a column of soldiers going *toward* the battle makes him almost weep with his longing to be one of their brave file. Increasingly, in short, Crane makes us see Henry Fleming as an emotional puppet controlled by whatever sight he sees at the moment. He becomes like Conrad's Lord Jim, romancing dreams of glory while he flinches at every danger. As his spirits flag under physical exhaustion, he hopes his army will be defeated so that his flight will be vindicated.

The climax of irony comes now, when, after a stasis of remorse in which he does indeed despise himself (albeit for the wrong reason of fearing the reproaches of those who did not flee), he sees the whole army come running past him in an utter panic of terror. He tries to stop one of them for information, and is bashed over the head by the frantic and bewildered man. And now, wounded thus, almost delirious with pain and exhaustion, he staggers back to his company—and is greeted as a hero! Henry is tended by the loud soldier, who has become stronger and steadier. Henry's reaction to his friend's care and solicitude is to feel superior because he still has the packet of letters the loud one gave him a day before, in his fear: "The friend had, in a weak hour, spoken with sobs of his own death. . . . But he had not died, and thus he had delivered himself into the hands of the youth." He condescends to his loud friend, and "His self-pride was now [so] entirely restored" that he began to see something fine in his conduct of the day before. He is now vainglorious; he thinks himself "a man of experience . . . chosen of the gods and doomed to greatness." Remembering the terror-stricken faces of the men he saw fleeing from the great battle, he now feels a scorn for them! He thinks of the tales of prowess he will tell back home to circles of adoring women.

The youth's reaction to his spurious "red badge of courage" is thus set down with close and ironical detail. Crane does not comment, but the picture of self-delusion and vainglory is meticulously drawn. In the following chapter Henry does fight furiously, but here he is in a blind rage that turns him into an animal, so that he goes on firing long after the enemy have retreated. The other soldiers regard his ferocity with wonder, and Henry has become a marvel, basking in the wondering stares of his comrades.

The order comes for a desperate charge, and the regiment responds magnificently, hurling itself into the enemy's fire regardless of the odds against it; and here Crane devotes a paragraph to a careful and specific analysis of their heroism:

> But there was a frenzy made from this furious rush. The men, pitching forward insanely, had burst into cheerings, moblike and barbaric, but tuned in strange keys that can arouse the dullard and the stoic. It made a mad enthusiasm that, it seemed, would be incapable of checking itself before granite and brass. There was the delirium that encounters despair and death, and is heedless and blind to the odds. It is a temporary but sublime absence of selfishness. And because it was of this order was the reason, perhaps, why the youth wandered, afterward, what reasons he could have had for being there.

Heroism is "temporary but sublime," succeeded by dejection, anger, panic, indignation, despair, and renewed rage. This can hardly be called, for Henry, gaining spiritual salvation by losing his soul in the flux of things, for he is acting in harried exasperation, exhaustion, and rage. What has seemed to him an incredible charge turns out, presently, to have been a very short one—in time and distance covered—for which the regiment is bitterly criticized by the General. The facts are supplemented by the tone, which conveys through its outrageous and whimsical language that the whole business is made of pretense and delusion: A "magnificent brigade" goes into a wood, causing there "a most awe-inspiring racket. . . . Having stirred this prodigious uproar, and, apparently, finding it too prodigious, the brigade, after a little time, came marching airily out again with its fine formation in nowise disturbed. . . . The brigade was jaunty and seemed to point a proud thumb at the yelling wood." In the midst of the next engagement, which is indeed a furious battle, the youth is sustained by a "strange and unspeakable hatred" of the officer who had dubbed his regiment "mud diggers." Carrying the colors, he leads a charge of men "in a state of frenzy, perhaps because of forgotten vanities, and it made an exhibition of sublime recklessness." In this hysterical battlefield the youth is indeed selfless and utterly fearless in "his wild battle madness," yet by reading closely we see that the opposing soldiers are a thin, feeble line who turn and run from the charge or are slaughtered.

What it all seems to come to is that the heroism is in action undeniable, but it is preceded and followed by the ignoble sentiments we have traced—and the constant tone of humor and hysteria seems to be Crane's comment on these juxtapositions of courage, ignorance, vainglory, pettiness, pompous triumph, and craven fear. The moment the men can stop and comment upon what they have been through they are presented as more or less absurd.

With all these facts in mind we can examine the Henry Fleming who emerges from the battle and sets about marshaling all his acts. He is gleeful over his courage. Remembering his desertion of the wounded Jim Conklin, he is ashamed because of the possible disgrace, but, as Crane tells with supreme irony, "gradually he mustered force to put the sin at a distance," and to dwell upon his "quiet manhood." Coming after all these events and rationalizations, the paragraphs quoted at the beginning of this discussion are a climax of self-delusion. If there is any one point that has been made it is that Henry has never been able to evaluate his conduct. He may have been fearless for moments, but his motives were vain, selfish, ignorant, and childish. Mercifully, Crane does not follow him down through the more despicable levels of self-delusion that are sure to follow as he rewrites (as we have seen him planning to do) the story of his conduct to fit his childish specifications. He has been through some moments of hell, during which he has for moments risen above his limitations, but Crane seems plainly to be showing that he has not achieved a lasting wisdom or self-knowledge.

If *The Red Badge of Courage* were only an exposure of an ignorant farm boy's delusions, it would be a contemptible book. Crane shows that Henry's delusions image only dimly the insanely grotesque and incongruous world of battle into which he is plunged. There the movement is blind or frantic, the leaders are selfish, the goals are inhuman. One farm boy is made into a mad animal to kill another farm boy, while the great guns carry on a "grim pow-wow" or a "stupendous wrangle" described in terms that suggest a solemn farce or a cosmic and irresponsible game.

If we were to seek a geometrical shape to picture the significant form of *The Red Badge*, it would not be the circle, the L, or the straight line of oscillation between selfishness and salvation, but the equilateral triangle. Its three points are instinct, ideals, and circumstance. Henry Fleming runs along the sides like a squirrel in a track. Ideals take him along one side until circumstance confronts him with danger. Then instinct takes over and he dashes down the third side in a panic. The panic abates somewhat as he approaches the angle of ideals, and as he turns the corner (continuing his flight) he busily rationalizes to accommodate those ideals of duty and trust that recur, again and again, to harass him. Then he runs on to the line of circumstance, and he moves again toward instinct. He is always controlled on one line, along which he is both drawn and impelled by the other two forces. If this triangle is thought of as a piece of bright glass whirling in a cosmic kaleidoscope, we have an image of Crane's naturalistic and vividly impressioned Reality.

STANLEY B. GREENFIELD

The Unmistakable Stephen Crane†

I

In a letter to a friend early in his brief writing career, Stephen Crane wrote, "I always want to be unmistakable"; and, at a later date, to another friend he explained retrospectively that "My chief-test [sic] desire was to write plainly and unmistakably, so that all men (and some women) might read and understand."[1] There is an irony in the critical fate that has befallen Crane's writings that perhaps that master ironist himself might have appreciated. For though the best criticism of his own time reveals a careful reading and understanding of his works, most recent criticism has seen Crane through a glass darkly.

I refer particularly to the body of commentary on Crane's war novel, *The Red Badge of Courage*, though the criticism of his other works is also lacking in clarity. An examination of the criticism of the novel reveals errors ranging from inadvertent though disturbing misstatements of fact to quotations out of context and gross distortion of sense. We find, for example, V. S. Pritchett avowing that Henry Fleming is never given a name, and Charles Walcutt, in the

† *PMLA,* LXXIII (December 1958), 562–63, 568–72. Reprinted by permission.
1. Cited by John Berryman, in *Stephen Crane* (New York, 1950), p. 99. In all fairness, it should be noted that Crane elsewhere expressed an artistic credo to the effect that the meaning of a story should not be made *too* plain. (See Robert Wooster Stallman, *Stephen Crane: An Omnibus,* New York, 1953, p. 218.)

most recent study of the novel, completely forgetting the tattered
man, saying that Henry deserts the dying Jim Conklin instead of
this forlorn figure.[2] These are indisputably simple lapses of
memory. But we read elsewhere, with more apprehension than
comprehension, remarks to the effect that Henry has "a complete
lack of appetite for glory," and that he deserts in protest "because
war wrenches young people out of their path of life, thwarting their
aspirations for work, education, love, marriage, family, self-develop-
ment."[3] Such interpretations are not only patently wrong but too
simple, for the human condition of the typical Crane character, as
John Berryman has pointed out (p. 280), is a combination of pre-
tentiousness and fear, as in the Swede of "The Blue Hotel," or the
New York Kid of "The Five White Mice," or Henry Fleming, who
throughout almost the entire novel is vainglorious and, when he
deserts, scared stiff. In another analysis we find the novel as a whole
regarded as defective because Henry's becoming a man "is largely a
matter of accident, [and] lacks the authority of a consciously willed
readiness to work out the hard way of salvation,"[4] a critical remark
that suggests a confusion of ethics with aesthetics and in the context of the whole article, a failure to perceive or understand irony.
In still another article we find the author confidently proclaiming
at the outset: "As one way of re-examining *The Red Badge of
Courage*, we would want to read it as myth and symbolic action."[5]
We may well wonder why we would or should.

I must examine at greater length the criticism of Crane by
Robert Stallman. We are indebted to a great degree to Stallman
for the revival of an interest in Crane. But his critical method and
interpretation I find very disturbing. His symbolic reading of *The
Red Badge of Courage*, with Jim Conklin emerging as Jesus Christ,
appears in his edition of the novel for the Modern Library and,
with some additional material, in his essay on Crane in *Critiques
and Essays on Modern Fiction* (ed. John W. Aldridge), and in his
Stephen Crane: An Omnibus; if I read aright the "For Members
Only" section of *PMLA*, it is now appearing in a Greek edition of
the novel. And this perseverance of the same argument and
method of criticism has led to converts.[6]

As an example of Stallman's method in his analysis of the novel,
we may look first at his purported objective summary of the action,

2. *The Living Novel* (New York, 1947),
p. 174; *American Literary Naturalism: A
Divided Stream* (Minneapolis, 1956), p.
81.
3. George D. Snell, *Shapers of American Fiction* (New York, 1947), pp. 225–
226; M. Solomon, "Stephen Crane: A
Critical Study," *Masses and Mainstream*,
IX (Jan. 1956), 38.
4. John W. Shroeder, "Stephen Crane

Embattled," *UKCR*, XVII (1951), 126.
5. John E. Hart, "*The Red Badge of
Courage* as Myth and Symbol," *UKCR*,
XIX (1953), 249.
6. See e.g., James T. Cox, "Stephen
Crane as Symbolic Naturalist: An Analysis of 'The Blue Hotel'," *Modern Fiction Studies*, III (Summer 1957), 147–
158.

which precedes the explicit formulation of his theory of salvation and redemption. In reviewing the sequence of events in the opening chapter, he describes the reception of Jim Conklin's rumor that the army is going into action the next day (italics, save for the word *tall*, are mine):

> But Jim Conklin's *prophecy* of hope meets with *disbelief*. "It's a lie!" shouts the loud soldier. "I don't believe this derned old army's ever going to move." No *disciples* rally round the red and gold flag of the herald. A furious altercation ensues; the *skeptics* think it just another *tall* tale. Meanwhile Henry in his hut engages in a *spiritual* debate with himself: whether to believe or disbelieve the word of his friend, the *tall* soldier. It is the *gospel truth*, but Henry is one of the *doubting apostles*.[7]

There are several comments this account calls for. There is an error of fact that is *not* negligible: Jim Conklin's rumor is *not* the gospel truth, or any truth at all, for the first sentence of Chapter II clearly states that "The next morning the youth discovered that his tall comrade had been the fast-flying messenger of a mistake." Another error of fact: Henry is not debating, spiritually or otherwise, about believing or disbelieving his friend; he has a more serious concern, trying "to mathematically prove to himself that he [will] not run from battle." Finally, consider the words I have italicized in the above quotation: not one of them appears in the part of the novel Stallman is describing. In brief, there is not the faintest hint of a religious question of faith versus doubt. Religious phrasing unfortunately predisposes the reader toward an interpretation of spiritual redemption.

This is not the only instance of such distortion. Let us consider a passage describing the climax of the book, the end of Chapter IX, where Henry watches Jim Conklin die: "[Henry] curses the red sun pasted in the sky 'like a wafer.' Nature, we are told, 'had given him a sign.' Henry blasphemes against this emblem of his faith, the wafer-like red sun" (*Omnibus*, p. 223). First, the Crane quotation about Nature giving Henry a sign is not from this part of the novel at all: it is from Chapter VII and is *Henry's* reaction to the squirrel's running when he threw a pine cone at him—a phrase, in other words, that is to be construed ironically in its proper context! Moreover, the text of the novel at this point is as follows:

> The youth turned, with sudden, livid rage, toward the battlefield. He shook his fist. He seemed about to deliver a philippic.
> "Hell—"
> The red sun was pasted in the sky like a [fierce] wafer.

Surely an unbiased reading of this passage reveals that Henry is blaspheming against the battlefield, against war. The shift in point

---

7. Pages xxiv–xxv of the Modern Library edition.

of view from Henry to an observer ("He seemed about . . .") suggests that Henry is not even aware of the sun.

Again, this time in connection with the last part of the novel, Stallman makes a statement about Henry's so-called spiritual change: "The brave new Henry, 'new bearer of the colors,' triumphs over the former one. The flag of the enemy is wrenched from the hands of 'the rival colorbearer,' the symbol of Henry's own other self, and as the rival colorbearer dies Henry is reborn." The implication in this passage is that Henry has done the wrenching; otherwise the comment is pointless. But it is Wilson who has actually grabbed the flag. The ambiguous passive voice ("is wrenched") is highly misleading.

* * *

III

The nature of heroic behavior and the state of mind of the courageous man lie at the heart of *The Red Badge of Courage*. The majority of critics accept the point of view that the novel is a study in growth, whether that growth be spiritual, social, or philosophic. These critics "concede" that the novel, especially in its earlier parts, has a strong naturalistic bias which tends to vitiate, most of them feel, its aesthetic integrity, though Berryman, a believer in Henry's ultimate heroism, asserts that it is the end of the novel that is deficient, since it fails to sustain the irony (p. 107).[8] Two critics, notably, depart from this opinion. Shroeder sees evidence of growth but feels it is inconsequential; he complains that the novel fails because Henry's heroism is largely accidental and because the pretty picture at the end "smacks too strongly of the youth's early impressions of the haunted forest; Crane seems to have forgotten everything that has gone before in his own book" (p. 126). Walcutt, on the other hand, claims that Henry, at the end of the novel, *is* back where he started from, naturalistic man still swelling with his ignorant self-importance (pp. 81–82).[9] I submit that neither interpretation of the novel—the heroic, with or without qualifications, or the antiheroic—gives proper credit to Crane's aesthetic vision. For though earlier than "The Open Boat" and "The Blue Hotel," *The Red Badge of Courage* exhibits the same interplay of

8. Berryman's interpretation of Crane as a whole is vitiated by his peculiar psychoanalytical view of Crane.

9. It is interesting to observe that Stallman, after examining the earlier manuscripts of *The Red Badge of Courage,* seems to have ·had a change of mind about Henry's "salvation." He sees the "images of tranquil skies" at the end of the novel as flatly sentimental and feels that they are given an ironic turn by the sun-through-clouds image: "[Henry] has undergone no change, no real spiritual development" (*Omnibus,* p. 221). I'm not sure where this "conversion" leaves the rest of Stallman's theory about Henry's rebirth when the rival colorbearer dies, but he himself has let it stand.

deterministic and volitional forces as the two short stories, and the same pervasive irony binding the heroic and the antiheroic themes. It reveals the same ultimate refusal to guarantee the effectiveness of moral behavior or the validity of man's interpretative processes. while simultaneously approving of the moral act and the attempt to gain insight into the meaning of experience.

To understand the novel, then, we must analyze Crane's handling of *behavior* and *attitude*. We may begin with the former. Its deterministic side has so often been commented on that a brief summary will suffice. It is enough to note that, like Scully's presumptuous behavior in "The Blue Hotel," Henry's presumption to patriotic motivation and ethical choice, in the guise of enlistment in the army, is ironically punctured by the circumstance of his enlistment, the "twisted news of a great battle";[1] to observe that Henry moves from tradition-conditioned behavior ("the moving box" of "tradition and law") to instinct-conditioned behavior as the atmosphere of battle overwhelms him; and to recall that Henry *awakes* to find himself a *knight* because he had gone on "loading and firing and cursing without the proper intermission," and had acted like "a barbarian, a beast."

The use of animal imagery to reinforce the determinism of the novel and to deflate man's pretensions to heroic conduct has also often been noted. The similar use of eating and drinking, both in deed and in imagery, has not, however, been given sufficient attention. What is most interesting is the variety of ways in which Crane stresses the survival theme by his handling of food and drink.

When Henry returns home with the news of his enlistment, his mother is milking the brindle cow, and when he departs, "she . . . doggedly [peels] potatoes." Here, food and drink are shown on the simple level of existence, as staples of life, and they point up by understatement the contrast between normality and the excited Henry's impressions of war. As the men march along, they shed all superfluous equipment: " 'You can now eat and shoot,' said the tall soldier to the youth. 'That's all you want to do'." Here, war as an eat-or-be-eaten affair is stated explicitly. When Jim Conklin and Wilson dispute about the running of the army, the former eats sandwiches "as if taking poison in despair. But gradually, as he chewed, his face became again quiet and contented. He would not rage in fierce argument in the presence of such sandwiches. During his meals he always wore an air of blissful contemplation of the food he had swallowed. His spirit seemed to be communing with the viands." This passage is almost pure comedy, with its emphasis on the power of food to condition man's frame of mind. In contrast

1. Cf. Walcutt, pp. 76–77.

is the tragedy in the description of Jim Conklin's death: "As the flap of the blue jacket fell away from the body, he [Henry] could see that the side looked as if it had been chewed by wolves." According to Stallman, this wound is supposed to be an unmistakable hint, among others, that Jim Conklin is Jesus Christ, but clearly it is part of the same eat-or-be-eaten concept that pervades "The Open Boat" and that we find in the melon image in the description of the Swede's death. Still another way in which food and drink contribute to meaning is found in the scene in which Henry and Wilson, at a significant lull in the battle after Henry has awakened a knight, go looking for water. Instead of finding the water, which is only an illusion on Wilson's part, they discover their own insignificance. Finally, at the end of the novel, Henry turns "with a lover's thirst" to images of peace. An evaluation of this image must be saved for later.

If Henry's and the other soldiers' behavior is conditioned by tradition and the instinct for survival, their fate, unlike Maggie's in Crane's earlier novel, is not the product of circumstance and the cumulative effect of other people's behavior. Their destiny involves other elements.[2]

For one thing, there is Nature or the Universe. Henry visualizes Nature as being most concerned with his fate. She sympathizes or is hostile according to his mood and circumstance; and this impressionism is part of the philosophy and aesthetic of the novel. But Nature's involvement in the affairs of man is really, as in the two stories, noninvolvement, though in *The Red Badge of Courage* she is not flatly indifferent as in "The Open Boat," or malevolently indifferent as in "The Blue Hotel," but cheerfully so. Regularly throughout the book Crane provides glimpses of this cheerful reality, so that the reader does not lose sight of the illusions and delusions of Henry's limited perspective. The reader of the novel will recall the surprising "fairy blue" of the sky and the references to Nature's "golden process" and "golden ray" of the sun.[3] Henry sees this indifference, but he does not understand it.

Another element is man's will. Jim Conklin, for one, demonstrates that man has and makes ethical choices. Before the battle, he states that he will probably act like the other soldiers; but when many of them run, he nonetheless stands his ground. Wilson, too,

2. That Crane developed and matured in his art from *Maggie* to "The Five White Mice" is, I think, indisputable, but a demonstration of this maturation is beyond the scope of this paper.
3. As for the hotly-debated wafer image, although it cannot be said to be cheerful, it seems to me that Scott C. Osborn is perfectly right when he suggests that it is the seal of Nature's indifference to Jim's (and man's) fate ("Stephen Crane's Imagery: Pasted like a Wafer," *AL*, XXIII, 1951, 362). I believe it was to insure this meaning that Crane deleted the "fierce" from his final revision of this passage.

feeling as the battle joins that it will be his death, does not run. And there is a decided growth in Henry's moral behavior as the novel progresses. From running away and rationalizing his cowardice as superior insight, Henry moves through a series of actions in which he does the right thing. When he and Wilson, on their mistaken expedition for water, overhear the officer say that not many of the "mule-drivers" will get back, both keep the secret and do not hesitate to make the charge. When the two friends grab the flag from the dead colorbearer, Henry pushes Wilson away to declare "his willingness to further risk himself." And in the final charge, Henry "saw that to be firm soldiers they must go forward. It would be death to stay in the present place, and with all the circumstances to go backward would exalt too many others." Henry at these moments is more than an animal.

Ethical choice, then, is part of the novel's pattern: the moral act is admired. Yet Crane refuses to guarantee the effectiveness of moral behavior, even as he refuses in the two short stories. For there is the element of chance, finally, as in those stories, that makes the outcome unpredictable. Jim Conklin, for all his bravery, is killed. The tattered man, who watches with Henry Jim's death struggle and who is concerned over Henry's "wound," has acted morally, but he is dying and is, additionally, deserted for his pains. Wilson, on the other hand, who has also done the right thing, is rewarded by chance with life and praise; but Henry's immoral behavior, not only in running but later in lying about his head wound, is equally rewarded.

The complexity and withal the simplicity in the nature of man's behavior and its effect upon his destiny is crystallized, it seems to me, in the figure of the cheery soldier. This man, before whom obstacles melt away, guides Henry back to his regiment after Henry has received a "red badge" from the rifle butt of one of his own men. As they move along, he talks blithely of the mixup in the battle and of another's death; he comes out of nowhere but takes Henry "firmly by the arm"; and as he leaves, whistling audaciously, the youth realizes that he has not once seen his face. This disembodied jovial voice is, like Nature, cheerfully indifferent. His materialization out of the blue seems to be an element of chance. His bringing Henry back to his regiment willy-nilly suggests a deterministic pattern. Finally, he seems to represent Henry's own will, arriving as he does at that point in the action when Henry really desires to return to his regiment.

Man's behavior, then, as viewed in *The Red Badge of Courage*, is a combination of conditioned and volitional motivation. Man has a freedom of choice, and it is proper from him to choose the right way; at the same time, much of his apparent choice is, in reality, conditioned. But even acting morally or immorally does not guarantee one's fate, for the Universe is indifferent and chance too has scope to operate. Crane is interested, however, in more than man's public deeds. He probes in addition the state of mind of the heroic man and the possibility of his interpreting experience. Again, as in the short stories, the light of his irony plays over the presentation of man's attitude toward life.

The heroic attitude is given to us in the early part of the novel at a relatively simple level. Jim Conklin, the tall soldier, exhibits a serene faith in himself and his opinions, even when he is wrong. He will not run like Henry's squirrel. If the other soldiers stand firm, he will. Self-confidence, that is the keynote of the heroic temperament. The reader is made to admire Jim's attitude and subsequent bravery, to approve his calm acceptance of the incomprehensible movements of the army forcing him to build and then abandon three breastworks, "each of which had been an engineering feat worthy of being made sacred to the name of his grandmother." At the same time, however, as this last quotation reveals, Jim's self-confidence is slightly pretentious. We first see Jim developing virtues by washing a shirt, and he is "'swelled with a tale he had heard from a reliable friend, who had heard it from a truthful cavalryman, who had heard it from his trustworthy brother." When this rumor is proved false the following morning, Jim feels called upon to beat severely a man from Chatfield Corners. And in a passage I have cited above, we see there is comic deflation in Jim's blissful and righteous eating of sandwiches.[4]

Wilson demonstrates this confidence in a somewhat different key. The loud soldier is brash, first in his optimism, then in his pessimism. But whether he is supremely confident that he will not be killed or, raising "his limp hand in a prophetic manner," that he will, his is the attitude of the hero. The bravura deflation involved in Wilson's switch from one kind of brashness to another is obvious. Even later, however, when Wilson has become nonassertive and more humbly and quietly confident, when we feel for him, as we did earlier for Jim, a warm approval, there is something a little too self-humiliating, at first, in his new relationship with Henry.

The tattered man furnishes a third glimpse of the heroic attitude. Although he has just seen Jim Conklin die, and he himself is badly wounded, he is very sure of his own destiny: "Oh, I'm not goin'

4. Stallman sees this shirt washing as a sign of the right way to achieve spiritual salvation, by immersion in the flux of things; but surely the context renders this interpretation invalid. Crane's ironic attitude toward Jim Conklin in the instances I have cited certainly militates against our seeing him as a Christ figure.

t'die yit! There's too much dependin' on me fer me t'die yit. No sir! Nary die! I *can't!*" He is more concerned over Henry's "wound" than over his own. But his mind wanders and we know he is going to die as Henry deserts him in the fields. Again we find a mixture of admiration for and ironic puncturing of this state of mind, though the ultimate effect in this scene is one of pathos.

In these characters, however, we do not see development of attitude, and hence the possibility of understanding experience. Even Wilson, who undergoes a metamorphosis, is not developed; we are merely shown the results of his change. It is through Henry, of course, that Crane shows us growth. To see it, we have only to compare Chapter II, where Henry fails to understand what a box of cigars has to do with war, with the "mule-driver" scene, where Henry overhears the officer speak of his regiment "as if he referred to a broom. Some part of the woods needed sweeping, perhaps, and he merely indicated a broom in a tone properly indifferent to its fate. It was war, no doubt, but it appeared strange." The word *properly* and the phrase "no doubt," which give us Henry's point of view, as well as Crane's explicit statement that Henry learns here that he is very insignificant, leave no room for doubt of the growth in Henry's insight and attitude. Indeed, by the time of this later scene, Henry is no longer worried about running away or pondering the question of death. Even when he reverts in the crises of action to illusions about himself and the nature of his accomplishments, his thoughts reveal the confidence that Jim, Wilson, and the tattered man had before him. To mention but one instance: when he is holding the colors, Henry resolves not to budge. "It was clear to him that his final and absolute revenge was to be achieved by his dead body lying, torn and glittering, upon the field. This was to be a poignant retaliation upon the officer who had said 'mule drivers,' and later 'mud diggers'." The fact that he does not recall Jim Conklin's torn body and that he has, in fact, only once thought about or alluded to Jim's death is not only ironic but an indication of self-confidence in the extreme.

There would seem to be, then, despite the naturalistic light in which Henry's behavior and attitude are bathed, growth and development on both counts. Most of the critics of this novel, as I have observed, note a fading away of the irony as the novel draws to an end. But Walcutt, in his dissenting theory, claims that if we take Henry's thoughts about his new manhood in the context of the whole novel, we see that his motives always have been and still are vain; that he "has never been able to evaluate his conduct," and he is still deluded about himself (pp. 81–82). There *is* irony in the end of the novel; in fact, if one examines the longer version in the earlier manuscript of *The Red Badge of Courage,* he can have no doubt that there is. For there are long passages there, later excised by Crane, which clearly reveal a delusion in Henry's thoughts. For example, a passage which Crane later omitted has Henry musing that "Fate had in truth been kind to him; she had stabbed him with benign purpose and diligently cudgelled him for his own sake"; another passage has Henry feeling that though he is insignificant, he is "not inconsequent to the sun. In the space-wide whirl of events no grain like him would be lost"; and a third reveals him thinking, "He had been to touch the great death, and found that, after all, it was but the great death, and was for others." In his revision of this last sentence, Crane excised the telltale "and was for others." These pretentious thoughts about his role in the universe, coupled with the image of Henry turning "with a lover's thirst [to] an existence of soft and eternal peace" and the enigmatic last sentence, "Over the river a golden ray of sun came through the hosts of leaden rain clouds," reveal an irony similar to that in the endings of "The Open Boat" and "The Blue Hotel."

But at what is this final irony directed? Not, as Walcutt would have it, at Henry's evaluation of his conduct, but at the presumption in his false impressions of Nature and the Universe; at his *philosophical* self-confidence. Just as earlier Jim Conklin's, Wilson's, and the tattered man's supreme confidence in themselves had been held up to ironic scrutiny, so here is Henry's, only on a befittingly larger scale. But even as the minor characters' confidence has its approbation from Crane, even as in "The Blue Hotel" man's conceit was shown to be the very engine of life, so has Henry's. It seems to me that what Crane was trying to do in his revision was to eliminate the too obvious irony and redress the tonal balance of the novel.

This tonal balance is seen in Crane's handling of Henry's final evaluation of his conduct. Shifting from the apparency of things to positive statement in Henry's recapituation of his conduct, Crane abandons the word *seems,* so pervasive in the novel. "His mind was undergoing a subtle change. . . . Gradually his brain emerged from the clogged clouds, and at last he was enabled to more closely comprehend himself and circumstances." As Henry reviews his deeds, Crane writes: "From his present viewpoint he was enabled to look upon them in spectator fashion and to criticize them with some correctness, for his new condition had already defeated certain sympathies." No *seems* here; the tone is entirely sympathetic, though the refusal to guarantee interpretation is still here with "to more closely comprehend" and "with some correctness." There is no vain delusion about the past. As for the future—well, that is a **different** matter, highly ambiguous: "at last his eyes *seemed* to open to some new ways," and he "thirsts" for the obviously impossible, unchanging, "eternal peace." But however insecure the basis of Henry's thoughts about his future actions may be, Henry still has emerged from his experience with a new assurance of which Crane obviously approves: "He felt a quiet manhood, nonassertive but of sturdy and strong blood."[5]

The achievement of Crane in *The Red Badge of Courage* may be likened, it seems to me, to Chaucer's in *Troilus and Criseyde*, despite the lesser stature of the novel. Both works are infused with an irony which neatly balances two major views of human life—in *Troilus and Criseyde*, the value of courtly love versus heavenly love; in *The Red Badge of Courage*, ethical motivation and behavior versus deterministic and naturalistic actions. Both pose the problem, "Is there care in Heaven?" One is concerned with human values in a caring Universe, the other in an indifferent Universe. It is the age-old question of human values appearing in both, though the context varies. Too many critics of both works have suffered from an inability to see the validity of both of the conflicting sets of values. Chaucer shows us earthly love at its best. Alas that it is ephemeral against the backdrop of eternity and Christ's love for us and ours for Him: the perdurable quality of the poem that teases us out of our senses (and provokes so much critical commentary) is precisely the interplay throughout the poem of the two sets of values, so that even though Chaucer "guarantees" in the palinode that the love of "thou oon and two and three eterne on lyve" is ultimately more rewarding, the lovely though perishable quality of human love is not effaced. Crane's magnum opus shows up the nature and value of courage. The heroic ideal is not what it has been claimed to be: so largely is it the product of instinctive responses to biological and traditional forces. But man does have will, and he has the ability to reflect, and though these do not guarantee that he can effect his own destiny, they do enable him to become responsible to some degree for the honesty of his personal vision. It is this duality of view, like Chaucer's, that is the secret of the unmistakable Crane's art.

5. I must dispute Walcutt's interpretation of this famous passage: "With all these facts [the juxtaposition of courage, ignorance, vainglory, etc.] in mind we can examine the Henry Fleming who emerges from the battle and sets about marshaling all his acts. He is gleeful over his courage. Remembering his desertion of the wounded Jim Conklin, he is ashamed of the possible disgrace, but, as Crane tells with supreme irony, 'gradually he mustered force to put the sin at a distance,' and to dwell upon his 'quiet manhood' " (p. 81). The mistaken identification of character is negligible. But two points are, I think, crucial: Henry is not gleeful about his courage, but "He was gleeful when he discovered that he now despised [the brass and bombast] of his earlier gospels." And Henry doesn't *dwell* upon his quiet manhood (the word is, I feel, prejudicial): "He felt a quiet manhood . . ."

MORDECAI MARCUS
The Unity of *The Red Badge of Courage*†

Three recent publications have helped to clear the path for reassessment of *The Red Badge of Courage*. Most important is the publication of passages which Crane canceled or later excised from a manuscript of the novel.[1] These passages provide clues to some of Crane's intentions and problems, and throw light on the novel's often criticized resolution. Also important are articles by Stanley B. Greenfield[2] and by Norman Friedman[3] which exactingly refute interpretations of the novel as a symbolic presentation of Henry Fleming's religious communion, with Jim Conklin as the supposed sacrificial god.

The greatest critical problem in *The Red Badge of Courage* remains the apparent discrepancy between the almost consistently instinctive motivation of Henry Fleming and the concluding assertion that he has gained a quiet but assertive manhood. Despite the obvious sincerity of Crane's tone, some readers propose that the concluding four paragraphs of the novel represent only Henry's point of view and that Crane is ironically condemning a consistently self-deluded youth. Greenfield not too successfully attempts to cite evidence that Henry indeed grows in battle and comes to exhibit selfless courage. More to the point, Friedman maintains that Henry has changed not in character (the moral basis of action), but in thought: through perceiving his own smallness in the scheme of things, he comes at last to accept the necessity of his dangerous lot. To reassess the novel, I propose to study the various devices which give it unity, and the closely related problems of its resolution, and its partial failure to sustain interest to the end.

The Red Badge of Courage gains unity primarily through three forces: (1) Various repetitions of image, idea, and action. (2) Henry Fleming's changing relations to himself and to his fellows. (3) Several patterns of major and minor ironies. Separate analysis of these devices must overlook some of their constant interaction and must make some repetitions. The patterns of irony are the strongest unifying force, but since they culminate in the problematic resolution of the novel, they must be discussed last.

† *The Red Badge of Courage: Text and Criticism*, ed. Richard Lettis et al. (New York: Harcourt, Brace, 1960), pp. 189–95. Copyright Mordecai Marcus. Reprinted by permission of the author. Another close study of Crane's ironic method can be found in the essay by Marston LaFrance.

1. *Stephen Crane: An Omnibus*, ed. Robert Wooster Stallman (New York, 1952), pp. 225–370.
2. "The Unmistaken Stephen Crane," *PMLA*, LXXIII (1958), 562–72.
3. Criticism and the Novel," *Antioch Review*, XVIII (1958), 343–70.

Imagery presenting the actoins of men as animal-like creates the dominant image pattern in the novel. Very significantly Henry and his comrades are chiefly compared to domestic and timid animals during their early engagements, and to fierce wild animals during the later and more successful engagements.[4] As I will show, this image pattern contributes to a major structural irony of the novel. Other important patterns compare men to machines, and to floods and streams. Frequent references to Henry's legs, which stand for instinctive forces he cannot control, create a pattern emphasizing his self-division and fear, and often showing bitter irony. Before battle Henry plans "to watch his legs to discover their merits and faults." He is often dominated by his legs, and when his instincts keep him from fleeing, Crane writes that nothing would "have been able to have held him in place if he could have got intelligent control of his legs." Later, as he rationalizes the necessity of his terrified flight, Henry reflects that his actions were "the work of a master's legs," but it is his legs which have mastered him. When soon after returning to his regiment Henry stands "with braced and self-confident legs," Crane is mocking his baseless pride.

A significant pattern of actions is the series of altercations in which Henry and Conklin, Henry and Wilson, and finally an unnamed soldier and Henry try to puncture pretensions: (1) "Well, you don't know everything in the world, do you?" "Didn't say I knew everything in the world. . . ." (2) "You ain't the bravest man in the world, are you?" "No, I ain't . . . and I didn't say I was the bravest man in the world, neither." (3) "Mebbe yeh think yeh fit th' hull battle yestirday, Fleming. . . ." "Why no . . . I don't think I fought the whole battle yesterday." Besides giving a realistic tone to the relations between the men, this series culminates in the irony of Henry's awkward position, and the mild rather than blatant reply which this position compels. Many other repetitions of action and idea must be discussed as parts of larger patterns.

Henry's relationships to himself and to his fellows form a pattern which in turn closely connects to the novel's major ironies. In the early chapters centering on Henry's initial fears, first engagement, and subsequent flight, he is self-divided most of the time. His fears mock his dreams of glory; pride and fear clash almost constantly. In battle Henry temporarily suspends self-division, but he is unified only by becoming part of a machine and fighting instinctively. His instincts serve both to unify his motivation and to make him at one with his fellows. When others flee, he panics and imitates them. Then self-division returns in the form of wounded pride and a stream of rationalizations. Henry's relationship to his friends and

4. *Cf.* Mordecai and Erin Marcus, "Animal Imagery in *The Red Badge of Courage," Modern Language Notes*, LXXIV, 2 (Feb., 1959), 108–11.

fellows is usually incidental; only his fear of their opinion is crucial. In the early chapters, Conklin and Wilson are used to initiate the plot through conflict over a rumor. Conklin's death temporarily and gratefully relieves Henry's probing by the tattered soldier, but it plants very small seeds of conscience, for later he thinks of Conklin only once.[5] Wilson's entrusting his packet of letters to Henry prepares for the irony of Henry's gloating over Wilson's fears when the letters are returned. This irony also helps to focus the ironic reversal of character by which Henry, a coward, becomes boastful and loud, while the formerly loud Wilson, now a staunch soldier, becomes quiet and mild.

In the second half of the novel, Henry again experiences unity and self-division. Now, however, they exist in a subtle and ambivalent relationship with each other. Fighting bravely, as do Wilson, his ever-present comrade, and most of his fellows, Henry again behaves like a machine and a fierce animal, and loses his individuality. As he discovers that he is acting like a hero—the attentions of his lieutenant and colonel, as well as his successes, convince him of this—his animal-like motivation is joined by a compulsive pride. The memory of an officer's jibes against him and his fellows as "mule drivers" exacerbates Henry's pride. His pride is a force which lashes him on and then congratulates him. Acting along with his animal-like motives, this pride suggests that both animal fierceness, and compulsive pride create a kind of alienation from self. From the perspective of the immediate situation, Henry's fierceness and pride create psychological unity which enables him to act bravely, but a larger perspective reveals that these forces alienate him from his humanness. This complexity is fully revealed only in Crane's concluding chapter.

The dominance of pride in Henry's successful fighting casts convincing doubts on the thesis that Henry now acts with self-willed courage. Numerous passages demonstrate the fury and importance of Henry's pride. However, of the two passages which Greenfield cites to show that Henry is now more than an animal, one clearly shows that Henry's dominant motivations are still fear and pride. Henry "saw that to be firm soldiers they must go forward. It would be death to stay in the present place, and . . . to go backward would exalt too many others." Certainly the pride in question would rarely apply to animals, but it is hardly an intelligent and self-willed motive. One must admit that the other incident cited by Greenfield, Henry's and Wilson's determination to keep the secret that they must charge, and to go through with the charge, does illustrate a deliberate courage. Crane also shows some men in Henry's com-

5. Unless one also counts his remembrance that the tattered soldier had helped Conklin.

pany succumbing to fear and hysteria. Nevertheless, this growth in Henry has a negligible effect on his general motivation.

Although Henry does show courage, there is decisive evidence that it is motivated chiefly by animal fierceness and competitive pride. Even his relationship to Wilson, which helps to sustain the plot of the last eight chapters, is often competitive. They keep the secret of the charge almost as if it were a boy's game. They are fiercely competitive over the possession of their own and the enemy flag, and they congratulate each other on their successes. It seems unlikely that Crane deliberately planned a series of alternations between unity and self-division in his central character. Nevertheless, his psychological acumen perceived that such an alternation might rule a sensitive boy's response to war. The combination rather than alternation of unity and self-division in Henry's second series of engagements appears psychologically penetrating and prepares for the more profound psychological unity demonstrated in the denouement. The novel thus reveals a basic psychological pattern: (1) Self-division (forethought). (2) Unity (early engagement). (3) Self-division (flight). (4) Combination of unity and self-division (return and second engagement). (5) Unity (discovery of the human situation in denouement).

Henry's relationships to himself and to others discussed thus far all contribute to the major structural ironies of the novel, which may be classified as dramatic irony and irony of manner. Dramatic ironies are those created by reversals of events and by juxtapositions. Ironies of manner show characters misunderstanding their own motivation. In addition to these, Crane uses some verbal irony, which presents his viewpoint with relative directness. This verbal irony usually involves overstatement or understatement about men or machines in action, as when Crane writes of "reliable" and "trustworthy" bearers of rumor or describes guns which "were assembling for a grim conference." Such irony contributes to the novel's tonal rather than its structural unity.

The ironies which help most to unify the novel are dramatic ironies, revealed by the sequence of events. The most comprehensive of these is implicit in the consistently animal-like and herd responses of the central character. As I have noted in discussing Henry's alternating feelings of unity and self-division, he fights instinctively and mechanically when his fellows do, and he is terrified and flees like an animal in imitation of his fellows. Later he fights according to the instincts of a fierce animal, as do most of his fellows, although he is also driven by pride. Undeniably Crane has further complicated the motivation by showing traces of selflessness in Henry and occasional cowardice in his fellows, but Henry's motivation remains primarily unreflective and imitative. Thus the

two main engagements ironically show cowardice and courage to be
similarly unreflective, bestial, and perhaps purposeless.

Another unifying dramatic irony stems from the novel's central
symbol, the head wound which Henry receives from a blow by a terrified and fleeing fellow soldier. That his wound enables him to
regain his regiment without explaining his actions, to grow boastful,
and then to become a hero has often been noted. The least conspicuous of the novel's unifying dramatic ironies occurs at the end
when Henry's regiment withdraws from the ground it has taken at
great cost and goes back across the river. All of these unifying dramatic ironies, as well as numerous ironic juxtapositions throughout
the novel, serve to deflate the pretensions of man and the glory and
purposiveness of war. They also help to shape the plot.

The Red Badge of Courage also makes major use of irony of
manner, irony which reveals the thoughts of Henry Fleming to be
self-deceptive, contradictory, and pretentious. Some of these ironies
contribute more to structural unity than do others. Henry's discovery of the smallness of himself and his regiment, which ironically
punctures his pretensions, develops after his first engagement and
continues during his second one. Also ironic are Henry's intermittent wishes to die; before his first battle, after his flight, and during
his successful second battle. Significantly, his motives each time are
similar: he is driven by pride to wish for glory and for release from
the stupidity of his superiors. Only his dead body will prove his
worth.

A comprehensive irony involving Henry's attitude toward nature
is perhaps less consistently worked out. Occasional descriptions early
in the novel suggest that Henry feels nature to be sympathetic. A
little later nature is described as impassive. The sequence showing
Henry frightening a squirrel, after which he sees a small animal
seize a fish and then comes upon a corpse in a "chapel of boughs,"
presents famous ironic juxtapositions. In subsequent passages we see
Henry experiencing nature as hostile, or forgetting, as Crane says,
that it is a process. Several excised paragraphs in Chapter XV show
Henry congratulating himself on being greatly favored by nature.
This passage correlates with an excised passage in the last chapter,
in which Crane mocks Henry for fraternizing with nature. Greenfield believes that this excised passage is ironical only about Henry's
optimistic view of his fate, and not about his earlier cowardice, but
this qualification seems to me mistaken. Crane wrote in this excised
passage:

> Fate had in truth been kind to him; she had stabbed him with
> benign purpose and diligently cudgeled him for his own sake. In
> his rebellion, he had been very portentious, no doubt, and sin-
> cere, and anxious for humanity, but now that he stood safe, with

no lack of blood, it was suddenly clear to him that he had been wrong not to kiss the knife and bow to the cudgel.

Since these thoughts refer back to an excised remark about "his terrible combat with the arrayed forces of the universe," and also clearly parallel the passage on nature's favor which Crane removed from Chapter XV, Crane must have intended irony about Henry's cowardice as well as about his delusions regarding his fate, for Chapter XV emphasizes Henry's luck in being spared public shame for his flight. These passages suggest that Crane planned a terminal irony both about Henry's early cowardice and later delusions of his importance to the universe. That Crane later changed his plan, as other excisions also indicate, suggests something more basic than the attempt to "redress the tonal balance" which Greenfield sees in these revisions. It suggests an ambiguity in Crane's attitude toward his material, an ambiguity he probably found it difficult to resolve.

Vital to the problem of the novel's resolution is John Berryman's observation that Crane "is simultaneously *at war* with the people he creates and *on their side*—and displays each of these attitudes so forcibly that the reader feels he is himself being made a fool of. . . ."[6] If Crane were not on the side of Henry Fleming, it would be impossible for the reader to identify with the youth and with his human weaknesses. Crane's problem, however, was not only to maintain the reader's identification but to express the compassion he so obviously felt for man in both his everyday and cosmic dilemmas. At the end Crane had to make an important choice: either Henry was to continue in delusions about his cowardice and his favored place in the universe, or he was to arrive at an understanding and acceptance of the perilous but unavoidable human lot. The most revealing of Crane's revisions dropped the final four words from this sentence: "He had been to touch the great death, and found that, after all, it was but the great death *and was for others*" (italics mine). Although Greenfield notes this change, he underestimates its significance, regarding the key words merely as added pretension. The difference, however, is between accepting the human lot and persisting in delusions. Without the last four words, as Crane's final version stands, the sentence resembles Shakespeare's "By my troth, I care not, a man can die but once. We owe God a death . . . and he that dies this year is quit for the next" (*II Henry IV*, III, ii, 250–55). Had he included the final four words, Crane would have portrayed a Henry who completely misses the most important thing he could have learned.

Other details, both in the final version and in excisions, show Crane hesitating between portraying a truly chastened and wiser

6. *Stephen Crane* (New York, 1949), p. 269.

Henry, and a still deluded one. Crane's excisions, I believe, clearly show that his final decision was to present a Henry who has accepted his place in the universe and thus become a man. The tone of the last four paragraphs, in the final version, is perfectly straightforward. They show no trace in the exaggeration characteristic of Henry's thought when Crane is ironic about it. The description of "tranquil skies, fresh meadows, cool brooks—an existence of soft and eternal peace" does not jar with Crane's description of predatory nature, as has been claimed both by some who find it ironic and by some who find it straightforward. Although the nature which Crane depicts is an indifferent process, men do not fool themselves when they take pleasure in its lovelier manifestations. In these final paragraphs Crane is seeking a catharsis after the horror and initiation which have dominated Henry's experience. The reappearance of rain and mud bring a temporary halt to action, a time for reconsideration and hope. The images of peace represent values to which man may turn after he is no longer compelled to be "an animal blistered and sweating in the heat and pain of war." Nor do I take Crane's final image to be either ironic or sentimental: "Over the river a golden ray of sun came through the hosts of leaden rain clouds." Again the tone provides no justification for seeing a correlation between this sun and the suns which introduced and shone upon battle. Although there is some triteness of phrasing here, Crane seems to be symbolizing the hope of a world of peace to which the purged and enduring soul may be lucky enough to survive.

Doubtless the general affirmation of Crane's conclusion still jars slightly with some of the preceding narrative, especially with the ironic treatment of Henry. His assumption of manhood may seem an unjust reward for his cowardice and rationalizations, even though that manhood is centrally an acceptance of the human lot. Although Henry's increase in self-confidence does help to make acceptable his final change, it is of first importance to observe that this final change is a result of all the action that precedes it, and is a revolt against both his cowardly and his fierce behavior. Henry's discovery of his precarious human lot comes as a flash of insight which is prepared for by the peacefulness after battle and by his ruminations about all of his previous behavior. The suddenness of Henry's insight, the traces of irony in the final chapter, and Crane's departure from naturalism are, I believe, the causes of scepticism about the effectiveness and straightforwardness of the denouement.

Norman Friedman sees Henry's change as one of thought rather than character. This distinction raises problems too complex for brief discussion, but one may suggest that since acceptance of the human situation may promote a calmer behavior in the future and a juster understanding of the motives of others, it may well lead to moral decisions, and thus can be seen as a change in character. One might also argue that authentic self-understanding always creates a change in character.

It is obvious that Crane has vastly improved his conclusion by his excisions. Without these excisions the final chapter would be quite ambiguous and would suggest that Crane regarded Henry ironically to the very end. Had Crane clearly shaped the final chapter to show Henry still deluded, his conclusion would have been even weaker, for the reader's bond of sympathy with Henry would then be snapped, and the anti-war feeling of the novel would be greatly diminished. Apparently Crane's momentum in depicting a youth driven by terror and pride, and prone to dreams and delusions, almost led him to continue intense irony to a point at which it would have weakened his general intention. His final problem was to make us accept some intellectual self-transcendence in Henry so that our sympathies—no matter how they have been tried—will remain with him. Crane's success with this problem was, I think, only moderate.

Certainly there are many devices that give a visible structure to *The Red Badge of Courage*. In addition to the numerous patterns which I have discussed, one may note the underlying scheme of forethought, failure, and successful engagement, which scheme pivots on Henry's receipt of the spurious wound. But despite these elements of design, the plot is still largely episodic, and the final eight chapters are distinctly weaker than the first sixteen. Before Chapter XVII Crane has exhausted all of his greatest scenes and his most intense ironies. Henry's worst battles of conscience are in the past. The great scenes involving fear and flight, the tattered man, the death of Jim Conklin, the false wound and the return it brings about—all are over. The most intense ironies created by Henry's wound—his gloating over Wilson's embarrassment and his worst boasting—occur in Chapters XV and XVI. After them the immediate ironies are always comparatively unobtrusive.

The ironies which pattern the whole book also become less noticeable: wild courage seems less exceptional than wild cowardice, and the division of self created by aggressive pride is less noticeable than the division of self resulting from self-torturing pride. As a result, it is possible to overlook the irony of the fact that Henry is still driven by instinct and pride. Rather than a sense of one magnificent scene after another, one has a stronger sense of loose episodes, although the competition of Henry and Wilson, and various ironies, are designed to maintain the tension. This partial decrease in tension from Chapters XVII to XXIII doubtless leads to a certain weariness which may increase one's scepticism about

Crane's resolution. Many of these weaknesses seem inevitable given the kind of plot which Crane constructed, but the general weakening of interest and cohesion in the last eight chapters, as well as the somewhat problematic resolution, add up to a serious defect in a generally magnificent work of art.

EDWIN H. CADY

The Red Badge of Courage†

* * *

II

It has been variously asserted that Crane's way of imagining and constructing *The Red Badge of Courage* was realist, naturalist, impressionist, or symbolist. It would make a difference if it could be demonstrated that one of them, or any other, was *the* method. One would then expect to interpret particular parts, and the whole, in certain ways, and one's reading and response would be affected accordingly. But the conviction with which these various views have been urged by sensitive and intelligent critics might in itself warn the reader that no unitary view is exclusively right. The very secret of the novel's power inheres in the inviolably organic uniqueness with which Crane adapted all four methods to his need. *The Red Badge*'s method is all and none. There is no previous fiction like it.

The narrative point of view, however, is nothing new. James and Howells had been developing the technique used in *The Red Badge* for years; they repeatedly displayed it with an easy virtuosity which Crane could hardly have missed in the big magazines. In the earliest pages of *The Red Badge*, the story-teller's point of view, the narrative line-of-sight along events which will afford the readers' perspective, is permanently established. The voice is that of a third-person, "objective" narrator—not a first-person, "subjective" teller who says "Call me Ishmael" or "You don't know me without you have read a book. . . ." But the point of view is located at almost the same place as if this were a first-person narrative: it is just behind the eyes of "the youthful private." The reader sees through Henry Fleming's eyes, and he is able to reflect backwards somewhat to record what goes on in Henry's mind (though never, of course, to overhear his "stream of consciousness"). But for the most part the reader is limited to seeing and hearing the life of the fiction as the narrator does; he can never "go behind" into the mind of another character.

† From *Stephen Crane* (New York, Twayne, 1962), pp. 118–44. Copyright 1962 by Twayne Publishers, Inc. Reprinted with the permission of Twayne Publishers, a division of G. K. Hall & Co., Boston.

These limitations make the experience afforded by the novel seem objective and thus credible, very intense, yet also somewhat detached and impersonal. The reader is not invited to "identify" wholly with young Fleming—a fact Joseph Hergesheimer recalled mourning over in his youth.[1] Fleming is part of a drama. He is to be subject to criticism, to judgment unintrusively unmoralized, established dramatically and ironically, but forcefully there. Essentially this is a perspective—but upon what? And to what end? What finally is the force of its proportion, its total form?

One way to begin to answer these questions is to notice some distinctions about the problem of point of view in this or any modern fiction which have not always been observed in discussing *The Red Badge*. At least four classes of "point of view" function in fiction. In simplest forms these are the author's, as he imagines and builds the work; the narrator's, which in any sophisticated fiction is not the author's way of looking at his work but an instrument of his technique in presenting it; the character's (or characters'), in the interplay of which—with one another and the narrator's viewpoints —lies a great deal of the craftsman's resource; and, finally, the reader's. Author's and reader's points of view are external to the novel. It may turn out that the reader's has been very skillfully played upon by the author who uses as instruments the internal points of view of narrator and characters.

The distinction in *The Red Badge of Courage* between the narrator's point of view and that of Henry Fleming, the sole character's view which the reader knows at all directly, is subtle for the reasons already suggested. The narrator's point of view is through Fleming's eyes. But though the reader sees what and as Fleming does, the reader is not he. Henry's point of view is that of his own experience; the reader knows it as, with the narrator, he goes reflexively "behind" for reports on that experience.

Material for observation of all this experience is very rich in the first four or five pages of the novel. It starts with a swiftly telescoped atmospheric registering of the context. Morning and early spring are telescoped in the first sentence:

The cold passed reluctantly from the earth, and the retiring fogs revealed an army stretched out on the hills, resting. As the landscape changed from brown to green, the army awakened, and began to tremble with eagerness at the noise of rumors. It cast its eyes upon the roads, which were growing from the long troughs of liquid mud to proper thoroughfares. A river, amber-tinted in the shadow of its banks, purled at the army's feet; and at night, when the stream had become of a sorrowful blackness, one could see across it the red, eye-like gleam of hostile camp-fires set in the low brows of distant hills.

It might, parenthetically, be possible to argue that the foregoing "one could see" establishes a narrative point of view distinct from Fleming's. But such as argument is unnecessarily messy and less than appreciative of Crane's artistic achievement. He handles point of view more like a movie camera than perhaps any predecessor had done. The reader stands to see somewhere back of Fleming's eyes. Sometimes the reader gets the long "panning" shot, sometimes the view only Henry could see, sometimes an interior view limited only by Crane's ignorance of methods Joyce would discover.

So the reader moves at once to a spirited, comic camp scene as tall Jim Conklin falsely reports imminent action. Then he retires with Fleming to ponder his emotions "in a little trance of astonishment" within the security of his hut. And suddenly his memory flashes back to the scenes and thoughts of his enlistment at home months before. It is the content of that flashback—seen by the reader through the narrator's double perception of what Fleming's point of view is now and what it was earlier—that presents the basic problem of the novel.

The reader begins, then, with a perspective upon the perspectives of "the youth." They go back to dreams of battle and personal magnificence in war, dreams he has classed with "thought-images of heavy crowns and high castles"—the cloudy symbols of a high romance. Awake, this adolescent Minniver Cheevy "had long despaired of witnessing a Greek-like struggle. Such would be no more, he said. Men were better, or more timid. Secular and religious education had effaced the throat-grappling instinct, or else firm finance held in check the passions." On the farm, Fleming was a perfect neo-romantic.

Tales of "the war in his own country" inevitably began to move him, however. "They might not be distinctly Homeric, but there seemed to be much glory in them." In the face of his mother's Christian pacifism and her quietly effective ironic undercutting of his egotisms, he eventually enlisted and left for camp with a soaring conviction "that he must be a hero." But the monotonous realities of camp life had taught him to concentrate on personal comfort and retreat "back to his old ideas. Greek-like struggles would be no more." Now, perhaps on the edge of the real thing, new possibilities of truth emerge. Maybe he will be a coward! "He felt that in this crisis his laws of life were useless. Whatever he had learned of himself was here of no avail. He was an unknown quantity. He saw that he would again be obliged to experiment as he had in early youth." When it turned out that the battle was not on the morrow, he had days to make "ceaseless calculations . . . all wondrously unsatisfactory." Examination of self and scrutiny of others were defeated. Only experience would help: "to go into the blaze, and then figuratively to watch his legs to discover their merits and faults . . . he must have blaze, blood, and danger, even as a chemist requires this, that and the other."

Except for the initial paragraph, the method and issues so far established are those of the realists. The emphasis on point of view, on vision, is theirs; and the establishment of a problem of knowledge, which will require an exercise in discovery and revelation is theirs. So, too, is the pragmatic dependence on experience: answering the question by watching whether one's legs ran or stayed might have come straight from James's *Principles of Psychology*. And raising the issues of romanticism—the heroic, the glamorous, the egotistical, exalted and sentimental—was a confirmed habit of the realists. Anti-romanticism, the reduction by ridicule and irony of the romantic to the common, negative realism, was the first and always the easiest way for the realists to define themselves. Positive realism, finding the beauty, power, and meaning of life in the commonplace —a green farm boy among his peers in an unblooded regiment, for instance—was much more difficult. But the wrangling amateur military experts in the company street and the soldiers' hut are scenically presented—they talk and act—with a humorous precision dear to the heart of any lover of the common American man.

III

One does not read far into *The Red Badge of Courage*, however, without discovering that it is very different from the traditional realistic novel. The extended and massive specification of detail with which the realist seems to impose upon one an illusion of the world of the common vision is wholly missing. Equally absent is the tremendous procession of natural and social "forces" characteristic of naturalism—of Frank Norris or Dreiser trying to be Zola. Detail is not absent, but it is comparatively sparingly deployed on a light, mobile structure; and it is used for intensive, not extensive effects. Reference to "forces" is there, but no effort at all to show them steaming in their mighty currents, floating the characters as tracers, as chips on the steam whose signifiance is to reval the trending of the currents.

One of the most reliable ways, indeed, to distinguish romantic from realistic and both from naturalistic fiction is to examine the way each handles its characters. To the romancer the significance of his people is symbolic; they are representative men and women who reveal, by the doctrine of correspondence, spiritual truths (*viz.*, Chingachgook, Chillingworth, Goodman Brown, Captain Ahab and all his men). The reductive, agnostic realist, however, cannot believe in the spiritual sublimity, the ideality, of his characters. He levels his vision to the human, fascinated by the paradoxes of the common person: his individuality, his commonplace mediocrity, the representative, perhaps universal, meaning of his "common" moral problems. To the naturalist, finally, humanity means only animality. This is the ultimate reduction. Where the romancer's concern was superhuman and the realist's humane, the naturalist's is infrahuman. And in a sense the naturalist joins hands with the romancer (no matter how the latter might cringe) again in looking not so much to what the man is as to what he can be made to reveal about realities far larger, stronger, more important and more abstract than man.

In this intent, too, Crane stands with the realists, but he stands historically in advance of them toward the coming future of the novel. The critics of his own day who wondered if Crane did not represent a "new realism" may have been more than a little right.[2] It was natural, if not inevitable, that the realism of the generation previous to Crane should develop to prepare the way for its own displacement. The shift was toward an increasingly psychological realism, and it was propelled by at least two major forces. One of these was the displacement of positivism from its dominance of late nineteenth-century thought. A decade like the 1890's, which began with William James's *Psychology* and ended with the unleashing of the new, electronic factors in physics which produced Henry Adams' image of "himself lying in the Gallery of Machines at the Great Exposition of 1900, his historical neck broken by the sudden irruption of forces totally new," was bound at the least to loosen the grip of positivism on the imagination. The second force, however, arose from the practice of realistic fiction itself. The more one confronted the mystery of men as persons living out their fates and struggling toward their deaths, the more one's scrutiny turned from the outward sign to the inward process itself. Howells noticed in 1903, when he was writing a novel Freudian in all but specifically Viennese terminology for the main concept, that all the realists had of late been turning to psychology. Indeed, many of them had been flirting with psychic phenomena as farflung as the claims of spiritualism. What he did not seem to notice was that he himself had been working largely in psychological realism since *The Shadow of a Dream* in 1891.

For the better part of thirty-five years, Howells had fought at the foremost point in a great battle to capture American taste for real-

2. See *New York Tribune,* January 20, 1897, and *Rochester Post Express,* February 22, 1897 (Stephen Crane Scrapbook, Barrett Collection, University of Virginia), commenting on H. D. Traill, "The New Realism," *Fortnightly Review,* January 1, 1897.

ism. He had defined realism as the objective truth in art about the
visible aspects of human life. But in 1903 he registered his realization that a change had occurred among the great realists of the
world. God seems to love the game of the pendulum in man's
affairs, he observed. And now "A whole order of literature has
arisen, calling itself psychological, as realism called itself scientific
... it is not less evident in Tolstoi, in Gorky, in Ibsen, in Björnsen,
in Hauptmann, and in Mr. Henry James, than in Maeterlinck
himself."[3]

It was like Howells to leave himself out of the account. The surprising thing is his so registering the change almost fifteen years
after he had launched himself into it. What he apparently did not
see was that what he called "the present psychologism" was not just
a providential swing of the pendulum but a fairly predictable outcome of the earlier realism—and that it was already bridging the
way for the interior, stream of consciousness, and therefore symbolic
fiction which would succeed it. The realism of which Howells had
been the chief American prophet had been, as he said, "scientific"
in the mid-nineteenth century sense of factualistic and "objective."
It has also been intensely humanistic, fixing its focus on persons, on
characters, in their human dimensions, qualities, conflicts, problems,
and fates. The more it fastened on characters and the visible evidence of inner conditions, the more that realism would be tempted
to "go behind" as James said. The further behind the veil of sense
it went, the less normally and normatively visible its evidences
would be. After a while it would no longer be the realist's appeal to
the common vision which would win the reader's suspension of
disbelief, but only a faith in the realist's honesty of covert vision
secured, perhaps, by his faithfulness to that common vision in overt
matters. The turn to psychology opened important and exciting
vistas to the accomplished realist like Henry James. It also paved
the way for the displacement of realism by such masters to come as
Joyce, Anderson, Lawrence, and Faulkner.

The Red Badge of Courage was the first masterpiece of that transition, as Howells imperfectly saw while reviewing it. Most commendable, he said, was "the skill shown in evolving from the
youth's crude expectations and ambitions a quiet honesty and self-
possession manlier and nobler than any heroism had imagined . . .
and decidedly on the psychological side the book is worth while as
an earnest of the greater things that we may hope for from a new
talent working upon a high level, not quite clearly as yet, but
strenuously.[4] In a lifetime devoted to part-time criticism, Howells
had a high batting average, but this time he hit only a part of the
ball. He may have been told or have divined Crane's interest in the

psychological. Crane was able to be overt about it from Greece, telling John Bass that "Between two great armies battling against each other the interesting thing is the mental attitude of the men." Or, as he explained himself to his English readers, people "think they ought to demand" of "descriptions of battle" that they be placed "to stand in front of the mercury of war and see it rise or fall . . . but it is an absurd thing for a writer to do if he wishes to reflect, in any way, the mental condition of the men in the ranks. . . ."[5]

"To reflect . . . the mental condition of the men in the ranks," representing them especially with one youth, is an exact definition of the achievement—and probably the intention—of The Red Badge of Courage. Its formal structure is rather simply Aristotelian. It has a beginning (Chapters I–IV), which gets the youth to real battle; a middle (Chapters V–XIII), which witnesses his runaway and return; and an end (Chapters XIV–XXIII), which displays his achievement of "heroism" at climax, followed by a certain understanding of it in a coda-like final chapter. The middle and end sections are replete with notations of Fleming's psychological responses to fear, stress, and courage. There are progressively at least ninety such notations of Fleming's state of nerves-mind-psyche (it is not at all clear that Crane had any coherent psychological theory to exploit). They occur in pairs or triads of alternating or developmental stages as well as singly and are sometimes recurrent. If only by mere weight, the ninety constitute a major part of the substance of a short novel.

Actually, of course, psychological notations count for far more than mere bulk in The Red Badge. They are fascinating in themselves. For instance, Crane recorded something he no doubt picked up from football (as psychologists are said to have done later, naming the phenomenon "scrimmage blackout"). In the depth of combat, Crane supposed, Fleming would pass into an absorptive trance in which he was conscious of little but performed with intense automatism in a "battle-sleep" during which he might occasionally "dream" impressions. Essential to the achievement of the novel are the psychological patterns Crane divined for Fleming's combat experience. One is the obverse of the other. In the one, fear leads to panic, panic to guilt, guilt to rationalization and eventually to frustration and acquiescence. In the other, resentment produces rage, and rage "battle sleep"; resolution, including willingness to die, follows and leads in turn to "heroism" and at last to adumbrations of emotional realism and modesty. Equally striking are Crane's observations of the complexities of individual-group relations.

If this psychologism carried Crane past realism, it also defined

5. John Bass, "How Novelist Crane Acts on the Battlefield," New York Journal, May 23, 1897; "With Greek and Turk, III," Westminster Review.

his sense of naturalism, at least for this novel. Philosophic naturalism in *The Red Badge of Courage* is used, not expounded. It is
identified as a form of romanticism, a buttress to the ego, a means
of escape from moral reality and responsibility. In the end it is
rejected. It is referred to—in the final state of the novel more
obliquely than directly—so often as to leave little doubt that Crane
was quite aware of its patterns of explanation and their potential
uses. But it is at last only a foil for the pragmatic, relativistic ideas
toward which the novel finally points.

It may also indicate Crane's decision about naturalism at this
point to note that he cut most of the explicit references to its ideas
out of *The Red Badge* at various stages of revision. No thorough
collation of all the states of the emergent text of the novel has ever
been published; and one is badly needed. But examination of the
Barrett manuscript tends to confirm Professor Stallman's steps
toward a variorum text[6] in *A Stephen Crane Omnibus*. Contrary
to the notion that Crane never revised, one can work out at least
seven states of *The Red Badge* text. Without knowing what preceded the text which Crane's poverty preserved in cancelled fragments on the versos of a later state, one starts with the earliest
extant draft which Stallman labelled "SV." Next, presumably
comes the Bacheller syndicated text (which may have been excised
from "SV"), then the extant manuscript (Stallman's "LV") which
stands in four states, having been revised in pen, in pencil, and
finally in blue crayon. Before the first edition, there was a lost typescript revised nobody knows how often.

Rather boldly explicit in draft but variously suppressed and left
implicit in the final text was Crane's association of philosophic naturalism with Henry Fleming's panic syndrome. One may guess that
he thought to make the resultant theme central to the novel's development and then changed his mind.

Early in the morning of his first battle day, Fleming dashes, wild
with curiosity, upon the scene of what he expects will be immediate
combat. But it is bathos, nothing really is happening; and as the
regiment presses on into a silently ominous landscape, his courage
oozes away: "This advance upon Nature was too calm . . . absurd
ideas took hold upon him. . . . It was all a trap." With this comes
the idea associated throughout: he must become a prophet of the
truth "Nature" reveals. "He thought that he must break from the
ranks and harangue his comrades. . . . The generals were idiots. . . .
There was but one pair of eyes in the corps." But fear of ridicule
silences him as the tense ranks advance "to look at war, the red animal—war, the blood-swollen god."[7] However, nature is no constant

6. Stallman, *Stephen Crane: An Omnibus*   7. *Work*, I, 50–52.
(New York, 1952), p. 225 *et seq.*

for Fleming; she varies with his psychic states. After his first and successful combat, he wakes from his battle-sleep with "a flash of astonishment at the blue pure sky and the sun gleaming on the trees and fields. It was surprising that Nature had gone tranquilly on with her golden process in the midst of so much devilment."[8]

Fleming's later efforts to appeal to nature as a constant and as a source of comforting revelation (or rationalization) are therefore doomed. If one were to argue from *The Red Badge of Courage* about Crane's attitudes toward the naturalistic argument for man's animal irresponsibility toward duty and morality he would, in fact, have to conclude that Crane had considered but repudiated that argument.

Chapter VII is the first decisively interesting surviving example of Crane's revision of *The Red Badge*, and the revisions affect precisely this issue, shifting from explicit to implicit. This is the chapter in which Fleming is plunged from unworthy hope of personal justification into shame and self-pity by his deserted comrades' holding their line and repulsing the attack from which he had run. He seeks to "bury himself" in the thick woods, in nature. There he passes through swift changes of mood. "This landscape gave him assurance. A fair field holding life. It was the religion of peace. . . . He conceived Nature to be a woman with a deep aversion to tragedy." He shies a pine-cone at "a jovial squirrel" who dashes for safety: "The youth felt triumphant at this exhibition. There was the law, he said. Nature had given him a sign. . . . Nature was of his mind."

As he wends on, however, other signs obtrude. In a swamp he sees "a small animal pounce in and emerge directly with a gleaming fish." And finally, in what at first seems "a chapel" in a pine grove, he finds the disintegrating corpse of a Federal soldier from a bygone battle, with "black ants swarming greedily upon the grey face." The present text ends abruptly with Fleming fleeing the horror and leaving "the chapel" to the "soft wind" and "sad silence" of nature[9]— which ties in perfectly with an impressionistic bit of atmosphere about the onset of twilight which begins the next chapter.

Once, however, the text had been far more intellectually obvious, and Crane had kept it that way for quite a while. The "LV" manuscript, at least the third state, was revised first in pen, then in pencil. It was in that minimally fifth revision that Crane cancelled from the end of the chapter these words,

> Again the youth was in despair. Nature no longer condoled with him. There was nothing, then, after all, in that demonstration she gave—the frightened squirrel fleeing aloft from the missile. He thought . . . that there was given another law which far-

8. *Ibid.*, p. 70.   9. *Ibid.*, pp. 81–84.

overtopped it—all life existing upon death, eating ravenously, stuffing itself with the hopes of the dead. . . .[1]

That mood also passed. Shortly he is thinking as he heads back toward the battle that, because brambles restrain him, "Nature could not be quite ready to kill him."[2] But, of course, that alternation was lost from the revised text.

Fleming's nightmare agony in the middle part of *The Red Badge* climaxes in Chapter IX with the macabre death of Conklin, "the tall soldier," and in Chapter X with Fleming's desertion of "the tattered man" on being asked where his own wound was. Crane tried hard to provide Fleming with reflections adequate to his shocked and shame-sodden state but he failed, cancelling, rewriting, and cancelling again. He had Henry reflect, in utter opposition to his old romantic ideas, that soldiers were really "Nature's dupes." Nature went seducing men with "dreams" of "glory," defeating their ingenuity of devices to stave off death by planting a treacherous sentiment in their hearts. "War, he said bitterly to the sky, was a makeshift created because ordinary processes could not furnish deaths enough." From hints in "SV" Crane seems to have developed this and Fleming's derisive fury about it or five pages in "LV."[3] He cancelled the effort out only in the blue-crayon revision of "LV" which appears to have gone to the typist.

That cancelled experience of Fleming's lay behind the returned motif of his exaltation of self-justification at seeing, at the beginning of Chapter XI, the routed troops on the road. That feeling is followed at once by his feeling like a sinner in Hell watching angels "with weapons of flame and banners of sunlight"[4] when a disciplined column of infantry butts its glorious way through the chaos. Crane stops to put Fleming through nine progressive states of psychosomatic and imaginary response to his situation in the least dramatic (and so perhaps least satisfactory) chapter in the book. And it was clearly Crane's intention in "SV" to follow the "analytic" chapter with a twelfth which would bring to an early climax both the theme of natural irresponsibility and the several times repeated theme of Fleming's prophetic role toward his comrades and the world.

Since the relative slackness of the previous chapter makes it clear that discursive patches mar *The Red Badge*, it is not surprising that Crane suppressed his intended Chapter XII. He was right to do so, and the principal use of considering it is to see that in it he unmistakably derided the naturalistic diagnosis of Fleming's condition

1. Barrett MS., p. 65 ("LV"). (Cf. Stallman, *Omnibus*, p. 276.)
2. *Work*, I, 86.
3. Barrett MS, "SV" p. 75 on verso of "LV" p. 118; "SV" p. 76 on verso of "LV" p. 97; "LV" p. 85. (Cf. Stallman, *Omnibus*, pp. 291–92).
4. *Work*, I, 105 ff.

together with Henry's Dreiser-like urge to proclaim its gospel. And he left (now submerged) that rejection as the pivot upon which Fleming could turn again, now fit to be delivered by kindly (but by no means unique, as it turned out) fates to his outfit.

That aborted chapter begins, "It was always clear to Fleming that he was entirely different from other men," and now he consoles himself that his suffering has been "unprecedented" in the awful opposition of his tiny self to the universe. But then he sees that there is no malice really, "merely law," and that there were compensating principles—what might be called the squirrel's law recurred to him:

> Nature had provided her creations with various defenses and ways to escape . . . that the things might resist or hide with a security proportionate to their strength and wisdom. It was all the same old philosophy. He could not omit a small grunt of satisfaction as he saw with what brilliancy he had reasoned it all out.

Soon he is ready to avail himself of that brilliancy and apply his findings to the incident of his own flight from the battle: "It was not a fault; it was a law. It was—But he saw that when he had made a vindicating structure of great principles, it was the calm toes of tradition that kicked it all down about his ears." In bitter rebellion he then resolves to save mankind from the worship of "the gods of the ashes," and he begins to see himself "the growing prophet of a world-reconstruction. Far down in the pure depths of his being . . . he saw born a voice. He conceived a new world, modelled by the pain of his life, in which no old shadows fell darkening upon the temple of thought. And there were many personal advantages in it."

He thinks of "piercing orations" and "himself a sun-lit figure upon a peak." But gradually his enthusiasm burns out as he thinks of mankind's bovine habitude—"he would be beating his fists against the brass of accepted things." He rails abuse "in supreme disgust and rage. . . . To him there was something terrible and awesome in these words spoken from his heart to his heart. He was very tragic."[5]

Crane's irony is obvious from the bathetic anti-climaxes of this; "And there were many personal advantages . . . a sun-lit figure. . . . He was very tragic." But even though this has disappeared from the text, its irony remains operative in the pivotal next chapter. There Fleming suddenly sees that all-enviable, heroic-angelic column charging back from the fray "like terrified buffaloes." He feels

5. Barrett MS, "SV" p. 84 on verso of "LV" p. 113; p. 85 on p. 108; p. 86 on p. 112. (Cf. Stallman, *Omnibus*, pp. 298–300).

"horror-stricken" and stares "in agony and amazement." Then, most significantly, "He forgot that he was engaged in combating the universe. He threw aside his mental pamphlets on the philosophy of the retreated and rules for the guidance of the damned." He loses himself in concern for the stricken angels, thinks absurdly of rallying them, tries to detain one to ask what happened, and gets his red badge of courage from the rifle-butt in the hands of a hysterical ex-hero. His knockout is virtually a death, and for a while after he goes "tall soldier fashion." His first day of combat draws on to sunset, and in the dark he is rescued by the selfless and faceless "cheery soldier" and delivered back to the 304th New York where he belongs.

There he is met with cheer and sympathy. His lie about being shot readily believed, he is nursed and cared for by a suddenly mature, modest and no longer loud Wilson. In the morning he discovers that perhaps half the regiment had been missing after the action but turned up by morning with stories—" 'Jest like you done,' " Wilson tells Fleming. Then, in a very late, blue-crayon cancellation surviving from two suppressed pages at the end of Chapter XIV ("LV"), he thinks "with deep contempt of all his grapplings and tuggings with fate and the universe." He sees how ridiculous had been the cherished uniqueness and novelty of his thought. But he begins to feel self-respect returning, since he is safe and "unimpeached."[6]

It will take all the rest of the last part of the book to try that egotism in the fire of a real, if minor, heroism and reduce it to the human modesty achieved by Wilson on the first day. From this point forward, however, nature will be no more abstracted, personified, or capitalized in *The Red Badge*, and Fleming's recollections of his prophetic ideas and role will be merely embarrassed. He will be glad nobody else knows. Intellectually, that seems to be what there is to naturalism in the novel, and the symbolic or impressionistic uses of it are keyed to the intellectual.

It seems clear that *The Red Badge* is not a work of naturalism; and it is also certain that Fleming is *not* "guided by a naturalistic code of ethics." No more is a naturalistic "Henry's attitude . . . characteristic of Crane."[7] The true naturalist's truth must be that man is a part of nature and not other. Crane's sense of the indifference or hostility of nature to man was shared, for instance, by a Pilgrim Father (Brewster), a Massachusetts Bay Puritan (Win-

6. Barrett MS, "LV" p. 125. (Cf. Stallman, *Omnibus*, p. 317).
7. Winifred Lynskey, "Crane's *The Red Badge of Courage*," *Explicator*, VIII (December, 1949), 18. For variant ways of putting the naturalistic argument see also Harry Hartwick, *The Foreground of American Fiction*, New York, 1934, pp. 21–44; and Charles C. Walcutt, *American Literary Naturalism, A Divided Stream*, Minneapolis, 1956, pp. 66–86. J. B. Colvert, "Style and Meaning in Stephen Crane: 'The Open Boat,'" *University of Texas Studies in English*, XXXVII (1958), 34–45, casts fresh light on the problem.

throp), a rationalistic Calvinist (Edwards), a deist (Freneau, "The Hurricane"), by Melville (whatever he was), and by many varieties of non-naturalistic Darwinists. Like them, Crane did believe man was "other"—in Crane's case, man was human. That was a lesson Henry Fleming learned to see.

IV

Then it becomes possible to say that *The Red Badge of Courage* is a work of psychological realism deeply affected in style by the fact that the author was also an ironic, imagistic, metaphysical poet. And that brings one to the moot questions of Crane's impressionism and symbolism. If one could be sure of the qualities of these, it would be best to treat them apart. Since, in fact, their existence as well as their separability is obscure, it may be best to take them together. Actually, in Crane's case it might be impossible to define his impressionism and symbolism separately.

"Impressionism" was a potent and intensely controversial term in the 1890's. A war cry for those who sought escape from Victorianism, it stood for the liberation of the artist from the academy and tradition, from formalism and ideality, from narrative, and finally even from realism; for realism demanded responsibility to the common vision and impressionism responsibility only to what the unique eye of the painter saw. It was also a swearword for conservatives of every variety, of course. In painting there was a solid body of reference, forged in the heat of often vicious controversy, and a body of distinguished (no matter how controversial) examples to give substance to "impressionism."

But in literature the case is and was different. The world was early applied to Crane's work. The *San Francisco Examiner* was working toward it from the hostile side when its paragrapher on January 12, 1897, objected to Crane and Garland together for "affectation in style," making "a dead set against literary rules [*sic*]" and to Crane separately for "the blare of his word-trumpets." And the *Chicago Record* got there the same week, observing on January 16 that "Mr. Crane is not a scientist. . . . He is above all an impressionist . . .'"; "superficial," he was called, and also "flashy" in *The Little Regiment*; and the work was not up to "the fine psychological study" of *The Red Badge*.[8] On the other hand, it was repeatedly the highest praise of Joseph Conrad and Edward Garnett in England that Crane was an impressionist; it made him triumphantly avant garde. And that has given the word considerable currency in recent Crane criticism.

Nevertheless, it was and is difficult to know just what Crane's

8. Stephen Crane Scrapbooks, Barrett Collection.

"impressionism" means. In literature the term is so vague and so
devoid of explicit example as not even to make an entry in Wellek
and Warren, *Theory of Literature*, or in standard histories. Handbook definitions, when they occur, are conspicuous neither for clarity nor richness of reference. They seem roughly agreed that in literature "impressionism" means either absence of detail or else the
effect of the author observing himself in the presence of life, not
the life.[9] Neither applies illuminatingly to the work of Stephen
Crane. Yet it would be strange if there were nothing meant by all
the often impressive critics who have applied the term to Crane;
and of course that is not the case.

What they are talking about comes down, perhaps, to the vividness and intensity of Crane's notation of atmospheric textures and
to the striking economy, *multum in parvo*, of his form. No doubt
the effort to achieve psychological realism promoted what Willa
Cather brilliantly defined as "The Novel Démeublé."[1] Howells'
first attempts at it in *The Shadow of a Dream* (1890) and *An
Imperative Duty* (1892) were strikingly "disfurnished" after *A
Hazard of New Fortunes* (1890). Crane's own comment on literary
aims is characteristically minimal and apparently innocent of the
term "impressionism" until his significant work had been done—
and Conrad, Garnett, and others had explained the avant garde situation to him. Even then he carefully confined a striking use of it
to painterly reference:

> The church had been turned into a hospital for Spanish
> wounded who had fallen into American hands. The interior of
> the church was too cave-like in its gloom for the eyes of the oper-
> ating surgeons, so they had had the altar-table carried to the
> doorway, where there was a bright light. Framed then in the
> black archway was the altar-table with the figure of a man upon
> it. He was naked save for a breech-clout, and so close, so clear
> was the ecclesiastic suggestion that one's mind leaped to a fantasy
> that this thin, pale figure had just been torn down from a cross.
> The flash of the impression was like light, and for this instant it
> illumined all the dark recesses of one's remotest idea of sacrilege,
> ghastly and wanton. I bring this to you merely as an effect, an
> effect of mental light and shade, if you like; something done in
> thought similar to that which the French impressionists do in
> color; something meaningless and at the same time overwhelm-
> ing, crushing, monstrous.[2]

It has been persuasively argued that Crane must have learned
much and adapted to his writing what he learned of French

9. *The New Cenury Handbook of Eng-
lish Literature* (1956), p. 605; Thrall,
Hibbard, and Holman, *A Handbook to
Literature* (1960), pp. 237–38.

1. *Willa Cather on Writing* (1949), pp.
35–43.
2. "War Memories," December, 1899;
Work, IX, 245–46.

Impressionism.[3] Yet Linson, who should certainly have known, denies it flatly—and apparently by implication denies the name of "painter" to Vosburgh and the "Indians." Linson had been a fellow student of Gauguin but not wholly in sympathy with him. At least, however, Linson must be supposed to have known what Impressionism was all about:

> To the oft repeated query as to Crane's use of color: "Did he get it from his studio associates?" My answer is "No." I was the only painter among his early intimates; one or two others he met casually with me. The rest were illustrators or journalists. . . . The Impressionism of that day was to him an affectation, and all affectation was dishonesty, uncreative, and thus dead from the start.[4]

That statement can, of course, be regarded at most as authoritative only through Crane's establishment of himself in England.

Taken at fullest value, however, Linson indicates the same things shown by Crane's remark about Oscar Wilde: Wilde was "a mildewed chump." Crane was having none of the official *fin de siècle*. But he might equally well have had nonetheless his own sort of impressionism; and one can catch him at it. In "War Memories," again, there is a peculiar little moment when one almost feels embarrassed for Crane:

> "But to get the real thing!" cried Vernall, the war correspondent. "It seems impossible! It is because war is neither magnificent nor squalid; it is simply life, and an expression of life can always evade us. We can never tell life, one to another, although sometimes we think we can."[5]

Those Shelleyan cries and the slightly sissified self-consciousness about expression and the real thing are out of character for Crane. And, as a matter of fact, they constitute a strategic insincerity. He is embarking on a long series of pictures which will not "tell life" but present it unmistakably to a reader.

Actually Crane had, quite consciously, mastered the solution to that (as presented) pseudo-problem long before. In the *New York World* for October 15, 1896, for instance, he had lightened a bit of journalism for himself with a touch of virtuosity:

> We, as a new people, are likely to conclude that our mechanical perfection, our structural precision, is certain to destroy all quality of sentiment in our devices, and so we prefer to grope in the past when people are not supposed to have had any structural precision. As the terrible, the beautiful, the ghastly, pass contin-

3. J. J. Kwiat, "Stephen Crane and Painting," *American Quarterly*, IV (Winter, 1952), 331–38.

4. Corwin K. Linson, *My Stephen Crane*, ed. Edwin H. Cady, 1958, pp. 46–47.

5. *Work*, IX, 201.

ually before our eyes we merely remark that they do not seem to be correct in romantic detail.

But an odor of oiled woods, a keeper's tranquil, unemotional voice, a broom stood in the corner near the door, a blue sky and a bit of moving green tree at a window so small that it might have been made by a canister shot—all these ordinary things contribute with subtle meaning to the horror of this comfortable chair, this commonplace bit of furniture that . . . waits and waits.

The subject is the electric chair at Sing Sing, and the virtuosity is that he has solved the expressive problem in the act of describing it.

Not to choose any of the nature descriptions which set the atmospheric stage so perfectly over and again in *The Red Badge* or which tally Fleming's psychic gyrations, one bit of Crane's special impressionism, his way of conveying the real thing with extraordinary intensity, may stand for dozens. The 304th New York has not quite gone into action when nearby "Saunders" gets "crushed" by Confederates:

> The flag suddenly sank down as if dying. Its motion as it fell was a gesture of despair.
> Wild yells came from behind the walls of smoke. A sketch in gray and red dissolved into a mob-like body of men who galloped like wild horses.[6]

With minimal but exact detail, in an aura of psychological, not objective, reality, the experience is precisely, forcefully communicated. The method is more poetic than traditionally novelistic, as has been variously observed. It is Crane's impressionism of texture. For the rest, the question has been most usefully approached through William M. Gibson's citation of the letter from Thomas Wolfe to Scott Fitzgerald dividing great writers into "putter-inners" and "taker-outers."[7] Crane belongs with Flaubert, Hemingway, and Willa Cather's ideal as a "taker-outer," and that trait perhaps is the other aspect of his impressionism.

Inescapably, when one considers Crane's abruptly vivid effects, the question arises whether they are just impressionistically textural or symbolic as well. In some senses, of course, they are immitigably symbolic, just as any word, any significant cluster of words, is symbolic in any literary context. But surely that is not what is meant when Crane is called a "symbolist," for it would distinguish him not at all from any other author. In fact, to make the point one last time, it is hard to say what species, if any, of "symbolist" Crane was. No systematic discussion of that subject appears to exist. Cer-

6. *Work*, I, 59.
7. William M. Gibson, Introduction, *Stephen Crane: "The Red Badge of Courage" and Selected Prose and Poetry* (New York, 1956), p. 5.

tainly, as visionist, he represented the opposite of Charles Feidelson's "symbolistic imagination" and so he represents the opposite of Mallarmé, Baudelaire, et seq.[8] Crane was, that is, intensely concerned with the vision of realities, objective and subjective, which he regarded as independent of language but ideally susceptible of "unmistakable" communication through words. The evidence seems clear that he had no notion of any linguistically self-contained and unique literary "reality" and that he would have found that notion laughably conceited. One might, of course, argue, as exponents of some antirational schools of criticism appear to do, that, regardless of what Crane thought he thought, he was a "symbolist" because all good literature is such and so successful authors are this (or that) because their literature is good. But arguments of that sort are not available to discussion.

Thoroughly discussable, however, is what has become virtually a school of Crane criticism which follows the original ideas of the single most energetic, successful, and embattled of Crane scholar-critics, Robert W. Stallman. One can scarcely avoid concentrating discussion of the master, his disciples, and their doctrine on the problem of the most famous image in The Red Badge of Courage, now almost the best known image in American literature: "The red sun was pasted in the sky like a wafer."

Stallman's intuition that this is the central characterizing symbol of the whole work, from which the nature and stature of its artistry and the substance of its meaning must be interpreted, was promulgated in a forty-nine page introduction in the Omnibus (175–224). For Stallman the key to it all is that the "wafer" means the form of bread, circular, crisp, almost parchment-like, used in the celebration of the Eucharist in liturgical churches: "I do not think it can be doubted that Crane intended to suggest here the sacrificial death celebrated in communion." From this he argued back that Jim Conklin, the tall soldier who has died in the passages just preceding Crane's introduction of the image, is Christ, or a Christ-figure, and that the book then becomes, as Daniel Hoffman, accepting Stallman, says, "a chronicle of redemption.[9] The contention is that, as in Christian doctrine, Fleming is somehow redeemed by the sacrificial death of Conklin in a symbolic or "apocalyptic"[1] novel richly laden with Christian reference.

It should cause no wonder that such views have been not only doubted but challenged. A small critical war has been waged over

8. Charles Feidelson, Symbolism and American Literature (1953), esp. pp. 44–76.
9. Daniel G. Hoffman, Introduction,

"The Red Badge of Courage" and Other Stories by Stephen Crane (New York, 1957), p. xv.
1. Ibid., p. xix.

them, with the balance appearing to turn of late against them.[2] The symbolist critics have obviously been useful in correcting over-emphases on Crane's "naturalism," in stimulating study of his art-istry, and in calling attention to achievements in that art which rise beyond what is usually subsumed under "impressionism." One thinks twice before rejecting the discoveries of well-informed, criti-cally sensitive commentators. And it would be arrogant to deny that the childhood training and imaginative affinities of Stephen Crane should have led him to Christian imagery, or even perhaps to a pat-tern of Christian symbolism in The Red Badge. But, in all candor, many other critics simply cannot find such interpretations valid. The evidence adduced for the symbolic pattern breaks down at every point and at the first scrutiny. It is in fact not clear, first of all, that Crane as Crane is every truly a symbolist: the test case may be "The Open Boat." Perhaps one needs to extend the sense of "impressionism" to take in what Crane does with images.

It would require a separate book to argue the problem out, but one can sketch the approaches to the problem by sticking to the wafer and Jim Conklin. To begin with, it was inherently improba-ble that Crane (whether he conceived the image ab ovo or read it in Kipling) thought of a "wafer" as eucharistic. He had been reared in an antiliturgical, enthusiastically anti-Catholic church and had become hotly anticlerical. While one could not rule out his know-ing of the wafer of the Mass, he was much more likely to have thought of the word as denoting a confection or, as various critics have pointed out, an item of stationery common to and typical of the nineteenth century. As messy, expensive sealing wax passed out of use, it was replaced by a useful imitation of paper or other sub-stance. Round, with neatly serrated edges stylizing the irregularities of a wax seal, often a deep, solid red as wax had been, these often gummed "wafers" were used to seal letters, packages, documents, etc. Joseph Hergesheimer, reading Crane, "thought of an actual red wafer, such as druggists fixed to their bottles; it had a definite, a limited size for me, an established, clear vermilion color."[3]

2. See Scott C. Osborn, "Stephen Crane's Imagery: 'Pasted Like a Wafer,'" American Literature, XXIII (November, 1951), 362; John E. Hart, "The Red Badge of Courage as Myth and Symbol," University of Kansas City Review, XIX (Summer, 1953), 249–56; Isaac Rosen-feld, "Stephen Crane as Symbolist," Kenyon Review, XV (September, 1953), 311–14; R. W. Stallman, "The Scholar's Net: Literary Sources," College English, XVII (October, 1955), 20–27; Edward Stone, "The Many Suns of The Red Badge of Courage," American Literature, XXIX (November, 1957), 322–26; Eric W. Carlson, "Crane's The Red Badge of Courage, IX," Explicator, XVI (March, 1958), no. 34; Bernard Weisberger, "The Red Badge of Courage," Twelve Original Essays, ed. Charles Shapiro (Detroit, 1958), pp. 96–123; Stanley B. Greenfield, "The Unmistakable Stephen Crane," PMLA, LXXIII (December, 1958), 562–72; James T. Cox, "The Imagery of The Red Badge of Courage," Modern (Fiction Studies, V (Autumn, 1959), 209–19; Richard Chase, Introduc-tion, "The Red Badge of Courage" and Other Writings by Stephen Crane (Bos-ton, 1960).
3. Work, I, x.

Visualizing *that* kind of "wafer" expunges religious significance from the image, and it removes certain embarrassments, too. If the image were to be taken as seriously sacramental, why was it red? And if one strained toward a metaphysical answer to that, why, then, was it surrealistically "pasted"? Not to mention the most painful, there are embarrassments in the argument that the Lincoln-esque Conklin is meant to represent Christ. As with the wafer, the connections seem hopelessly imprecise. Conklin does not bear the stigmata of Christ—even in his side. Christ's side was pierced after death by the spear of a professional soldier, iconography shows a neat, clean incision. Conklin's "side looked as if it had been chewed by wolves."[4] Nor will it do to argue that the sign is Fleming's recognition scream, "Gawd! Jim Conklin!" Thirteen lines later, Conklin is saying, ". . . Lord, what a circus! An' b'jiminey, I got shot. . . ."[5] Soldiers in *The Red Badge*, like real soldiers, frequently take the name of the Lord their God in vain—speaking not with symbolic portentousness any more than with blasphemous intent but simply as they speak (not in *The Red Badge*) obscenities for the registration of stereotyped and often comically inappropriate emotions.

The decisive difficulties with the Christian-symbolist reading of *The Red Badge*, it seems, are that there appears to be no way to make a coherent account of the symbols as referential to Christian doctrine and then to match that with what happens in the novel. The Christian doctrines of redemption and atonement, however central to orthodox faith, have ever been theologically obscure, intellectually mysterious. But they have always also been vital to Christian experience. And there just isn't any evidence of that, particularly as associated with the wafer and Conklin's death, in the after development of *The Red Badge*. There is textually no evidence that Fleming so much as perceives the "wafer." He mentions Conklin only once, informing Wilson of Jim's death, and they mourn briefly in the fashion of combat soldiers in the midst of death, ". . . poor cuss!"[6] Restored to self-esteem on his safe return to the regiment, Fleming quickly soars into an arrogance unpleasantly contrasted with Wilson's quiet manliness. At the end he has self-admiration to place beside humiliation as objects of contemplation. But it is his desertion of the live but dying tattered man which stabs his conscience. Conklin's death is absent from his thoughts.

It may be, in short, that Crane had no notion conscious or unconscious of "redemption" for Fleming. That may not have been his point at all, and the fact that one can gather a great deal of religious reference—or any other sort of reference—from the

4. *Work*, I, 98.
5. *Ibid.*, p. 93.
6. *Ibid.*, p. 131.

text may imply no hidden cohesions of meaning. Or it may: perhaps it is more a matter of whether one cares for Miss Caroline Spurgeon's methods with Shakespeare or not.

But in the end, the trouble with a "symbolic" reading of *The Red Badge* is that it assumes some sort of operative attitude toward a referential reality on the part of the artist. No matter how one qualifies it, a literary symbol must somehow be an image which points to something else, something usually conceptual. That "other" may be an established mythology accepted by artist and public; but nobody supposes that sort of integrative symbolism possible to Crane with Christianity. Or the artist may be in revolt, and the symbols disintegrative of the mythology—as dominantly in Melville. Or the symbols may refer to an arcane, even unique, mythology of the artist— in which case the interpreter must either be blanked or find the key to the acranum.

The arcane way of a Blake or Yeats seems foreign to the temperament and known ideals of Crane. But it may be that symbolistic investigation of that possibility and of the disintegrative functions of Crane's religious imagery might prove more fruitful than those which have hitherto apparently assumed integrative patterns. Howells may well have been deeply perceptive in remarking that Crane had not yet got into the secret of himself. It might be possible to divine part of that secret by guessing at where Crane's religious insights were, perhaps unconsciously, leading him. On the other hand, humanistic and naturalistic interpreters have no doubt been right in seeing how the vision of *The Red Badge* scouted and reduced traditional religious as well as romantic securities. Perhaps such should pay more attention to the imagery as symbol.

In any case, symbolic or not, Crane's imagery has obviously only begun to be comprehended. With a bewildering richness of reference (infraconceptual and so at first level imagistic and not symbolic), he wove a dense texture in *The Red Badge of Courage*. That, and not the often startling locutions, constitutes the triumph of its style. *The Red Badge* focuses only on three soldiers, Fleming and two who are obviously foils for him. One of them, Wilson, goes swiftly through the evolution from "loud soldier" to clear-sighted and therefore modest manhood which "The Veteran" testifies that Fleming also attained, perhaps by the end of the novel. But Wilson's transformation occurs while our eyes, which are Fleming's, are absent. Partly they are occupied with the death of "the spectral soldier," Jim Conklin.

If these common soldiers are representative as well as ordinary persons, Conklin is the representative sacrificed soldier, and he occupies in the novel a place equivalent to that of the Unknown Soldier in the national pantheon. His death deserves the emphasis its drama provides in *The Red Badge*. It is, as it must be, an occasion for shock and protest. Fleming incoherently registers it: "The youth turned, with sudden, livid rage, toward the battlefield. He shook his fist. He seemed about to deliver a philippic. 'Hell—'" And nature, as it generally does in the novel, registers Fleming—the awful intensity but faceless frustration of the shock which cannot yet be grief: "The red sun was pasted in the sky like a wafer."

V

If style be taken as texture and form as structure, the question of the equal success of the novel's form depends on deciding the much-discussed problem of the ending. Does the novel end well? Does it end or just disappear? Is there a climax? Is the ending of the novel satisfactory, in short, in emphasis and substance?

Debate has raged since the early reviews, and much of it around the last chapter. Though many critics have not troubled to mention it, few would deny the real achievement of a climax in personal victory which comes at the end of the next to the last chapter. Jeered at by veterans, scorned by their general as "mud-diggers" and "mule drivers," barely surviving after a temporary desertion rate of nearly fifty percent on the first day, close to a "pretty success" which they had funked by a hundred feet a little earlier, the regiment had stood exasperatedly under a last pressure. Fleming, now a color-bearer, had resolved "that his final and absolute revenge was to be achieved by his dead body lying, torn and guttering, upon the field." His lieutenant had continued to curse, but it was now "with the air of a man who was using his last box of oaths."[7]

Then the men are ordered to charge and at last, tough, determined, sacrificial, soldier-like, they really do. Fleming forces the way, banner in hand, and Wilson captures the colors of the enemy. There arose "wild clamorings of cheers. The men gesticulated and bellowed in ecstasy." They had even taken prisoners. Fleming and Wilson sat "side by side and congratulated each other." The narrative progression has been simple. Beginning in doubt about Fleming's—and the regiment's—courage, it had sunk to despair with his cowardice and Conklin's death. Now it rises to climax in their clear success, even, in a minimal sense, their heroism. The reversed curve is classic. And even more so is the reflective short downward curve of anticlimax at the end as the regiment is recalled and starts to wind its way back over the river and the men can suddenly realize that the battle is over.

As Fleming realizes this, his mind clears of "battle-sleep," and he is able to take stock. Crane trimmed quite a lot from the "LV"

7. *Ibid.*, pp. 186–87.

state of the last chapter, much of it reflecting too exactly the naturalistic debates he had earlier cut. But only one of the cuts was really important. What he was doing with Fleming, it seems clear, was not holding him up for judgment but rounding off the account of his experience. It was out of the question for Crane, insofar as he was a realist, to end a plot. It was neither with abstract structure nor with fable that he was concerned. The realists saw life as a continuum of the personal experiences of their characters. One broke in upon its flow at one significant point and left it at another. If in the course of this, one had any ulterior ideological motives, they should be planted out of sight and left for the reader to find.

As realist—psychological realist—as impressionist, perhaps even as metaphysician, Crane was, as we have seen, a visionist. The important thing was to see pellucidly and honestly. And what Crane is concerned with at the end of *The Red Badge* is what Fleming can see. By letting the readers see what Fleming sees, Crane will let them decide what to think of him. Henry struggles "to marshal all his acts. . . . From this present point of view he was enabled to look upon them with some correctness, for his new condition had already defeated certain sympathies."

Supposing that the defeated sympathies are the multitude of earlier romanticisms, what does Fleming's cleared sight now reveal in those three ultimate pages of the novel? That his "public deeds" are glorious and impart a "thrill of joy" to his ego. But that he has incurred real shame, however hidden, for "his flight" and real guilt for the tattered soldier, "he, who blind with weariness and pain, had been deserted in the field." This vision and the fear of some impossible detection balance his self-glorification with "a wretched chill of sweat" and "a cry of sharp irritation and agony."

In the end he sees that he is neither a hero nor a villain, that he must assume the burdens of a mixed, embattled, impermanent, modest, yet prevailing humanity. He has discovered courage:

. . . gradually he mustered force to put the sin at a distance. And at last his eyes seemed to open to some new ways. He found that he could look back upon the brass and bombast of his earlier gospels and see them truly. He was gleeful when he discovered that he now despised them.

With this conviction came a store of assurance. He felt a quiet manhood, non-assertive but of sturdy and strong blood. He knew that he would no more quail before his guides, wherever they should point. He had been to touch the great death, and found that, after all, it was but the great death. He was a man.

If capturing the enemy flag climaxes the action of *The Red Badge*, this discovery of manliness concludes its exploration of ideas. The third major theme could not be concluded, however, since Fleming

was not dead. It was the continuing notation of Fleming's psychological states which could only be harmonized in a sort of fade-out
chord as Milton had done with the last lines of "Lycidas." Trying
to force more out of these last sentences than Crane put there has
caused unnecessary trouble for critics.

As he trudged away from "blood and wrath" Fleming's "soul
changed"—as it had changed sometimes three times in a page earlier in the novel, though with more prospect of duration (not permanence) this time. Crane tried to end this three times before he
got it right.[8] Finally he showed Fleming turning to a vision—"with
a lover's thirst to images of tranquil skies, fresh meadows, cool
brooks—an existence of soft and eternal peace." And a nature-
image ends the book as one had begun it, the endlessly shifting nature registering the never settled psychological state in the last
words. "Over the river a golden ray of sun came through the hosts
of leaden rain clouds."

Was Henry Fleming then a hero? Well. yes—and no. It wasn't
quite Crane's business to say so in The Red Badge, and he let it go
to "The Veteran," which Eric Solomon very properly calls "A Gloss
on The Red Badge of Courage."[9] There the reader sees that modesty, candor about his "flight," and a quiet courage to do what a
man must do mark the veteran with the perspective of more battles
and many years—as in two days they could never plausibly have
marked "the youth." The ambiguities of Fleming's situation are
natural. But Crane's irony bites only at his past delusions. He has
become entitled to "images" of flowery peace.

The essence of that irony is that it would have been impossible
for the Early Fleming to judge whether the boy who had both "run"
and borne the colors was hero or poltroon. He wouldn't, in fact,
have known what he was talking about. He wouldn't have been able
to see. From another point of view, Henry's heroism at its last is
only common, the ordinary stock of courage among fighting men
(or among truly living men and women), where what the visionless
think "heroism" is as common as breathing. But from yet another
point of view, the courage it takes to be human in the face of all
the odds is magnificent, as only the extraordinarily sharp and realizing vision perceives. And it was Crane's sense of that in The Red
Badge, as in much of the best of his work, which gives it an elevation and a pungency often tragic and always memorable. He talked
about it overtly in "War Memories":

> On the morning of July 2, I sat on San Juan Hill and watched
> Laughton's division come up. . . . There wasn't a high heroic face
> among them. They were all men intent on business. That was all.

8. Stallman, Omnibus, pp. 219–21.
9. Eric Solomon, "A Gloss on The Red Badge of Courage," Modern Language Notes, LXXV (February, 1960), 111–13.

It may seem to you that I am trying to make everything a squalor. That would be wrong. I feel that things were often sublime. But they were *differently* sublime. They were not of our shallow and preposterous fictions. They stood out in a simple, majestic commonplace. It was the behavior of men on the street. It was the behavior of men. In one way, each man was just pegging along at the heels of the man before him, who was pegging along at the heels of still another man, who was pegging along at the heels of still another man who—It was that in the flat and obvious way. In another way it was pageantry, the pageantry of the accomplishment of naked duty. One cannot speak of it—the spectacle of the common man serenely doing his work, his appointed work. It is the one thing in the universe which makes one fling expression to the winds and be satisfied to simply feel.[1]

This passage was written at the end, when Crane was sick unto death and worn down to talking about it. In *The Red Badge of Courage* he was at a peak of his creative powers and could simply master the imaginations of readers with the power of an astonishing young genius presenting a masterpiece.

WILLIAM B. DILLINGHAM

Insensibility in *The Red Badge of Courage*†

When Henry Fleming, the youth of Stephen Crane's *The Red Badge of Courage*, charges ahead of his comrades and fearlessly carries his flag into the very jaws of death, he seems to be a romantic hero rather than the protagonist of a naturalistic novel. But for Crane appearance was seldom reality. Bearing the symbol of his country's cause, Henry is unquestionably courageous, but the underlying causes of his deeds are neither noble nor humane. Throughout his life Crane deeply respected heroic action. His attitude was, as Daniel G. Hoffman has said, that it was "among the very few means man has of achieving magnificence",[1] nevertheless, he considered courage the product of a complex of nonrational drives. The difference between the external act of courage and the internal process that leads up to that act created for Crane one of the supreme ironies of life.

The Red Badge has frequently been read as the story of how a

1. *Work*, IX, 238.
† *College English*, XXV (December, 1963), 194–98. Copyright © 1963 by the National Council of Teachers of English. Reprinted by permission of the publisher and the author. The nature of Henry's courage is also the subject of the essays by Kermit Vanderbilt and Daniel Weiss, John Fraser, and Robert Rechnitz, below.
1. Daniel G. Hoffman, *The Poetry of Stephen Crane* (New York, 1957), p. 150.

young soldier achieves some sort of spiritual salvation. One critic sees Henry Fleming's "growth toward moral maturity";[2] another, his "redemption" through "humility and loving-kindness."[3] His initiation has been called the successful search for "spiritual and psychological order," the discovery of a "vision of pattern."[4] Some readings emphasize Henry's new sense of brotherhood and call the book the story of a young man's developing awareness of social responsibility.[5] Such views as these offer more insight than may be indicated by a brief quotation and comment, but they also tend to obscure the central irony of the novel, that of the nature of courage, by making Henry Fleming as distinctive and as individually interesting a character as, say, Raskolnikov, Huckleberry Finn, or Isabel Archer. The young soldier whom Crane seldom calls by name is, as Alfred Kazin has suggested, Everyman—or at least every man who has the potentiality for courage.[6] The chief purpose of the novel is to objectify the nature of heroism through Henry Fleming. Through witnessing his actions and changing sensations we discover the emerging paradox of courage: human courage is by its nature subhuman; in order to be courageous, a man in time of physical strife must abandon the highest his human facilities, reason and imagination, and act instinctively, even animalistically.[7]

In developing and illustrating this paradoxical definition of courage, Crane used a simple structural arrangement. The novel is divided into two parts of twelve chapters each. The first twelve chapters tell of Henry Fleming's early insecurities about himself; his first battle, where he fights and then runs; his various adventures during his retreat; and finally his encounter with the fleeing soldier and then his wound. Chapter 13 begins with Henry's coming back to his own camp to begin anew, and the remainder of the book takes the reader through the battles of the next day, in which Henry fights with great courage.

The first part of the book deals with the anatomy of cowardice, which is in Henry the result of an active imagination and a disposi-

2. James B. Clovert, "Structure and Theme in Stephen Crane's Fiction," *Modern Fiction Studies*, 5 (Autumn, 1959), 204.
3. Robert Wooster Stallman, introduction to *The Red Badge of Courage*, Modern Library (New York, 1951), p. xxxii.
4. Earle Labor, "Crane and Hemingway: Anatomy of Trauma," *Renascence*, 11 (Summer, 1959), 195.
5. John E. Hart, *"The Red Badge of Courage* as Myth and Symbol," *University of Kansas City Review*, 19 (Summer, 1953), 249–56. See also M. Solomon, "Stephen Crane: A Critical Study," *Mainstream*, 9 (January, 1956), 25–42.
6. Alfred Kazin, *On Native Grounds*

(New York, 1956), p. 50.
7. Although the focus of his article is somewhat different from the present discussion, James Trammel Cox also states this central paradox of *The Red Badge*: ". . . the selfless behavior of heroism paradoxically emerges only from the grossest, most infantile, animalistic, fiery hatred born of the vanity of egocentrism." "The Imagery of *The Red Badge of Courage*," *Modern Fiction Studies*, 5 (Autumn, 1959), 219. Hoffman suggests the paradox in his treatment of Crane's indebtedness to Tolstoi: introduction to *The Red Badge of Courage and Other Stories* (New York, 1957), p. xii.

tion to think too much. Until he receives the head wound in Chapter 12, he is characterized by a romantic and thoughtful self-consciousness. In his anxiety about how he will conduct himself in combat, he speculates constantly about himself and the nature of battle: "He tried to mathematically prove to himself that he would not run from a battle." Trying to comfort himself through reason, he makes "ceaseless calculations" for days. Finally he had to admit that "he could not sit still and with a mental slate and pencil derive an answer." Henry's "own eternal debate" is frequently interrupted by the terrifying images of his imagination. In the darkness he sees "visions of a thousand-tongued fear that would babble at his back and cause him to flee." This constant activity of Henry's reason and imagination compels him to feel isolated until he experiences a vague sense of unity with his fellows during the first battle. Here he becomes suddenly caught up in the fight almost by accident. In contrast to his insensibility in later battles, "he strenuously tried to think," but he is luckily carried along by the momentary excitement of his comrades. The first encounter with the enemy is very brief, and his courage is not seriously tested. In the second engagement, his imagination is rampant: "He began to exaggerate the endurance, the skill, and the valour of those who were coming." He imagines the enemy as dragons and sees himself as being "gobbled." No longer feeling enclosed in the "moving box" of his first encounter and now stimulated by wild imaginings, Henry runs in terror from the battle.

In "The Veteran," a short story written as a sequel to *The Red Badge*, Henry, now an old man, reminisces about his war experience and tells how his imagination and his reliance on reason compelled him to run; "The trouble was . . . I thought they were all shooting at me. Yes, sir, I thought every man in the other army was aiming at me in particular, and only me. And it seemed so darned unreasonable, you know. I wanted to explain to 'em what an almighty good fellow I was, because I thought then they might quit all trying to hit me."[8]

After his retreat, he wanders behind the lines, still relying upon his reason and imagination, attempting to convince himself that he is the reasonable man, "the enlightened man," who "had fled because of his superior perceptions and knowledge." When he comes upon the group of wounded men, he is still debating his case. He then witnesses the death of his friend Jim Conklin. But even at this point he shows no significant change.[9] Shortly thereafter, his imagination still controls him as he magnifies "the dangers and horrors of the engagement" from which he fled. Until he is wounded in Chapter 12, he is still rationalizing, still trying mathe-

8. *The Work of Stephen Crane*, ed. Wilson Follett (New York, 1925), I, 204.

9. For an opposite opinion, see Stallman, p. xxxiii.

matically to prove to himself that his cowardice was "in truth a symmetrical act."

The episode in which Henry is struck by a retreating Union soldier occurs at the center of the novel both physically and thematically. The incident has frequently been called the ironic peak of the story. A Union soldier, not the enemy, gives Henry his wound, and unlike his comrades he is wounded with the butt of a gun, not with a bullet. Upon this highly ironic "red badge" Henry builds his courage. In addition to its function as irony, the wound serves as the chief symbol of the book. Significantly, the wound is inflicted on the *head*. Almost from the moment he is struck, Henry starts to set aside his fearful and potent imagination and his reason. Symbolically, the head wound is the damage the experience of war gives to these highest human faculties. The chaos of war teaches the necessity of insensibility. After the symbolic wound, Henry finds his way back to his regiment, and the last half of the book portrays a youth initiated into the ways of courage. From here on, Henry runs from himself; he escapes his essential humanity in order to avoid running in battle.

Henry's inner voices and visions, then, are obliterated by the head wound. Through one half of the story, his mind has been tried and found wanting. Henry's wound forces his attention to his physical being. The only voices now heard are those of the body. After he returns to camp, "he made vague plans to go off into the deeper darkness and hide, but they were all destroyed by the voices of exhaustion and pain from his body." When he awakes, "it seemed to him that he had been asleep for a thousand years, and he felt sure that he opened his eyes upon an unexpected world." The Henry Fleming who before looked into the future, saw imagined horrors, and speculated constantly about himself, now thinks little of the future: "He did not give a good deal of thought to these battles that lay directly before him. It was not essential that he should plan his ways in regard to them." He has become instinctively aware of a truth taught by intense experience, that man can and must cultivate a dullness which will serve as armor against the stings of fear and panic. The totality of Henry's war experience thus far has helped to show him that "retribution was a laggard and blind."

In contrast to the thoughtful and romantic boy of the first part of the book, the young warrior of the last twelve chapters is capable of unreason, even self-abandon. At the first sight of the enemy, he "forgot many personal matters and became greatly enraged." He becomes a prideful animal, seeking the throat of the enemy with self-forgetfulness. The feelings of the imaginative young soldier, who once thought of war as a glorious Greek-like struggle, now are constantly described in terms of bestiality, unreason, and even insanity. He "lost sense of everything but his hate." Suspending all thought, he fights as a "barbarian, a beast . . . a pagan." His actions are frequently described as "wild." He is "unconsciously" out in front of the other troops, looking "to be an insane soldier." "There was the delirium that encounters despair and death, and is heedless and blind to the odds. It is a temporary but sublime absence of self-ishness." The selflessness implied here is not self-sacrifice but insensibility, which enables Henry to escape thoughts and suspend imagination, to get outside of himself while the emotions of rage and hatred control his actions. As he cultivates personal insensibility his mental position as an observer becomes more and more pronounced: "He was deeply absorbed as a spectator; . . . he did not know that he breathed." Henry's self-abandon spreads to the others, who were "again grown suddenly wild with an enthusiasm of unself-ishness." Henry is no longer aware of the personal element in the danger that he faces. Now he does not think of the enemy as attempting to kill him personally. He looks upon their bullets vaguely as "things that could prevent him from reaching the place of his endeavour." So separated from meditation and imagination is Henry that he finds it difficult after the battle to become himself again: "It took moments for it [his mind] to cast off its battleful ways and resume its accustomed course of thought. Gradually his brain emerged from the clogged clouds, and at last he was enabled to more closely comprehend himself and circumstances."

Henry's change is thus the result of intensely dangerous experience which reveals to him intuitively the impersonal nature of the forces that defeat men. After glimpsing the powers of "strange, squalling upheavals" he is able to control his fear. This ability comes to men not through intellectual or spiritual processes but through habit in being exposed to violence. As Henry becomes more accustomed to battle and the sight of death, he no longer thinks about the implication of these overwhelming experiences. He sinks into a subhuman dullness and is thereby able to act courageously. He does not learn to know himself, as one critic asserts,[1] but to escape himself—to make his mind blank, to become a "spectator."

Otherwise, Henry remains essentially unchanged during the course of the novel. It is a mistake to think of him as having become rejuvenated through humility or in any way changed into a better person morally. He has simply adapted himself through experience to a new and dangerous environment.[2] When the last battle

1. Norman Friedman, "Criticism and the Novel," *Antioch Review,* 18 (Fall, 1958), 356–61.
2. Crane never ceased to be interested in the molding influence of environment. His favorite situation shows man pitted against a new and quite different environment. In some cases, as in "The Blue Hotel" and "The Bride Comes to Yellow Sky," characters find it impossible to undergo the necessary change to survive and are either destroyed or disillusioned. In *The Red Badge* as in "The Open Boat," however, the chief characters manage to adapt to the dangerous new environment and thus to survive.

is over, he is the same prideful youth, bragging on himself as he reviews his deeds of valor. The Christian references, which have so frequently been a subject of controversy, do not point to "rebirth" or "salvation" for Henry. The pattern of religious imagery built up through the use of such words as "sacrifice," "hymn," and "cathedral" is part of the pervasive irony of the book.[3] Just as Henry is not "selfless" in the usual sense of the word, neither is he "saved" in the Christian sense. It is his body that is saved, not his soul. He is trained by war to realize, in contradiction of Christian ideals, that he must desert the mind and spirit and allow his physical being—even his animal self—to dominate. Through Henry, Crane is saying with St. Matthew that whosoever will lose his life will find it. But the Christian paradox is in direct opposition to Crane's. Henry finds and retains his physical life by losing that sensibility characteristic of the highest forms of life.

The evidence for a "naturalistic" interpretation of *The Red Badge is* overwhelming.[4] Creating, chiefly through irony, a considerable degree of aesthetic distance, Crane studies the change in the behavior of a soldier. Through half the book this character is a sensitive youth. But sensitivity is incompatible with physical courage and the ability to kill. In the center of the story occurs the symbolic head wound, which damages the youth's sensibility and causes him to rely more on the physical and instinctive, less on the mental. For the rest of the book, Henry is brave in battle, having arrived at that state of self-discipline which makes one in danger resemble more an animal than a man. An iconoclast, Crane enjoyed laughing as he destroyed the illusions of a former tradition. He does not rejoice that Henry has found courage; he does not change him into a better person. Nor does he mourn as did Wilfred Owen for the tenderness and the innocence that war destroys in those who must kill.[5] With a keen sense of the incongruity of things, he simply shows that courage has been misunderstood. In order to be a Greek (in a Greek-like struggle), one must be a barbarian.

3. Two critics have made similar statements about the Christian imagery of the book: Bernard Weisberger, "The Red Badge of Courage," in *Twelve Original Essays on Great American Novels*, ed. Charles Shapiro (Detroit, 1958), pp. 104–105; and Cox, pp. 217–18.
4. Several naturalistic interpretations are available. See, for example, Winifred Lynskey, "Crane's *The Red Badge of Courage*," *Explicator*, 8 (Dec., 1949), 3; Richard Chase, introduction to Riverside Edition of *The Red Badge* (Boston, 1960); and Charles Child Walcutt, *American Literary Naturalism, A Divided Stream* (Minneapolis, 1956).
5. Owen's poem "Insensibility" is, however, a remarkably similar statement of the definition of courage:
Dullness best solves
The tease and doubt of shelling,
And Chance's strange arithmetic
Comes simpler than the reckoning of
their shilling.
. . . .
Happy are these who lose imagination:
They have enough to carry with ammunition.
. . . .
Having seen all things red,
Their eyes are rid
Of the hurt of the colour of blood for ever.

SERGIO PEROSA
Naturalism and Impressionism in Stephen Crane's Fiction†

One of the most interesting aspects of Stephen Crane's fiction lies in its characteristic combination of naturalistic and impressionistic elements. The composite nature of his work has given rise to many one-sided interpretations; but the novelty, significance, and representative quality of his fiction is to be found in its combination and, as it were, symbiosis, of some freely-accepted naturalistic premises with an impressionistic method of presentation, at first instinctively, then consciously applied to his work.

* * *

Written in 1893, shortly after the "naturalistic" *Maggie*, *The Red Badge of Courage* shares with the earlier novel the theme of a young person's initiation into life, or indeed the wider theme of the individual's relation to a hostile world, over which, in this case, the protagonist triumphs. "It was an effort born of pain—despair, almost; and I believe that this made it a better piece of literature than it otherwise would have been. It seems a pity that art should be a child of pain, and yet I think it is," Crane was to write in his letter to the editor of *Leslie's Weekly*. He considered *The Red Badge* as the amplification of a mere episode; elsewhere he was to call it a psychological portrait of fear. All these definitions are fairly accurate and useful: the novel can be seen as an amplification of a mere episode—a crucial episode that marks the transition from the illusions of adolescence to an acceptance of responsibility in life. It is a psychological portrait of fear: but it is artistically valid exactly because it is "realized" in a context of vivid and concrete sense impressions, of physical references to the field of battle. The "mere episode" achieves all the conspicuousness and the resonance bestowed upon it by an impressionistic rendering of the details within the scenes, and of the scenes within the general framework.

Although Crane had no personal experience of war, he had probably read Tolstoy and Ambrose Bierce on the subject, and had listened to his brother William recounting episodes of the Civil War. But he was more than ever dealing with "imagined reality," and this was bound to lead him to a kind of evocative, rather than descriptive, writing. The novel belongs to the tradition of the *Lehrjahre* and the *Bildungsroman*; but the story of Henry Fleming's victory over himself achieves a perfect thematic *and* formal unity

† From *Stephen Crane: A Collection of Critical Essays*, ed. Maurice Bassan (Englewood Cliffs, N.J.: Prentice-Hall, 1967), pp. 80, 87–94. Reprinted by permission of Sergio Perosa. (First published in Italian in 1964.)

thanks to the impressionistic quality of its texture. According to Agostino Lombardo (in his introduction to the Italian edition of the Tales), this kind of impressionism is an instrument for the representation of the moral and psychological inner life of the protagonist. But the contrary is also true: the inexhaustible ferment of Henry Fleming's moral and psychological inner life achieves its own peculiar kind of "epiphany" by being rendered in concrete and physical terms—in terms of light and shadow, sounds and colors, images and sense impressions.

The *Red Badge of Courage* is indeed a triumph of impressionistic vision and impressionistic technique. Only a few episodes are described from the outside; Fleming's mind is seldom analyzed in an objective, omniscient way; very few incidents are extensively *told*. Practically every scene is filtered through Fleming's point of view and seen through his eyes. Everything is related to his *vision*, to his *sense*-perception of incidents and details, to his *sense*-reactions rather than to his psychological impulses, to his confused sensations and individual impressions. Reality exists and can be artistically recreated in that it affects his eyes, his ears, his touch—his sensory, rather than mental, imagination. The battlefield is to Henry Fleming colorful and exciting, new and phantasmagoric, mysterious and unforeseen; it stimulates beyond measure, it exasperates his sensations. Thus stimulated, his impressions—above all his visual and auditory impressions—give *substance*, not only vividness, to the picture. Even his meditations on the psychological dilemma of fear are rendered as a staccato sequence of mental *impressions*, typical of a young mind dismayed by the spectacle of war.

It is basically a question of sight. Henry Fleming's is, first of all, a point of *view*: he is a source and a receptacle of impressions, and it is in their disconnected sequence that the phantom, and the meaning, of life is gradually brought to light. A simple statistical analysis on the linguistic level is quite revealing in this respect. One is struck at first glance by the recurrence of terms indicating visual perceptions. Verbs like *to see, perceive, look, observe, gaze, witness, watch, stare, peer, cast eyes, discover*, etc. appear on practically every page, indeed, no less than 350 times in this fairly short novel. Expressions like *to seem, appear, look like, exhibit, glare, gleam, shine, flash, glimmer, display, loom, show, reveal*, etc. occur no less than 200 times. Less numerous, but still quite frequent, are verbs of auditory perception (like *to hear*, etc.) or those expressing inner feeling (*to feel*, etc.), especially when Henry Fleming is wounded or regaining consciousness. Examples like the following are quite common and, indeed, quite revealing:

The youth *turned quick eyes* upon the field. He *discerned* forms begin to swell in masses out of a distant wood. He again *saw* the tilted flag speeding forward.

He *saw* that the ground in the deep shadows was cluttered with men, sprawling in every conceivable posture. *Glancing* narrowly into the more distant darkness, he *caught* occasional *glimpses* of visages that *loomed* pallid and ghostly, *lit* with a phosphorescent glow.

The youth's *eyes* had instantly turned in the direction indicated by the awakened and agitated lieutenant, and he *had seen* the haze of treachery *disclosing* a body of soldiers of the enemy. They were so near that he could *see* their features. There was a *recognition* as he *looked at* the types of faces. Also he *perceived* with dim amazement that their uniforms were rather gay in effect, being light gray, accented with a brilliant-hued facing. Too, the clothes *seemed* new.

He stood, erect and tranquil, *watching* the attack begin against a part of the line that made a blue curve along the side of an adjacent hill. His *vision* being unmolested by smoke from the rifles of his companions, he had opportunities to *see* parts of the hard fight. It was a relief to *perceive* at last from whence came some of these noises which had been roared into his ears.

The rhythm of perception is ceaseless and pressing, continual and almost obsessive. We get the impression of life displaying itself to the apprehension of human conscience. Henry Fleming's "mind took a mechanical but firm impression, so that afterward everything was pictured and explained to him." The impression can be mechanical, but it is firm and allows us to form the picture; once the picture has been formed, everything can be explained. It sounds almost like a definition of Crane's own method, if it is true that he identifies himself with Fleming's point of view and consciousness. By faithfully recording *his* sensations, Crane gives substance and shape to the dramatic scene or the evoked picture, and the gradual unfolding of the meaning coincides with the slow process of perception. The total picture is the sum of the infinite touches and sense impressions, and must be focused anew at each step or turn of the process: it is the characteristic manner of impressionistic rendering.

Crane sticks to this method also in those parts which are not seen through Fleming's limited point of view and in which only the *sense* of his *possible* perceptions is given. And such a method, of course, as appears from the previous quotations, deeply affects the stylistic texture. It forces language to an unprecedented terseness of diction and conciseness of statement, breaking it down into very short sentences, whose *progression d'effet* is cadenced and leads in each case to an intense revelation of reality:

He lay down on a wide bunk that stretched across the end of the room. In the other end, cracker boxes were made to serve as furniture. They were grouped about the fireplace. A picture from an illustrated weekly was upon the log walls, and three rifles were paralleled on pegs. . . . A folded tent was serving as a roof. The sunlight, without, beating upon it, made it glow a light yellow shade.

The fire crackled musically. From it swelled light smoke. Overhead the foliage moved softly. The leaves, with their faces turned toward the blaze, were colored shifting hues of silver, often edged with red.

When another night came the columns, changed to purple streaks, filed across two pontoon bridges. A glaring fire wine-tinted the waters of the river. Its rays, shining upon the moving masses of troops, brought forth here and there sudden gleams of silver or gold. Upon the other shore a dark and mysterious range of hills was curved against the sky. The insect voices of the night sang solemnly.

Crane himself had written to John N. Hilliard: "My chiefest desire was to write plainly. I endeavoured to express myself in the simplest and most concise way." The fleeting image of life is here captured and recreated in a phantasmagoric "panorama" of lines, colors, forms, and tones. The paragraphs break down into mere sentences, and the sentences are reduced to the simplest statements, according to a stylistic principle that was to influence, among others, Ernest Hemingway, and is the counterpart of the touch of pure color directly applied to the canvas by the impressionist painter.

This fragmentation of syntax, in fact, aims at the precision and terseness of the visual impression and leads to a "pictorial" achievement—to an airy "picture of life" which is the sum of the single impressionistic details: a lively and colorful picture of life apprehended, as it were, in action, in its displaying itself to Henry Fleming's, the writer's, and the reader's, perception.

What matters, of course, behind and beyond the inner vibration of Crane's impressionistic rendering, is the quality and the significance of the total achievement. But it is important here to stress the nature of the technical method that makes it possible and gives a particular flavor to the underlying theme of the novel. In this respect, it is clear that Fleming's basic experience can be identified with the gradual process of his perception and recognition of reality —a process which becomes all the more meaningful and significant in that it is impressionistically presented *as such*. His ordeal is the ordeal of fear; his dilemma is whether to face or to escape reality: but the moral victory he achieves over himself is strictly related to the gradual disclosing of his perception over the spectacle, and the meaning, of life.

A few naturalistic remnants are still to be found in the novel: Crane's avowed intention of making Fleming as "representative" as possible; his resorting to types, rather than full characters, for the secondary roles; the use of descriptive, rather than proper, names (the "tall soldier" etc.); the use of slang for documentary purposes; and the attempt to present the common soldiers as "underdogs" in a careless and ruthless world (the officers call them "mule drivers" or "mud diggers") and therefore trampled on and irresponsibly sent to a useless death.

But the cultural and historical context in which the novel was written and the inspiration sustaining it remain basically impressionistic: and this explains why, when in 1897 Crane moved to England, he was hailed by English writers and critics as "the chief impressionist of the age" (Edward Garnett), as "the impressionist par excellence" (Joseph Conrad). They referred of course to the fiction-writer, but it is also to be remembered that Crane's recent collection of poems (*The Black Riders and Other Lines*, 1895, which he seemed to value more than *The Red Badge of Courage*) gave further proof of his mastery of the short, impressionistic notation and of the sharp formulation of thoughts and images. It was clearly influenced by Emily Dickinson's taste for the short lyric; but it also paved the way for the Imagist poets, leaving no doubt as to Crane's double role as an innovator.

His fiction seemed indeed to conform to the new principles of impressionistic writing which were being developed at the time in England by Conrad, Garnett, and Ford Madox Hueffer (Ford). The best definition of its aims and methods is to be found in Conrad's well-known preface to *The Nigger of the "Narcissus"* (1897). Fiction, Conrad wrote,

> if it at all aspires to be art—appeals to temperament. . . . Such an appeal to be effective must be an impression conveyed through the senses. . . . All art, therefore, appeals primarily to the senses, and the artistic aim when expressing itself in written words must also make its appeal through the senses. . . . It must strenuously aspire to the plasticity of sculpture, to the colour of painting, and to the magic suggestiveness of music—which is the art of arts.

The writer's task is to render and convey to the reader the sense impression in all its terseness and conspicuity, to capture the fleeting image of life in order to reveal its underlying secret:

> My task which I am trying to achieve is, by the power of the written word to make you hear, to make you feel—it is, before all, to make you *see*. . . .

To snatch in a moment of courage, from the remorseless rush of time, a passing phase of life, is only the beginning of the task. The task approached in tenderness and faith is to hold up unquestioningly, without choice and without fear, the rescued fragment before all eyes in the light of a sincere mood. It is to show its vibration, its colour, its form; and through its movement, its form and its colour, reveal the substance of its truth—disclose its inspiring secret: the stress and passion within the core of each convincing moment. . . .

And when it is accomplished—behold!—all the truth of life is there: a moment of vision, a sigh, a smile. . . .

Ford Madox Ford was later to repeat incessantly the same concepts and to provide the epistemological grounds of the new technique ("We saw that Life did not narrate, but made impressions on our brains. We in turn, if we wished to produce on you an effect of life, must not narrate but render . . . impressions"). They both aimed at conciliating objective reality with subjective vision; in both cases, the final meaning and the total effect was to be achieved by reproducing the process of perception and discovery; each "moment of vision" led to the revelation of the whole truth.

The Red Badge of Courage appeared right in the middle of this tranquil literary revolution, embodying all the features of the new impressionistic novel. Crane was taken for a follower and a disciple: he was in fact a forerunner, instinctively applying to his work all the new principles that were being formulated in England. His novel can be read in the light of Conrad's poetics, which seems to account perfectly well for its method and its achievement.

It is based, as we have seen, on an impressionistic rendering of sense perceptions (its appeal is "made through the senses"); it tries strenuously to make us hear, to make us feel, to make us, before all, *see;* by showing the vibration, the color, the form of the rescued fragment, it gradually reveals the substance of its truth, its inspiring secret—"the stress and passion within the core of each convincing moment." In Crane, too, the truth of life is revealed in the "moment of vision" incessantly repeated. If art, as Conrad maintained, could be defined as "a single-minded attempt to render the highest kind of justice to the visible universe," this was indeed Crane's achievement; Crane too was trying to bring to light the truth underlying its aspects, its forms, its colors, its lights and shadows—as Conrad had required of the artist in the same preface. Through his impressionistic rendering he aimed at discovering what is "fundamental, lasting and essential" in the fleeting aspects of life; and if he succeeded in capturing it, then the final picture is a composite, and at the same time unified, revelation of life—an interpretation, almost, of its secret, as it is given in terms of human suffering and moral conscience.

The fact is that the technical method is not only perfectly suited to express the theme of the novel: it actually merges and *coincides* with it. Henry Fleming has to undergo his initiation into life and achieve a moral victory over himself: but the *leitmotiv* of his adventure lies first of all in his gradual discovery of reality. He has to discover what is "fundamental, lasting and essential" in the rescued fragments of life which are offered to his perception: this is what he does, and what the writer himself does, through the gradual unfolding of Henry Fleming's process of perception. Capturing the phantom of life in its many-colored and mysterious aspects is for Fleming an initiation into life; the sum of his impressions leads him to a recognition of the world and to an acceptance of his own role in it. This is the meaning of his experience, but also a description of Crane's rendering of the theme. Theme and process coincide.

This is why Crane's impressionistic rendering is perfectly in keeping with the theme of the novel and embodies it in the best possible way. Henry Fleming's initiation into life coincides and is one with his perception of it; by assuming Fleming's point of view and sticking to *his* process of perception, Crane can succeed in unfolding the meaning of his experience and in conveying its ultimate sense to the reader. In this way *The Red Badge of Courage* can be regarded as a triumph of impressionistic rendering: it is not merely a question of technical devices and expressive vehicles, but of a perfect coincidence of aims and means, of formal intention and thematic substance. A formal method strictly consistent with the theme enhances and enlivens in an original way an artistic vision which is, by its very nature, an experience of life.

JOHN BERRYMAN

Stephen Crane: *The Red Badge of Courage*†

The wars of men have inspired the production of some of man's chief works of art, but very undemocratically. Napoleon's wars inspired Goya, Stendhal, Beethoven, Tolstoy; a prolonged bicker of 1100 B.C. inspired the poet of the *Iliad*, who celebrated and deplored three centuries later a little piece of it near its end; the Wars of the Roses resulted in Shakespeare's giant effort, again long afterward; the Athenian empire's ruin was adequately dramatized by a participant, the greatest of historians; Picasso made something of

† Chapter 8 of *The American Novel: From James Fenimore Cooper to William Faulkner*, ed. Wallace Stegner (New York: Basic Books, 1965), pp. 86–96.

the soul-destroying Civil War in his native country. But what came of Cromwell's war? Or of the atrocious conflict between North and South in the United States?

Thirty years after it ended came a small novel by a very young man, called *The Red Badge of Courage.* The immediate literature of the Civil War has been beautifully studied of late in Edmund Wilson's *Patriotic Gore,* but no one would claim for that literature any such eminence as belongs, after almost seventy years, to Stephen Crane's novel. A critic seems to be faced, then, with alternative temptations: to overrate it, as an American, because it chronicles our crucial struggle, or to underrate it, in the grand perspective of the artists just mentioned, because it appears to assert neither the authority of the experienced warrior nor the authority of the historical artist—Tolstoi having both, Thucydides both. Crane was no scholar and had seen no battle. Yet some authority should be allowed him, and identified, for his work has not only brilliantly survived but was recognized instantly abroad—in England—as authentic; professional military men were surprised to learn that he was not one.

It is hard to see how anyone, except a casual reader, could overrate *The Red Badge of Courage* for patriotic reasons, because, though the book does indeed handle parts of the battle of Chancellorsville, it is not really about the Civil War. For instance, it shows no interest in the causes, meaning, or outcome of the war; no interest in politics; no interest in tactics or strategy. In this book, these failures are a merit, in opposition to the supreme fault of *War and Peace,* which is philosophical and programmatic. Here we have only parts of one minor battle, seen from one ignorant point of view, that of a new volunteer. One would never guess that what has been called the first modern war was being studied. All the same, as from the weird diagrams of Samuel Beckett emerges the helpless horror of modern man, we learn, as we learn from few books, about the waiting, the incomprehension, rumor, frustration, anxiety, fatigue, panic, hatred not only of the enemy but of officers; about complaints of "bad luck" and the sense of betrayal by commanders. This is a losing army. Since every intelligent man has to be at some point afraid of proving himself a coward—which is what the ordeal of Crane's protagonist is about—the story presents itself to us initially as making some claim to universality. The claim is strengthened by Crane's reluctance to divulge the name of the hero (it is Henry Fleming) or the names of the only other two people who matter— the tall soldier (Jim) and the loud youth (Wilson)—or the identity of the regiment, or the geography. By *leaving things out* the author makes his general bid for our trust.

But of course he has put in things too, and our problems are where he got them and how he put them. The main things he put in are reflection and action. Much of the book really is battle. Crane had read *Sebastopol*, Tolstoi's short novel, and declared that he learned what war was like from football; after starring in baseball at the two colleges he briefly attended, he coached a boys' football team in New Jersey. One of the staff at his military academy, a major-general, had seen action at Chancellorsville and liked to talk about it. Crane had played war games as a child, and talked with veterans, and read (with disappointment and contempt) magazine articles on the Civil War. Later, after witnessing substantial parts of the Greco-Turkish War, he said, "*The Red Badge* is all right." I don't know that we can say precisely how he learned what he knew, except to recognize in him an acute visual imagination and an inspired instinct for what happens and what does not happen in conflict. Here is a short passage:

> He expected a battle scene.
> There were some little fields girted and squeezed by a forest. Spread over the grass and in among the tree trunks, he could see knots and waving lines of skirmishers who were running hither and thither and firing at the landscape. A dark battle line lay upon a sunstruck clearing that gleamed orange colour. A flag fluttered.
> Other regiments floundered up the bank.

Some of the features of Crane's *style* appear: his convulsive and also humorous irony ("expected," as if he would not see it but he saw it, and "firing at the landscape"), its violent animism ("squeezed") its descriptive energy ("knots and waving lines"—like an abstract-expressionist painting). But a Tolstoyan sense also of futility and incomprehension is swiftly conveyed, and this is only partly a product of the style. He is inventing, he is experimenting. Crane himself goes in for this language—several times he speaks of "experiment" and says of the youth, "He tried to mathematically prove to himself that he would not run from a battle." In the action, then, the fantastic and the literal cooperate. The reflective aspects of the novel are another matter.

The scene of this extremely simple novel is laid in a single mind. It starts with soldiers speculating loudly about whether there is going to be a fight or not. Then "a youthful private" goes off to his hut: "He wished to be alone with some new thoughts that had lately come to him." This has the effect of understatement, putting so flatly the youth's debate with himself about his honor, but it is literal, besides introducing the theme of intense isolation that dominated Crane's work until a later story, his masterpiece, "The Open Boat," where human cooperation in face of the indifference of nature is the slowly arrived-at subject. In *Red Badge* his youth broods in private, having crawled into his dilemma, or hut, "through an intricate hole that served it as a door"—and the rest of the book provides a workout of the plight. On the first day he does well, and then runs away. A Union soldier clubs him in the panic retreat; Crane's ironic title refers to the "badge" of that wound; the youth is taken for a good soldier. He witnesses the death of his boyhood friend, the tall soldier, a true hero. Returned, by the kindness of a stranger, to his regiment, he is cared for as a combatant by the loud youth, toward whom he is also enabled to feel superior in that, scared earlier, Wilson entrusted him with letters to be sent in the event of his death and has now, shamefacedly, to ask for their return. Next day he fights like a hero or demon. Such is the story. Perhaps many readers take it as a novel of development, a sort of success story, and this view is encouraged by the climactic passage:

> He felt a quiet manhood, non-assertive but of sturdy and strong blood. . . . He had been to touch the great death, and found that, after all, it was but the great death. He was a man. . . .

It is possible to feel very uncomfortable with this way of looking at the book. For one thing, pervasive irony is directed toward the youth—his self-importance, his self-pity, his self-loving war rage. For another, we have only one final semiself-reproach for his cowardice and imposture:

> He saw that he was good. . . . Nevertheless, the ghost of his flight from the first engagement appeared to him and danced. There were small shoutings in his brain about these matters. For a moment he blushed, and the light of his soul flickered with shame.

I find it hard to believe that in this passage Crane is exonerating his hero without irony. Finally, we have very early in the book an indication of his pomposity (his mother's "I know how you are, Henry"), and there is pomposity in his final opinion of himself as a war demon. That would suggest a circular action, in the coward middle of which he appeared to reveal his real nature, or in fact did reveal it, by running. The irony embraces, then, all but the central failure.

It is easy to feel uncomfortable with this view, too—more particularly because the apparent wound of the first day is indeed a real wound, and its silent pretension is later justified. On the other hand, the irony never ends. I do not know what Crane intended. Probably he intended to have his cake and eat it too—irony to the end, but heroism too. Fair enough. How far did he fail?

Again I invoke, as praiseworthy, that which is not done. The youth is frantically afraid of being found out (he never is found out) but except in the passage just quoted he never suffers the remorse one would expect. Intimate as Crane is with his hero psychologically, still the view he takes of him is cold, unsentimental, remote. This certainly preserves him from any full failure (though there have been many reliable readers from the day the book was published to now who have not liked it, because they regarded it as artificial and sensational).

The coldness leads to a certain impersonality, and it is a striking fact that some of Crane's deepest private interests find no place in the novel; in fact, they are deliberately excluded. Three of them are worth singling out. In his earlier novel, or long story, called *Maggie*, laid in New York's Bowery, Crane dramatized a distinct social philosophy—environmentalist, deterministic, and convinced that "the root of slum-life" was "a sort of cowardice." Yet his indifference to society in *The Red Badge* is complete, and it would not do to say "Of course it would be," for an army *is* society.

So with the matter of personal philosophy. We happen to know Crane's views perfectly, because he put them at length in letters to a girl (Nellie Crouse) by whom he was fascinated in 1895–96. He wrote:

> For my own part, I am minded to die in my thirty-fifth year [he died at 28, in 1900]. I think that is all I care to stand. I don't like to make wise remarks on the aspect of life but I will say that it doesn't strike me as particularly worth the trouble. The final wall of the wise man's thought however is Human Kindness of course.

Exceptionally for him, Crane capitalized the two words. Now it might have been supposed that, bringing his hero through to maturity in *The Red Badge*, he would have concentrated in this area. But no. It seems impossible not to conclude that the splendid burst of rhetoric with which the novel concludes is just that, *in part*—a burst of rhetoric—and that Crane retained many of his reservations about his hero. As the wisest of modern British novelists, E. M. Forster, once observed, novels almost never end well: character desires to keep on going, whereas remorseless plot requires it to end. I hardly remember a better instance. Yet the last page is confidently and brilliantly done:

> It rained. The procession of weary soldiers became a bedraggled train, despondent and muttering, marching with churning effort in a trough of liquid brown mud under a low, wretched sky. Yet the youth smiled, for he saw that the world was a world for him, though many discovered it to be made of oaths and walking-sticks. He had rid himself of the red sickness of battle.

But *then* comes a sentence in which I simply do not believe. "He turned now with a lover's thirst to images of tranquil skies, fresh meadows, cool brooks—an existence of soft and eternal peace." In short we are left after all with a *fool*, for Crane knew as well as the next man, and much better, that life consists of very little but struggle. He wrote to Miss Crouse of

> . . . a life of labor and sorrow. I do not confront it blithely. I confront it with desperate resolution. There is not even much hope in my attitude. [Perhaps I should mention that at this time Stephen Crane was an international celebrity.] I do not even expect to do good. But I expect to make a sincere, desperate, lonely battle to remain true to my conception of my life and the way it should be lived. . . . It is not a fine prospect.

The shutting out of his hero from his personal thought redeems for me, on the whole, the end of the book.

The absence of interest in religion in *The Red Badge of Courage* is even more surprising than the other indifferences, whether seen in a critical way or in a biographical way. Henry Fleming, orphan of a farm widow, was seminary-trained. What emerges from the training is scanty indeed. "He would die; he would go to some place where he would be understood. It was useless to expect appreciation of his profound and fine senses from such men as the lieutenant." This is a fine and funny passage, not deeply Christian. Then there is the famous passage about the wafer, long quoted as a war cry for modernism in American fictional art. Unutterably wounded, upright, the tall soldier has sought a private ground away from the retreat, in a field mysteriously chosen, followed by the youth and a tattered soldier, for his dance of death:

> As the flap of the blue jacket fell away from the body, he could see that the side looked as if it had been chewed by wolves.
> The youth turned, with sudden, livid rage, toward the battlefield. He shook his fist. He seemed about to deliver a philippic.
> "Hell—"
> The red sun was pasted in the sky like a wafer.

Pasting is a failingly temporary operation (for the pagan god of the sky?) handed us here as an overpowering rebuke to the youth's rebellion. A wafer is thick nourishment, too, is it not? Disdain and fury against the prerogatives of majesty seem to be the subject. Even here it is hard to decide just how far Crane is sympathetic with the youth and how far critical of him. Revolt, in a seminary youth, should have been better prepared: one would welcome a *trace* of his Christian history, pro or con; that Crane never provides. Shortly afterward we hear:

He searched about in his mind for an adequate malediction for the inadequate cause, the thing upon which men turn the words of final blame. It—whatever it was—was responsible for him, he said. There lay the fault.

Crane did not here believe in evil. Henry Fleming is not evil, nor is anyone. A strange setup for an ambitious novel. Determinism is in control: "It . . . was responsible for him." Or is it? For the next little words are "*he said*"—which may be a repudiation. Again we are in the seesaw, which is not a bad place to be, so long as one trusts the writer.

Crane's religious history can be treated briefly. He could not help being the son of a cleryman and of a madly missionary woman. He told an interviewer:

> That cooled off and when I was thirteen or about that, my brother Will told me not to believe in Hell after my uncle had been boring me about the lake of fire and the rest of the side-shows.

Another time he said:

> I cannot be shown that God bends upon us any definable stare, and his laughter would be bully to hear out in nothingness.

I think we may conclude that neither this personal opinion nor the fierce scorn of Christianity that flashes in many of Crane's brilliant poems really has anything to do with the purely naturalistic framework—from this point of view—of *The Red Badge of Courage*.

With the word "naturalistic," however, we turn to some consideration of the artistic affiliations of the novel. All the categorical terms that have been applied to Crane's art are slippery, but let me deny at once that he was a naturalist. The naturalists—Frank Norris, say, and Theodore Dreiser—are accumulative and ponderous. Crane's intense selectivity makes him almost utterly unlike them. Crane's himself, when hardly more than a boy, allied his creed to the realism preached—in revolt against the slack, contrived, squeamish standards of popular American fiction in the nineties—by his first admirers, William Dean Howells, then the country's leading critic, and a younger writer, Hamlin Garland. But Crane's work does not resemble theirs, either, and he seems to have meant, in his alliance, only that art should be "sincere" (one of his favorite words) and truthful. Like many another young genius he regarded most writers as frauds and liars, and in fact perhaps most writers *are* frauds and liars. But epithets so vague as "sincere" and "truthful" tell us very little. The best term is undoubtedly that of his close friend, the far greater novelist, Joseph Conrad (though

whether a *better* writer it is probably too soon to say), who
observed in a letter to a mutual friend that "He is *the* only impressionist, and *only* an impressionist."

If we can accept this characteristically exaggerated but authoritative judgment, we are in a position to make some reservations.
Conrad and Crane, when they met in England in 1897, immediately recognized an affinity for one another; Conrad was soon
charged by reviewers with imitating Crane (a charge he denied, to
Crane). In truth, parts of *Lord Jim* are much indebted to *The Red
Badge*; yet Conrad clearly did not regard himself as an impressionist. Next, there exist in Crane's work obviously realistic and fantastic elements (as in Conrad's and in that of their friend, Henry
James, also domiciled in the south of England at this time), two
Americans and a Pole re-creating English fiction, which was lan-
guishing, so far as form was concerned, in the powerful hands of
Thomas Hardy and Rudyard Kipling. The power of experiment
came from abroad, as later from Joyce and Hemingway and Kafka,
and in poetry from T. S. Eliot and Ezra Pound.

Finally, the use of irony enters so deeply into most of Crane's
finest work (all five latter authors are ironists) that the simple term
"impressionist" will hardly do, and my uncertain feeling is that
Crane is best thought of as a twentieth-century author. Authorities
date modern American literature, some from *The Red Badge* in
1895, some from the re-issue in the following year of *Maggie*. This
critique is not the place for an exposition of the nature of irony in
relation to Crane, but perhaps something of that will emerge from a
summary study of his style. By way, though, of winding up the
impressionist reservations, let me reinforce Conrad's label with a
quotation from Crane:

> I understand that a man is born into the world with his own pair
> of eyes and he is not at all responsible for his vision—he is
> merely responsible for his quality of personal honesty. To keep
> close to this personal honesty is my supreme ambition.

Ill, dying indeed, hard-pressed with guests and fame and need for
money, working incessantly, he said to a journalist visitor during his
last year of life: "I get a little tired of saying, 'Is this true?'" He
was an impressionist; he dealt in the way things strike one, but also
in the way things are.

This famous style is not easy to describe, combining as it does
characteristics commonly antithetical. It is swift, no style in English
more so, improvisatorial, manly as Hazlitt; but at the same time it
goes in for ritual solemnity and can be highly poetic. For example,
as an illustration of the speed of his style:

> For a moment he felt in the face of his great trial like a babe,
> and the flesh over his heart seemed very thin. He seized time to
> look about him calculatingly.

Here we are already into something like the poetic tone which is
well illustrated in the opening sentence of the novel: "The cold
passed reluctantly from the earth, and the retiring fogs revealed an
army stretched out on the hills, resting." This is a high case of the
animism already referred to. The color of the style is celebrated;
maybe he got it from a theory of Goethe's, but the style is also
plain, plain. Short as it is, it is also unusually iterative; modern and
simple, brazen with medieval imagery; animistic, dehuman, and
mechanistic; attentive—brilliantly—to sound:

> As he ran, he became aware that the forest had stopped its music,
> as if at last becoming capable of hearing the foreign sounds. The
> trees hushed and stood motionless. Everything seemed to be
> listening to the crackle and clatter and ear-shaking thunder. The
> chorus pealed over the still earth.

Adverbs are used like verbs, word order deformed: somebody leans
on a bar and hears other men "terribly discuss a question that was
not plain." But the surest attribute of this style is its reserve, as its
most celebrated is its color. Crane guarantees nothing. "Doubtless"
is a favorite word. The technique of refusal is brought so far forward that a casual "often" will defeat itself: "What hats and caps
were left to them they often slung high in the air." Once more we
hear a Shakespearean contempt, as in *Coriolanus*. In a paradoxical
way, if he will not vouch for what he tells us, if he does not push
us, trying to convince, we feel that he must have things up his
sleeve which would persuade us if we only knew them. As for color:
"A crimson roar came from the distance" is the mildest example I
have been able to find. His employment of it here is not only not
naturalistic (what roar was ever red?) but is solely affective, that is,
emotional, like his metaphorical use, in the novel, of devils, ghouls,
demons, and specters. Crane made use of a spectrum. A final item
is his rueful humor: "He threw aside his mental pamphlets on the
philosophy of the retreated and rules for the guidance of the
damned."

On that note we might end, except for a poem written by Stephen Crane several years after the novel, called "War Is Kind"; it is
one of his major poems, and one of the best poems of the period.
In the novel there is little of the pathos of which he had already
shown himself a master in *Maggie*, and little of the horror informing his best later war stories. These qualities come to life in the
poem.

Crane makes a sort of little bridge between Tolstoi—supreme—

supreme?—and our very good writer Hemingway. But these superior gentlemen are not competitors. One of the most cogent remarks ever made about the poet of the *Iliad* is that he shared with Tolstoi and with Shakespeare both a virile love of war and a virile horror of it. So in his degree did Crane, and before he had seen it.

KERMIT VANDERBILT and DANIEL WEISS

From Rifleman to Flagbearer: Henry Fleming's Separate Peace in *The Red Badge of Courage*†

The significance and to some extent the excellence of a literary work can be measured by the volume of critical debate which it has provoked. By this gauge, Stephen Crane's *The Red Badge of Courage* stands virtually unsurpassed among American novels. The critical issues have ranged from the meaning of Jim Conklin's death on the first day of battle to Crane's ironic or non-ironic intention on the second day when Henry Fleming presumably arrives at a quiet, unflinching manhood. Beyond these matters, a larger question of meaning has centered on whether Crane placed his youthful soldier in a world of naturalism, of Christian morality, or of primordial myth.

This wide disagreement over the intended meaning of an author who aimed to write "plainly and unmistakably" can be partly explained when one isolates a major frustration which critics of *The Red Badge of Courage* seem to have shared. It is this: after Henry, on the second day, has at last hurled himself into the cannon's mouth, and then only briefly (Chapter XVII), he abandons the role of rifleman and soon becomes a flagbearer. He gives up the psychic advantage of the soldier who can shoot back at the enemy and chooses, instead, this highly dangerous but auxiliary role in the final extended action of the second day. How does one account for Henry's self-election as standard-bearer in the final one-fourth of the novel (Chapters XVIII to XXIII)? Readings of *Red Badge* have consistently passed over these flagbearing chapters with, at most, a passage or two cited to provide a convenient transition from Chapter XVII to concluding Chapter XXIV.[1]

† *Modern Fiction Studies*, XI (Winter, 1965–66), 371–80. Copyright © 1966 by Purdue Research Foundation, West Lafayette, Indiana. Reprinted by permission.

1. A notable exception is John E. Hart's *"The Red Badge of Courage* as Myth and Symbol," *University of Kansas City Review*, XIX (Summer, 1953), 249–256. Mr. Hart tries to give a total reading of the novel by interpreting Henry as a mythic hero whose arduous quest is fulfilled when he attains the "beautiful maiden," symbolized by the flag. Mr. Hart, however, overlooks Henry's basic self-concern and spectator-interest which are fully renewed during his second day's role as flagbearer.

The present confusion over the unity of *The Red Badge of Courage* might have been partly avoided had Crane's later critics been more willing to accept his own stated intention, to present "a psychological portrayal of fear."[2] Cosmic issues aside, *Red Badge* is clearly what Crane said that it was, an extended dramatic portrayal of fear. He apparently intended to characterize a youth who is trying to maintain an equilibrium within himself and with relation to his own comrades and a fearsome enemy. The culmination of Henry Fleming's ordeal of fear, the point where Henry's essentially dependent, sensitive nature finally becomes reconciled to aggressive warfare, occurs not in his experience of Jim Conklin's death on the first day. Nor does it happen, again anticlimactically, during the initial charge of the second day, when Henry fights momentarily with blind and ferocious abandon. Rather, the climax of the novel occurs when Henry suddenly has a revelation later on the second day and elects to replace the slain flagbearer. This fourth and final act of the novel is a consistent, climactic, and in a qualified sense an ironic, culmination of Henry Fleming's ordeal as a soldier. In addition to illuminating Henry's psychological defenses against fear in the previous chapters of the novel, this final action also helps to reveal Crane's meaning in the final chapter of the book. By understanding Henry Fleming's self-appointed commission as flagbearer, we also discover the structural and psychological unity of Crane's novel.

I

Henry Fleming's major concern as a soldier is to cope with his fear of death by discovering what his basic nature is and, in the process, to preserve his esteem within the regiment. His preliminary anxieties (Chapters I to III, to "one gray dawn") are followed by a many-sided test of his fear during the first day of battle (Chapters III through XIII). Briefly summarized, this first day depicts Henry in an opening charge which reveals him to be neither courageous nor cowardly. He is borne along in a "battle-sleep." But an unexpected second wave of attack suddenly floods Henry with panic fear. He drops his rifle and runs. He next receives several grisly views of death close up, culminating in the death-ceremony of Jim Conklin. He invites his harmless "red badge of courage" by his annoying

2. Robert W. Stallman discounted Crane's statement and also criticized Thomas Beer's early study of Crane for its influential and misleading emphasis on fear in Crane. That Beer and later Crane critics failed to analyze in any detail the nature of fear in *Red Badge* might be more justly charged. Mr. Stallman's own "Notes Toward an Analysis of *The Red Badge of Courage*" which, not surprisingly, has been scored for being fragmentary, and thereby forced, insists that the novel "is about the self-combat of a youth who fears [sic] and stubbornly resists change, and the actual battle is symbolic of this spiritual warfare aaginst change and growth" (*Stephen Crane: An Omnibus* [New York, 1952], pp. 582, 193).

questions to a retreating Union soldier. So "wounded," he acts out in fancy several guilty and unsatisfactory daydreams of heroic courage, together with a death Jim-Conklin-fashion. He is finally reunited with his regiment through his childlike dependence on a magic helper, the "cheery soldier." And we see him at the close of the first day behaving with "doglike obedience" toward Wilson, who protectively cares for the receptive Henry with "the bustling ways of an amateur nurse."

Before giving a soomewhat more detailed account of Henry's fear on this first day of battle, we can first draw two tentative conclusions. One is that Henry's continuing defenses against fear after the death of Jim Conklin can dismiss the argument that Jim's death has produced any significant change in Henry. Second, Crane has given us no reason whatsoever to believe that his fearful youth is ready to awaken on the following morning the happy warrior. Henry's actions on the second day, with certain exceptions to be noted, will be, in fact, suspiciously like those of the first day. After his sudden and short-lived bravado and one brief, demonic charge (Chapters XIV to XVII), Henry will again be threatened with overwhelming panic. But he will be rescued once more through the aid of a fantasied protector—this time the Union flag. In short, Henry experiences neither change nor regeneration in his two days of soldiering. Rather, he discovers the conduct proper to his native qualities as a man, which includes his relative unfitness as an aggressive rifleman.

Henry Fleming at the opening of the second day of battle does appear to be a new man, an aggressive, hell-for-leather fighting soldier. The main differences in Henry's attitude are two. First, he is encouraged by his "wound" to adopt an equally spurious pose of masculine aggressiveness—in returning Wilson's farewell letters of the previous day "with condescending pity"; in constructing a private fantasy of being back home a hero recounting his war exploits to a worshipful audience; and in noisily criticizing the officers in authority. But a soldier unwittingly calls Henry's bluff, and "his mind shrank from going nearer to the danger, and thereafter he was silent. The significance of the sarcastic man's words took from him all loud moods that would make him appear prominent. He became suddenly a modest person." When Henry briefly returns to his criticism of the operational procedures, the "savage-minded lieutenant" quickly sets Henry down. The second difference in Henry's behavior is more significant, the degree of anger which he now has been able to cultivate against the enemy. Gregory Zilboorg, writing about troop morale in World War Two, his described the sanction of anger:

> It is a well-observed fact that "green" troops become "seasoned" as soon as they become angry—that is, as soon as they begin to

288 · *Kermit Vanderbilt and Daniel Weiss*

convert their fear of death into hatred and aggression. This usually happens after the baptism of fire, not so much because the soldiers become accustomed to the fire of the enemy, but primarily because their anger begins to be aroused after they have lost some of their brothers in combat. It is the mechanism of revenge, of overcoming death by means of murder, that proves here too the most potent psychological force.[3]

But Henry's is a rage with a difference. The "mechanism of revenge" on behalf of comrades lost in battle plays no recognizable part at all. The anger which Henry feels when confronted by the relentlessly advancing enemy belongs to the passive, contemplative youth of the day before: "There was a maddening quality in this seeming resolution of the foe to give him no rest, to give him no time to sit down and think. Yesterday he had fought and had fled rapidly. There had been many adventures. For to-day he felt that he had earned opportunities for contemplative repose." Notice also that the cruel and saddening death of Jim Conklin has now become only one among the "many adventures" of the first day. So Henry is different on this second day because of anger, but it is an anger inspired directly by his continuing self-concern. It will, however, prove valuable as a temporary defense against overwhelming panic in his third charge.

One must conclude, then, that Henry's responses here are not substantially different from the first day. In the first charge of the second day, Henry's aggressive pose and "loud moods" are quickly supplanted by his old sense of personal impotence and of existing in a battle-sleep. He wishes that his rifle were "an engine of annihilating power. . . . When, in a dream, it occurred to the youth that his rifle was an impotent stick, he lost sense of everything but his hate. . . ." Again, he returns to the delirium of his first-day battle experience: "The youth was not conscious that he was erect upon his feet. He did not know the direction of the ground. Indeed, once he even lost the habit of balance and fell heavily. He was up again immediately. One thought went through the chaos of his brain at the time. He wondered if he had fallen because he had been shot."

And again, this helplessness and delirium suggest the behavior of a young boy. What makes Crane's grasp of the psychology of soldiering a marvel of intuition throughout the novel lies in his recognition of what servicemen know from direct observation, that war invokes infantile responses, a primitive level of mind which is archaic to the uses of mature and peaceful culture. Army life decrees a moratorium on maturity in the mental lives of individual soldiers. The army becomes for the soldier a substitute family, an institutionalized version of both the protective and the punishing

3. "Fear of Death," *Psychoanalytic Quarterly*, XII (October, 1943), 474.

parents. In exchange for giving up his independence, the soldier entrusts his life and well-being to his superiors, fashioning the relationship out of its analogy with his earlier dependence on his parents. And so on the first day of battle, Henry finds his protective security not in the enveloping concern of his strong-minded mother for her only son, but in the collective activity of the army. When the battle forms, Henry is engulfed in the collective security of the "moving box," the "common personality . . . superior to circumstances . . . with a mighty power." He also appears both to be seeking and rebuking his lost father in the images of those officers whom Crane isolates, now here, now there, who represent aggression, authority, assurance, and an active omnipotence, but who also threatened to leave Henry to face his anxieties alone. Before battle, Henry feels that he can concern himself with "his personal comfort. For recreation he could twiddle his thumbs and speculate on the thoughts which must agitate the minds of the generals." He presently blames these paternal figures, however, for not protecting him against his anxiety: "In his great anxiety his heart was continually clamoring at what he considered the intolerable slowness of the generals." But when Henry conjures a fearful, impressionistic image of "the red eyes across the river . . . growing larger, as the orbs of a row of dragons advancing," he turns to the colonel on the horse and sees him, a looming, authoritarian, Kafkaesque figure, "lift his gigantic arm and calmy stroke his mustache." When this omnipotence seems to falter and Henry feels cast out on his own, he resents the officer who rebukes him and orders him to march ahead. To punish the officer, as well as to appease his own wounded conscience, Henry thinks like the dependent and angry small boy—he will die and then the unfeeling parent will be sorry: "He would die; he would go to some place where he would be understood. It was useless to expect appreciation of his profound and fine senses from such men as the lieutenant." The fantasy passes. The officer, as Crane notes, is necessary to Henry's and the regiment's safety, and his voice speaks to a soldier with something of "divinity . . . stern, hard, with no reflection of fear in it."[4]

4. The omnipotent officer of *Red Badge* appears elsewhere in Crane. In "The Price of the Harness," written out of Crane's experience in the Spanish-American War, the unassailable officer returns in the following scene: "The whole scene would have spoken to the private soldiers of ambushes, sudden flank attacks, terrible disasters, if it were not for those cool gentlemen with shoulder-straps and swords who, the private soldiers knew, were of another world and omnipotent for the business." (*Stephen Crane: Twenty Stories*, ed. Carl Van Doren [New York, 1940], p. 436).

John Berryman's *Stephen Crane* (New York, 1950) first hypothesized Oedipal fixations in Crane's life and work. Maxwell Geismar, *Rebels and Ancestors: The American Novel, 1890–1915* (Cambridge, Mass., 1953), supported Berryman's thesis, and attempted also to give it social and religious significance. Whether or not Henry Fleming's conflicts within the military family are derived in part from Crane's own childhood is not crucial to the present analysis of the novel.

The first day of battle is replete with even more specific references to the regressive nature of soldiering in general, and of Henry Fleming in particular. Henry feels "like a babe" as he is carried along in the security of the moving box. Henry's perspiring face is "like that of a weeping urchin." He fights for air in the midst of the smoke "as a babe being smothered attacks the deadly blankets," while the soldier next to him is "babbling . . . like the monologue of a babe." At the end of the first charge, Henry is filled with the sensations of collective omnipotence and liberation from the "red, formidable difficulties of war." In his battle-sleep, he has been carried along to safety within the family of his "subtle battle brotherhood," the "mysterious fraternity" of the collective regiment. And now, as "the youth awakened slowly," he "felt the bonds of tied hearts." But he is also filled with the sense of being something special within the brotherhood, of being not only secure from danger but of being privately "magnificent," and he goes into "an ecstasy of self-satisfaction." But a few moments later, he is suddenly confronted by the Rebel Army in a second wave, and in a trance of astonishment and helplessness, he suddenly grows numb with fear and runs "like a rabbit."

Returning to the opening wave of attack on the second day, one finds Henry still behaving like a fearful young boy. What Crane suggests this time, in addition, is the essential paradox of men at war who are most "heroic" when they have become heedless, demonic children. Henry becomes the infantile berserker, shooting wildly at an enemy who seems more like a swarm of "flies sucking insolently at his blood" than like men. He even continues to fire when the retreating enemy is no longer there. Henry's flight to activity on the second day, in short, leads him briefly to deny fear and danger by the paradoxical strategy of exposing himself to the very thing he fears. To prevent or forestall the terror of surprise and sudden annihilation, he plunges headlong into the feared situation, preferring even destruction to the dread of destruction. He is like Ovid's fear-crazed men in the plague-ridden city who

> Hung themselves
> Driving the fear of death away by death
> By going out to meet it.[5]

Henry Fleming's old need for reassurance of his own immunity is bound up with his obsessive and very short-lived display of fierceness in the first charge of the second day. He dimly and ironically recognizes soon afterwards, when he has received the admiration of his comrades and the praises of his officer, that he has been a som-

5. *Metamorphoses*, trans. Rolfe Humphries (Bloomington, 1955), Book Seven, lines 604–606.

nolent schoolboy commanding a phantom enemy to fall dead on command: "By this struggle he had overcome obstacles which he had admitted to be mountains. They had fallen like paper peaks, and he was now what he called a hero. And he had not been aware of the process. He had slept and, awakening, found himself a knight." What Henry senses here is that fear is a strictly personal emotion which may lie behind either cowardice or "courage." His central problem of mastering his fear has now taken the two extremes of adjustment—cowardice in flight from the dangerous object, and barbaric "courage" through flight toward the danger.

II

It is here, precisely, at what would seem to be the moment of his apotheosis as the soldier-hero that Henry Fleming makes his final adaptation, not only to his continuing fear of death but also to his basic nature as a man. After this third charge of his battle career, Henry, far from being the seasoned veteran who kills without scruple, now turns gradually to regain the softer emotional sensibilities of the non-combatant.

Henry's abdication from his brief role as the aggressive rifleman begins when he and Wilson go in search of water to fill their comrades' canteens. During the search, Henry once more resumes his earlier role of the curious spectator. He is again filled with anxiety over his helpless vulnerability: he has overheard the two officers of his division refer to his regiment as "a lot 'a mule drivers," and now "new eyes were given to him. And the most startling thing was to learn suddenly that he was very insignificant."

In the action of the fourth charge that follows, Henry's fear of death returns in its original form when he concurs with the fearful soldier who says "in a meek voice, 'We'll git swallowed.'" The angry, reckless Henry of the previous charge, who had tried to swallow the enemy alone, has become again the passive fearful youth: "The youth stared at the land in front of him. Its foliages now seemed to veil powers and horrors." He is momentarily in the moving box, and then "directly he lunged ahead and began to run." He is again in a dazed condition until the young lieutenant "grappled with him as if for a wrestling bout." Henry is soon running "like a madman to reach the woods before a bullet could discover him. He ducked his head low, like a football player. In his haste his eyes almost closed, and the scene was a wild blur. Pulsating saliva stood at the corners of his mouth." More dazed and helpless than the day before, Henry suddenly has a revelation: he discovers a new source of immunity from the mounting terrors of death on the battlefield:

Within him as he hurled himself forward, was born a love, a despairing fondness for this flag which was near him. It was a creation of beauty and invulnerability. It was a goddess, radiant, that bended its form with an imperious gesture to him. It was a woman, red and white, hating and loving, that called him with the voice of his hopes. Because no harm could come to it he endowed it with power. He kept near, as if it could be a saver of lives, and an imploring cry went from his mind.

That the color sergeant is suddenly struck dead does not alter Henry's belief in the efficacy which the flag will hold especially for him. In a brief rivalry over the flag with Wilson, Henry gains possession of his new magic helper. Just as the "cheery soldier" came along after Jim Conklin's death, seemingly with "a wand of a magic kind," to save the submissive Henry after the debacle of the first day, the flag serves Henry's need for a protector during the critical juncture of the second day. The flag, which he endows so obviously with intermingled trappings of invulnerability, maternity, and divinity, is, in effect, the protective Athena for this delicate young Achilles, and war becomes the "Homeric" game Henry had initially fancied it to be. He is clearly employing once more a delusional system linked to the reality of warfare as magic formulae are linked to the phenomena they control. In actuality, Henry has become the most conspicuous moving target on the battlefield. But the flag, in becoming his fantasied charm against danger, will allow Henry in the remaining charges of the second day to protect himself from fear and to maintain his self-respect within the regiment. To the young lieutenant rallying the troops, Henry becomes the helpmeet, not an identification this time but an independent, auxiliary relationship with the man of action. Henry can also charge along with his comrades and shout encouragement without incurring the risk of their vulnerability or their "misty-eyed" panic and confusion in the face of the aggressor: "He veiled a glance of disdain at his fellows who strewed the ground, choking with dust, red from perspiration, misty-eyed, disheveled." In short, the irony of Henry's final stance is that he is now praised by the colonel as the good soldier, a 'jim-hickey," and he has, in fact, returned to his original self-concern, his propensity for make-believe, and his preferred role of an absorbed spectator at a "great drama," at a "matched game."[6]

6. Hemingway, who admired Crane and whose war career and writings about fear parallel Crane's in many respects, has Yogi Johnson in *The Torrents of Spring* liken war-combat to a football game; Crane has Henry Fleming, on the second day, race over the battlefield ducking "his head low like a football player." The similitude of the "matched game" in *Red Badge* recurs on the second day: the soldiers are like "sprinters before a signal;" the opposing armies exchange "blows in the manner of a pair of boxers." Suggested here is that Crane and Hemingway, both athletes, knew privately what psychologist Abram Kardiner has since verified: that fear generally and battle sickness in particular have a way of working themselves out through the spectator experience, actual or fantasied, of the ritualized sports event. (See *War Stress and Neurotic Illness* [New York, 1947], pp. 206 ff.)

III

At the end of *The Red Badge of Courage*, Henry Fleming has constructed his own mental defenses against the "thousand-tongued fear," and so has learned how to control and master it. That he has gradually come to terms with "reality" through various fantasies, culminating with his being both a spectator at a controlled and ritualized "game" of war, and a non-aggressive participant divinely protected from danger through his magic helper, the flag—these are only a part of Crane's mild ironies at the end. Henry is also given to feel "a quiet manhood, nonassertive but of sturdy and strong blood. He knew that he would no more quail before his guides wherever they should point. He had been to touch the great death, and found that, after all, it was but the great death. He was a man." But this "manhood" does not include the aggressiveness which characterizes the good hard-boiled soldier, the primitive Fortinbras. Henry remains essentially the young Hamlet, the contemplative youth whose responses to danger could never be hammered into the merciless reflexes of the hardened veteran. Briefly at the opening of the second day, Henry's fear had driven him into aggressive activity; but it was inevitably a spurious flight, a pantomime of the fierce soldier from which he turned with a sense both of helplessness and relief back to his old dependencies. As flagbearer, he clearly has not thrown off the swaddling bands; instead, he has extended their coverage. He has gained a female protectress who will enclothe with total invulnerability her favored and dependent only son. He has once again become someone magnificent and special. (In the passage just quoted, Crane had originally made unmistakable the irony of Henry's sense of special immunity: Henry had discovered that the great death "was for others.") Now feeling exalted within the regiment, he discovers that he can put at a convenient distance the haunting memory of his panic flight and his shameful inability to help the tattered soldier on the previous day. He has rid himself of the "red sickness of battle" without suffering the loss of self-esteem or social alienation from his fighting comrades. Henry has adopted his unique and final role as bearer of the colors because it is entirely in accord with his unconscious sense of himself.

Returning to the critical debate over *The Red Badge of Courage*, one must conclude that the structure of Crane's "psychological portrayal of fear" has been developed, naturally enough, around Henry Fleming's instinct of fear. The alternating rhythms of the novel on both days have been defined by Henry's sleeps and wakings, his separations from and reunions with some form of omnipotence, his alternating flights (both real and imagined) into activity and then back into passivity. In the flagbearing chapters, these rhythms have been brought into unity and the discords of battle activity privately resolved for Henry. Crane's final chapter fails to support the reading of Henry either as a seasoned military man or as a mythical hero dominated by altruistic concern for his people. Nor does one discover here the concluding scene in a Christian drama of spiritual growth and change: Henry's private vision suggests the late nineteenth-century universe not of Tolstoy but of Mark Twain. At the end, the novel and its central character turn away from the problems of courage and cowardice, from delirium, battle sleep, and the chaos of human warfare.

> He turned now with a lover's thirst to images of tranquil skies, fresh meadows, cool brooks—an existence of soft and eternal peace.

> Over the river a golden ray of sun came through the hosts of leaden rain clouds.

The landscape images the separate "golden" peace which Henry has arrived at through his fantasied election as flagbearer, while the "leaden rain clouds" of war exist for Union soldiers less fortunate. Henry Fleming's final stance suggests both a return to himself and a farm boy's private reunion with a world of beneficent nature, a separate existence of security and peace in the midst of war.

DONALD PIZER

Late Nineteenth-Century American Naturalism†

Most literary critics and historians who attempt definitions are aware of the dangers and advantages inherent in this enterprise. But few, I believe, recognize that many literary genres and modes have their barriers of established terms and ideas to overcome or outflank. The writer who seeks to define tragedy usually finds that his definition takes shape around such traditional guideposts as the tragic hero, the tragic flaw, recognition and catharsis, and so on. American naturalism, as a concept, has two such channelled approaches to its definition. The first is that since naturalism comes after realism, and since it seems to take literature in the same direction as realism, it is primarily an "extension" or continuation of realism—only a little different. The second almost inevitable approach involves this difference. The major distinction between

† From *Realism and Naturalism in Nineteenth-Century American Literature* (Carbondale: Southern Illinois University Press, 1966), pp. 11–14, 24–30. Copyright © 1966 by Donald Pizer.

realism and naturalism, most critics agree, is the particular philosophical orientation of the naturalists. A traditional and widely accepted concept of American naturalism, therefore, is that it is essentially realism infused with a pessimistic determinism. Richard Chase argues that American naturalism is realism with a "necessitarian ideology," and George J. Becker (defining all naturalism, including American) considers it as "no more than an emphatic and explicit philosophical position taken by some realists," the position being a "pessimistic materialistic determinism."[1] The common belief is that the naturalists were like the realists in their fidelity to the details of contemporary life, but that they depicted everyday life with a greater sense of the role of such forces as heredity and environment in determining behavior and belief.

This traditional approach to naturalism through realism and through philosophical determinism is historically justifiable and has served a useful purpose, but it has also handicapped thinking both about the movement as a whole and about individual works within the movement. It has resulted in much condescension toward those writers who are supposed to be naturalists yet whose fictional sensationalism (an aspect of romanticism) and moral ambiguity (a quality inconsistent with the absolutes of determinism) appear to make their work flawed specimens of the mode.

I would like, therefore, to propose a modified definition of late nineteenth-century American naturalism.[2] For the time being, let this be a working definition, to be amplified and made more concrete by the illustrations from which it has been drawn. I suggest that the naturalistic novel usually contains two tensions or contradictions, and that the two in conjunction comprise both an interpretation of experience and a particular aesthetic recreation of experience. In other words, the two constitute the theme and form of the naturalistic novel. The first tension is that between the subject matter of the naturalistic novel and the concept of man which emerges from this subject matter. The naturalist populates his novel primarily from the lower middle class or the lower class. His charac-

1. Richard Chase, *The American Novel and Its Tradition* (Garden City, N.Y., 1957), p. 186 n; George J. Becker, "Modern Realism as a Literary Movement," in *Documents of Modern Literary Realism*, ed. George J. Becker (Princeton, 1963), p. 35. See also the definitions by Lars Ahnebrink, *The Beginnings of Naturalism in American Fiction* (Cambridge, Mass., 1950), pp. vi–vii; Malcolm Cowley, "A Natural History of American Naturalism," *Documents*, pp. 429–30; and Philip Rahv, "Notes on the Decline of Naturalism," *Documents*, pp. 583–84.
2. The discussion of naturalism in the next two paragraphs resembles in several ways that by Charles C. Walcutt in his *American Literary Naturalism, A Divided Stream* (Minneapolis, 1956), pp. 3–29. In general, I accept Walcutt's analysis of naturalism's philosophical and literary ambivalences. I believe, however, that his discussion of the naturalists' divided view of nature and of their maintenance of the idea of free will by implicitly encouraging their readers to social action are ways of describing these ambivalences historically and socially—by source and effect—rather than as they function within the naturalistic novel itself.

ters are the poor, the uneducated, the unsophisticated. His fictional world is that of the commonplace and unheroic in which life would seem to be chiefly the dull round of daily existence, as we ourselves usually conceive of our lives. But the naturalist discovers in this world those qualities of man usually associated with the heroic or adventurous, such as acts of violence and passion which involve sexual adventure or bodily strength and which culminate in desperate moments and violent death. A naturalistic novel is thus an extension of realism only in the sense that both modes often deal with the local and contemporary. The naturalist, however, discovers in this material the extraordinary and excessive in human nature.

The second tension involves the theme of the naturalistic novel. The naturalist often describes his characters as though they are conditioned and controlled by environment, heredity, instinct, or chance. But he also suggests a compensating humanistic value in his characters or their fates which affirms the significance of the individual and of his life. The tension here is that between the naturalist's desire to represent in fiction the new, discomforting truths which he has found in the ideas and life of his late nineteenth-century world, and also his desire to find some meaning in experience which reasserts the validity of the human enterprise. The naturalist appears to say that although the individual may be a cipher in a world made amoral by man's lack of responsibility for his fate, the imagination refused to accept this formula as the total meaning of life and so seeks a new basis for man's sense of his own dignity and importance.

The naturalistic novel is therefore not so superficial or reductive as it implicitly appears to be in its conventional definition. It involves a belief that life on its lowest levels is not so simple as it seems to be from higher levels. It suggests that even the least significant human being can feel and strive powerfully and can suffer the extraordinary consequences of his emotions, and that no range of human experience is free of the moral complexities and ambiguities which Milton set his fallen angels to debating.[3] Naturalism reflects an affirmative ethical conception of life, for it asserts the value of all life by endowing the lowest character with emotion and defeat and with moral ambiguity, no matter how poor or ignoble he may seem. The naturalistic novel derives much of its aesthetic effect from these contrasts. It involves us in the experience of a life both commonplace and extraordinary, both familiar and strange, both simple and complex. It pleases us with its sensationalism without affronting our sense of probability. It discovers the "romance of the common-

3. Erich Auerbach's *Mimesis: The Representation of Reality in Western Literature* (Princeton, 1953) deals with the representation of these ideas in imaginative literature from antiquity to our own day.

place," as Frank Norris put it. Thus, the melodramatic sensational-ism and moral "confusion" which are often attacked in the natural-istic novel should really be incorporated into a normative definition of the mode and be recognized as its essential constituents.

* * *

The Red Badge of Courage also embodies a different combina-tion of the sensational and commonplace than that found in *McTeague*. Whereas Norris demonstrates that the violent and the extraordinary are present in seemingly dull and commonplace lives, Crane, even more than Dreiser, is intent on revealing the common-place nature of the seemingly exceptional. In *The Red Badge* Henry Fleming is a raw, untried country youth who seeks the romance and glory of war but who finds that his romantic, chivalric preconcep-tions of battle are false. Soldiers and generals do not strike heroic poses; the dead are not borne home triumphantly on their shields but fester where they have fallen; and courage is not a conscious striving for an ideal mode of behavior but a temporary delirium derived from animal fury and social pride or fear. A wounded officer worries about the cleanliness of his uniform; a soldier sweats and labors at his arms "like a laborer in a foundry"; and mere chance determines rewards and punishments—the death of a Conklin, the red badge of a Fleming. War to Crane is like life itself in its injus-tice, in its mixing of the ludicrous and the momentarily exhilarat-ing, in its self-deceptions, and in its acceptance of appearances for realities. Much of Crane's imagery in the novel is therefore con-sciously and pointedly antiheroic, not only in his obviously satirical use of conventional chivalric imagery in unheroic situations (a sol-dier hearing a rumor comes "waving his [shirt] banner-like" and adopting "the important air of a herald in red and gold") but also more subtly in his use of machine and animal imagery to deflate potentially heroic moments.

Crane's desire to devalue the heroic in war stems in part from his stance as an ironist reacting against a literary and cultural tradition of idealized courage and chivalry. But another major element in his desire to reduce war to the commonplace arises from his casting of Fleming's experiences in the form of a "life" or initiation allegory. Henry Fleming is the universal youth who leaves home unaware of himself or the world. His participation in battle is his introduction to life as for the first time he tests himself and his preconceptions of experience against experience itself. He emerges at the end of the battle not entirely self-perceptive or firm-willed—Crane is too much the ironist for such a reversal—but rather as one who has encoun-tered some of the strengths and some of the failings of himself and others. Crane implies that although Fleming may again run from battle and although he will no doubt always have the human capacity to rationalize his weaknesses, he is at least no longer the innocent.

If *The Red Badge* is viewed in this way—that is, as an antiheroic allegory of "life"—it becomes clear that Crane is representing in his own fashion the naturalistic belief in the interpenetration of the commonplace and the sensational. All life, Crane appears to be saying, is a struggle, a constant sea of violence in which we inevitably immerse ourselves and in which we test our beliefs and our values. War is an appropriate allegorical symbol of this test, for to Crane violence is the very essence of life, not in the broad Darwinian sense of a struggle for existence or the survival of the fittest, but rather in the sense that the proving and testing of oneself, conceived both realistically and symbolically, entails the violent and the deeply emotional, that the finding of oneself occurs best in moments of stress and is itself often an act of violence. To Crane, therefore, war as an allegorical setting for the emergence of youth into knowledge embodies both the violence of this birth and the commonplaces of life which the birth reveals—that men are controlled by the trivial, the accidental, the degradingly unheroic, despite the preservation of such accoutrements of the noble as a red badge or a captured flag. Crane shows us what Norris and Dreiser only suggest, that there is no separation between the sensational and the commonplace, that the two are coexistent in every aspect and range of life. He differs from Norris in kind and from Dreiser in degree in that his essentially ironic imagination leads him to reverse the expected and to find the commonplace in the violent rather than the sensational beneath the trival. His image of life as an unheroic battle captures in one ironic symbol both his romanticism and his naturalism—or, in less literary terms, his belief that we reveal character in violence but that human character is predominantly fallible and self-deceptive.

Much of Crane's best fiction displays this technique of ironic deflation. In *Maggie*, a young urchin defends the honor of Rum Alley on a heap of gravel; in "The Open Boat," the stalwart oiler suffers an inconsequential and meaningless death; in "The Blue Hotel," the death of the Swede is accompanied by a derisive sign on the cash register; and in "The Bride Comes to Yellow Sky," the long-awaited "chivalric" encounter is thwarted by the bride's appearance. Each of these crucial or significant events has at its core Crane's desire to reduce the violent and extraordinary to the commonplace, a reduction which indicates both his ironic vision of man's romantic pretensions and his belief in the reality of the fusion of the violent and the commonplace in experience.

As was true of Norris and Dreiser, Crane's particular way of combining the sensational and the commonplace is closely related to the second major aspect of his naturalism, the thematic tension or complexity he emboidies in his work. *The Red Badge* presents a vision of man as a creature capable of advancing in some areas of knowledge and power but forever imprisoned within the walls of certain inescapable human and social limitations. Crane depicts the similarity between Henry Fleming's "will" and an animal's instinctive response to crisis or danger. He also presents Fleming's discovery that he is enclosed in a "moving box" of "tradition and law" even at those moments when he believes himself capable of rational decision and action—that the opinions and actions of other men control and direct him. Lastly, Crane dramatizes Fleming's realization that although he can project his emotions into natural phenomena and therefore derive comfort from a sense of nature's identification with his desires and needs, nature and man are really two, not one, and nature offers no reliable or useful guide to experience or to action. But, despite Crane's perception of these limitations and inadequacies, he does not paint a totally bleak picture of man in *The Red Badge*. True, Fleming's own sanguine view of himself at the close of the novel—that he is a man—cannot be taken at face value. Fleming's self-evaluations contrast ironically with his motives and actions throughout the novel, and his final estimation of himself represents primarily man's ability to be proud of his public deeds while rationalizing his private failings.

But something has happened to Fleming which Crane values and applauds. Early in the novel Fleming feels at odds with his comrades. He is separated from them by doubts about his behavior under fire and by fear of their knowledge of his doubts. These doubts and fears isolate him from his fellows, and his isolation is intensified by his growing awareness that the repressive power of the "moving box" of his regiment binds him to a group from which he now wishes to escape. Once in battle, however, Fleming becomes "not a man but a member" as he is "welded into a common personality which was dominated by a single desire." The "subtle battle brotherhood" replaces his earlier isolation, and in one sense the rest of the novel is devoted to Fleming's loss and recovery of his feeling of oneness with his fellows. After his initial success in battle, Henry loses this quality as he deserts his comrades and then wanders away from his regiment in actuality and in spirit. His extreme stage of isolation from the regiment and from mankind occurs when he abandons the tattered soldier. After gaining a "red badge" which symbolically reunites him with those soldiers who remained and fought, he returns to his regiment and participates successfully in the last stages of the battle. Here, as everywhere in Crane, there is a deflating irony, for Henry's "red badge" is not a true battle wound. But despite the tainted origin of this symbol of fraternity, its effect on Henry and his fellows is real and significant. He is accepted gladly when he returns, and in his renewed confidence and pride he finds strength and a kind of joy. Crane believed that this feeling of trust and mutual confidence among men is essential, and it is one of the few values he confirms again and again in his fiction. It is this quality which knits together the four men in the open boat and lends them moral strength. And it is the absence of this quality and its replacement by fear and distrust which characterizes the world of "The Blue Hotel" and causes the tragic denouement in that story.

Crane thus points out that courage has primarily a social reality, that it is a quality which exists not absolutely but by virtue of other men's opinions, and that the social unity born of a courageous fellowship may therefore be based on self-deception or on deception of others. He also demonstrates that this bond of fellowship may be destructive and oppressive when it restricts or determines individual choice, as in the "moving box" of the regiment. Fleming, after all, at first stands fast because he is afraid of what his comrades will do or think, and then runs because he feels that the rest of the regiment is deserting as well. But Crane also maintains that in social cohesion man gains both what little power of self-preservation he possesses and a gratifying and necessary sense of acceptance and acknowledgement difficult to attain otherwise. Crane therefore establishes a vital organic relationship between his deflation of the traditional idea of courage and his assertion of the need for and the benefits of social unity. He attacks the conventional heroic ideal by showing that a man's actions in battle are usually determined by his imitation of the actions of others—by the group as a whole. But this presentation of the reality and power of the group also suggests the advantages possible in group unity and group action.

There is, then, a moral ambiguity in Crane's conception of man's relationship with his fellows, an ambiguity which permeates his entire vision of man. Henry Fleming falsely acquires a symbol of group identity, yet this symbol aids him in recovering his group identity and in benefiting the group. Man's involvement with others forces him into psychic compulsion (Henry's running away), yet this involvement is the source of his sense of psychic oneness. Henry is still for the most part self-deceived at the close of the novel, but if he is not the "man" he thinks he has become, he has at least shed some of the innocence of the child. Crane's allegory of life as a battle is thus appropriate for another reason besides its relevance to the violence of discovery. Few battles are clearly or cleanly won or lost, and few soldiers are clearly God's chosen. But men struggle, and in their struggle they learn something about their limitations and capacities and something about the nature of their relations with their fellow men, and this knowledge is rewarding even though they never discover the full significance or direction of the campaign in which they are engaged.

JAMES B. COLVERT

Stephen Crane's Magic Mountain†

The weaknesses of Stephen Crane's *The Red Badge of Courage* are important clues to the real issue raised in the novel—indeed, to the fundamental issue raised in all of Crane's important work. These weaknesses all stem, actually, from one weakness: Crane's inability to control the metaphor which is not only central to his novel but is also the master symbol of his characteristic attitudes, ideas, and feelings about man, God, and the universe. I refer to the constantly recurring image in his work—both poetry and fiction—of the little man in conflict with the hostile mountain. The meaning of the figure is complex, and I shall deal with it directly later on. But I should like first to approach it indirectly by examining the consequences of Crane's imperfect mastery of it in *The Red Badge of Courage.*

Although the novel might appear to be a straightforward account of how a self-centered young man acquires, as a result of his war experiences, a measure of redeeming wisdom, the problems raised in the story are not clearly defined or resolved. As a consequence the ending is confused and unconvincing. We are told that Henry Fleming is a changed man, but we are told how he is supposed to have met the conditions implicity required of him in the first sixteen chapters. In the first part of the story Henry is the target of the narrator's relentless ironic criticism, scored for his delusions of grandeur, his assumption that he somehow merits a special place in the regard of the universe. And though Crane labors in the final chapter to convince us that his hero has rid himself of these delusions, the deterioration in the quality of the writing—the appearance of a tendency toward incoherence—shows that the task is too much for him. The tone shifts inappropriately, the irony is erratic and often misdirected, and the hero is permitted certain assumptions inconsistent with his previous characterization and Crane's established attitudes toward him.

Here is an example of Crane's treatment of Henry early in the

† *Stephen Crane: A Collection of Critical Essays*, ed. Maurice Bassan (Englewood Cliffs, N.J.: Prentice-Hall, 1967), pp. 95–105. Copyright by James Colvert. Reprinted by permission of the publisher and the author.

novel, when the hero is under the spell of his sentimental image of himself as a conquering hero:

> In visions he had seen himself in many struggles. He had imagined peoples secure in the shadow of his eagle-eyed prowess. . . . He had burned several times to enlist. Tales of great movements shook the land. They might not be distinctly Homeric, but there seemed to be much glory in them. He had read of marches, sieges, conflicts, and he had longed to see it all. His busy mind had drawn for him large pictures extravagant in color, lurid with breathless deeds.

It is just such sentimental hallucinations, Crane makes clear, that render Henry unfit by upsetting his moral balance. This being the case, the reader of course expects to be shown a corrected state of mind proper to the redemption claimed for him at the end of the book. But Crane disappoints us. Consider, for example, Henry's state of mind as he leads the regiment in a magnificent charge against the enemy:

> Within him, as he hurled himself forward, was born a despairing fondness for this flag which was near him. It was a creation of beauty and invulnerability. It was a goddess, radiant, that bended its form with an imperious gesture to him. It was a woman, red and white, hating and loving, that called him with the voice of his hopes. Because no harm could come to it he endowed it with power. He kept near, as if it could be a saver of lives.

Now there may be irony in Crane's treatment of Henry in this, but if so it is a different kind of irony. Crane approves the deed, and so we must assume that he approves the attitudes which motivate it. But the emotions here are not very much different from those Henry experiences in his self-glorifying daydreams. They do not seem appropriate. They are, one suspects, not the hero's feelings but Crane's; and if so, the passage suggests that the author's own heroic ideal is hardly more viable than that he mocks in his naïve hero. Even at best, the sense of the passage is ambiguous.

This tendency in Crane's treatment of Henry is not always obvious, but it represents fairly enough, I think, the insecurity of the author's control over his point of view. The tendency is also revealed in another, perhaps more significant, way. We recall that Crane's irony is directed not only against Henry's heroic reveries, but also against his egotistical assumptions about his relation to Nature. When things go badly, Henry believes unquestioningly that Nature is against him; when things go well, he believes just as deeply that Nature is friendly and sympathetic. Humiliated when he proves a coward in his first battle, he turns to Nature for solace and comfort. Wending his way in a forest, he is gratified by his reflection that Nature is "a woman with a deep aversion to tragedy"; he believes that She has provided in the high, arching boughs of the trees a little chapel for the refreshment of his spirit. Entering the chapel-like bower he is suddenly transfixed with horror and loathing. Sitting on the gentle brown carpet in the religious half-light, is a rotting corpse. When he tries to flee, it seems to him that nature has suddenly turned against him all its malice and fury, that the branches of the bower are now trying to throw him over on the unspeakable corpse.

Now at the end of the book when we are told that Henry's eyes are "at last opened to some new ways," that he "could look back upon the brass and bombast of his earlier gospels and see them truly," we must expect to be shown that he has cast off the crippling burden of this senseless subjectivism. Surely, we think, the lesson in the forest has been so well driven home that he would no longer find it strange to see a pure blue sky over the carnage of battle, no longer be astonished that Nature goes "tranquilly on with her golden process in the midst of so much devilment." Yet in the very last paragraphs of the novel we find him still on personal terms with Nature, turning "with a lover's thirst to images of tranquil skies, fresh meadows, cool brooks—an existence of soft and eternal peace." The last sentence is notoriously sentimental: "Over the river a golden ray of sun came through the hosts of leaden rain clouds." Thus Crane approves in Henry once again what he criticizes relentlessly up to the very turning point of the novel; and when Crane throws away in this manner the issue of his hero's conflict with Nature, he throws away also the richest theme in the story —and the basic theme of all his work.

Perhaps Crane suspected how inappropriate this resolution was to the true theme of the book, for as the manuscript shows, he edited the last pages heavily, deleting from Henry's final thoughts all references to his experience with Nature. In effect, Crane was attempting to eliminate the emphasis on Henry's struggle against a hostile Nature and the issue of the hero's sentimental misreading of Nature's meaning. One omitted sentence reads: "Echoes of his terrible combat with the arrayed forces of the universe came to his ears. . . ." Henry's thought that Nature might be capable of moral judgment—that "he had been wrong not to kiss the knife and bow to the cudgel"—is also edited out. References to the possible indifference of Nature are omitted, and a mocking observation that Henry, whose mood grows self-congratulatory at one point, "was . . . fraternizing again with nature" is likewise penciled out. In short, the moral issue which Crane raises in his treatment of Nature in the novel is abandoned—or rather Crane attempts to abandon it.

We should think that Henry's reflection that he could "no more stand upon places high and false, and denounce the distant planets" would be one of the essential earned insights, but Crane, trying to avoid the whole issue, struck the passage out, as if he himself had little faith in what he was really in effect claiming for his hero. Crane surely could not have accepted Henry's sentimental faith in a benign and sympathetic universe; yet this is the faith Crane gives him: "Over the river a golden ray of sun came through the hosts of leaden rain clouds."

The failure of the book then is a failure in tone and theme, and although the two weaknesses are related, they must be explained in different ways. The failure in tone is relatively easy. Crane's biography makes it clear that for all his cool skepticism and irony he was an imperfectly suppressed sentimentalist laboring under the spell of a naïve heroic ideal. A member of his family described him once as one of those "terribly romantic young men who would think it delightful to be shot at dawn and all that sort of thing." He was addicted to a certain romantic attitudinizing; he followed wars compulsively all his life, and his despatches from the battlefield often reflect the kind of sentimental chauvinism we sense in the "flag" passage quoted above. Still, Crane distrusted this in himself, and if we may judge from his letters, ironic self-criticism was habitual with him. Addicted himself to sentimentality, his ironic mockery of Henry is in effect self-censorship. So long as Crane's secret sympathies are exposed to the correction of his irony, the critical sense of his writing is clear enough. But how was Crane really to portray Henry as a genuine hero when his own conception of the heroic was undermined by a naïve and spurious sentimentalism? This is Crane's problem at the end of *The Red Badge*, and he has no real solution for it: he is forced to fall back upon the only conception of the heroic available to him, and stripped of its correcting irony it turns out after all to be not too much different from Henry Fleming's.

The uncertainty in the treatment of the Nature theme is harder to account for, but it is also more interesting because it leads directly to the most important issue in the study of Crane's work, throwing light not only on the flawed novel but on all of his important fiction and poetry.

A starting place is a passage in Chapter XVII of *The Red Badge* the description of Henry's first reactions on discovering that he is suddenly a hero:

> He had been a tremendous figure, no doubt. By this struggle he had overcome obstacles which he had admitted to be mountains. They had fallen like paper peaks, and he was now what he called a hero. And he had not been aware of the process. He had slept and, awakening, found himself a knight.

The passage is interesting for several reasons. It contains the main elements of the novel: the vainglorious hero, the image of Nature as antagonist, the critical irony of the narrator. It summarizes the situation up to this point and marks the turning point in the narrative. But the most interesting point is that Henry, at this crucial moment, should think of himself as securing a victory, not over the enemy or his fear of them, but over Nature. It is almost as if, in his imagination, he sees it as a revengeful victory over the traitorous forest which refused him the solace of its cathedral-like bower.

We are reminded, reading this passage, that Nature from the very beginning has been the real source of Henry's terror. Mountains, fields, streams, the night, the sun, appear in his disordered fancy in the guises of living creatures, monstrous and terrible. He sees the "red eyelike gleam of hostile campfires set in the low brows of distant hills," the "black columns [of enemy troops] disappearing on the brow of a hill like two serpents crawling from the cavern of night." Crossing a little stream he fancies that the black water looks back at him with "white bubble eyes," and that "fierce-eyed hosts" lurk in the shadow of the woods. When he deserts in his first battle he flees, not the attack of enemy troops, but the "onslaught of redoubtable dragons," the approach of the "red and green monsters."

Images of a hostile Nature may take a variety of metaphorical forms—monsters, dragons, ogres, demigods, and other such grotesqueries—but the most characteristic is the figure of the sinister mountain. It occurs several times in *The Red Badge*: "A dark and mysterious range of hills . . . curved against the sky," "the low brows of distant hills," huge careening boulders, "a cliff over which one tumbles at midnight." In one variation or another the mountain turns up somewhere in almost all of Crane's writings, always as an inimical force or spirit. The horizon in "The Open Boat" is "jagged with waves that seemed thrust up in points like rocks." Life's problems confront the hero of *George's Mother* like "granite giants" and he is "no longer erect to meet them." George shrinks from "chasms with inclined approaches" and "peaks" that "leaned toward him." The buildings in the sketches of slum life appear to the little people at their feet in "pitiless hues sternly high, forcing regal heads into the clouds, throwing no downward glances." But once the hero of *George's Mother*, like Henry Fleming, had a vision in which he saw himself as a conqueror, "a stern general pointing a sword at the nervous and abashed horizon."

Most of the stories in Crane's earliest work, *Sullivan County Sketches*, two years earlier in composition than *The Red Badge*, show its hero in conflict with various natural presences—black caves, bears, ghostly forests—but the most interesting is "The Mesmeric Mountain." The unnamed hero is "the little man." Hiking through the wild countryside he becomes lost and climbs a tree to get his bearings. In the distance he sees a mountain, glowering so angrily that he falls out of the tree in a fit of terror. After a time he approaches cautiously and sits under a tree to watch. The mountain looks harmless enough, and the little man returns, watchful and wary. The mountain attacks again, and again the hero is overwhelmed with terror—and this time, rage.

As he felt the heel of the mountain about to crush his head, he sprang again to his feet. He grasped a handful of small stones and hurled them. "Damn you!" he shrieked loudly. The pebbles rang against the face of the mountain.

The little man then made an attack. He climbed with hands and feet wildly. Brambles forced him back and stones slid from beneath his feet. The peak swayed and tottered, and was ever about to smite with a granite arm. The summit was a blaze of red wrath.

But the little man gains the summit, at last, and when he does, he experiences the wild emotions of a conqueror of the world. He struts grandly across the peak, strikes a heroic pose, and surveys the universe. He is no longer lost. "There," he says grandly, "is Boyd's house." The last sentence of the story reads: "But the mountain under his feet was motionless."

The relation of the fable to *The Red Badge* is obvious. It is at once a summary of the plot of the novel and an expansion of the metaphor by which Henry interprets his victory. There are the familiar elements—the terror and rage of the hero, the hallucinatory imagery, the antagonism of Nature, the delusive victory, the heroics, the narrator's ironic commentary. By the time Crane started writing *The Red Badge* in 1893 he had repudiated the Sullivan County stories as immature and unworthy; but he was never to repudiate the basic elements of these tales, for they are expressive of his deepest sense of the meaning of life. When we trace the metaphor of the mountain through his poems, especially those in *The Black Riders*, we get further indication of its meaning.

The Black Riders was Crane's favorite of all his books. He once described it as "an ambitious effort" in which it was his "aim to comprehend [his] thoughts about life in general." Almost all of the nearly 70 poems are on religious themes—the inscrutability of God, man's futile quest for God, God's wrath, the terrors of a Godless universe, human pride, and human impotence. One poem, oddly, is a mockery of romantic idealism, the hero being a medieval young man who dreams of his noble death in full armor, sword in hand, in a forest fight with a black assassin. Several give versions of the fable of the little man and the angry mountain:

> On the horizon the peaks assembled;
> And as I looked,
> The march of the mountains began.
> As they marched, they sang,
> "Ay! we come! we come!"

The opening lines of another read:

> Once I saw mountains angry.
> And ranged in battle-front.
> Against them stood a little man;
> Ay, he was no bigger than my finger.

Another poem implies that the mountain is the cruel way to an unattainable heaven;

> The hard hills tore my flesh;
> The ways bit my feet.
> At last I looked again.
> No radiance in the far sky,
> Ineffable, divine;
> No vision painted upon a pall;
> And always my eyes ached for the light.

In a manuscript version of still another poem where the image appears in a variation as housetops, the hero flings a challenge at the sun and God appears leading an army:

> Once a man clambering to the housetops
> Appealed to the empty heavens.
> With strong voice he called to the imperturbable stars;
> A warrior's shout he raised to the higher suns.
> Lo, at last, there was an indication, a dot,
> Then—finally—God—the sky was filled with armies.

And still again the central image of a poem is mountains in lofty communion with God, indifferent to man:

> In the night
> Grey heavy clouds muffled the valleys,
> And the peaks looked toward God alone.

The poem goes on to contrast the imperturbable vigil of the mountains with the daytime scurry of humanity in their "little black cities"; at the end it is night again. Man is shrouded in darkness once more and the silent peaks still "look toward God alone."

Finally, the image appears in a more hopeful poem on the resurrection theme:

When a people reach the top of a hill,
Then does God lean toward them,
Shortens tongues and lengthens arms.
A vision of their dead comes to the weak.

The single-minded earnestness with which Crane pursues his disturbing visions is remarkable. Clearly, these poems express a state of profound spiritual unrest. Is God dead in heaven, the questioning runs, and man alone in a heedless universe? Or is He terribly alive, breathing malice and hatred on helpless little men? Or is He perhaps a kindly God, screened from the view of man? What hope has man, burdened with sin and guilt, pride and self-love, to enter His Kingdom, if it does exist? Worrying these questions, Crane is torn between blasphemy and piety. "I hate Thee, unrighteous picture," he rages against the God of Wrath. But to the man who says the roaring thunder is the voice of God, he says, "Fool. No so. The voice of God whispers in the heart." Crane's skepticism, nevertheless, seems to tip the balance: the idea of a personal God, either wrathful or kindly, he cannot accept; his reluctant conclusion is that God, whoever He might be, is simply unknowable to man. The bitter irony he turns on the blind little men of earth who strut and rage and cry out for Him is at once the mockery of their outrageous presumption and his own painful disbelief.

Considering the facts of Crane's biography, we find nothing surprising in this. His father was the Reverend Jonathan T. Crane, a gentle-hearted minister of the Methodist faith who bolted the Presbyterian Church as a young man because he refused to believe that God punished unconfirmed infants in the fires of hell. He wrote books inveighing against the evils of card-playing and dancing, and arguing, with the self-sufficient logic of the theologian, the existence of a benign, though inscrutable, God. "God could," he wrote in his book *Holiness the Birthright of All God's Children*, "if he deemed it best, so reveal himself that unbelief would be impossible. He might write his laws upon the azure skies. . . . He could smite every sinner at the very moment of his transgression with so stern and visible a hand that obedience would have little moral value. . . . That moral liberty may not be destroyed, God withdrew himself from human vision." Mrs. Crane's religion was not so gentle. Descended of a long line of fire-breathing Methodist preachers of the "old ambling-nag, saddle-bag, exhorting kind" (as Crane described her), she was herself a writer of religious tracts. Her views, apparently, were represented in a book by her uncle, Bishop Peck, titled *What Must I Do to Be Saved?* "Your sins are remembered," Bishop Peck warned. "Every one charges upon your soul its infinite wrong, and demands the wrath of your offended Sovereign without mixture of mercy forever. . . . The Savior himself has condescended to inform you of the fearful doom which awaits you. You shrink from it with indescribable terror."

But we see Crane as a boy refusing the faith. "I used to like church and prayer meetings when I was a kid but that cooled off and when I was thirteen or about that, my brother Will told me not to believe in Hell after my uncle had been boring me about the lake of fire and the rest of the sideshows." We see him as a young man, Puritan turned Bohemian, in the old Art Students League Building in New York, living with a crowd of painters—"irresponsibles," a contemporary called them. We see him suffering because of his reputation for vicious living, hunted by the scandal of his common-law marriage to the madam of a Jacksonville bordello. We see him writing his brother Will of his "unworthiness," confessing from England that he had "managed his success like a fool," reporting only three years before he died that he felt that he was "slowly becoming a man." His biography reminds us of his characteristic way of turning his irony against his own egotism and pride. "I saw," he wrote in reference to his growing fame, "the majestic forces which are arrayed against man's true success—not the world—the world is silly, changeable, any of its decisions can be reversed—but man's own colossal impulses more strong than chains and I perceived that the fight was not going to be with the world but with myself."

It is to all this—the spiritual unrest, the sense of guilt, the Christian abhorrence of pride, the fear of the thrusting ego—that the metaphor of the little man and the mountain refers. The angry mountain is an egostistical projection of the little man's demand upon the notice of God, his bid for a place in God's personal affection and sympathy. And God, thus peremptorily summoned, sends him green dragons and armies in the sky and rotting corpses in the nave of Nature. The ironic narrator, taking a cue from the Reverend Crane on the inscrutability of God, prompts the little man to note the pure, blue unconscious sky, and heaps upon him his uneasy scorn.

The meaning of the fable is amplified elsewhere in Crane's fiction. The Swede in "The Blue Hotel," his mind swarming with terror at the threat of an unknown menace is, we discover, really at war with himself and an angry Nature. "We picture the world," Crane writes in his description of the Swede battling his way through a storm,

> as thick with conquering and elate humanity, but here, with the bugles of the tempest pealing, it was hard to imagine a peopled earth. One viewed the existence of man then as a marvel, and

conceded a glamor of wonder to these lice which were caused to cling to a whirling, fire-smitten, ice-locked, disease-stricken, space-lost bulb. The conceit of man was explained by this storm to be the very engine of life.

"This weather," the Swede boasts later to the bartender, "I like it. It suits me." The little man on the mountain. A few minutes later, the Swede is dead, his open eyes fastened melodramatically on the words on the saloon cash register: "This registers the amount of your purchase."

And again we find the symbols of the fable in "The Open Boat," the story of the correspondent's anguished speculation about the meaning of an ambivalent Nature. Is Nature the sign of God's malice, as the angry waves, the sinister gulls, the deadly shark suggest? Or is it the sign of God's benevolence, as the gentle swells, the beauty of the sea-birds sweeping across the sky suggest? Or is it merely impersonal and indifferent as the high cold star says? The correspondent is the only one of Crane's heroes who is allowed to see beyond the curtain of his conceit. And yet how little comfort in what he sees. "When it occurs to a man," he poignantly reflects,

> that Nature does not regard him as important . . . he at first wishes to throw bricks at the temple, and he hates deeply the fact that there are no bricks and no temples. Any visible expression of nature would surely be pelleted with his jeers. Then, if there be no tangible thing to hoot, he feels, perhaps, the desire to confront a personification and indulge in pleas, bowed to one knee, and with hands supplicant, saying, "Yes, but I love myself."

But the hero of *The Red Badge* conjures up tangible things to assault—the baleful sun at which he shakes his fist, the green dragons he charges at the head of his regiment, the angry mountain. As he stands victorious over the fallen peaks, he perceives, like the nameless hero of "The Mesmeric Mountain," that he is the conqueror of the world. But—to return at long last to the failure in the resolution of the novel—the idea is unthinkable. It violates the meaning of Crane's master symbol—the metaphor of the little man before the mountain. There are, after all, only victories in secular wars, inspired by flags; but there are no victories in wars against heaven. The contradiction, arising out of the rich implications of Crane's metaphor, brilliantly developed throughout the first sixteen chapters, is impossible to resolve. If Henry must be a victor, there is nothing to do but to revise him downward to an earthly hero, credit him with insights he has not earned, place on his shoulder the comforting arm of a tender mother Nature, and march him, serene and confident, out of the novel.

JOHN FRASER
Crime and Forgiveness: *The Red Badge* in Time of War†

War is waged by men; not by beasts, or by gods. It is a peculiarly human activity.[1]

In a period of such rampant formalism as our own it seems especially necessary to keep affirming, however unphilosophically, that literature is inseparable from life and that one can learn quite directly about the latter from it. The work that I am concerned with here seems particularly to invite such an affirmation, and it is largely that invitation that has prompted yet another article on so notoriously overanalyzed a novel, and so brief a novel at that.

If *The Red Badge of Courage* is brief, it also quivers with life in a way that partly accounts, no doubt, for the disproportionately large body of criticism that it has provoked. No other classic American novelist has so masterfully rendered the immediacy of consciousness, the impingement of data on the mind, the *creative* activity of the perceiving mind in respect to that data, the tricks and hiatuses and sudden shifts in direction that an ordinary mind is capable of. None, furthermore, has created an experiencing consciousness with so little analytical guidance to the main changes of direction in it and yet with what feels like so high a degree of meaningful unconscious or semi-conscious logic informing those changes. And accordingly a very salutary tension can be set up for the reader between trying simultaneously to elucidate that logic and to preserve his own openness to the presented experiences. The novel is to a considerable extent, indeed, precisely "about" the dangers of mental rigidity and the disruption (sometimes for the worse, more often for the better) of premature orderings, so that it is especially ironical if in analyzing it one comes up with overly neat and academic formulations oneself. And the tension deserves to be especially acute at the present time.

To lecture to undergraduates on *The Red Badge* even three or four years ago was a somewhat disquieting experience. It felt strangely presumptuous, I mean, to be a well-fed academic ensconced behind a lectern and comfortably analyzing the intimate mental processes of a young man being shot at and breaking down under the strain of battle; and if one recoiled alike from the curiously pharisaical moralizings about them by a number of critics and from

† From *Criticism*, IX (Summer, 1967), 243–56. Copyright 1967 Wayne State University. Reprinted by permission.

1. Frederic Manning, from prefactory note to *The Middle Parts of Fortune: Somme & Ancre, 1916* (London, 1929).

the sort of pattern-hunting and symbol-mongering by others that seemed to negate the intense reality of the rendered experience of battle, it was tempting to fall instead into a too easy neo-Nietzschean celebration of Man Fighting. Whatever one's approach may be, however, one's critical sincerity is surely being put to the test now that one is lecturing to young men who may themselves have to face death or mutilation in a war. And if studying literature is indeed directly relevant to living, here surely is a place where it should be demonstrable.

One major way in which the relationship obtains in fiction generally, I take it, is prognostically. That is to say, the sort of things that happen to this or that imagined character may sometime, in however subtilized a form, happen to *us*, and in works that matter we are presented either with workable modes of responding to them or with erroneous ones so explored as to enable us to formulate more workable ones for ourselves. Hence it is that any way of reading that draws us away from the vitality of the presented experiences is not simply a chance missed but an insidious psychological injury, in that because one has responded inappropriately to the imagined experience now, one will be the more likely to respond inappropriately to actual ones in the future. In the general spirit of these remarks I would like, then, to look once again at certain key aspects of Henry Fleming's experience of the complexities of battle and his coming to terms with them and with himself, since I judge the way in which he comes to terms to be a successful one with implications going considerably beyond the presented battlefield.

That Henry's accommodation to battle conditions is indeed estimable is still, it seems safe to say, by no means a truism. It would be hard, for instance, to guess at the number of readers who have learned from the introduction to the Riverside edition of the novel that "Crane 'makes us see Henry Fleming as an emotional puppet controlled by whatever sight he sees at the moment,' that when Henry does return to the battle it is not as a valiant adult but 'in a blind rage that turns him into an animal,' [and] that if there is 'any one point in the book' it is that 'Henry has never been able to evaluate his conduct' . . ."[2] Faced with comments of that order, moreover—faced, for instance, with such judgments elsewhere as "Henry is unquestionably courageous, but the underlying causes of his deeds are neither noble nor humane,"[3] and "Although Henry does show courage there is decisive evidence that he is motivated chiefly by animal fierceness and competitive pride"[4]—it is hard not

2. Richard Chase, ed., quoting approvingly Charles Child Walcutt (Boston, 1960), p. xv.

3. William B. Dillingham, "Insensibility in *The Red Badge of Courage*," *College English*, XXV (December, 1963), 194.

4. Mordecai Marcus, "The Unity of *The Red Badge of Courage*," in Richard Lettis *et al.*, eds., *Stephen Crane's The Red Badge of Courage: Text and Criticism* (New York, 1960), p. 191.

to feel that a certain naive liberalism is brought into play by the novel for a good many readers. War is an abomination, Henry Fleming adjusts himself wholeheartedly to war, therefore the mental processes involved cannot be very creditable ones—thus, one suspects, the unspoken argument runs, intensified perhaps by a feeling that improvement ought to involve introspection, increased self-understanding (which is to say, in this case, understanding of one's errors), and no doubt some kind of abnegation and general "withering into truth." Viewed from such an angle, of course, Henry most decidedly doesn't improve. Not only does he continue to delight throughout in the thought of winning glory, he actually *does* win it, and does so when by rights he should have been exposed in a very different sort of light. After all, he has not only allowed his comrades after he rejoins them to assume that he is respectably wounded, he has even had the nerve to take advantage of his wounded-hero role to pick on the chastened and now tenderly helpful Wilson. In fact he has become positively *jaunty*. And yet— "who should 'scape whipping?" To speak in the kinds of terms I have been employing is to feel the niggling ungenerosity of the implied ethics when one stops and considers the boy's age and inexperience, the shock of battle, the abrasive torments of his wanderings behind the lines, and the fact that in its effects the blow from the fleeing soldier's swung rifle butt is just as much a wound as an actual graze from a bullet would have been. And a good deal more is at issue than mere pharisaism.

To approach Henry in the kind of moral fashion I have sketched in is especially ironical in that it is to approach him in very much the terms in which he himself was operating up until the time when he rejoined his regiment—and from which, I shall be arguing shortly, he is thereafter very beneficially liberated. To complain as one critic does apropos of Henry's encounter with the walking wounded that "the guilt he feels among these frightfully wounded men . . . should be enough to make him realize his brotherhood, his indebtedness, his duty; but his reaction as he watches the retreat swell is to justify his early flight,"[5] is in fact to miss the point by a very sizeable margin. The novel up to and including that episode has been a brilliant study of psychological disintegration as a direct result of certain ethical over-intensities, and Henry's abandonment of the tattered soldier in particular (quite properly it is the thought of *that* that returns momentarily to haunt him at the end of the novel) is produced directly by his crippling sense of guilt and dread of exposure. It is from those feelings too that he becomes liberated with what seem to me unquestionably beneficial consequences, and

5. Charles Child Walcutt, *American Literary Naturalism: A Divided Stream* (Minneapolis, 1956), p. 79.

if one acknowledges those consequences one is in a position to move further into the moral significance of the novel.

That both George Wyndham and Joseph Conrad among the novel's admirers should have responded so sympathetically to the change in Henry bears witness to a good deal more, I take it, than the strength of certain *fin-de-siècle* preoccupations (I mean, the growing weariness with rationalistic and ego-denying democratic liberalism, and the reviving esteem for violent and physically dangerous action of one kind or another). Both men knew the stresses of violent action at first hand, and when Conrad reworked the basic situation of *The Red Badge* in *Lord Jim* he seems to me to have been testifying to a perception that Henry's restoration involves something considerably weightier than simply the attainment of military effectiveness. Henry *is* effective now, of course; he fights instead of running, he fights with great energy and success, and in the course of so doing he helps to rally his panicking comrades and save them from being overwhelmed. But "effectiveness" is too narrow a term, even though one may well feel that when fighting is called for the first necessity for a soldier is to fight as well as possible. Henry's change has also been unquestionably an improvement psychologically in a broader way, at least if one regards a unified state of consciousness as superior to a fragmented one. Henry back with his regiment is free of both the modes of estrangement displayed so brilliantly earlier—the emotional estrangement from his comrades and officers caused by his exacerbated broodings, and the stultifying self-estrangement, the inability to settle on any single reading of his circumstances and conduct and act accordingly, that had left him in a seemingly hopeless impasse just before he was engulfed by the fleeing soldiers and received his own "wound." And again, to speak in these terms is really to be speaking in moral ones too. "One can love and one can work" was one of Freud's definitions of health, I believe, and it is plain that the Henry who is back with his comrades—the Henry who can now take note of the change in Wilson, and can feel a healthy indignation on behalf of his unjustly abused regiment and "a love, a despairing fondness" for its flag—is far closer to other people and in a far better position to act in a conventional sense morally than the egoistically brooding youth of the earlier part. "He had been taught that a man became another thing in a battle. He saw his salvation in such a change." The change that in fact occurs can surely be summed up in a preliminary way by saying that a man—or at least much more of a whole one—is precisely what Henry has become; and when Crane writes of his comrades that "The impetus of enthusiasm was theirs again. They gazed about them with looks of uplifted pride, feeling new trust in the grim, always confident weapons in their hands.

And they were men," there seems no reason to think that he is speaking ironically. True, Henry hasn't become impeccable—but then, why should he?

If, then, I am right about the improvements, we would seem to be invited to consider rather carefully the causes of Henry's breakdown in the first place, and the nature of the process by which he becomes liberated from them. This I now propose to do.

To say that in the first engagement Henry is basically in trouble because of the sort of Christian pacificism ingrained in him by his mother would be over-simple, of course; among other things it wouldn't allow for his disposition to preconceive situations overrigidly and then to be increasingly set off balance by the discrepancies between preconceptions and actualities. (E.g., "The youth stared. Surely, he thought, this impossible thing was not about to happen. He waited as if he expected the enemy to suddenly stop, apologize, and retire bowing. It was all a mistake.") But it wouldn't be a gross over-simplification, and I wish to try and refine it. More precisely—given Henry's romantic craving for distinction— the destructive tensions would seem to result from the clash in him between that Christian pacifistic ethic and the kind of neo-pagan ethic pointed to in the well-known and, in its essentials, twice-repeated assertion that "He had long despaired of witnessing a Greeklike struggle. Such would be no more, he had said. Men were better, or more timid. Secular and religious education had effaced the throat-grappling instinct, or else firm finance held in cheek the passions." And this is where the equally well-known supernatural imagery is invaluable as an index to the way in which the currents of Henry's feelings are flowing. That the forthcoming engagement presents itself to him almost excusively in terms of an ultimate test of his moral worth is obvious enough; and that he has a sense of the test as taking place in some measure under the eyes of *someone* emerges in his lagging "with tragic glances at the sky" and reflecting that "he would die; he would go to some place where he would be understood." (See too his later reflection that the intelligently self-preserving squirrel at which he has thrown a pine-cone "did not stand stolidly baring his furry belly to the missile, and die with an upward glance at the sympathetic heavens.") Yet the proliferation of the "infernal" imagery, and the impartial distribution with respect to the enemy and his own side of the comparisons to serpents, imps, monsters, dragons, and the like, surely indicates how much the reverse of innocent and "Greekline" the military scene is appearing to the deeper reaches of his mind, and testifies to a growing unconscious anxiety as to the meritoriousness of the activities that he has committed himself to with such initial neo-pagan enthusiasm. He himself is entangled now with those balefully serpentine

columns and those figures "dodging implike around the fires"; and
when the fighting comes and he breaks, the fact that at that point
the enemy onslaught figures to him in terms of ravening demonic
monsters coming inexorably towards him bears witness, surely, to an
overwhelming upsurge of guilt-feelings. The destructive power of
the enemy's persistency is presumably heightened by his general
feeling that if he himself is to be morally tested it must somehow
be under "fair" conditions, and that conditions are proving increasingly very much the reverse of fair. That is to say, the failure of
battle conditions to conform to his expectations functions as a further subliminal intimation that morally the battlefield is the wrong
sort of place for him to be and that he was radically in error in his
initial neo-pagan commitment to its values—though of course his
conscious sense of the battle as a straightforward moral test isn't
affected thereby.

Viewed in this general light, Henry's overwhelming perturbation
and sense of guilt after he has broken don't call for much explica-
tion. It is significant in an obvious enough way when he conceives
of his separation from the unbroken soldiers in such terms as, "He
felt that he was regarding a procession of chosen beings. The separation was as great to him as if they had marched with weapons of
flame and banners of sunlight." So it is too when we learn, apropos
of the questioning of him by the tattered soldier, that "he was continually casting sidelong glances to see if the men were contemplating the letters of guilt he felt burned into his brow" and that "his
. . . companion's chance persistency made him feel that he could
keep his crime concealed in his bosom. It was sure to be brought
plain by one of those arrows which cloud the air and are constantly
pricking, discovering, proclaiming those things which are willed to
be forever hidden. He admitted that he could not defend himself
against this agency." And when one puts these and all the other
supernatural references together they point unmistakably (despite
Crane's canny avoidance of any specific reference to the Christian
deity)[6] to Henry's dominant sense of a supernaturally penetrated
universe in which crimes are absolutely and inescapably crimes
because known inescapably to *someone*, and so are almost certain to
be visited by retribution.

What we see Henry getting liberated from, I suggest, is his whole
disposition to view what he is up to in terms of such a universe
and seek, unavailingly, to justify himself to it. The most revealing
fact, it seems to me, is that after he has rejoined his regiment—and
nothing, it should be recalled, has happened to validate his conduct

6. Stanley Wertheim's "Stephen Crane
and the Wrath of Jehova," *The Literary
Review*, VII (Summer, 1964), 499–508,
can help to bring home to one, if further
evidence than that of the novel itself is
needed, the kind of psychological mine
field through which Crane was making
his way.

in terms of his earlier set of rules—the supernatural imagery disappears virtually altogether, and with it his sense of his own worthlessness and the inevitability of his exposure. And the nature of the change in him gets spelled out in certain rightly much quoted passages that can be consolidated into a single one here:

> His self-pride was now entirely restored. In the shade of its flourishing growth he stood with braced and self-confident legs, and since nothing could now be discovered he did not shrink from an encounter with the eyes of judges, and allowed no thoughts of his own to keep him from an attitude of manfulness. He had performed his mistakes in the dark, so he was still a man. . . . He had been taught that many obligations of a life were easily avoided. The lessons of yesterday had been that retribution was a laggard and blind. . . . He had been out among the dragons, he said, and he assured himself that they were not so hideous as he had imagined them. Also they were inaccurate; they did not sting with precision. A stout heart often defied, and, defying, escaped. . . . Yesterday, when he had imagined the universe to be against him, he had hated it, little gods and big gods; today he hated the army of the foe with the same great hatred. He was not going to be badgered of his life, like a kitten chased by boys, he said. It was not well to drive men into final corners; at those moments they could all develop teeth and claws. . . . He had a gigantic hatred for those who made great difficulties and complications. . . . He had been to touch the great death, and found that, after all, it was but the great death. He was a man.

If my account thus far has been reasonably correct, Henry is no longer bothered by the presumed hostility of the "big gods and little gods" because he has ceased to bother about the "gods" in any Christian sense at all; and because he has ceased to bother about them he has ceased, too, to bother about retribution or to introduce supernatural values into the activities of battle. Hence the act of fighting is no longer some kind of ultimate moral testing of the self (is he in fact one of the "elect" or not?), and even death becomes simply death and not a stage en route to further judgment. We are not, it seems to me, being invited to react with patronizing irony when informed that "He saw that he was good. He recalled with a thrill of joy the respectful comments of his fellows upon his conduct." And the fact that we can indeed refrain from so reacting testifies to a deeper moral validity in what has been going on, and brings me back to the question of the novel's "lessons."

I have not, of course, been arguing that *The Red Badge of Courage* is valuable because it demonstrates that to be a good soldier one should not be a good Christian. It demonstrates nothing of the sort, for Henry is not a *good* Christian at all. He is something more familiar to most of us, and perhaps more relevant, namely someone in whom certain religion-induced dispositions persist in a vulgarized form and without any strong accompanying affirmations and consolations, and who is in a state of muddle, perplexed by impulses towards a (seemingly) non-moral self-affirmation on the one hand and a (seemingly) moral self-denial on the other, and by a conflict between a view of the world as rationally ordered and superintended and demanding reasonableness in return, and a view of it as not ordered at all. By putting an intellectual (albeit a very inept one) into the situation of battle where certain attitudes have much weightier direct consequences than they normally do, Crane has very usefully clarified the undesirability of that kind of muddle. He has also, it seems to me, effectively contributed to one's achieving an intelligent attitude towards war when one is in it, by treating it as a normal aspect of human existence. By "normal" I do not mean inevitable. Nor, of course, do I mean commonplace; part of the brilliance of the novel consists precisely in its continual demonstrations of the immense *strangeness* of battle. But war itself is treated by Crane, as it is by Tolstoy and Shakespeare and Homer, as a state in which so many of the deeper problems of existence are present that when one is in it it is no longer something to be set against "life," it *is* life; and he has brought out, I think, that if a value system is to be fully tenable it must somehow be adequate to both peace *and* war, not least because many of those problems are present in an intensified and paradigmatic form. The same kind of thing, as I have just indicated, can be said of other distinguished presentations of war.[7] But one of the temptations for the "enlightened" American consciousness is to pique itself on its moral superiority to foreign and less idealistic ones and hence quietly to slide non-protesting responses to war into the category of the morally underdeveloped. Crane, however, has dealt with war in terms that not only include that kind of consciousness but transcend it, and he seems to me to have effectively precluded the concession, "Well, perhaps as a matter of *expediency* a temporary transformation of the psyche may be necessary!"[8]—a concession which of course, with its moral reser-

---

7. See especially D. W. Harding's "The Poetry of Isaac Rosenberg," *Scrutiny*, III (March, 1935), 358–369, with its development of the thesis that 'What most distinguishes . . . Rosenberg from other English poets who wrote of the [1914–18] war is the intense significance he saw in the kind of living effort that the war called out, and the way in which his technique enabled him to present both this and the suffering and the waste as inseparable aspects of life in war. Further, there is in his work, without the least touch of coldness, nevertheless a certain impersonality: he tried to feel in the war a significance for life as such, rather than seeing only its convulsion of the human life he knew." It seems significant that the best poetry to come out of that war was Rosenberg's and the best novel Frederic Manning's *The Middle Parts of Fortune*, and that the latter likewise was not a work of "protest." The nearest twentieth-century American equivalents are probably David Douglas Duncan's superb photographs from Korea assembled in *This Is War* (New York, 1951).
8. Even Eric Solomon doesn't escape it in his sympathetic and perceptive "The Structure of *The Red Badge of Courage*," *Modern Fiction Studies*, V (Autumn, 1959), 220–234.

vations, thrusts one right back into the muddles of Henry's state before he breaks. In the terms of the novel there are not two moralities, a lower and a higher, but one, and it seems to me intellectually an eminently respectable one. I would like to develop that point.

That Henry has travelled from one intellectual position to another without passing through any kind of normal argumentation except of the most rudimentary kind[9] is essentially of no consequence if it can be granted that, contemplating the experiences presented in the novel, people with much better minds could arrive quite validly at the same position. It seems to me that they could, and that we are not in fact even compelled to choose in the novel between religion and mere naturalism. If we are indeed presented with a journey from a certain kind of Christianizing to a certain kind of naturalism, the naturalism is so rich that it is not only not "mere," it is in fact perfectly compatible with a superior—or at any rate an existentialist—way of being religious, even though the novel is manifestly written by someone who is in no sense a Christian himself. And this brings me to what is intellectually perhaps the most remarkable aspect of the whole remarkable book, namely that Crane, in a period in which absolutes were notoriously disintegrating, was able himself to assist in the process without in the least falling into the "amoral extremism or . . . sheer objectivism or romantic nihilism"[1] that have been imputed to him. In comparison to *The Red Badge*, *Lord Jim*, for example, seems philosophically crude, the product of someone who, driven out of the possibility of believing that there is some kind of supernatural sanction for values, can only fumble around with the notion that accordingly all values are simply the products of man-made systems and hence are all equally meaningless when one really reflects on them. Of course the events in *Lord Jim* to a considerable extent give the lie to the naive Marlovian pessimisms; in some sense it does indeed matter very much when a shipload of pilgrims are abandoned to a fiery or watery death, or when a native community is saved from predators. But in *The Red Badge* the language of events is a good deal clearer and more compelling, and I wish now to point out how in Henry's wanderings between his flight and his return to his regiment, events speak to him in such a way as to block his attempts to escape from ethical claims by invalid philosophical moves. It is to these moves that the term "naturalism" can properly be applied pejoratively.

What I have especially in mind are the "chapel" scene and the scene of the death of Jim Conklin. In the former, what is put a

9. E.g., "He searched about in his mind for an adequate malediction for the indefinite cause, the thing upon which men turn the words of final blame. It— whatever it was—was responsible for him, he said. There lay the fault."
1. Chase, p. xiv.

stop to is Henry's attempt to shut out the ethical exactions of the battle (and hence the torments of his own failure in terms of it) by reconceiving nature so that peacefulness and a quiet self-preservation become the "natural" order of things and the battle a mere remote aberration incapable of moral claims. The hideously solid corpse in the "chapel" serves as an irrefutable witness to the continuing reality of the battle, and the ants busily at work on its face furnish a reminder that predatoriness is as much a part of the natural as the reassuring self-preservation of the *sympathique* squirrel. Presumably they further serve as a subliminal reminder of the battle's scale, since what Henry then attempts is a conversion of it into something that is ethically harmless because vast and inhuman, a mere machine-like activity that one can remain emotionally detached from and in fact assert one's superiority to by contemplating—by positively seeking it out, indeed—as an aesthetic spectacle. This second and very *fin-de-siècle* move, of course, is countered by the sudden confrontation not with ant-like distant figures but with the human warmth and decency and courage of the tattered soldier and the appalling fact of Jim Conklin. The comforting metaphor of the battle as an "immense and terrible machine" producing corpses vanishes when juxtaposed not with an anonymous corpse (however shocking and incongruously located) but with a man, and worse, a known man, going through the awesome and untranslatable act of dying.

It is in this latter scene, too, with its culmination in the wafer image, that Crane's dissolving of the conventional disjunction between "religion" and "naturalism" reaches its climax. There is, of course, an agreeable irony in the notorious attempt to appropriate the wafer image for conventional Christian purposes. Wafers are flat, and things to which they are pasted are also more or less flat, and what the image surely does is simultaneously destroy the numinousness of the sun as an external agent giving life to the earth and convert the bowl of the sky into an opaque surface holding the mind's eye back from penetrating into the space of the "heavens." In terms of the deeper currents of Henry's mind, in other words, we could hardly be further from that moment earlier when the quasi-patriarchical figure of the mounted general "beamed upon the earth like a sun" and three times in the space of some twelve lines exclaimed jubilantly "By heavens!"—and "the youth cringed as if discovered in a crime. By heavens, they had won after all!" Yet if Henry's fist-shaking protest now would seem to point to a rejection of the claims of the universe to being informed with a Presence whose severities must be respected because of its paternal benevolences,[2] it has just been unforgettably demonstrated that no

2. It is not, of course, a complete rejection at this point, as the continuance of the supernatural imagery testifies.

diminishment of the mysteriousness and numinousness of life need be entailed therein. One of the most valid objections to certain ways of being religious is precisely that they *do* diminish those qualities. In *Paradist Lost*, for instance, it is especially noteworthy how unmysterious are the presented depths of the heavens and how commonplace their chief occupant, and how it is only in and through the consciousnesses of the two humans that one experiences any sense of genuine mysteries and profundities in existence. In *The Red Badge*, similarly, in contrast to the tritely physical supernaturalism of Henry's guilt-ridden imagery it is the truly marvellous, the sense of immense human lonelinesses and intensities in the face of existence, that gets reaffirmed in the account of the death of Jim Conklin.[3] In a very small compass one has been led from the ostensibly broad—and false—view of human activities, via the presences and pressures of men en masse and the greater intimacies of decent fraternal concern, to the impenetrable isolation of the individual confronting the unknown.

In the title of this paper I mentioned forgiveness, and it is concerning that that I wish to close. I have spoken already of the language of events and of how events in the novel speak to Henry, in a sense, humanly and judicially. What I wish to point out now is how they can comfort as well as lacerate, forgive as well as condemn. That Henry, apparently in a complete impasse after Jim Conklin's death, with every mental escape route blocked by his own arguings, is able to awake the following day a completely free man is certainly the strangest thing in the novel; and yet the mechanisms at work seem both entirely convincing and very heartening. Having witnessed the formidable ability of the mind to construct a reality in terms of which it appears hopelessly and permanently condemned, we now see the power of life to disown such a construction and relax abruptly the death-grip of the past. When Henry is overwhelmed by the fleeing men he is shocked out of his sense of the fixity of the battle lines and of his own uniqueness in running. With the blow from the rifle butt the seeming moral order of things is further loosened: in the place of Henry's doing unjust things to just people in an ostensibly just universe, someone else is now behaving unjustly to *him*—and doing so impersonally too, so that the blow seems to come simply from life itself like a random bullet, instead of like one of those carefully aimed retributive arrows he had been imagining earlier. And in his encounter with the cheerful soldier he is confronted with the demonstrated possibility of

3. Concerning whom, it seems pertinent to add, one commenator has been able to assert bluntly, "His loyalty consists of braggadocio and clichés, and his death is without meaning." (Max Westbrook, "Stephen Crane and the Personal Universal," *Modern Fiction Studies,* VIII [Winter, 1962–1963], 351–360.) The remark testifies obliquely, I suspect, to the dehumanizations involved in the kind of symbol-hunting against which Westbrook is reacting.

someone's having deserted like himself and yet being able to function with unabashed equanimity, good human, and kindliness. It
seems a profound gesture of benevolence from life, finally, that he
should be guided so skillfully through the woods by his new companion in a manner that recalls, albeit in a wholly secular way, the
loving figure of the Good Shepherd, and that on his arrival he
should be welcomed with such tender consideration by his comrades, the latter changed both from what they had actually been
earlier and from the implacable judges of his imaginings. Moreover,
more than an illustration of Paul Tillich's formula about being
accepted because unacceptable seems to be involved. In view of the
fullness with which he has exposed himself to the tumults of existence, Henry in a sense has *earned* his acceptance and his subsequent wholeness and success. Especially significant in this connection, I think, is the episode at the end of the book in which the
thought of his abandonment of the tattered soldier returns to haunt
him and, after experiencing pain at it, he "gradually mustered force
to put the sin at a distance. And at last his eyes seemed to open to
some new ways." It is as if here were the final heartening affirmation of the change in him; quite rightly he is now able to reject the
claims on him for a renewed sense of guilt that could be crippling
in the same sort of way, though presumably not to the same extent,
as the guilt he had felt after his first—and lesser—moral failure.
The book, in sum, demonstrates that if one remains fully responsive
to existence the possibility is always there of becoming to some
extent "another thing,"[4] and not just in battle either.

The Red Badge of Courage, as I have indicated earlier, does not
in the least mitigate the atrociousness of war. Indeed, to reread it
is to be made more thankful than ever that one does not have to go
into battle oneself, and more humblingly uncertain as to what one's
own conduct would be under conditions like those faced by Henry
Fleming. But to insist on the affirmative quality of Crane's treatment of war is not to diminish those facts. Crane has neither ex-
ploited war in the interests of nourishing a self-pitying fatalism
about the inexorable destruction of the good and beautiful by life,
nor indulged in a facile indignation about human brutishness and
folly. Like B. Traven in *The Death Ship*—and like almost no other
American novelist—he has succeeded in writing with unforgettable
vividness about the atrocious in a way that yet makes it simply a
part of life and not an indictment of it, or an indictment of "man,"
or any sort of indictment at all. In its psychological richness and its
truly religious openness, *The Red Badge* is not only one of the most
remarkable of American novels, it is one whose wisdoms seem

4. That the change in Henry would be
likely to be a lasting one seems suggested
by the striking rsemblances between it
and what William James describes in
Varieties of Religious Experience as
"conversion."

especially valuable among the philosophical confusions of the present time. In exploring war as a closed situation in which an intellectual cannot escape from the moral claims of events merely by willing it—escape by focusing only on the kinds of events that feed his vanities—Crane has helped to show up the fashionable nihilisms of today as the effete and schizophrenic things that they are.

JOHN W. RATHBUN

Structure and Meaning in *The Red Badge of Courage*†

Stephen Crane's *The Red Badge of Courage* has been continually sifted for up-to-date techniques, until now we are all aware of its grim ambiguities, its persistent ironies and paradoxes, and its often extraordinary imagery and diction. These techniques establish Crane as a complex writer. In the last decade, however, Crane's complexity has discouraged us from viewing the novel as anything more than an ironic equivocation that undercuts and ultimately checks earnest attempts to uncover a single (not multiple) thread of meaning. Scholars have increasingly tended to focus on plastic and formal values in the novel, with the intention of relating these values to a very sophisticated strain of metaphysical speculation in Crane that I think was likely foreign to his temperament.[1] I propose a modest but clear alternative. That is to turn to the traditional writer's technique of narrative organization, and to explore the novel in terms of patterns of action. Following that exploration, we might then invoke a traditional scholarly technique and check our conclusions against what we know of Crane's other work.

This mode of approach assumes that an author has consciously worked through a process of elaborating his theme by shrewdly disposing the parts in such a way as to lead cumulatively to a conclu-

† *Ball State University Forum*, X (Winter, 1969), 8–16. Copyright 1969. Reprinted by permission of the publisher and the author.
1. The tendency is especially marked after Isaac Rosenfeld's review of Robert Wooster Stallman's *Stephen Crane: An Omnibus,* published in *Kenyon Review,* XV (1953), 311–14. Although the large number of particular insights of scholars working on the novel become lost in a process of categorizing, in general, conflicts in critical interpretation may be reduced to three positions represented by Stallman, Charles Walcutt, and Stanley Greenfield. Stallman finds a basic pattern of symbols and of alternating contradictory moods that finally result in spiritual regeneration for Fleming. Walcutt, on the other hand, thinks the novel is naturalistic and emphasizes the vain and selfish motives of Fleming. And Greenfield, in a well-argued essay, concludes that Crane used imagistic patterns to reconcile the polarities of volition and necessity. Stallman, Introduction to *Stephen Crane: An Omnibus* (New York, 1952); Walcutt, *American Literary Naturalism, a Divided Stream* (Minneapolis, 1956), pp. 66–86; and Greenfield, "The Unmistakable Stephen Crane," *PMLA,* LXXIII (December, 1958), 562–72.

324 · John W. Rathbun

sion. The assumption concentrates attention on those basic building blocks that most writers use to give their work structural coherence. Structure, in other words, can be viewed as an objective property of literary works to which such suggestive properties as tone, mood, and imagery are subordinate. If we remain properly aware of the narrative organization of a literary work, we are not apt to be misled into such contemporary critical pitfalls as over-generalization, ingenious symbol hunting, or even what may strike us as perversities of reading more artful than the work they profess to study.

Three studies deal explicitly with the structure of *The Red Badge*.[2] All make their contributions to our understanding of the novel, but of the three only Eric Solomon's is directly involved with its narrative continuity. Solomon's more important conclusions are hardly to be quarreled with, but the thematic rationales of action *within* his three divisions are not sufficiently explored to point irrevocably to the deductions that Solomon draws from the novel. Of other studies of *The Red Badge*, James Trammell Cox's article seems the most persuasive in terms of argument and consistency, and my own study of structure may be viewed as a companion piece to Cox's analysis of imagery in the novel.[3]

I would suggest that if the novel is divided into four main blocks of action, a pattern of meaning emerges which checks out with the prevailing imagery and patterns of meaning in Crane's other work. The first block consists of chapters 1 through 5. Here a kind of counterpoint is developed between Fleming as an untried introspective soldier and the regiment as a collective mob. The second block, chapters 6 through 12, provides us episodes in Fleming's flight that serve to introduce him to collateral aspects of death in war and nature. Chapters 13 through 16, which constitute the third block, associate Wilson and Fleming against the vague backdrop of battle, and contrast Wilson's newly won maturity with Fleming's continued adolescent uncertainty. Then finally, in the fourth block, consisting of chapters 16 through 23, Wilson and Fleming become virtually inseparable, take on essentially the same qualities of courage, and merge with the massed army to participate in the "thumping of gigantic machinery" which parallels the "complications among the smaller stars." The final chapter serves as a coda to the novel.

Even this brief statement of the blocks of action serves to reveal

2. James B. Colvert, "Structure and Theme in Stephen Crane's Fiction," *MFS*, V (1959), 199–208; Eric Solomon, "The Structure of *The Red Badge of Courage*," in the same issue of *MFS*, pp. 220–34; and Thomas M. Lorch, "The Cyclical Structure of *The Red Badge of Courage*," *CLA Journal*, X (1967), 229–38. Colvert is concerned with the larger issue of structure in Crane's fiction, and when he examines *The Red Badge* it is largely in terms of Fleming's maturation rather than narrative organization. Lorch's illuminating study finds repetitive patterns in various chapters of the novel that serve to point up not only the similarity of experience but significant variations in response to experience.
3. "The Imagery of *The Red Badge of Courage*," *MFS*, V (1959), 209–19.

that Crane is chiefly interested in simply working Fleming out of a state of enervating self-analysis and into a state of unreflecting group participation. More particularly, as I hope to show, the blocks disclose no interest, singly or cumulatively, in such problems as "regeneration," man's "volitional abilities," or the possibility for "ethical choices." Fleming achieves little more than awareness of what the world is like: a kind of consciousness on which we traditionally put a high price. No one incident is critically important. In general, and solely in terms of his experience, Fleming becomes aware that nature, war, and men's collective actions all testify to a grotesque, incredible world in which death, striking at random and without meaning, is the one constant.

The first block, chapters one through five, juxtaposes the mob-like regiment, with its seeming collective assurance, to the indecision of the single young and untried soldier. Within his hut, in a "trance of astonishment," Fleming ponders his coming participation in "one of those great affairs of the earth," a battle. Fighting and death are concealed in ignorance. Despite his youthful fantasies of heroic actions, Fleming had been schooled to believe, as indeed had many of Crane's contemporaries in that period of "progress," that modern "secular and religious education" had combined with "firm finance" to check the "aggressive and passionate instincts"[4] Those early "laws of life" on which he had been nurtured were predicated on the assurance of peace and reason. Yet here is war, so fresh an experience in terms of aggression and passion that Fleming sees himself an "unknown quantity."

Conjecture is no help in resolving this anxiety-ridden doubt. Fleming must, as he himself admits, experience "blaze, blood, and danger" in order to construct a new life based on a model that recognizes the primitive instincts. As for the model itself, we can be sure that one constituent, at least in terms of war, is the loss of self and the subsequent sharing in a collective psychology when part of a crowd. This latter is played off against the personal loneliness and "eternal debate" of Fleming. On the march, brigades grin and regiments laugh. More often, the view, which is ambiguously both Fleming's and the narrator's, is a presentiment of evil.[5] A great deal of animal imagery, as Mordecai and Erin Marcus have demonstrated, informs the novel.[6] Images of "dragons," "red eyes," and foreboding representations of nonobjective threats establish the tone

4. This point, although critics may sometimes refer to it, is curiously slighted in criticism of the novel. Crane thought it sufficiently important to reiterate the view several pages later.
5. The question of narrative point of view, which is responsible for much of the seeming ambiguity of the novel, is just now beginning to be fully appreciated. See especially Robert C. Albrecht, "Content and Style in *The Red Badge of Courage*," *CE*, XXVII (1966), 487–92.
6. "Animal Imagery in *The Red Badge of Courage*," *MLN*, LXXIV (1959), 108–11.

of the early chapters. But despite the use of what are basically organic images, Fleming persists in dissociating war and nature. Nature appears gentle, composed of soft browns and greens. In contrast, the battalions are "woven red." But once arrived on the battlefield, Fleming also thinks that this advance upon nature is too calm, and he ascribes a portentous significance to the scene. He expects to see death.

Much of this expectation is given in religious terms. Evidences of Crane's early nurture in the Methodist household of his minister father are everywhere apparent in Crane's writing. Usually such religious references are inverted. In *The Red Badge*, war replaces the Christian god. War, whose agent is death, is pictured as the "blood-swollen god," the "red animal" men propitiate only to be devoured. Introduced in the third chapter, the red god dominates the book. The battlefield is his place of public worship. As the regiment prepares for battle it stops in the "cathedral light" of the forest, where it can look down the "aisles" of the woods to see the smoke of battle. For his part, Fleming hopes that the stress of battle will provide him "salvation" in the eyes of the red god. That salvation seems assured as the men, Fleming included, revert to the instinctive rage of animals, and chanting the chords of a "wild, barbaric song" find themselves welded into a "common personality." At the section's end, Fleming notes that nature has remained tranquil in the midst of "so much devilment."

Summing up, the first block of action is chiefly devoted to contrasting an individual against the group. On the one hand is Fleming, torn by doubt and indecision. He has been a child of his century in assuming the "civilized" view that man had progressed beyond blood-letting. Thus he is psychologically unprepared to meet the demands of the red god of war and suspicious that he lacks the resources of courage to act bravely. On the other hand is the regiment. It gains in composite strength in proportion to the loss of personal identity. Existing for the sole purpose of killing, the regiment in action develops a "subtle battle brotherhood." In battle, reason is singularly absent, and the regiment reverts to the instinctive rage of animals serving a monstrous god.

The second block of action, which consists of episodes in Fleming's flight, is, as almost all critics recognize, a critical section of the book. But not for the reasons usually given. Its separate incidents have been extensively sifted and explicated with all the erudite remoteness of the higher criticism. What is lost to sight is that these separate incidents seem to have little more than an immediate and passing effect on Fleming.[7] It is only in the aggregate that they

7. A point made very well by Norman Friedman in reference to Conklin's role in the novel. See Friedman's "Criticism and the Novel," *Antioch Review*, XVII (1958), 343–70.

assume meaning to the youth, and this later and only in the most general way.

The purpose of the second block of action is to extend the range of meaning (for the reader, not Fleming) by revealing that nature and war are reciprocally related through the agency of death. The first chapter (chapter six) continues the red god and monster imagery developed in the first section. As the enemy returns to the attack, the soldier "slaves" toiling in the "temple" of the red god feel an intense resentment. Fleming, seeing the enemy simultaneously as "machines of steel" and as "redoubtable dragons"—which blends organic nature and mechanized war—panics, deserts his comrades, and rushes terror stricken to the rear. And then occurs an important statement generally passed over in the critical literature. As Fleming thinks about it "later," he concludes that the fear of facing death is better than the fear of hearing death at one's back: one should stand up to "the appalling than to be merely within hearing." We don't know when the "later" is, but the sentence intimates that at some point in the novel Fleming has the resources for objectively assessing his earlier terror.,

But at the moment, fleeing, Fleming is only aware of the "dragons" about to devour him. Ironically, the enemy attack is held. He rationalizes that he was the only one who possessed the capacity for "intelligent deliberation." But actually irrational fear had moved him like a puppet. Now, having fled the religion of war of the red god, Fleming rushes into the forest grove, where he anticipates a "religion of peace." Nature seems to sanction his view by giving him a "sign" in the form of the fearful squirrel. But the mood does not last. Moving on, he sees a "small animal" pounce into the "black" water after a fish, and shortly after, in the "religious half-light" of the grove chapel, he comes across the horrible sight of the dead man with eyes the hue of a "dead fish." No more than an implied suggestion, death seems to be an agent of nature as well as of the red god.[8]

The point is reinforced when one realizes that nature now disappears as an element in the novel until the restful peace of the final chapter. For the next approximately two thirds of the novel, we are given only the roars of the "celestial battle," which strike both Fleming and the narrator as the thunder of an "eloquent being" describing death.

Conklin's impressive agony, which has misled many critics into thinking it the climactic chapter in the novel, is qualitatively no

8. The tone of the passage does not seem to me to support the interpretation of John E. Hart that "After the burial of himself in the forest, it is his unconscious awareness of the nature of death that restores the strength and energy he had felt in his dream at home." *"The Red Badge of Courage* as Myth and Symbol," *University of Kansas City Review*, XIX (1953), 251.

more important than Fleming's other experiences in the second block of action.[9] A "devotee of a mad religion" who proceeds in a "rite-like" way to his doom, Conklin's death is graphic and immediate. But it constitutes no "redemption" for Fleming. Within the context of the section, as well as of the novel's narrative organization, it is hard to see the relevance of any Christ imagery. At best we might agree with J. T. Cox's observation that "in this red world Jesus Christ is a grim joke."[1] What emerges is simply another experience of war, and not even the most important experience at that. Fleming refers to Conklin's death only once, when he briefly informs Wilson. A more critical episode, as we shall see in examining the last chapter, is his desertion of the tattered man, left to wander aimlessly in the field.

The belief that "war, the red animal, war, the blood-swollen god, would have bloated fill" of men is pervasive in the events following Conklin's death and Henry's desertion of the tattered soldier. Against this belief, Fleming's poor attempts at rationalizing his predicament are ineffective. In reality, as indeed throughout the second block, he is motivated by nothing more than a dim, generalized instinct, as a "mothlike quality" keeps him near the battle. The two kinds of death witnessed in the forest chapel, Conklin's death, the approaching unattended death of the tattered man, the random movements of fleeing men, the butt on the head, all against the background of battle noise, provide precious little enlightenment to Fleming. What emerges from this second section is an impression of absolute contingency upon a chaotic and unstructured world in which death is the common agent of war and nature.

With Fleming's return to the regiment there is a lull, and the third block of action takes over. For the next four chapters we dwell on Fleming's thoughts and especially on his discovery of a new Wilson, who now begins to serve as a foil to Fleming. Fleming had gotten some inkling the night before that Wilson's solicitude for his "wound" was a far cry from the braggart Wilson he had known in the early chapters. Wilson seems possessed of new virtues. This change, of course, is all seen through the eyes of Fleming. But there is no reason to discount what Fleming sees, and even the narrator seems to agree. Before, Fleming had viewed Wilson, as had the other men, as a "child," a "swaggering babe" who had nothing more than a tinsel courage. But now new eyes have been "born" to Wilson. He has gained wisdom, self-reliance, and new purposes and

9. R. W. Stallman in his Introduction to *The Red Badge of Courage* in *Stephen Crane: An Omnibus* (1952) and John E. Hart in the article just cited especially emphasize the relevance of Conklin's death to Fleming's "regeneration." I doubt that most critics any longer seriously entertain this view, although it is true that in his "philippic" Fleming momentarily recognizes that war has its own ritual, against which he rebels.

1. "The Imagery of *The Red Badge of Courage*," p. 217.

abilities. The key to Wilson's new state is his apparent realization that he is a "very wee thing," not at all important when viewed from any "peak of wisdom," and therefore no more important than the general run of men with whom he must associate and no longer try to dominate. Wilson has gained what others have not. Conklin's death cuts him short of conclusion, as the description of his hanging babe-like on Fleming is intended to imply. And Fleming's own emergence from the babe-like state presumably depends on winning through to the attributes now possessed by the new Wilson.

Just how far in the future the acquisition of these new attributes lies can be seen in the little interlude where Fleming gives Wilson the packet of letters the latter had entrusted to his care before the first engagement. Fleming's self-deceit, adolescent arrogance, and self-pride are all laid out for the reader. He treats Wilson with great condescension. In addition, he ascribes "discretion and dignity" to his flight. Yet there is a hint of change. A "little flower of confidence" is secretly blossoming within Fleming, according to the narrator. It has two elements. First, in actually fronting the "dragons" of war, Fleming has not found them so "hideous" as he had anticipated. Second, and probably more important, the "dragons" are seen to lack precision. They are inaccurate. Retribution seems "a laggard and blind." Such thoughts constitute only a small advance, but it is an advance nonetheless.

The tone of the novel does not appreciably shift at this point, but the ironic undercutting of Fleming, which before has been minute, particular, and heavily circumstantial, largely disappears in the last block of action. Consequently, those critics who profess to find irony rising climactically to the very end become increasingly ingenious, with the result that their analyses seem unnecessarily abstruse and finally unconvincing. Looked at objectively, the last section gives us a straightforward presentation of the actions of the last day of battle. The organization of the section is in terms of a small detailed picture of the two comrades-in-arms, Wilson and Fleming, as this is superimposed on the larger picture of the animality and unreflecting conduct of fighting armies. The customary images of religious and instinctive involvement continue to prevail. In their "moblike and barbaric" assaults, the soldiers are in a "delirium" which makes them heedless and blind. They are possessed of a "mad enthusiasm"—the counterpart to Christian evangelical fervor. During the pauses of battle, the soldiers become cautious, but otherwise they show a "vicious wolflike temper," yell and scream like "maniacs," burst into barbaric cries of rage and pain, fight with "despairing savageness," and generally exhibit a wild and malevolent recklessness. Serving the red god, they become "men."

In these actions, Fleming is at one with the regiment. There is hardly a trace of irony in the narrator's transcription of his actions. Early in the engagement he fights "like a pagan who defends his religion." Later, he feels the "daring spirit of a savage religion mad." The day before, Henry had hated the controlling god of the universe. Today he hates only the opposing army. He has committed himself to the red god. This commitment becomes clearer in the various episodes where the flag figures. Here the two youths act in unison. To Fleming, the flag appears to be beautiful, invulnerable, womanly imperious in gesturing him on. He endows it with a supernatural power to save lives, which is immediately dispelled when the color-sergeant himself is hit. Far from being dispirited, as he might have the day before, Fleming leaps to clutch the pole, as does Wilson, and for a moment the two friends and the dead color-bearer engage in a grim encounter finally won by Wilson. A few minutes later they again compete for possession of the flag, simply to show one another their willingness to bear further risks. Finally, they compete for the enemy flag, which is won by Wilson. The capture signifies the end of action on this part of the line, and as the two friends sit together with their respective flags, they exchange congratulations joyously. It requires an unnecessary wrenching of the text to see this section as anything less than Henry's belated acquisition of those virtues of self-reliance and ability earlier assigned to Wilson, whose person in the third block contrasted so sharply with Fleming's It remains, however, to be seen whether Fleming has also won through to Wilson's wise insight into himself as a "very wee thing."

The final chapter, an epilogue to the novel, closes out and clarifies the novel's narrative organization. The enemy has departed, and the battle is over. Fleming has to shake himself free of his battle mind in order to focus on what has happened. He becomes reflective and, says the narrator, his mind is "undergoing a subtle change." Fleming understands that he has dwelt in a strange land, identified in the two yoked images of "red of blood" and "black of passion." He has survived and "come forth." Now, in the aftermath of battle, he struggles to add up his account, including his deeds, his failures, and his achievements. He can do this with "some" correctness, says the narrator, because he has a "new condition" capable of defeating the "certain sympathies" he had previously held.

Nevertheless, the memory of his ignominious flight returns to Fleming, and he remembers with particular shame his desertion of the tattered soldier. This is the one memory that continues to rankle. After all, his views of death in the forest grove and the spectacle of Conklin dying were repeated in infinite variation all about him. But his desertion is a moral shame, a "dogging memory" and a "somber phantom" that could accompany him through life.

Earlier, he would have feared the obloquy that discovery would have visited on him. He is of course sensitive to this possibility, but he also thinks of a hurt done a fellow soldier, and in the thought there is a kind of selflessness.

But at last Fleming manages to muster strength to keep the memory at a distance. Some critics have interpreted this act ironically; Charles Walcutt, for instance, thinks that the passage is a "climax of self-delusion."[2] Undoubtedly elements of irony are present, for Crane was ironic by temperament, suspicious of situations in which the ambivalent did not play its accustomed role. And too, when one is as introspective as the young Fleming, this constant self-consultation cannot help revealing to the consciousness the shifting patterns of feeling and opinion that lie below the threshold of will.

Nevertheless, Fleming's action in putting aside the rankling memory can accommodate another construction, one that is consonant with the general structural movement of the novel. Within that movement, two facts present themselves to which we must adjust: first, the new Wilson in the third block; second, the concerted efforts of Wilson and Fleming in the last block, symbiotic in character. So far as the second fact is concerned, we should be alert in reading the last chapter to those outlines that are consistent with the suggested development of Fleming. As for the first fact, no critic, so far as I know, has ever seriously doubted that Wilson has really changed under the stress of battle, and this despite the fact that there are incidents, such as his mournful and self-indulgent expectation on the last day that he will surely be killed, which serve to strike off the edges on his new maturity. Presumably Wilson adjusts to these conditional checks by recognizing them and then refusing to brood on them.

When Fleming pushes aside the memory of his wrong, I think he might well be following a similar course. Man, we have heard often enough, cannot abide by his sins alone, and too rigorously dwelling on them leads only to despair. It takes courage to acknowledge one's frailties and to incorporate them into a larger vision. In effect, Fleming follows the temperate theology of Crane's father in refusing to be paralyzed by the knowledge of sin. He looks to the future. When he does glance back on the "brass and bombast of his earlier gospels," he finds that he despises them.

What, then, is the new gospel? Nothing too complicated. Fleming has touched death, and found it only death. Because death is very real, it is neither awesome nor to be feared. For the rest, reality hardly exists. The red god is simply a metaphor. It is consequently to little purpose to talk, as some critics have, of the disparity

2. *American Literary Naturalism*, p. 81.

between Fleming's illusions and "reality." We should be careful not to attribute too much philosophical subtlety to the young Crane. His "reality," if we must use the term, is actually unstructured, morally indifferent, and essentially unreadable. For all his vaunted reason, man best meets the conditions of life when he does not think on them but trusts instead to his irrational self. As for his ideas, as Bertrand Russell has said, they are comforting convictions trailing behind man like an accompanying swarm of summer flies. The fact that so much of the novel is couched in religious language testifies to the importance that Crane attached to his vision.

Strictly speaking, the narrator of the novel and we the readers attain the vision. The strength of Fleming's conviction comes from "sturdy and strong blood," not from what his insight tells him. Fleming is simply on his way; whatever he faces, he likely will not quail. In this sense, Fleming is a fore-runner of the modern hero and anti-hero, that man who is stoical before adversity, often taciturn, frequently bewildered, who sometimes possesses no more than the bestiality of the cornered animal, who at other times cherishes visions of a soft, eternal peace that he knows, deep down, is at best wondrously fragile.[3]

The virtue of this reading, which as I said earlier complements the article of J. T. Cox, is that it lodges the book squarely in the Crane canon. The Crane canon constantly ridicules the public illusion that consciousness is a factor in human affairs through the radical alteration of its environment. To Crane, consciousness does not alter things, nor is it a mode of control. Consciousness simply identifies, or creates awareness. But even awareness can be tentative and incomplete, so that neither Fleming nor Collins in "A Mystery of Heroism" quite knows why he should be an intruder in the "land of fine deeds." Fleming's red world, aside from the color, is the world of "The Blue Hotel," in which the very existence of man is a kind of marvel. Like the survivors in "The Open Boat," Fleming's sharpened awareness of the nature of this world puts him in the class of "interpreters," whether or not he ever utters a word.

Even the religious references are used in a manner fairly habitual to Crane. *Maggie*, as William Stein has pointed out, abounds in inverted religious imagery.[4] So does *The Red Badge*. Its purpose is the same: to reinforce the picture of man's predicament in a world which is a maze of contradictory and often treacherous "signs" that finally turn out to be so terrifying because they are so meaningless. There is also *George's Mother*, where the "dead altars" of the

3. Daniel Weiss in a very interesting study points specifically to Hemingway parallels. See "The Red Badge of Courage," *Psychoanalytic Review*, LII, ii (1965), 32–52; iii, 130–54. Stallman also dwells on the Hemingway parallel in his Introduction to *Stephen Crane: An Omnibus*, p. 191ff.

4. "New Testament Inversions in Crane's *Maggie*," *MLN*, LXXII (1958), 268–72.

mother are contrasted with the son's equally crude "new religion" that exalts the "impenetrable mystery" of the city. And, as one last example, there is "An Experiment in Misery," in which the youth comes to "certain convictions" that oppose the romantic, unreal aspirations of the city and nation. *The Red Badge of Courage* explores richer experience, and it is Crane's finest achievement. But it does not differ in kind from his other work.

MARSTON LaFRANCE

Private Fleming: His Various Battles†

* * *

Crane's view of the human situation, set forth more clearly in *The Red Badge* than in his earlier work, is that man is born into an amoral universe which is merely the external setting in which human moral life is lived,[1] and that if moral values are to exist and man's life is to be meaningful, morality must be the creation of man's weak mental machinery alone; but even the best of men, the most personally honest, is prone to error and thus liable to bring misery upon himself and others because the mental machinery often distorts that reality which he must perceive correctly if his personal honesty is to result in morally significant commitment. Thus, Crane's essential subject, in *The Red Badge* as in the *Sullivan County Sketches, Maggie,* and the 'Experiment in Misery', is man's weak mental machinery as it labours under the stress of some emotion, usually fear, to perceive correctly an area of reality which is not yet within the compass of the perceiver's experience. And if so, *The Red Badge* does have an obvious source which is available to anyone who wishes to investigate it; but the assumption of a naturalistic, a factually realistic, or a specifically literary context leads in the wrong direction. The real source of this novel and any other important Crane work seems to me simply the ironist's incredible

† From *A Reading of Stephen Crane* (New York: Oxford University Press, 1971), pp. 98–99, 104–24. Copyright © 1971 by Oxford University Press. Reprinted by permission of the Oxford University Press, Oxford.
1. This view of the universe can reasonably be called naturalistic; but Crane's acceptance of it no more makes his work naturalistic than Matthew Arnold's acceptance of ultimately the same view makes his poetry naturalistic.
   "If this seems a pessimistic view of nature, it is not the logical end of Crane's concern with the subject, it is the logical end of America's concern. When Hawthorne and Melville questioned Emerson's view of nature as the benevolent image of the Over-Soul, they revealed an ambiguity in nature that begged closer inspection. Stephen Crane's examination showed nature to be as unmotivated as a machine with which man had come only accidentally in contact." (R. B. West, Jr., 'Stephen Crane: Author in Transition', *American Literature,* XXXIV [May, 1962], 227.)

awareness of human nature. Our amazement should not be directed at Crane's mastery of the techniques of naturalism, or knowledge of the Civil War, or Jamesian grasp of Western literature, but at so young a man's ability to create so superb a psychological portrayal as Henry Fleming.[2]

* * *

The novel opens with that sense of uncertainty which plagues Fleming until the last two or three pages. He hears Conklin's rumour that the regiment is about to engage in combat, and immediately withdraws to his hut to think about his own problems—and not at all about Conklin's rumour, by the way; he merely assumes the rumour will prove true (as it does not) and gives his whole attention to worrying about how he will act during his first battle. Thus, Fleming's intensely active imagination is presented at once: the really significant battles in this novel are already raging in full career within Henry's mind long before the first shot is fired in any external skirmish. He had dreamed of 'bloody conflicts that had thrilled him with their sweep and fire'; and, like George Kelcey,[3] his dreams feature great visions of personal glory in which he imagines 'peoples secure in the shadow of his eagle-eyed prowess'. Henry had enlisted, had voluntarily fled his dull farm life, because of these vainglorious desires set in the impossibly romantic picture of war which his imagination has evoked from village gossip and luridly distorted news reports.

The flashback to the farewell scene can serve almost as a structural précis of the novel. Henry had 'primed himself for a beautiful scene. He had prepared certain sentences which he thought could be used with touching effect'. But his mother merely peels potatoes and talks tediously of shirts and socks. The result is Crane's usual deflation of vanity, comic here because of Henry's romantic and sentimental foolishness. Nevertheless, buried in his mother's prosaic commonplaces is precisely the view of himself and his duty to which Henry has to inch his way in painful experience throughout the remainder of the novel: 'Yer jest one little feller amongst a hull lot of others, and yeh've got to keep quiet an' do what they tell yeh. . . . Never do no shirking child, on my account. If so be a time comes when yeh have to be kilt or do a mean thing, why, Henry, don't think of anything 'cept what's right'. Fleming is not the undiscovered Achilles of his grand illusions; he is just another lad who has to learn to be a man. And to be a man in Crane's world is to perceive the human situation as it is, accept it, and remain personally honest in fulfilling the commitments such a perception

2. Cf. James B. Colvert, 'Stephen Crane: The Development of His Art.' Ph.D. dissertation, Louisiana State University, 1953, p. 145.
3. The principal figure in Crane's novel George's Mother (1896).

demands of the individual. The fact that Henry has to suffer the experiences of the whole novel even to approach this simple truth merely reveals, again, the most bitterly ironic aspect of Crane's psychological pattern: as in *Maggie* and the Sullivan County tales, the protagonist of *The Red Badge* also has to undergo all his suffering in order to perceive, to 'see', a constant reality which is present and available to him before his progression through experience to the perception of it even begins.

Henry's weak mental machinery is at this point so busy with visions of glory and he is so impatient to leave that he hardly hears his mother's advice; but his shame, when he turns to see her praying and weeping among the potato parings, distinguishes him from Crane's earlier protagonists, and implies that eventually he will learn the truth of what he has just been told—that the real hero, in such a world as this, is the quiet, nameless man who can discern what is right and do it, simply because it is right and because he is a man.

Henry's education has already begun before the reader first encounters him. He has experienced the dreariness, boredom, filth, and part of the misery of a soldier's life. The prolonged inaction has left his imagination free to concentrate on that part of his problem which experience has not yet clarified for him, and thus he is first seen lying in his bunk trying 'to mathematically prove to himself that he would not run from a battle'. He contemplates the 'lurking menaces of the future', in the only way he can, as these menaces exist within his own mind; and given Henry's imagination, it is no wonder that his thoughts scare him. When Conklin's rumour proves false and still more waiting has to be endured, Henry's tension becomes almost unbearable; and his imagination evokes two illusions which Crane exploits throughout the novel: the notion that moral qualities exist in external nature—'The liquid stillness of the night enveloping him made him feel vast pity for himself. There was a caress in the soft winds; and the whole mood of the darkness, he thought, was one of sympathy for himself in his distress'—and the belief that he is unique, separated (at this point by fear) from the other men in the regiment. After timidly broaching the hint of fear to Wilson only to have the conversation end in an abrupt quarrel, Henry 'felt alone in space. . . . No one seemed to be wrestling with such a terrific personal problem'. Henry is wrong, of course. The other men are also afraid; but without Henry's imagination they fear only the *fact* of combat, and hence they can play poker while he suffers. Henry no longer fears the actual fact: 'In the darkness he saw visions of a thousand-tongued fear that would babble at his back and cause him to flee, while others were going coolly about their country's business. He admitted that he would

not be able to cope with this monster.' Such is Henry's state of
mind when he is suddenly awakened one morning and sent running
towards his first skirmish.

Crane introduces the 'moving box' episode with the flat statement that Henry 'was bewildered'. Barely awake and intensely
excited, he has to use 'all his faculties' to keep from falling and
being trampled by those running behind him. The passage in question constitutes Henry's *first* reaction to this situation:

> he instantly saw that it would be impossible for him to escape
> from the regiment. It inclosed him. And there were iron laws of
> tradition and law on four sides. He was in a moving box.
> As he perceived this fact it occurred to him that he had never
> wished to come to the war. He had not enlisted of his free will.
> He had been dragged by the merciless government. And now
> they were taking him out to be slaughtered.

This passage is pure rationalization without a hint of naturalism in
it. The 'iron laws of tradition and law' are made by men and
changed by men. And Henry did enlist of his own free will; he was
not dragged to this commitment by any force except his own wish
to go to war. All that this passage really reveals is that Henry is so
badly frightened he is considering flight even before a shot is fired.

When Henry's curiosity leads him to charge over a rise only to be
confronted with still more inaction, Crane unambiguously presents
his basic trouble: 'If an intense scene had caught him with its wild
swing as he came to the top of the bank, he might have gone roaring on. This advance upon Nature was too calm. He had opportunity to reflect. He had time in which to wonder about himself and
to attempt to probe his sensations'. Hence, a house acquires an
'ominous look', shadows in a wood are 'formidable', and Henry feels
he should advise the generals because 'there was but one pair of
eyes' in the regiment. In the afternoon he tells Conklin the truth
when he says, 'I can't stand this much longer'. Henry's inner turmoil again obscures his perception: he no more grasps the significance of Wilson giving him the packet than he had heard his mother's advice. He soon witnesses the rout of some troops who run
blindly back through his own regimental line, and he intends to
wait only long enough to see the 'composite monster' which has
frightened these men. But when the charge finally comes, he does
not run; he stays and fights.

This episode must have taken considerable thought, for Crane
had to find a means of letting Henry engage in battle, an incident
to which the four previous chapters have pointed, and still not
undergo the unknown experience he fears. In other words, Crane's
treatment at this point would commit him one way or the other: if

Henry experienced the unknown here the result would be a short story; if this experience could be further delayed the result would be a novel. Crane solved his problem by having Henry fight this skirmish in a trance, a 'battle sleep' induced by fatigue and rage; and because of this Henry later does not accept this combat as that attainment of the experience he has been anticipating.

Thus, Crane in this episode is able to repeat the irony of Henry's farewell scene. When the fight begins, Crane allows Henry to attain the real bearing of responsible manhood at war—for a few moments:

> He suddenly lost concern for himself, and forgot to look at a menacing fate. . . . He felt that something of which he was a part —a regiment, an army, or a country—was in a crisis. He was welded into a common personality which was dominated by a single desire. . . .
> There was a consciousness always of the presence of his comrades about him. He felt the subtle battle brotherhood more potent even than the cause for which they were fighting. It was a mysterious fraternity born of the smoke and danger of death.
> He was at a task.

This is a quiet statement, without any irony, of the ideal which Crane was to honour repeatedly in his writings about the Spanish-American War. But at this point Henry enters his battle sleep. Then, after the charge has been repulsed, and before Henry emerges from his trance, he feels 'a flash of astonishment at the blue, pure sky and the sun gleamings on the trees and fields. It was surprising that Nature had gone tranquilly on with her golden process in the midst of so much devilment'. And this statement implies the mature man's unsentimental view of nature as an amoral external mechanism. But then, when Henry emerges from his trance, his old weaknesses reassert themselves, and he is entirely unable to recall either the achievement or the perception which came to him at either edge of his battle sleep. Once again the reality he is seeking lies within his grasp; and once again his mental turmoil prevents his awareness of it.

This episode also contains some of Crane's famous animal imagery; and, provided it is read correctly, Crane's *use* of this very imagery argues against naturalism. Crane does not use animal images until Henry begins to slip into his battle sleep; before this, there is only a single animal image in the three pages of this chapter: 'the colonel . . . began to scold like a wet parrot'. And, more important, there is no hint of such imagery in the above description of Henry's moment of manhood before his trance begins. But as Henry descends from full consciousness and becomes something less than a man he abruptly begins to perceive in terms of nonhuman images; he feels 'the acute exasperation of a pestered animal, a well-meaning cow worried by dogs'; he rages like a 'driven beast'; men 'snarl' and 'howl'; a coward's eyes are 'sheeplike . . . animal-like'. And this sort of imagery ends when Henry regains full consciousness. The *use* of imagery is fairly consistent throughout the novel. Hence, the demands of dramatic propriety are as insistent here as they are in the flophouse scene in the 'Experiment in Misery', and for the same reason: the primary function of the imagery in *The Red Badge* is, again, to represent the protagonist's agitated mind as it struggles from lurid distortions to an understanding that reality is, after all, but reality. The imagery in the novel always becomes most vivid when Henry's perception is most distorted, and such a state of mind is the extreme of the condition which Henry labours to transcend by applying his awareness, conscience, and force of will to his experience. Crane's use of such imagery in this novel, in short, strongly implies that he is a humanist, not a naturalist.[4]

When Henry awakens from his battle sleep to find that the charge has been withstood, he becomes vain in complacent admiration of his part in this success; and all his self-congratulation is illusory. Nothing is 'over' for him; no trial has been passed. He uncritically admires actions which were done in a trance; and no Crane character ever feels such pompous self-satisfaction, even for real accomplishment, unless he is a vain fool. Complacency is a delusion in a world where nothing but death is final, where no ideal can ever be possessed because man has to reckon with externalities beyond his control, a stoic's world in which a continuous present poses a continuous demand upon man's moral and physical endurance. The attack is immediately renewed; and this time, after having seen so many others flee that he believes he will be left alone, Henry runs away. One must insist that he runs only nominally from the advancing enemy; what he really runs from is his own imagination. Crane's statement could hardly be more bluntly unambiguous: 'On his face was all the horror of those things which he imagined'.[5] Even as he flees, his busy mind rationalizes his flight in terms of his previous feeling of uniqueness, and thus he loiters in the rear long enough to learn that the line held and repulsed the charge a second time. Then, miserably ashamed, cringing 'as if discovered in a crime', he moves into the forest.

Henry's journey through this forest, like Marlow's journey up the river into the heart of darkness, charts a pilgrimage within the

4. Max R. Westbrook, 'Stephen Crane and the Personal Universal', *Modern Fiction Studies*, VIII (Winter, 1962–3), 353.
5. See Gordon O. Taylor, *The Passages of Thought: Psychological Representation in the American Novel 1870–1900* (New York: Oxford University Press, 1969), p. 126.

mind. This moral forest clearly suggests the 'direful thicket' through which the brave man of the poems has to plunge to find truth, and its 'singular knives'—fear, guilt, shame, hatred of those who remained and fought, vanity, self-pity, rage, his suffering as he sympathetically experiences Conklin's death, the self-loathing evoked by the tattered man—slash at Henry's ego just as the brush and vines entangle his legs. This section of the novel probably required more virtuosity and sheer craftsmanship than any other because, in terms of Crane's structural pattern, no further progress can occur until Henry returns to face his commitment: the unknown experience is thus beautifully delayed while the protagonist undergoes an intense struggle within himself, the outcome of which merely returns him to the position from which he had fled when this section began.

Thus, Crane begins with considerable care. Henry's guilt first evokes rationalization of his cowardice as superior intelligence, and from this premise his mind moves through anger at his 'stupid' comrades who had 'betrayed' him, to vanity, self-pity, and finally to a general 'animal-like rebellion against his fellows, war in the abstract, and fate'. The adjective is significant because with rationalization Henry has abandoned moral responsibility and again has become less than a man. Such is his state of mind as he enters the metaphorical forest of his inner self and the ensuing scenes portray his struggles to claw his way back up to the human condition again. His terrible journey through this forest can be divided into four parallel scenes or episodes—the craftsman's device of *Maggie* used here with much greater subtlety—which are easily identified: each begins with a specific illusion, a direction of Henry's thought which is followed until the pathway becomes blocked; when the illusion is destroyed, or when the barricade is encountered and Henry has to seek a new direction, the episode ends and the next one begins.

His first illusion arises directly from his attempts to rationalize his cowardice. It begins when he attempts to draw illusory justification from sentimentalized nature, and it expands to include an equally sentimental religious feeling. The 'landscape gave him assurance. A fair field holding life. It was the religion of peace. It would die if its timid eyes were compelled to see blood. He conceived Nature to be a woman with a deep aversion to tragedy'. He throws a pine-cone at a squirrel, and the squirrel, to Henry's immense satisfaction, runs away: 'There was the law, he said [conveniently forgetting that a man is not a squirrel]. Nature had given him a sign'. Although he then observes a 'small animal' pounce into black water and 'emerge directly with a gleaming fish', Henry needs stronger medicine and, moving 'from obscurity into promises of a greater obscurity', he soon gets it. He blunders into the forest 'chapel' with its 'gentle brown carpet', its 'religious half light'; and the way in which he perceives this mere hole in the woods should recall his earlier view of death as a means of getting 'to some place where he would be understood'. This sentimental religious feeling is thus equated with Henry's sentimental view of nature, and both illusions are brutally shattered when he finds a rotting corpse in the 'chapel' where one would expect to find the altar. This putrid matter being eaten by ants does not suggest that death is any gateway to understanding, that nature has any aversion whatsoever to such tragedies, or that some sort of Christian doctrine is the theme of the novel. Rationalization which overrides one's personal honesty can only lead to moral death (as George Kelcey also demonstrates); death literally blocks Henry's way at this point, and he has to find a new direction.

His new direction comes when out of curiosity he runs towards a great roar of battle. This first tentative step towards emerging from the forest is consciously determined, and Henry is aware that it is 'an ironical thing for him to be running thus toward that which he had been at such pains to avoid'; but he now wants 'to come to the edge of the forest that he might peer out'. However, Henry then meets the tattered man—one of Crane's finest characters—whose question, 'Where yeh hit, ol' boy?' causes him to panic; and his guilt and sense of isolation immediately lead him to another illusion: 'he regarded the wounded soldiers in an envious way. He conceived persons with torn bodies to be peculiarly happy. He wished that he, too, had a wound'. To reveal to Henry the real absurdity of such thoughts, to puncture this insane illusion, Crane lets him witness the appalling death of Jim Conklin. And if this seems too slight an accomplishment for so intensely written a scene, one should remember that this whole section of the novel is, after all, a virtuoso performance in prolonging the delay of Henry's actual experience of combat. Also, Conklin's death is as necessary to Henry's education as his parallel encounter with the corpse was. In its presentation of human suffering considered specifically against the infinite back-drop of the amoral universe this scene is a young author's first attempt at coping with a theme that immensely interested him; hence, as only one critic has noted, there is absolutely no irony in the portrayal of Henry in this passage. 'Although Fleming cuts a rather pitiful figure under the towering sky, Crane's intention is not satirical. In fact this is one point in the book where the author seems to identify himelf wholly with his character.'[6] Henry rebels against the universe at this grotesque and meaningless death of a man he has known since boyhood, and his rebellion is simulta-

6. Olov W. Fryckstedt, 'Henry Fleming's Tupenny Fury: Cosmic Pressimism in Stephen Crane's *The Red Badge of Courage*', *Studia Neophilologica*, XXXIII (1961), 276.

neously as futile, as absurd, and as understandable as the belief of
the men in an open boat who think that fate will not drown them
because they have worked so hard to get within sight of shore. The
implicit truth behind the destruction of Henry's illusion is that
man's position in this world is bleak enough as it is without wishing
for any wounds to make it worse. Finally, it must be stated that the
text offers no evidence of Conklin's death accomplishing anything
else. Shortly thereafter, Henry commits his greatest sin: he deliberately deserts the tattered man who selflessly worries about others
even when he is himself at the edge of the grave.

Because of the importance of the tattered man in Henry's journey to awareness, this episode can reasonably be considered a parallel scene comparable to the two just examined. That is, the desertion of this dying man is in itself Henry's illusion. His bitter and
immediate self-loathing—'he now thought that he wished he was
dead'—foreshadows what Crane makes explicit in the final chapter:
the tattered man will always haunt Henry, not because of anything
he does to Henry, but because of what Henry does to him. This
desertion is the limit of Henry's penetration into the direful thicket
of cowardice, selfishness, and immaturity; and as he can go no further, he must once more seek a new direction—metaphorically the
only one left to him—a way out of the 'forest' and back to his original commitment.

Henry's subconscious desire to find his way back is revealed by
his envying the men of an advancing column so intensely that 'he
could have wept in his longings'. He immediately pictures himself
as 'a blue desperate figure leading lurid charges with one knee forward and a broken blade high—a blue, determined figure standing
before a crimson and steel assault, getting calmly killed'. These asi-
nine visions, in this context, are evoked by Henry's desire as a psychological thrust to counteract the opposing force of fear. Thus,
Henry begins a debate with himself: he wants to go forward, his
fear invents excuses, and his reason overcomes these excuses one by
one as they are raised. This debate ends in defeat only because
Henry believes there is absolutely no way in which he can return to
his regiment with self-respect. And this belief, of course, turns out
to be the illusion which forms the basis of his final episode in the
forest.

However, Henry's mental debate itself accomplishes two important results: it enables Henry to transcend by an effort of will his
most absurd selfishness—his wish for the defeat of his own army—
and it sufficiently calms his mind for him to realize, for the first
time since his original flight, that his physical condition—hunger,
thirst, extreme fatigue—suggests he is actually 'jest one little feller',
ordinary, weak, fallible. His inner debate ends when he sees the very

men with whom he had lately identified himself flee back through the woods in terror. He leaps into the midst of these panic-stricken men *in an attempt to rally them*, and receives his red badge of courage when one of them clubs him in the head with a rifle butt.

Crane probably seized upon this incident for his final title because of the complex ironies woven into it, because of its centrality to a story about courage and various sorts of wounds, and because Henry has to win his way to manhood by struggle as one wins a badge:

> he does not receive his wound in flight, but in the performance of an act of courage! Henry is struck down (by a coward) while inarticulately striving 'to make a rallying speech, to sing a battle hymn.' He is in a position to suffer such a wound because he has originally fled from his regiment, but he is going against the current of retreating infantry, *towards* the battle, when he gains the red badge.[7]

He has already revealed his intent, his desire to return. The external fact of the wound changes nothing whatsoever within Henry's mind. Chance merely provides the means for which he has already been searching, the means of returning to his regiment secure from outward ridicule. He is guided back by the cheery-voiced soldier, a man who helps others without vanity or even a wish for thanks, exactly as Henry should have helped the tattered man. Henry tells his lie —which ironically proves unnecessary—is nursed by Wilson and, being both physically and emotionally exhausted, is put to bed in his friend's blankets.

In terms of Crane's structural pattern, Henry is now back in his original position and again about to confront the unknown, still untried in battle—so he believes—still afraid. Nevertheless, the short story has become a novel, and within Henry's mind a major battle has been fought and won. Although he still does not know how he will act when he confronts the unknown, the bitter experience of this fantastic day's journey through the moral forest has brought Henry to secure knowledge of what he can *not* do when the time for this confrontation comes, for him, on the morrow.

His actions the next morning, however, are not reassuring. His vanity returns with his sense of security, he complains loudly, and he treats Wilson quite shabbily. This reassertion of the old Henry is demanded by dramatic necessity (if growth of character is contingent upon awareness Crane cannot very well make much of a change in Henry before he experiences actual combat), and Crane justifies it with great care by making it serve at least three functions.

7. Eric Solomon, 'The Structure of "The Red Badge of Courage" ', *Modern Fiction Studies*, V (Autumn, 1959), 230–1. See also John J. McDermott, 'Symbolism and Psychological Realism in *The Red Badge of Courage*', *Nineteenth-Century Fiction*, XXIII (Dec., 1968), 324–31.

Henry's undesirable traits first provide a necessary contrast in order to emphasize the change which has occurred in Wilson, who has already had his baptism of fire:

> He seemed no more to be continually regarding the proportions of his personal prowess. . . . He was no more a loud young soldier. There was about him now a fine reliance. He showed a quiet belief in his purposes and his abilities. . . . And the youth saw that ever after it would be easier to live in his friend's neighborhood.

Given Crane's technique of the parallel scene, this passage has to foreshadow the change which Henry will also undergo once he successfully faces up to his own commitment; it can have no other function.[8] Henry's vain foolishness at this point is also important as a contrast with his yesterday's view of himself—yesterday he had seen himself lower than all other men, and mocked by nature; today, like George Kelcey, he imagines himself 'a fine creation . . . the chosen of some gods', and he considers nature 'a fine thing moving with a magnificent justice'—and because these absurdities allow Crane to show that Henry is now capable of perceiving the falseness of his position. His 'pompous and veteranlike' thoughts are just as foolish, of course, as those he revealed during his flight; and neither passage presents Crane's own view of the universe and man's place in it.[9] But no one has noticed that these silly illusions form a carefully wrought sequence in themselves which begins with Henry's smug sense of power over Wilson because of the packet, rises to a climax of loud complaint, and ends suddenly when this swelling pomposity is 'pierced' by a fellow soldier's lazy comment: 'Mebbe yeh think yeh fit th' hull battle yestirday, Fleming.' Henry is *inwardly* 'reduced to an abject pulp by these chance words'. Henry, in short, has assumed a vain pose and has been acting out his role as if the external view of himself were all that mattered; the laconic comment pierces this pose by abruptly awakening Henry's conscience, and the whole external pose collapses before this inner voice's inflexible command that Henry view himself as he really is. This whole sequence, finally, helps Henry prepare psychologically to face up to the coming fight.

When the battle comes, Henry turns his reawakened self-loathing and self-hatred upon the enemy, and he chooses to stay and fight rather than run again into the terrible forest: 'He had taken up a first position behind the little tree, with a direct determination to

8. The precise parallel between Wilson and Fleming is discussed by William P. Safranek, 'Crane's *The Red Badge of Courage*', *Explicator*, XXVI (Nov., 1967), item 21.

9. Crane uses exactly the same device in a poem: two contrasting views of a morally neutral reality, the sea, are presented, and neither can legitimately be called Crane's own. See *The Poems of Stephen Crane*, ed. Joseph Katz (New York: Cooper Square, 1966), p. 84.

hold it against the world'. After making this willed commitment, Henry slips again into the trance of battle sleep, fights like a regular 'war devil', and after the skirmish he emerges from his trance with the praise of his comrades ringing in his ears.

> He had fought like a pagan who defends his religion. Regarding it, he saw that it was fine, wild, and, in some ways, easy. He had been a tremendous figure, no doubt. By this struggle he had overcome obstacles which he had admitted to be mountains. They had fallen like paper peaks, and he was now what he called a hero. And he had not been aware of the process. He had slept and, awakening, found himself a knight.

Henry has thus successfully *passed through* the unknown, the feared experience, and *this* time because he has not run he accepts the fact, even though, again because of battle sleep, he has not actually *experienced* the unknown itself. Hence, he has a great deal to ponder about. The excellent irony of this crucial episode is *not* that Henry has become a hero in his battle sleep—Crane never offers the reader such an absurd definition of heroism—but that during this sleep Henry has successfully passed through the very experience upon which his imagination and fear have been intensely centred since the beginning of the novel; the monumental irony is that Henry has endured all his suffering, all the tortures of his imagination, over an action which is so easily done that one can do it superbly while in a trance. The implications which follow from this ironic deflation should be clear to the reader, even if Henry is not yet capable of sorting them out: if the feared unknown, the hideous dragon of war, can be successfully encountered while one is in a trance, then Henry's former imaginings, fears, concepts of knightly heroism, all such feverish activity of his weak mental machinery, stand revealed as absurd. Henry, in other words, for the first time since the novel began, is now in a position to learn authentic self-knowledge, to perceive the reality which is actually before his eyes to be seen, and to acquire the humility which Wilson has already attained.

Henry's subsequent actions immensely favour this conclusion. He accepts his own insignificance when he overhears his regiment of 'mule drivers' ordered into an action from which few are expected to emerge alive. And, even though he knows the danger of the coming battle, there is no hesitation in Henry, no thought of flight. Hence, it follows reasonably from this deliberate courage that Henry should finally be able to experience actual combat in full possession of all his faculties. In fact, Crane insists upon Henry's awareness, both of the external and the inner reality, during this charge: 'It seemed to the youth that he saw everything. Each blade of the green grass was bold and clear . . . all were comprehended.

His mind took a mechanical but firm impression, so that afterward everything was pictured and explained to him, *save why he himself was there*' (my italics). The final phrase simply points to Henry's remembrance of his past failures. The frenzy of this charge, not a blind rage of battle sleep, is described as a 'temporary but sublime absence of selfishness. And because it was of this order was the reason, perhaps, why the youth wondered, afterward, what reasons he could have had for being there'. Henry, like the other men, still shows anger, pride, wild excitement; but such qualities are good ones for a soldier to have because they help him stand and fight, they could hardly be omitted from any realistic presentation of men at war, they do not make these men less than human, and Henry never again loses his grip on his consciousness because of them. These men reveal anger and pride in this situation precisely because they are men who hold themselves responsible for their own actions and seek the good opinion of their fellow men. Henry has yet to learn that if a man satisfies his own sense of personal honesty, this is enough; the opinions of others, just one more externality, will vary with the several views which others take of one's actions. Chapter 21 prepares Henry for this stoic lesson.

The elated regiment returns from their charge, only to be taunted by veterans who observe how little ground was covered. Henry soon accepts the view that the extent of the charge was comparatively 'trivial', even though he feels 'a considerable joy in musing upon his performances during the charge' (a joy which is not unreasonable when we recall that only yesterday Henry had fled in panic from this same situation). When a general states yet another point of view—that the charge was a military failure, and the 'mule drivers' now seem to him to be 'mud diggers'—the lieutenant's defence of his own men implies that a military failure is in itself no criterion of the performance of the men doing the fighting. And the chapter ends with Wilson and Fleming being told of the praise they have received from the lieutenant and colonel of their own regiment. Wilson and Fleming have every right to feel pleased at this praise; and the fact that they 'speedily forgot many things', that for them 'the past held no pictures of error and disappointment', does not indicate that they are mere automatons at the mercy of external circumstance: it indicates that in their first flush of pleasure they have not yet assimilated and considered this praise in the total perspective which is specifically demanded by the several points of view presented in this very chapter. There is no time for assimilation of anything at this point because the novel immediately roars on into yet another battle, a final skirmish in which Henry's actions confirm the self-control he has recently acquired. During this fight all the men act like veterans by tending strictly to business and Wilson even captures an enemy flag; after the battle he holds this prize 'with vanity' as he and Henry, both still caught up in the excitement of the moment, congratulate each other. The time for reflection and assimilation comes only with the final chapter when Henry walks away from the battle-field and is again free to probe into his own mind.

The endless critical squabbles which have arisen over this final chapter hinge upon a single question: does Fleming achieve any moral growth or development of character? Yet any Crane student should be able to answer this question almost without consulting this chapter at all—without reading Crane's description of Henry's change of soul which requires at least two pages in most editions. To claim that Fleming does *not* achieve any growth or development is to ignore many quite obvious statements of his gradual moral progress that are scattered throughout the novel, the entire function of Wilson's role, and the fact that Crane must have had some reason for endowing Henry—unlike the earlier protagonists—with awareness and a conscience. It is also well to remember that Crane is trying to be psychologically realistic: this is the *first* time Henry has full opportunity to reflect upon all the experiences which have crowded the past two days of his life, he is still a young lad not yet even twenty-four hours removed from the very nadir of self-abasement, and, like Wilson whose development preceded his own, Henry is still 'capable of vanity. Even in the final chapter of the novel, Crane still writes as of a process that is going on. Fleming's mind, he says, "was under-going a subtle change"; nevertheless, the final paragraphs describe that change in detail, and the unmistakable traits of genuine maturity . . . are present.'[1]

Crane devotes the first two pages, over a fourth of the chapter, to a careful preparation for the important matters which follow. The battle is over for the day, and, as the regiment ironically marches back over the same ground they had taken at great cost, the reader is taken directly into Henry's mind. He begins by rejoicing that he has come forth, escaped, from 'a land of strange, squalling upheavals'. The deliberately ambiguous language here should suggest *all* of Private Fleming's various battles, with the enemy, the 'arrayed forces of the universe', and his own weaknesses. Then Henry attempts to consider all that has happened to him from the point of view of the new perspective he has attained by living through these past two days. And here Crane is again explicit, neither ironic nor ambiguous:

he began to study his deeds, [both] his failures, and his achievements. Thus. fresh from scenes where many of his usual

1. Max R. Westbrook, 'Stephen Crane and the Revolt-Search Motif,' Ph.D. dissertation University of Texas, 1960, pp. 199–200.

machines of reflection had been idle . . . he struggled to marshal all his acts.

At last they marched before him clearly. From this present view point he was enabled to look at them in spectator fashion and to criticize them with some correctness, for his new condition had already defeated certain sympathies.

Henry's 'procession of memory' begins with the most recent events, his public deeds which are recalled with delight because they tell him 'he was good'. This recollection seems reasonable, so far as it goes; these public deeds, after all, have been good. But the next sentence reveals Henry's error a few moments before he himself corrects it: 'He recalled with a thrill of joy the respectful comments of his fellows upon his conduct'. Henry, in short, begins with his old error of judging himself by the opinion of others, by his external reputation. The entire remaining portion of his self-analysis consists of the assaults made upon this public image by the shameful recollections of his private deeds until, finally, an equilibrium is attained in which both public and private views of the self take permanent position in a realistic, balanced judgment. These emotionally powerful memories of his private misdeeds originally fell under three headings: his desertion from the regiment's first engagement, his "terrible combat with the arrayed forces of the universe', and his desertion of the tattered man. In the final version, the first act of desertion merged with the more vividly personal abandonment of the tattered man, and the resolution to the theme of Henry's battle with the universe was largely omitted.[2]

Thus, the great image which dominates these final pages as an inexorable 'spectre of reproach' is the 'dogging memory of the tattered soldier—he who, gored by bullets and faint for blood, had fretted concerning an imagined wound in another; he who had loaned his last of strength and intellect for the tall soldier; he who, blind with weariness and pain, had been deserted in the field'. The great care with which Crane makes Henry recall all the ramifications of this incident implies the deep impression it has made upon the youth. He cringes when this spectre looms before him: 'For an instant a wretched chill of sweat was upon him at the thought that he might be detected in the thing. As he stood persistently before his vision, he gave vent to a cry of sharp irritation and agony'. If read correctly this passage does not reveal a selfish vanity; it reveals only the continuity of Henry's thought. He is still basking in the

2. Although the resolution of this excised theme is presented ambiguously—Henry's 'deity laying about him with the bludgeon of correction' for whom 'no grain like him would be lost' can only be an illusion in Crane's amoral universe—Henry's conclusion resembles Crane's own view: 'those tempestuous moments were of the wild mistakes and ravings of a novice who did not comprehend. He had been a mere man railing at a condition. . . . The imperturbable sun shines on insult and worship'. See Fryckstedt, 'Tupenny Fury'.

warmth of his public deeds when this private horror suddenly
pierces and deflates, for him, his public image of himself. In order
to live with this awful ghost Henry has to redress his own judge-
ment of himself: he retains a concern for his external reputation—
few men of any age desire to have their shameful deeds made public
—but this vision finally forces him to accept the characteristic position of the mature man that his own inner view of himself is vastly
more important than the external opinions of others.

Henry never entirely banishes this ghost—an attainment which
would be as impossible in Crane's world as it would be in Hawthorne's—but he is able to place it in perspective, 'to put the sin at
a distance'. An excised passage which follows reveals that Henry
handles this sin as any intelligent man of conscience would handle
it, as a means of trampling upon his own ego to prevent his com-
mitting such a sin again. 'This plan for the utilization of a sin did
not give him complete joy but it was the best sentiment he could
formulate under the circumstances, and when it was combined with
his success, or public deeds, he knew that he was quite contented'.
Henry is being neither vain nor callous in this decision; he is merely
being practical and realistic. No better use of a past sin is possible
in Crane's world. And if this sin is a real and permanent part of his
past, so are his good actions during the day's fighting: if Henry is to
see himself as he really is, he must consider both 'his failures, and
his achievements'.

Once he attains this balanced view of himself, he is able to fore-
see 'some new ways' of life for him in the future: 'He found that he
could look back upon the brass and bombast of his earlier gospels
and see them truly. He was gleeful when he discovered that he now
despised them'. Henry's weak mental machinery, in short, has
undergone considerable readjustment. His eyes have finally opened,
and he is now able to begin perceiving correctly the reality which
has been before him and largely unchanged since the novel began.
Henry's personal honesty can now assert itself in morally significant
action, and he is ready to begin the difficult practice of manhood in
an amoral universe.

> *With this conviction* [my italics] came a store of assurance. He
> felt a quiet manhood, nonassertive but of sturdy and strong
> blood. He knew that he would no more quail before his guides
> wherever they should point. He had been to touch the great
> death, and found that, after all, it was but the great death. He
> was a man.

I am unable to find much irony in the closing paragraphs of the
novel. Henry is exhausted from all his battles and gratefully marching to a rest. Only the most romantically obtuse reader at this point
could believe in the actuality of 'an existence of soft and eternal

peace', but the image aptly describes how inviting the coming rest must seem to a weary young soldier. Certainly Henry is not fooling himself; his quiet confidence that he will 'no more quail before his guides wherever they should point' would be meaningless if he really anticipated an existence of soft and eternal peace. And the final image seems to me merely an emblem of what has just happened to Henry. He has attained authentic self-knowledge and a sense of manhood after long and fierce battles with his own moral weaknesses; hence it seems entirely appropriate that Crane should end this tale with the image of a golden ray of sunlight appearing through hosts of leaden rain clouds. Irony has its function earlier in Crane's pattern, before the protagonist becomes aware of the reality he struggles to perceive correctly.

ROBERT M. RECHNITZ

Depersonalization and the Dream in *The Red Badge of Courage*†

I

Studies of *The Red Badge of Courage* continue to question whether the intention of the novel's final paragraphs is literal or ironic. Most of the recent critics lean toward a literal interpretation and assert that Henry Fleming gains a measured and realistic understanding of himself and his world.[1] James B. Colvert's conclusion is representative: " . . . when he [Henry] sees them in spectator fashion . . . events in reality seem to fit into a comprehensible order."[2]

I believe that the possibility of Henry's gaining any such spectator-like objectivity is highly unlkely. In believing so, I am partially reverting to Charles C. Walcutt's judgment that the final four paragraphs of the novel

> are a climax of self-delusion. If there is any one point that has been made it is that Henry has never been able to evaluate his

† *Studies in the Novel*, VI (Spring, 1974), 76–87. Copyright by *Studies in the Novel*. Reprinted by permission of North Texas State University.

1. See, for example any of the following: Stanley B. Greenfield, "The Unmistakable Stephen Crane," *PMLA*, 73 (Dec., 1958), 562–72; John E. Hart, "*The Red Badge of Courage* as Myth and Symbol," *University of Kansas City Review*, 19 (Summer, 1953), 249–56; Maynard Solomon, "Stephen Crane: A Critical Study," *Masses and Mainstream*, 9 (Jan., 1955), 32–41; and, of course, R. W. Stallman, Introduction to the Modern Library edition of *The Red Badge of Courage*. For two more recent straightforward readings see John Fraser, "Crime and Forgiveness: The Red Badge in Time of War," *Criticism*, 9 (Summer, 1967), 243–56; and John J. McDermott, "Symbolism and Psychological Realism in *The Red Badge of Courage*," *Nineteenth-Century Fiction*, 23 (Dec., 1968), 324–31.

2. James B. Colvert, "Structure and Theme in Stephen Crane's Fiction," *Modern Fiction Studies*, 5 (Autumn, 1959), 207.

conduct. He may have been fearless for moments, but his motives were vain, selfish, ignorant, and childish. . . . He has . . . for moments risen above his limitations, but Crane seems plainly to be showing that he has not achieved a lasting wisdom or self-knowledge.[3]

Walcutt suggests that Henry's ultimate understanding is clouded because it is distorted by the subjective delusions which have infused his perceptions throughout the novel. I depart from Walcutt, and take the position that Henry, in the course of his experience, exchanges his subjective delusions for a socially derived and sanctioned vision, an alleged objectivity, which is as far removed from reality as was his abandoned private vision. In exchanging private delusion for public, Henry finds a home in the army, just as Jim Conklin had before him, but the price is exorbitant. Becoming the good soldier, he becomes less the individual being; and he emerges in the concluding paragraphs in serene possession of an unauthentic soldier-self, ominously ready to follow his leader.

The little autonomy he possesses at the beginning is immediately threatened. He had entered the army intent upon realizing youthful dreams of glory. These private delusions are soon replaced by the incommunicable anguish and fears which are a natural part of the lull before the battle. Along in the "light yellow shade" of his hut, he wonders whether he will have guts enough to stand and fight when his times comes. His imagination, which is nourishing this private fear, gains its matter not from Henry's own limited experience but from that of his society. The veterans have told him of the enemy, "gray, bewhiskered hordes . . . tremendous bodies of fierce soldiery who were sweeping along like the Huns." Though Henry does not "put a whole faith in veterans' tales," he does tend to give greater credence to their reports than to the witness of his own senses. The tales of the veterans follow and displace his own observation of the rebel picket who had called him a " 'right dum good feller.' "

This contest between individual and group perceptions, or, more precisely, between individual and social evaluation of personal perceptions continues throughout the novel. Much of the action depicts Henry's attempts to honor his personal interpretations, but the final outcome is foreshadowed in this present episode. The authority of personal interpretation crumbles under the massive testimony of the group. Eventually, Henry cannot believe his eyes.

He is by no means mere victim in this process. Henry is tempted to surrender his interpretive faculties to the group upon discovering that his fears are abated when leagued with those of his comrades.

3. Charles Child Walcutt, *American Literary Naturalism, A Divided Stream* (Minneapolis: University of Minnesota Press, 1956), pp. 81–82.

After hearing Jim Conklin say that he might run if the others did, Henry "felt gratitude for these words of his comrade. He had feared that all of the untried men possessed a great and correct confidence. He now was in a measure reassured." Henry can thus choose to sink his individuality in group anonymity and diminish his fear by partaking of the group's strength.

Since such a maneuver, demanding a surrender of autonomy, simultaneously appeals to and repels him, Henry compromises; he maintains an ambivalence toward his group allegiance, wryly dubbing his outfit "the blue demonstration." This ambivalence, this desire to assert his individuality and the equally pressing need to abandon it, runs through not merely the opening chapters but the entire book. Yet in the world of *Red Badge*, there can be no doubt whatsoever about the outcome. Henry must surrender his individuality for the sake of simple survival.

He does so, however, begrudgingly, his ambivalence always in evidence. For example, Henry relies upon and damns his officers with monotonous regularity. One morning, in the ranks of his regiment ready at last to march into the unknown under the red eyes of the enemy troops across the river, Henry gazes into the east, and in his need for leadership he sees against the sun "black and patternlike . . . the gigantic figure of the colonel on a gigantic horse." *Patternlike* is the key word here, the presence of the officer obliterating Henry's fear and confusion. But *black* is equally important, carrying as it does the threat of annihilation of self. This probability is forgotten though, as "the rolling crashes of an engagement come to his ears," and the officer, displaying beneficent self control, "lift[s] his gigantic arm and calmly stroke[s] his mustache."

The threat of lost individuality is also forgotten when the men finally move into combat and Henry yields himself totally to the saving embrace of the group:

> He became not a man but a member. He felt that something of which he was a part . . . was in a crisis. He was welded into a common personality which was dominated by a single desire. . . . [The noise of the regiment] gave him assurance. . . . It wheezed and banged with a mighty power. . . . There was a consciousness always of the presence of his comrades about him. He felt the subtle battle brotherhood more potent even than the cause for which they were fighting. It was a mysterious fraternity born of the smoke and danger of death.

Crane's description of the fearlessness his soldiers enjoy during this part of the battle is similar to an account of the loss of fear on the part of concentration-camp inmates given in Bruno Bettelheim's *Informed Heart.* Forced to stand in the cold without adequate clothing and any chance to help their dying friends, the prisoners con-

352 · *Robert M. Rechnitz*

fronted a "situation which obviously the prisoner as an individual could not meet successfully."

Therefore, the individual as such had to disappear in the mass. Threats by the guards become ineffective because the mental attitude of most prisoners was now changed. Whereas before they had feared for themselves and tried to protect themselves as well as possible, they now became depersonalized. It was as if giving up individual existence and becoming part of a mass seemed in some way to offer better chances for survival, if not for the person, at least for the group.[4]

But just as the prisoners are unable to sustain their fearlessness and sense of power, so Henry soon feels his courage drain from him, and in the following exchange of fire he runs away. Henry's flight has been foreshadowed by more than his fearful anticipations before the battle. His perception of the officers as benign authorities who promise an end to chaos and the comfort he has derived from the ambience of the "blue demonstration" has been qualified by his growing suspicion that the officers are idiots who send the men "marching into a regular pen." The "blue demonstration" threatens to rob him of his will; marching into battle he sees "that it would be impossible for him to escape from the regiment. It inclosed him. And there were iron laws of tradition and law on four sides. He was in a moving box."

Consequently, though motivated by fear, Henry's flight has implications of which Henry remains unaware but which suggest themselves to the reader because of the traditional nature of the flight itself. Like a great number of American literary figures—Huck, Rip, Goodman Brown, the *persona* of "Song of Myself," an endless list of others—Henry abandons his society and lights out for the territories. One more romantic egoist, Henry resigns his membership in the society which would demand from him the relinquishment of his perfect freedom. Though he is most assuredly no student, he would seem to have imbibed his share of Transcendentalism from the very air of nineteenth-century America and would claim for himself Emerson's "infinitude of the private man."

But in the following moment, the reader is reminded that this is *Red Badge* and not Emerson's *Nature*. Henry enters the forest chapel and learns, most hideously, that the woods will no longer serve as nursery to the burgeoning soul:

Near the threshold he stopped, horror-stricken at the sight of a thing.
He was being looked at by a dead man who was seated with his back against a column-like tree. The corpse was dressed in a

4. Bruno Bettelheim, *The Informed Heart* (Glencoe. Ill.: The Free Press, 1960), p. 137.

uniform that once had been blue, but was now faded into a melancholy shade of green. The eyes, staring at the youth, had changed to the dull hue to be seen on the side of a dead fish. The mouth was open. Its red had changed to an appalling yellow.

This scene marks the impasse at which, one after the other, the romantic heroes of the last half of the nineteenth century find themselves. Huck discovers that the Mississippi flows inexorably into the heartland of slavery, and James's Isabel Archer, to name only one other, discovers that the highroad of unlimited choice terminates within the walls of the Palazzo Roccanera. Henry Fleming learns to his horror that nature culminates in the forest chapel.

Nature and morality, once fused by the transcendentalists, are now divided, and the division has wide-ranging consequences. First, nature itself becomes foreign and treacherous. The branches in the forest chapel threaten to push Henry onto the corpse. Second, the individualism that Henry is capable of imagining as a substitute for his life in the army is no longer Emersonian, no longer expansive and life-enhancing, but isolating, atomistic. Self-reliance, drained of moral content by the time Crane is writing, has degenerated to mere selfishness. Whitman's "man in the open air" has become only a corpse propped against a tree. The third consequence is societal and needs a further paragraph of amplification.

Made aware of his experience with the corpse of the inadequacy of his individualism, Henry tries to rejoin the army. Marching up the road in a crowd of soldiers, Henry "regarded the wounded soldiers in an envious way. He conceived persons with torn bodies to be peculiarly happy. He wished that he, too, had a wound, a red badge of courage." This image appears in the first paragraph of chapter 9 and is paired at the end of the chapter with a highly similar image, the notorious: "The red sun was pasted in the sky like a wafer." The referent of "wafer" must remain a puzzle, but perhaps it is of little importance. The crucial fact about the sentence is its reductive effect. The setting sun is reduced to a trivial, two-dimensional dot merely pasted in the sky. This reduction may be considered as a further consequence of the lost transcendental fusion of nature and morality. Associating the paired images suggests, and added consideration confirms, that the image at the first part of the chapter is also perhaps reductive. To think of a wound as a badge is, indeed, to trivialize human suffering. Furthermore, we may say that if the nature-morality split diminishes nature, the same split brutalizes society. Henry knows that it is in society's eyes that a wound is a badge of courage. Society, stripped of morality, then, is not community, but is brutal collectivity. Consequently, Henry's hungering for a wound signifies a desire to surrender personal morality to the demands of collectivization, a sacrifice which perhaps Crane sensed might be increasingly demanded of men in the twentieth century.

Henry, on the other hand, has no comprehension of the moral implications of the wound, but he is a witness to its physical import when he sees Jim Conklin die. Conklin has served from the novel's opening as a warning, apparent only in retrospect, against whole-hearted identification with the group. Prior to their first battle, Conklin exhibits a blissful unconcern. This compliance with the dictates of the war machine marks him for destruction; and in the moments of his death, he remains in some hideous, indefinable way, a willing collaborator in the perverted mystic ceremony of war: "There was something ritelike in these movements of the doomed soldier. And there was a resemblance in him to a devotee of a mad religion, blood-sucking, muscle-wrenching, bone crushing." Like a "devotee of a mad religion," Conklin enacts the roles of both priest and sacrifice. The passive surrender of personal initiative in his early behavior culminates in a sort of self-destruction.

Having witnessed Conklin's death, Henry can no longer yearn for a red badge, that emblem of membership in the group, for he sees that the badge is deadly. He is forced in chapter 10 to take up the other alternative, which if not he then at least the reader already realizes is equally hopeless, his earlier atomistic individualism. In fact, so empty are the alternatives, that it is not until he is goaded into choosing by the mindless yammering of the zombie-like tattered soldier that Henry decides to run. But as the forest chapel scene demonstrated, individualism offers no adequate sanctuary, and in a short time Henry is led back to his regiment.

II

With Henry's return at the beginning of the second half of the novel, the dominant motif, that archetypal American movement of alternating escape and return, is several times repeated, even though there is no possibility of any genuine escape. The attempted escapes, however, are no longer physical; rather, they become a matter of allegiances and commitments. When Henry's individuality dominates, he curses the army. As the novel moves closer to its conclusion, he identifies increasingly with the army.

Quite understandably, Henry's initial loyalty upon returning is to the regiment. Wounded and exhausted, he sees in the figures of the sleeping men an image of content, and after having his wound dressed he sleeps among his comrades. But in chapter 14 he awakes; "He believed for an instant that he was in the house of the dead, and he did not dare to move lest these corpses start up, squalling and squawking." Only a moment passes before he realizes that "this

somber picture was not a fact of the present, but a mere prophecy."
The prophecy is accurate on two levels: first, of course, many of the
men will be killed in the forthcoming skirmishes. But, second, the
men are all doomed to die in a spiritual sense as they surrender
themselves more and more to the demands of the army.

With some sort of recognition of this second meaning, Henry is
unwilling to accept the officers' leadership. At the beginning of the
new day's combat, furious at the evidence of the Union defeat,
Henry cries out, " 'B'jiminey, we're generaled by a lot 'a
lunkheads.' " Wilson, however in terms reminiscent of Jim Conklin's, defends the commanding general: " 'Mebbe, it wa'n't all his
fault—not all together. He did th' best he knowed. It's our luck t'
git licked often,' said his friend in a weary tone. He was trudging
along with stooped shoulders and shifting eyes like a man who has
been caned and kicked." Wilson may have the better of the argument, but he is a beaten man. The great cost of what we may call
his collective vision is but partially revealed in this passage.

It is more fully revealed as further instances of the collective
vision are disclosed. In the following action, "deeply absorbed as a
spectator," Henry observed the battle:

> The regiment bled extravagantly. Grunting bundles of blue
> began to drop. The orderly sergeant of the youth's company was
> shot through the cheeks. Its supports being injured. his jaw hung
> afar down, disclosing in the wide cavern of his mouth a pulsing
> mass of blood and teeth. And with it all he made attempts to cry
> out. In his endeavor there was a dreadful earnestness, as if he
> conceived that one great shriek would make him well.

Though the events being described here are horrible, the style
drains them of emotional content. This is precisely the cost of the
collective vision—affectlessness. Throughout the novel, Crane's
famous irony insists upon the unspeakable lesson: as he continues
to surrender his autonomy to the overwhelming pressure of collectivization, modern man will most likely lose even the capacity to
feel.

Another characteristic of the collective view might be noted here.
Possibly, it is not so "enlarging and ruthlessly revealing" as critic
James Colvert says.[5] On their way to fill the canteens, Henry and
Wilson have a chance for a collective view of the battle:

> From their position . . . they could of course comprehend a
> greater amount of the battle than when their visions had been
> blurred by the hurling smoke of the line. They could see dark
> stretches winding along the land, and on one cleared space there
> was a row of guns making gray clouds, which were filled with

5. Colvert, p. 200.

large flashes of orange-colored flame. Over some foliage they could see the roof of a house. One window, glowing a deep murder red, shone squarely through the leaves. From the edifice a tall leaning tower of smoke went far into the sky.

It is true that this view is enlarging, but only in spatial terms, and with such a view one is bound to feel insignificant. But it should be noted that it is in such passages that Crane's style is at its most impressionistic. Though the view is broad, it consists of no more than a bundle of discrete images, for neither Henry nor the narrator supplies the conceptual strands which would weave the images into a fabric of meaning. The passage even suggests that meaning might be impossible to achieve on any plane more profound than the purely aesthetic one, impressionism having, as Richard Chase points out, "implications that are pessimistic, irrationalist, and amoral since its technique is to break down into a shimmering flow of experience the three dimensions that symbolized rationality and religious and social order in traditional art."[6]

Finally, on the psychological level, it must be noted that these paragraphs of the collective mass view follow immediately upon a passage that demands distancing and impressionism if one is to retain his sanity. Jimmie Rogers has been wounded: "He was thrashing about in the grass, twisting his shuddering body into many strange postures. He was screaming loudly. This instant's hesitation seemed to fill him with a tremendous, fantastic contempt, and he damned them in shrieked sentences." And off Henry and Wilson go with the canteens. The collective view here, then, seems motivated not by any desire to see reality, but rather to escape it. Motivation need not wholly determine perception, but it certainly qualifies it as we know. At any rate, all the considerations I am discussing here combine to suggest that the collective view may serve not only to humble a man but to delude and diminish him.

More references to man's diminished stature follow. The officers are referred to as "critical shepherds struggling with sleep." The regiment itself is lost in the noise of battle, the battle, in turn, lost in a world "fully interested in other matters." These images serve as background for Henry's and Wilson's crucial withholding from the men their knowledge of the great dangers involved in the impending charge. As a consequence, the virtues implicit in that decision are undermined. Without doubt, their choice to remain silent has elements of selflessness, loyalty, and certainly valor. But the context of the decision suggests that they remain mute also because they are feeling the pressures of the collective vision and its attendant, self-diminishing impressionism.

6. Richard Chase, Introduction to *The Red Badge of Courage* (Boston: Houghton Mifflin, 1960), p. xii.

In the climactic battle of the book, Henry yields to those pressures. Charging across the field "like a madman," Henry undergoes the change he had yearned for before the battle. Unprotected and essentially alone, thirsting for help and protection, he finds it in the flag, "a creation of beauty and invulnerability . . . a goddess, radiant . . . that called him with the voice of his hopes. Because no harm could come to it he endowed it with power." Unable to protect himself, Henry again chooses to submerge himself in the group; but this time he does so wholeheartedly, abandoning that remnant of individuality that had insisted earlier upon a wry aloofness from the group, derisively dubbing it the "blue demonstration." With the identification he makes now, Henry finds the strength to conduct himself nobly in battle, but there can be no mistake about the price he has unwittingly paid. The flag he carries, the emblem of group allegiance, does not belong to living men. The corpse from whom they wrest it tries to warn Henry and Wilson that to serve the flag is to die, but the warning is of no avail. "One arm [of the corpse] swung high, and the curved hand fell with heavy protest on the friend's unheeding shoulder."

In the final chapters, the ultimate consequences of Henry's unqualified identification with the group unfold. This is accomplished primarily by a continued alternation of two points of view, the private and the collective, until Henry wholly surrenders his belief in the validity of his own perceptions and memories.

Having driven off the light contingent of rebels, the regiment, at the end of chapter 20, regains the "impetus of enthusiasm." But when they return to their line and the mockery of the veterans, they quickly lose it. Henry looks back at the ground they have just covered:

> He discovered that the distances, as compared with the brilliant measurings of his mind, were trivial and ridiculous. The stolid trees, where much had taken place, seemed incredibly near. The time, too, now that he reflected, he saw to have been short. . . . Elfin thoughts must have exaggerated and enlarged everything, he said.
>
> It seemed, then, that there was bitter justice in the speeches of the gaunt and bronzed veterans.

Now the point is not that here, regarding his actions in spectator fashion, he is right and earlier wrong, for actually both impressions are correct. At the time of the battle, Henry's perception was accurate, the way was long and hard; in denying this, in accepting the point of view of the veterans, Henry betrays himself and his fellows. The glance of disdain he gives them is, however, not simply unjust. It is a tacit denial of the testimony of his own senses. Having made this, Henry is all the more vulnerable to the opinion of the general that the men are nothing but "a lot of mud diggers."

Of course the men all rage at this unjust treatment. Their personal perceptions are still weighty enough to prevent their utter abasement by the opinion of the officer. But Crane is extremely shrewd at this point. If the men are able to maintain their personal points of view in the face of the officers' condemnations, they are not able to hold out against their praise. Told that the colonel said they deserve to be "major generals," Henry and Wilson are elated, "and their hearts swelled with grateful affection for the colonel and the youthful lieutenant." Given what Crane has told us about the psychology of the battlefield, we question whether the officers' praise has any meaning. But the real importance of the chapter lies in its revelation of the degree to which Henry's opinion of himself is becoming increasingly determined by the official version of his behavior.

Therefore, after the following victory and subsequent retreat (the logic of the battlefield remaining absurd to the end) when Henry remembers his behavior, his reflections are not easily acceptable as reliable judgment of his past:

he began to study his deeds, his failures, and his achievements. Thus, fresh from scenes where many of his usual machines of reflection had been idle, from where he had proceeded sheeplike, he struggled to marshal all his acts.

At last they marched before him clearly. From this present viewpoint he was enabled to look upon them in spectator fashion and to criticize them with some correctness, for his new condition had already defeated certain sympathies.

By now there can be little doubt in our minds that viewing events in "spectator fashion" offers no assurance of discovering the truth. The spectator's way is the collective way, the way of the officers, remote, impressionistic, inhumanly dispassionate. Contrary to his opinion, Henry has not been "good," a moral term which has questionable validity as applied to men in the chaos of combat. And in a moment, his self-congratulations congeal as, in a "wretched chill of sweat," he recalls his desertion of the tattered soldier. "A specter of reproach came to him. There loomed the dogging memory of the tattered soldier—he who, gored by bullets and faint for blood, had fretted concerning an imagined wound in another; he who had loaned his last of strength and intellect for the tall soldier; he who, blind with weariness and pain, had been deserted in the field."

But this recollection, too, is inaccurate. It is true that Henry deserted him, and it is perhaps true that this was indeed profoundly criminal; but in being inaccurate, in constructing as he does here a sentimentalized version of the tattered soldier, a version replete with the sentimental cadences of the fundamentalist pulpit, he is being criminal again. He left the tattered soldier because of a complex of reasons and circumstances, which we can sum up by saying that he was being forced to take up the red badge of the mass man but chose at that desperate moment the alternative of atomistic individualism.

Perhaps the choice was wrong. It certainly served as no viable alternative. But in not adequately comprehending in this last chapter the stakes and circumstances that were then involved, and in "maturely" forgiving himself a little for that "sin"—without fully understanding its real nature—Henry runs a great risk of slipping ever more deeply into the role of mindless foot soldier. And we must consequently shudder when Henry, marching along with his fellows, knows "that he would no more quail before his guides wherever they should point." For we end almost where we began: to escape his fear of isolation, Henry will lose himself, not in the wryly dubbed "blue demonstration," but in something far more insidious, the "procession of weary soldiers" of the novel's final page.

III

Given the reading I have offered, it is impossible to take the final four paragraphs as either intentionally straightforward or ironic in tone. My insistence upon the wholly unambiguous implications of Henry's final commitment to his regiment nullifies the possibility of a straightforward reading and renders the irony so painfully obvious as to make of Crane a hopelessly inept artist. That being emphatically not the case, I conclude with Richard Chase that these paragraphs reflect Crane's embarrassment "about the necessity of pointing a moral."[7]

Yet, I would go further and suggest the possibility that Crane was a victim of more than just the demands of the reading public of his time. In including these final paragraphs, Crane is being strongly prompted to refuse to acknowledge the logic of his own art by a cultural force. In spite of the corpse in the forest chapel, the death of Emersonian self-reliance it symbolizes, Crane is compelled to insist upon his anti-institutional legacy, the anarchic dream of Emerson and Thoreau. Henry again escapes, if only in thought, to roam fields of clover and fresh meadows.

Crane insists in these last paragraphs upon Emersonian individualism, upon the impossible American dream of escape from history. Though it tear art works apart, as it does the last of this one, as it does the final fifth of *Huckleberry Finn*, and though it sink the nation, as it does the *Pequod*, the dream persists, measuring our institutions and, no less important, our lives. Having dramatized the

7. Ibid., p. xiii.

forces in modern America which were increasingly demanding the subservience of human needs to those of the machine, Crane insists at the final moment—unconvincingly—that man might escape his self-imposed servitude. By doing so, Crane in effect redefines the dream, showing in the vastly limited possibility of its realization how precious is its vision of Emersonian individualism.

Red Badge, then, takes its place with those other works in our literature that constitute an evolving definition of that complex, protean American Dream of anarchic freedom. Wildly extravagant, certainly no proper goal if we are to survive as a free society, that dream must yet be cherished, indeed now more than in the past, as the profoundly valuable counterweight to the increasingly urgent search for community that is properly bound to occupy Americans in the decades to come.

Selected Bibliography

STEPHEN CRANE

Novels
Maggie: A Girl of the Streets (1893)
The Red Badge of Courage (1895)
George's Mother (1896)
The Third Violet (1897)
Active Service (1899)
The O'Ruddy (with Robert Barr) (1903)

Short Stories and Sketches
The Little Regiment (1896)
The Open Boat (1898)
The Monster (1899)
Whilomville Stories (1900)
Wounds in the Rain (1900)
Last Words (1902)

Poetry
The Black Riders (1895)
War Is Kind (1899)

Collected Editions
The Complete Novels of Stephen Crane. Edited by Thomas A. Gullason. Garden City: Doubleday, 1967.
The Complete Short Stories and Sketches of Stephen Crane. Edited by Thomas A. Gullason. Garden City: Doubleday, 1963.
The Poems of Stephen Crane: A Variorum Edition. Edited by Joseph Katz. New York: Cooper Square, 1966.
Stephen Crane: Letters. Edited by R. W. Stallman and Lillian Gilkes. New York: New York University Press, 1960.
The Work of Stephen Crane, ed. Wilson Follett. 12 vols. New York: Alfred A. Knopf, 1925–27. Reprinted New York: Russell & Russell, 1963.
The Works of Stephen Crane. Edited by Fredson Bowers. 10 vols. Charlottesville: University Press of Virginia, 1969–.

LATE NINETEENTH-CENTURY LITERARY HISTORY

Berthoff, Warner. *The Ferment of Realism: American Literature, 1884–1919*. New York: Free Press, 1965.
Martin, Jay. *Harvests of Change: American Literature, 1865–1914*. Englewood Cliffs: Prentice-Hall, 1967.
Pizer, Donald. *Realism and Naturalism in Nineteenth-Century American Literature*. Carbondale: Southern Illinois University Press, 1966. Reprinted New York: Russell & Russell, 1976.
Walcutt, Charles C. *American Literary Naturalism, A Divided Stream*. Minneapolis: University of Minnesota Press, 1956.
Ziff, Larzer. *The American 1890s: Life and Times of a Lost Generation*. New York: Viking, 1966.

GENERAL BIBLIOGRAPHY, BIOGRAPHY, AND CRITICISM

Bibliography
Blanck, Jacob. "Stephen Crane." In *Bibliography of American Literature*, Vol. II. New Haven: Yale University Press, 1957.
Stallman, R. W. *Stephen Crane: A Critical Bibliography*. Ames: Iowa State University Press, 1972.

Collections of Criticism
Bassan, Maurice, ed. *Stephen Crane: A Collection of Critical Essays*. Englewood Cliffs: Prentice-Hall, 1967.

Gullason, Thomas A., ed. *Stephen Crane's Career: Perspectives and Evaluations.* New York: New York University Press, 1971.

Katz, Joseph, ed. *Stephen Crane in Transition: Centenary Essays.* DeKalb: Northern Illinois University Press, 1972.

Weatherford, Richard M., ed. *Stephen Crane: The Critical Heritage.* Boston: Routledge & Kegan Paul, 1973.

Books

Beer, Thomas. *Stephen Crane: A Study in American Letters.* With an Introduction by Joseph Conrad. New York: Alfred A. Knopf, 1923. Reprinted New York: Octagon, 1972.

Berryman, John. *Stephen Crane.* New York: Sloane, 1950. Reprinted New York: Octagon, 1975.

Cady, Edwin H. *Stephen Crane.* New York: Twayne, 1962.

Cazemajou, Jean. *Stephen Crane (1871–1900) Ecrivain-Journaliste.* Paris: Librairie Didier, 1969.

Gilkes, Lillian. *Cora Crane: A Biography of Mrs. Stephen Crane.* Bloomington: Indiana University Press, 1960.

Hoffman, Daniel G. *The Poetry of Stephen Crane.* New York: Columbia University Press, 1957.

Holton, Milne. *Cylinder of Vision: The Fiction and Journalistic Writing of Stephen Crane.* Baton Rouge: Louisiana State University Press, 1972.

LaFrance, Marston. *A Reading of Stephen Crane.* New York: Oxford University Press, 1971.

Linson, Corwin K. *My Stephen Crane.* Syracuse: Syracuse University Press, 1958.

Solomon, Eric. *Stephen Crane: From Parody to Realism.* Cambridge: Harvard University Press, 1966.

Stallman, R. W. *Stephen Crane.* New York: George Braziller, 1968.

Articles and Parts of Books

Brennan, Joseph X. "Stephen Crane and the Limits of Irony." *Criticism,* XI (Spring, 1969), 183–200.

Colvert, James B. "Structure and Theme in Stephen Crane's Fiction." *Modern Fiction Studies,* V (Autumn, 1959), 199–208.

———. "Style as Invention." In *Stephen Crane in Transition: Centenary Essays,* edited by Joseph Katz. DeKalb: Northern Illinois University Press, 1972.

Geismar, Maxwell. "Stephen Crane: Halfway House." In *Rebels and Ancestors: The American Novel, 1890–1915.* Boston: Houghton Mifflin, 1953.

Johnson, George W. "Stephen Crane's Metaphor of Decorum." *PMLA,* LXXVIII (June, 1963), 250–56.

Knapp, Daniel. "Son of Thunder: Stephen Crane and the Fourth Evangelist." *Nineteenth-Century Fiction,* XXIV (December, 1969), 253–91.

Kwiatt, Joseph J. "The Newspaper Experience: Crane, Norris, and Dreiser." *Nineteenth-Century Fiction,* VIII (September, 1953), 99–117.

———. "Stephen Crane and Painting." *American Quarterly,* IV (Winter, 1952), 331–38.

Leaver, Florence. "Isolation in the Work of Stephen Crane." *South Atlantic Quarterly* LXI (Autumn, 1962), 521–32.

Overland, Orm. "The Impressionism of Stephen Crane." In *Americana Norvegica,* Vol. I, edited by Sigmund Skard and Henry H. Wasser. Philadelphia: University of Pennsylvania Press, 1966.

Rogers, Rodney O. "Stephen Crane and Impressionism." *Nineteenth-Century Fiction,* XXIV (December, 1969), 292–304.

Shroeder, John W. "Stephen Crane Embattled." *University of Kansas City Review,* XVII (Winter, 1950), 119–29.

Stein, William B. "Stephen Crane's *Homo Absurdus.*" *Bucknell Review,* VIII (May, 1959), 168–88.

Weimer, David R. "The Landscape of Hysteria: Stephen Crane." In *The City as Metaphor.* Gloucester: Peter Smith, 1966.

Wells, H. G. "Stephen Crane from an English Standpoint." *North American Review,* CLXXI (August, 1900), 233–42.

Wertheim, Stanley. "Stephen Crane and the Wrath of Jehovah." *Literary Review,* VII (Summer, 1964), 499–508.

Westbrook, Max. "Stephen Crane's Social Ethic." *American Quarterly,* XIV (Winter, 1962), 587–96.

———. "Stephen Crane: The Pattern of Affirmation." *Nineteenth-Century Fiction,* XIV (December, 1959), 219–30.

———. "Stephen Crane and the Personal Universal." *Modern Fiction Studies,* VIII (Winter, 1962–63), 351–60.

THE RED BADGE OF COURAGE

Articles included in this volume are omitted here.

Significant Editions

The Red Badge of Courage. Edited by John T. Winterich. London: The Folio Society, 1951. (Uncanceled passages restored.)

Stephen Crane: An Omnibus. Edited by R. W. Stallman. New York: Alfred A. Knopf, 1952. (Uncanceled passages restored.)

The Red Badge of Courage. Edited by R. W. Stallman. New York: Signet Books, 1960. (Some rejected draft passages published.)

The Red Badge of Courage. Edited by Joseph Katz. Columbus: Charles E. Merrill, 1969. (A facsimile of the 1895 first edition.)

The Red Badge of Courage: A Facsimile Edition of the Manuscript. Edited by Fredson Bowers. Washington, D.C.: NCR/Microcard, 1972.

Sources of *The Red Badge of Courage*

Ahnebrink, Lars. *The Beginnings of Naturalism in American Fiction, 1891–1903.* Cambridge: Harvard University Press, 1950. Reprinted New York: Russell & Russell, 1961.

Anderson, Warren D. "Homer and Stephen Crane." *Nineteenth-Century Fiction,* XIX (June, 1964), 77–86.

Dusenberg, Robert. "The Homeric Mood in *The Red Badge of Courage.*" *Pacific Coast Philology,* III (April, 1968), 31–37.

Eby, Cecil D. "The Source of Crane's Metaphor, '*Red Badge of Courage.*'" *American Literature,* XXXII (May, 1960), 204–207.

Gullason, Thomas A. "New Sources for Stephen Crane's War Motif." *Modern Language Notes,* LXXII (December, 1957), 572–75.

Hough, Robert L. "Crane and Goethe: A Forgotten Relationship." *Nineteenth-Century Fiction,* XVII (September, 1962), 135–48.

O'Donnell, Thomas F. "John B. Van Petten: Stephen Crane's History Teacher." *American Literature,* XXVII (May, 1955), 196–202.

Pratt, Lyndon U. "A Possible Source of *The Red Badge of Courage.*" *American Literature,* XI (March, 1939), 1–11.

Solomon, Eric. "Another Analogue for *The Red Badge of Courage.*" *Nineteenth-Century Fiction,* XIII (June, 1958), 63–67.

Webster, H. T. "Wilbur F. Hinman's *Corporal Si Klegg* and Stephen Crane's *The Red Badge of Courage.*" *American Literature,* XI (November, 1939), 285–93.

Wertheim, Stanley. "*The Red Badge of Courage* and Personal Narratives of the Civil War." *American Literary Realism,* VI (Winter, 1973), 61–65.

The Wafer Controversy

Carlson, Eric W. "Crane's *The Red Badge of Courage,* IX." *Explicator,* XVI (March, 1958), no. 34.

Eby, Cecil R. "Stephen Crane's 'Fierce Red Wafer.'" *English Language Notes,* I (December, 1963), 128–30.

Marlowe, Jean. "Crane's Wafer Image: Reference to an Artillery Primer?" *American Literature,* XLIII (January, 1972), 645-47.

Stallman, R. W. "The Scholar's Net: Literary Sources." *College English,* XVII (October, 1955), 20–27.

Stone, Edward. "The Many Suns of *The Red Badge of Courage.*" *American Literature,* XXIX (November, 1957), 322–26.

Criticism

Albrecht, Robert C. "Content and Style in *The Red Badge of Courage.*" *College English,* XXVII (March, 1966), 487–92.

Cazemajou, Jean. "*The Red Badge of Courage:* The 'Religion of Peace' and the War Archetype." In *Stephen Crane in Transition: Centenary Essays,* edited by Joseph Katz. DeKalb: Northern Illinois University Press, 1972.

Cox, James T. "The Imagery of *The Red Badge of Courage.*" *Modern Fiction Studies,* V (Autumn, 1959), 209–19.

Free, William J. "Smoke Imagery in *The Red Badge of Courage.*" *CLA Journal,* VII (December, 1963), 148–52.

Friedman, Norman. "Criticism and the Novel." *Antioch Review,* XVIII (Fall, 1958), 343–70.

Frohock, W. M. "*The Red Badge* and the Limits of Parody." *Southern Review,* VI (January, 1970), 137–48.

Fryckstedt, Olov W. "Henry Fleming's Tupenny Fury: Cosmic Pessimism in Stephen Crane's *The Red Badge* of Courage." *Studia Neophilologica,* XXXIII (1961), 265–81.

Hough, Robert L. "Crane's Henry Fleming: Speech and Vision." *Forum* (Houston), III (Winter, 1962), 41–42.

Labor, Earle. "Crane and Hemingway: Anatomy of Trauma." *Renascence*, **XI** (Summer, 1959), 189–96.

Lorch, Thomas M. "The Cyclical Structure of *The Red Badge of Courage*." *CLA Journal*, X (March, 1967), 229–38.

McDermott John J. "Symbolism and Psychological Realism in *The Red Badge of Courage*." *Nineteenth-Century Fiction*, XXIII (December, 1968), 324–31.

Marcus, Mordecai and Erin. "Animal Imagery in *The Red Badge of Courage*." *Modern Language Notes*, LXXIV (February, 1959), 108–11.

Pizer, Donald. "A Primer of Fictional Aesthetics." *College English*, (April, 1969), 575–80.

Solomon, Eric. "The Structure of *The Red Badge of Courage*." *Modern Fiction Studies*, V (Autumn, 1959), 220–34.

Taylor, Gordon O. "The Laws of Life: Stephen Crane." In *The Passages of Thought: Psychological Representation in the American Novel, 1870–1900*. New York: Oxford University Press, 1969.

Tuttleton, James W. "The Imagery of *The Red Badge of Courage*." *Modern Fiction Studies*, VIII (Winter, 1962–63), 410–14.

Weisberger, Bernard. "*The Red Badge of Courage*." In *Twelve Original Essays on Great American Novels*, edited by Charles Shapiro. Detroit: Wayne State University Press, 1958.

Weiss, Daniel. "*The Red Badge of Courage*." *Psychoanalytic Review*, LII (Summer, 1965), 176–96; (Fall, 1965), 460–84.

Williams, G. L. "Henry Fleming and the 'Cheery Voiced Stranger.'" *Stephen Crane Newsletter*, IV (Winter, 1969), 4–7.

Wogan, Claudia C. "Crane's Use of Color in *The Red Badge of Courage*." *Modern Fiction Studies*, VI (Summer, 1960), 168–72.

NORTON CRITICAL EDITIONS

HOMER   *The Odyssey*   translated and edited by Albert Cook
HOWELLS   *The Rise of Silas Lapham*   edited by Don L. Cook
IBSEN   *The Wild Duck*   translated and edited by Dounia B. Christiani
JAMES   *The Ambassadors*   edited by S. P. Rosenbaum
JAMES   *The American*   edited by James A. Tuttleton
JAMES   *The Portrait of a Lady*   edited by Robert D. Bamberg
JAMES   *The Turn of the Screw*   edited by Robert Kimbrough
JAMES   *The Wings of the Dove*   edited by J. Donald Crowley and
      Richard A. Hocks
Ben Jonson and the Cavalier Poets   selected and edited by Hugh Maclean
Ben Jonson's Plays and Masques   selected and edited by Robert M. Adams
MACHIAVELLI   *The Prince*   translated and edited by Robert M. Adams
MALTHUS   *An Essay on the Principle of Population*   edited by Philip Appleman
MELVILLE   *The Confidence-Man*   edited by Hershel Parker
MELVILLE   *Moby-Dick*   edited by Harrison Hayford and Hershel Parker
MEREDITH   *The Egoist*   edited by Robert M. Adams
MILL   *On Liberty*   edited by David Spitz
MILTON   *Paradise Lost*   edited by Scott Elledge
MORE   *Utopia*   translated and edited by Robert M. Adams
NEWMAN   *Apologia Pro Vita Sua*   edited by David J. DeLaura
NORRIS   *McTeague*   edited by Donald Pizer
Adrienne Rich's Poetry   selected and edited by Barbara Charlesworth Gelpi and
      Albert Gelpi
The Writings of St. Paul   edited by Wayne A. Meeks
SHAKESPEARE   *Hamlet*   edited by Cyrus Hoy
SHAKESPEARE   *Henry IV, Part I*   edited by James J. Sanderson   *Second Edition*
Bernard Shaw's Plays   selected and edited by Warren Sylvester Smith
Shelley's Poetry and Prose   edited by Donald H. Reiman and Sharon B. Powers
SMOLLETT   *Humphry Clinker*   Edited by James L. Thorson
SOPHOCLES   *Oedipus Tyrannus*   translated and edited by Luci Berkowitz and
      Theodore F. Brunner
SPENSER   *Edmund Spenser's Poetry*   selected and edited by Hugh Maclean
      Second Edition
STENDHAL   *Red and Black*   translated and edited by Robert M. Adams
STERNE   *Tristram Shandy*   edited by Howard Anderson
SWIFT   *Gulliver's Travels*   edited by Robert A. Greenberg   *Revised Edition*
The Writings of Jonathan Swift   edited by Robert A. Greenberg and
      William B. Piper
TENNYSON   *In Memoriam*   edited by Robert Ross
Tennyson's Poetry   selected and edited by Robert W. Hill, Jr.
THOREAU   *Walden and Civil Disobedience*   edited by Owen Thomas
TOLSTOY   *Anna Karenina* (the Maude translation)   edited by George Gibian
TOLSTOY   *War and Peace* (the Maude translation)   edited by George Gibian
TURGENEV   *Fathers and Sons*   edited with a substantially new translation by
      Ralph E. Matlaw
VOLTAIRE   *Candide*   translated and edited by Robert M. Adams
WATSON   *The Double Helix*   edited by Gunther S. Stent
WHITMAN   *Leaves of Grass*   edited by Sculley Bradley and Harold W. Blodgett
WOLLSTONECRAFT   *A Vindication of the Rights of Woman*   edited by
      Carol H. Poston
WORDSWORTH   *The Prelude: 1799, 1805, 1850*   edited by Jonathan Wordsworth,
      M. H. Abrams, and Stephen Gill
Middle English Lyrics   selected and edited by Maxwell S. Luria and
      Richard L. Hoffman
Modern Drama   edited by Anthony Caputi
Restoration and Eighteenth-Century Comedy   edited by Scott McMillin

and knotted so that the child is sewing with a double thread. Needles do not constantly become unthreaded and lost. Very fine sewing is not needed, simple running stitch is used. Aim to be fairly even in stitch size and draw seam lines with a ruler in pencil if it helps the child keep straight. This should be creative fun as the pieces are chosen and the colours blended. A child should not have to agonise over the stitching, but be encouraged to relax and make progress as part of the whole.

The design is the placing of strips (logs) of a constant width but gradually increasing length around the centre square in concentric rings.

Allocate one or two children as cutters. Their job is to cut long lengths of logs as wide as a ruler width from the fabrics you are using.

1 Begin with a square of 1"/2.5cm. Join the first log to the square along one edge, right sides together. Cut the log to the exact length of the square after it is sewn on.

2 Now open out the log and square and lay flat. Take a second log and join, face down, to the square and first log, with a seam at right angles to your first.

3 Cut log 2 to the length of the square plus log 1 and then open out.

4 Continue adding logs around the central square, always seaming at right angles to the previous seam, and trimming the length of the log after it is joined to the work.

It is traditional to put strips of a darker shade on two adjacent sides of your patchwork square, and lighter ones on the opposite two sides. When you come to join completed squares together, patterns are created by the juxtaposition of these dark and light areas as dark and light 'diamonds' form.

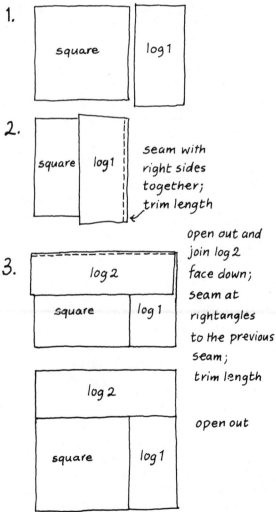

1.

square   log 1

2.

square   log 1   seam with right sides together; trim length

3.

log 2
square   log 1

open out and join log 2 face down; seam at rightangles to the previous seam; trim length

log 2
square   log 1

open out

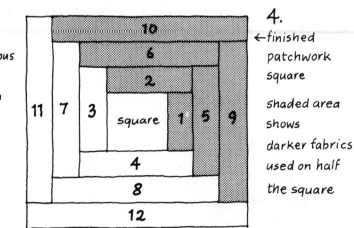

4.
←finished patchwork square

shaded area shows darker fabrics used on half the square

modelling
· · · · · · · · · · · · · · · · ·

For rolling, carving and pinching into shape, clay and homemade playdough come top of my list. The smooth cool touch of the material in your hands can calm down most people, and children of all ages will soon be rolling it into sausages and printing their thumbnails into it!

· · · · ·

playdough

Keep this dough in a plastic tub in the fridge.

> 1 mug of cold water
> 1 mug plain flour
> ½ mug salt
> 1 tablespoon vegetable oil
> 2 teaspoons cream of tartar
> colouring (optional)

Mix all the ingredients together and form a smooth paste. Place in a saucepan and cook slowly until the dough forms a ball. Allow to cool and then knead for a few minutes. If you add colouring at the kneading stage you will produce streaked marbled dough.

papier mâché

Perhaps this is the messiest activity of all, but children love it and it can be used for a wide variety of modelling ideas. Use papier mâché to create model railway landscapes, slowly building up layers to form hills and valleys. Or apply the papier mâché layers to a blown up balloon and remove it when dry, leaving a mask curved to fit your head. (Be sure to remove all bits of balloon as they are dangerous if swallowed.)

Tear up several newspapers into tiny pieces and soak thoroughly in a bucket of hot water to soften. Then, with both hands, rub the bits into a pulp and squeeze out the moisture. Strain and wring in a cloth. Mix with the following paste recipe and model before the mixture becomes dry.

paste

> ½ mug flour
> 1 tablespoon salt
> cold water

Put in a small pan and add water until it has the consistency of thick cream. Bring slowly to the boil and simmer, stirring for 5 minutes. Keep in an airtight jar in the fridge.

Mix this paste with the paper pulp to form lumps such as noses or raised areas in a landscape. For other flatter parts of the work, use layers of torn up paper and paint on the paste between each layer of paper. In this way you can build up layers gradually, using small pieces of paper to keep control of your work.

Where you build up layers on a mould or form, such as a glass bottle, cover your mould with a wet cloth first to prevent the papier mâché sticking too firmly to it. Then it will be easy to detach after the layers have dried.